A
Husband's
Regret

THE UNWANTED SERIES

A Husband's Regret

THE UNWANTED SERIES

NATASHA ANDERS

Published by Montlake Romance, Seattle

www.apub.com

ISBN-13: 9781477818374
ISBN-10: 1477818375

Cover design by Laura Klynstra

Library of Congress Control Number: 2013919711

Printed in the United States of America

To my wonderful family. Thank you for
always believing in me.

Rest in Peace, Fidel. You were the best little dog in the
world. I miss you so much, my beautiful boy.

PROLOGUE

What do you mean, you're *pregnant*? What about your studies? We were going to wait, Bronwyn, remember? Just tell me you're joking?" Bronwyn felt her husband's furious words strike her like boulders. She stared up into his livid face and didn't recognize the man standing in front of her. He was shocked, that was all. He was thrown by her news. Her words would sink in soon enough and he'd go back to being the man she adored, the wonderful man to whom she had entrusted her heart. She just needed to give him time to get over his shock. The more she tried to rationalize his inexplicable reaction to what should have been joyous news, the more the insidious little voice in the back of her mind kept telling her that she was lying to herself. This was a side of Bryce that she had never seen before—one that he had never *allowed* her to see—and she was terrified of what that said about their two-year marriage.

"I know that it's sooner than we'd planned," she said softly, trying to maintain an even tone of voice. "But this is the reality of our situation now, and it can't be changed. We're having a baby . . . a *baby*, Bryce. Don't you get how wonderful that is?"

"I can't believe you did this. I can't believe you would stoop to this," he gritted out bitterly. "This was supposed to be a joint decision. I'm not ready for this, Bronwyn. I don't want a kid, damn it!"

"But it's our baby. We made it together," she protested, trying and failing to keep the pain and confusion from her voice. She tried to find a glimmer of her kind and loving Bryce beneath the mask of anger and frustration that he was displaying, but he wasn't there. She wondered if he had ever been there.

"You mean *you* made it, without my consent." He could barely meet her eyes, and she was grateful for that because the tears that she had been struggling to keep at bay were finally winning the battle.

"I don't know why you're being like this," she cried. "I didn't plan this; it just happened. Our birth control failed. I asked the doctor and he said that if I'd had a stomach virus or anything like that it could have provided a window of opportunity. And remember? I was sick a couple of days before your company party three months ago." He strode out of the conservatory without a word and she followed him as he made his way downstairs to their en suite. She watched in sick disbelief as he opened the medicine chest and yanked out her birth-control pills.

"*What are you doing?*" She tried to maintain her composure as he counted the pills left in the box and felt the hope that she had been clinging to shrivel up into a tiny ball inside her chest and die. She felt nauseated as she watched the man she had married turn into a monster right in front of her. Slowly the confused mortification turned to fury. How could he do this to her? How could he *humiliate* her like this?

"God, have you been chucking pills down the drain every night?" he wondered out loud, and she found herself almost hating him for asking the question.

"You know I wouldn't do that."

"Do I? Well I obviously don't know you as well as I thought I did, do I?"

"Of course you know me, Bryce." She tried to appeal to the reasonable man who had to be in there somewhere and laid a tentative hand on his rigid forearm, but he yanked his arm away and turned away from her.

"Get out of here," he whispered harshly, and Bronwyn felt something give way and break at those four words.

"What?" She *must* have misheard him. Still she tried to give him the benefit of the doubt.

"Get the hell out," he said before turning to face her. Bronwyn tried not to flinch when she saw his face. There was nothing there— no anger, no regret, just a blank mask. She didn't know this man at all. "Go *now*."

She sobbed, whirled from the room, and did as he had commanded. She fled.

CHAPTER ONE

She had been working for less than two hours and already she knew that it had been a mistake to come in. But not showing up for work meant not getting paid, and that would be disastrous. She needed her job desperately and couldn't risk losing it.

A bout of flu had wiped her out for nearly a week, leaving her without an income and dangerously low on resources. Though she still felt a bit shaky, she had dragged herself in to work that morning. But no sooner had she walked through the front door of the busiest, trendiest beachfront restaurant in Plettenberg Bay, than she comprehended what a grave error in judgment she had made. She was muddling up her orders, breaking dishes, and walking blindly into her fellow servers. She knew that the manager—who already felt that her personal circumstances were incompatible with her working environment—was just itching to fire her. Now she was basically handing him an excuse to get rid of her.

She valiantly soldiered on, hoping against hope that Gerhard would, by some miracle, take pity on her and keep her on his books. A young couple with a baby cart made their way into her section and she shuffled over to them, her lack of enthusiasm obvious with every reluctant step. The couple were leaning into one another, whispering and laughing intimately, while the baby slept peacefully in its stroller.

The pair looked very much in love and pretty much oblivious to the rest of the world.

"Good afternoon," she murmured, so focused on keeping her nausea at bay that she barely glanced at them. "Would you like anything to drink?" The woman looked up and started to say something, but she was interrupted by her companion, who swore viciously before jumping to his feet like a scalded cat.

"Oh my *God*! Bronwyn?"

Bronwyn gasped and raised one shaking hand to her mouth to stifle a shocked cry when she recognized the handsome man standing in front of her. Her vision blurred and she blinked rapidly to clear it. The baby, clearly startled by the man's harsh voice, started crying.

"So this is where you have been hiding out all this time?" The shock had disappeared from his voice to be replaced by contempt.

"Ricky," she moaned shakily, overwhelmed by love, fear, and relief all at the same time.

"Don't call me that!" he growled in warning, and she flinched. "God, you're an ice-cold bitch, aren't you? How could you stay away all this time? How could you *live* with yourself?"

"Please," she implored in the smallest whisper. "Please don't . . ."

"Don't what? Call a spade a spade?" He sneered.

"Rick," the woman, whom Bronwyn had forgotten about, spoke up. She kept her voice low, while she rocked the still-crying baby. "Take it easy, for heaven's sake, she doesn't look well. What's going on here?"

"Of course she doesn't look well," he scoffed, his harsh tone of voice totally unfamiliar. "Why would she look well when she has finally been caught, like the miserable little sneak that she is?"

Bronwyn swayed even more. Rick had never spoken to her like this before—it wasn't in his gentle nature to be deliberately cruel—but he was firing on all cylinders today, and Bronwyn flinched with each terrible barb.

"Rick." The woman was speaking again, but her voice sounded hollow, like it was coming from down a long tunnel. "Rick, *stop* it . . ." She was saying something else but this time her voice had disappeared behind the angry buzzing in Bronwyn's head. She shook her head but the sound got worse and louder until it was as deafening as a chainsaw. She groaned weakly and lifted her hands to her ears. That didn't help, and she sobbed as her field of vision got narrower and narrower, until she could not see them at all, until there was only blackness.

Voices faded in and out of her consciousness and Bronwyn struggled to make sense of what they were saying. She was comfortable again, no longer dizzy and no longer achy. She felt like she was floating and was enveloped by an incredible sense of well-being. But this feeling was not *quite* right, and that awareness prevented her from being entirely at ease. She was sure that this uneasiness stemmed from the raised voices in the background, and again she attempted to filter out the garbled speech from the few words that she could understand.

". . . Don't get . . ." it was a man's voice, recognizable and well loved but unfamiliarly harsh. ". . . What she did . . . unforgivable . . . left him . . . *bitch*!" An unfamiliar female voice intervened, her gentle voice soothed Bronwyn's overwrought nerves.

" . . . Is she? What . . . she do . . . so bad?" Bronwyn strained to open her eyes but it felt like a colossal effort.

". . . Deserted Bryce . . . needed her most . . ."

Bronwyn managed a weak gasp at that, outraged by this blatant lie. The couple went abruptly silent.

". . . Waking up," the woman said urgently. ". . . The doctor! *Now, Rick!*"

Doctor? Bronwyn frowned. Why a doctor? For the first time since regaining consciousness she wondered where she was and managed to drag her heavy lids apart with great effort. She stared up into the vaguely recognizable features of a pretty woman who seemed to be a couple of years younger than Bronwyn's twenty-eight. The woman's warm smile transformed her gentle features from plain to almost pretty and had the effect of immediately calming Bronwyn down.

"Try not to panic," she instructed gently. "You passed out at work. At first we assumed it was shock but your fever and pallor soon made it pretty clear that you're seriously ill." Her sea-green eyes were grave behind the lenses of her trendy prescription eyeglasses, and her voice took on a chastising tone. "You should never have been at work in that condition. You should take better care of yourself."

Bronwyn frowned, wondering who the woman was, before deciding that being offended by her admonishment would require way too much of her strength. Clearly she was going to need that strength in the face of Rick's unexpected and unprecedented hostility. An alarming thought struck her, and she sat up in a blind panic, ignoring the sudden onslaught of dizziness.

"Passed out at work?" Her voice sounded weak, even to her own ears. "Oh no . . . I have to call my boss!"

"Bronwyn." The woman placed gentle hands on her shoulders to push her back onto the cot, her lovely eyes brimming with sympathy. "I'm afraid that he wasn't very sympathetic about any of this. He said something about having had enough of your drama and that you shouldn't bother coming back. I'm so sorry."

"Oh no," she moaned. "No, no. I needed that job!"

"Well if you wanted to keep it, you shouldn't have gone to work in the condition you were in today, young lady." A stern voice intruded from the doorway, where a harried-looking older man in a white coat stood framed. "Are you trying to kill yourself? You're just barely over a *very* bad bout of flu, possibly even pneumonia from what I can gather, and you were so dehydrated when they brought you in that I'm amazed you didn't pass out sooner! The mere fact that you've been out like a light for nearly five hours is proof of how close you are to relapsing. You're completely run-down." She went dramatically pale at that bit of news, and the doctor wrongly assumed that he had shocked her into taking her illness seriously. "I would like to keep you overnight to monitor your condition."

"*No!*" They were all taken aback by her sudden, shrill vehemence. "No, I can't stay here. I have to go home. I should be there right now. My shift would have ended an hour ago; I should be at home."

"That would be stupid and downright dangerous in your condition, Mrs. Palmer," the doctor admonished, and Bronwyn's world reeled.

"What did you call me?" she asked in a shocked whisper.

"He called you Mrs. Palmer," Rick taunted from where he stood in the doorway with his arms folded across his broad chest. "That *is* still your name, isn't it?" She stared at Richard Palmer helplessly, not knowing what to say and suddenly hating him with a ferocity that shook her.

"*Well?*" he prompted sarcastically, and she nodded mutely, not understanding this hostility from someone who had always loved and respected her.

"Please . . ." she whispered. "Please, Rick, I have to go home."

"You're going home all right," Rick informed her coldly. "Just as soon as it can be arranged."

"Mr. Palmer, I strongly advise against that," the doctor interjected firmly, but Rick ignored him, keeping his eyes on Bronwyn.

"Just prescribe whatever medication she'll need, Doctor," he ordered in a manner that went completely against his usual easygoing nature. "We'll make sure that she gets plenty of rest." The doctor glared at them before shaking his head and leaving the room abruptly.

"Rick, do you think this is a good idea?" The other woman asked worriedly, and he raised his eyes to her anxious face before smiling gently, his expression now reminiscent of the Rick that Bronwyn knew and loved.

"It'll be fine," he murmured reassuringly, but the woman made an irritated sound and shook her head angrily.

"I've had enough, Rick," she seethed, revealing claws beneath the sweet exterior. "You'd better tell me what's going on and fast. I've been sitting here for hours without getting a single straight answer from you, and I'm fed up with it. Tell me what's going on, or I'll pack up and head off to Knysna *on my own!*" Bronwyn watched in fascination as his eyes flared in panic and he lost all semblance of his previous icy coolness.

"Lisa," he choked. "You wouldn't go off on your own when we just . . ."

"*Don't* test me," she warned. "Now I think that it's past time you did some proper introductions and try to be civil, please." He frowned sullenly, looking about as menacing as a little boy with his hand caught in the biscuit tin.

"Lisa, meet Bronwyn Palmer. Bron, my wife, Lisa." Bronwyn's eyes lit up with genuine pleasure as her eyes flew from one face to the other. His *wife*? Well, then, that would explain the baby. She glanced around the room, looking for the child. She smiled when she saw the pram parked close to the window on the other side of the room and marveled at how much his life had changed in the last two years.

"Your *wife*? Ricky, you got married?" He winced in response to her words.

"Bron, don't call me that," he muttered uncomfortably, sounding so much like his old self that Bronwyn's heart swelled with love for him. She smiled and turned her attention to the slender woman who stood beside him.

"I'm so glad that he married someone like you," she managed weakly, wishing she could be more eloquent but suddenly feeling quite drained. She leaned back against the pillows and smiled up at them both. "Ricky deserves someone lovely . . ." Her eyes drifted shut. "I'm so tired. Take me home. Please. I need to go home . . ."

"She's my brother's errant wife," she heard Rick telling his wife, but he sounded so far away that she frowned. Where was he going? "And, as I said before, she's the heartless bitch who abandoned him when he needed her most!" Her eyes flew open in horror, and she was shocked to find that he was closer than his distant voice had suggested. Confused, she tried to gather her thoughts.

"I didn't," she protested vehemently. "I wouldn't. Why would you say something like that, Rick? Why would you *lie*?" She heard the bewildered hurt in her voice and was ashamed to reveal how much his lies had wounded her. "I thought we were friends."

"Our friendship ended when you did what you did to my brother," he snarled. She jumped when his voice caught up with him and the volume increased dramatically on the last word.

"I didn't do anything to Bryce," she whimpered, her own voice still far away. "He didn't want me anymore . . . so I left. I left him."

"You left him for *dead*!"

The woman, Lisa, laid a restraining hand on Rick's arm as he made a frustrated move toward Bronwyn. Bron blinked at the fury on his face; she had no idea where all of this anger was coming from.

"Take me home . . ." she entreated again, keeping her eyes on the other woman's face. "Please. I have to go home . . ." Just then an intimidatingly large figure suddenly loomed in the doorway, and when Bronwyn's eyes lifted, she was filled with a sense of impending doom.

He stood there. Quiet, graceful, and fierce, and Bronwyn cowered at the sight of him.

"You *called* him?" she said, exhaling, the hurt and betrayal she felt evident in her voice and face. Despite everything, she had still steadfastly clung to the belief that Rick was her friend. She lifted her wounded doe eyes to his furious face. "You called him? Oh, Ricky, how could you?"

"He called me because I'm his brother and his loyalties lie with me." The beautiful dark voice was calmer than she would have expected and drifted over her like a gentle caress. She closed her eyes at the sound of that voice. It was the first time she had heard it in over two years, and God how she had missed it. She had hungered for the sound of his voice and had often thought of calling him just to hear it but had dismissed that impulse as a dangerous and forbidden luxury.

When she opened her eyes, she was shocked to find that he had moved. He was standing right beside her bed and much too close for comfort. She shifted somewhat, lowering her eyes to the bed covers, afraid to meet his glacial gaze. She was terrified of what she would see in those eyes and sneaked a peek at him from beneath her half-mast lids.

He was so big. She had forgotten that about him, forgotten the sheer bulk of this man who had once been her love and her life. He stood six feet four and had the brawn to match the height, huge shoulders, trim waist, and slim hips. He resembled a Norse god of old with the darkly golden hair and the grim features that looked carved from granite. The only hints of softness in that roughly hewn face were his long, long lashes and his beautifully shaped mouth. She had always wondered what a gorgeous, successful man like him had seen in a plain nobody like her. She was an awkward and gangly woman who had long legs, a skinny body, and the gracelessness of a giraffe. There was nothing remarkable about her, save that a man like

Bryce Palmer had chosen her to be his wife, had seemed to love her and want her.

He looked older than his thirty-three years. He had obviously aged since she had last seen him, but it wasn't unflattering and it added even more character to an already strong face. Now he hovered over her like an avenging angel, beautiful and intimidating. He had all the power in the world to hurt her and—according to him—all the reason on Earth to hate her.

"Look at me!" he hissed furiously. She lifted her head to meet his cold eyes head-on and quaked before the sheer, unadulterated hatred she saw there. "You took everything from me when you left. You stripped me of all dignity, left me bleeding by the roadside, and you never once looked back. I will *never* forgive you for that, Bronwyn."

"You *told* me to go," she defended herself weakly, looking down as she spoke, and was shocked when his huge hand reached out and grasped her fragile jaw. His grip was so unexpectedly fierce that she cringed a bit. She sensed Rick moving to intervene, but Bryce let her go abruptly.

"*Look* at me when you talk to me," he gritted out savagely. "You did this to me. The least you can do is look at me when you have something to say."

"Bryce," she managed weakly, looking up at him, even though it terrified her to meet his eyes. "You told me to go. Remember?" He made an impatient sound and turned his back on her. Bewildered, she stared at the broad expanse of his back and tried again, tears spilling from her eyes and her voice thickening with despair. "You didn't want me anymore. You said . . . I t-tricked you . . . said . . ."

"Where is my baby?" He cut through her words coldly, spinning around to face her again, his eyes locked onto her tearful face with an intensity that unnerved her. She was aware of Rick making a shocked sound and Lisa quietly taking the stroller and leaving the room. "Where is the child you so cruelly deprived me of knowing?" The tears streaming down her face did not move him at all, and his vicious gaze was unwavering.

"Please," she whispered, and his eyes dropped to her mouth. "Please, Bryce . . . you said you didn't want a child . . . said I'd tricked you. I don't understand why you're being like this."

"For *God's* sake, Bronwyn," he all but shouted, suddenly and quite spectacularly losing his cool. "You knew that I was angry! You knew that I would calm down eventually. But you chose to run out of there, chose to jump into your car when you weren't the best of drivers, and then you sped down that hill so fast that I was terrified you'd kill yourself. You *knew* that I'd follow . . ." He gritted his teeth and tilted his head back, and she could see the muscles in his neck and throat work as he forced himself back under control. It took him longer than she would have expected. Bryce had always been quite adept at mastering his temper. Not this time, it seemed. While he managed to damp down the rage, she could still feel it simmering dangerously below the surface and it unsettled her. She didn't quite understand where all this anger was coming from.

"*Where is my child?*" he growled dangerously, and Bronwyn's eyes flooded as she thought of her beautiful little girl. Kayla had every right to know her father and vice versa. It was just that, up until now, Bronwyn had had no clue that Bryce *wanted* to know his daughter. She thought of the two weeks she'd spent at their holiday home in Knysna, waiting for him to come. Yes, she had known that he would need time to calm down and she had known that once he thought things through he would come for her. There had never been a doubt in her mind that he would want her and their baby.

But he hadn't come . . . he hadn't come to the most obvious place, the one place that she had been certain he would look, the place where they had spent so many happy hours together. And as the hours had turned into days and then into weeks, Bronwyn had been forced to face the reality of her situation: he had meant every cruel word. Bryce did not want their child, and as a consequence, he no longer wanted her. She would never have believed it of him, would never have expected him to abandon her to care for their baby on her own.

He had never once during their two-year-long marriage *said* that he loved her, but he had shown her in so many ways that she had believed that was enough. In the face of his abandonment, she had come to question that love and had been forced to acknowledge that the words would have meant more; the words would have meant *everything*. They would have set his love in stone.

Now he was standing here telling her that he had wanted Kayla after all? What was she supposed to believe? Why was he treating her like the villain for leaving, when *he* was the one who had driven her away? In the midst of her turmoil, she heard an unmistakable sound—the familiar irrepressible chatter and giggle of a toddler . . . of a *particular* toddler. Bronwyn's panicked gaze swung to the open door and she was horrified to see the babysitter leading her beautiful daughter toward the room. Her anxious gaze swung toward Bryce but he seemed oblivious. He was watching her intently, still wanting an answer to his previous question. Rick had heard though and his gaze was riveted on the doorway as well. Oh *God* how could Katrina bring her here? How had the woman even known where to find Bronwyn?

"*Answer* me, damn you!" Bryce was growling. How could he remain unaware of the approaching babble of an effervescent eighteen-month-old baby? He had his back to the door and so did not see when Kayla and the now-faltering Katrina crossed the threshold. The young woman hesitated as her gaze swept around the room, immediately picking up on the tension. The toddler had no such reservations and upon seeing her mother, her face lit up and she made a beeline for the cot. She was muttering incoherently under her breath, as was her wont, and her nappy-clad bottom waddled comically as she toddled her way toward Bronwyn. Bryce still seemed to have no idea that she was there, and as Kayla passed by the bemused Rick, barely sparing him a glance, she was suddenly confronted by an obstacle in the form of her tall father. She frowned up at the big man who had his back to her, looking so much like him in that moment that Bronwyn smiled.

"What do you find so *funny* about this Bronwyn?" he hissed.

"Man big," Kayla said, her first two clear words since entering the room, and it sounded more like criticism than compliment. When he still didn't get out of her way, she gave him a measuring look, drew back her leg, and . . .

"Kayla, *no!*" Bronwyn shouted in horror, just as the little girl kicked her father on his calf. Bryce staggered a little, shocked rather than hurt, and whirled around, scanning the room desperately for a few seconds before dropping his gaze to the mutinous tiny girl before him. Not even knee-high to him and still in nappies, but she refused to back down.

"Kayla go . . ." she stated like a queen, sweeping by her enthralled father. When she reached her destination, she stopped and stared up at her next obstacle with a fulminating glare. The bed was too high for her to climb on to, so the beautiful little imp with her mop of silky brown hair and her big ice-blue eyes swept beguilingly back to the tall man she had just slighted and undid him with a charming smile before lifting her arms demandingly.

"Up, peese!" she commanded with the air of one accustomed to getting her way. The "please" was just a formality, and her father was helpless to do anything but obey. He picked her up reverently, holding her close for just an instant longer than she liked and she squirmed uncomfortably until he settled her onto the cot beside her mother, before shifting his piercing scrutiny to the babysitter whom he had only just noticed.

"I'm sorry, Bronwyn," Katrina spoke uncertainly from the doorway, unnerved by Bryce's direct stare. "When you were late I called the restaurant and they told me what had happened. I spoke to the doctor before bringing her here, and he said that you weren't contagious. I have a date . . . and I thought . . ."

"You thought that you'd leave a little girl in hospital with her sick mother?" Bryce completed incredulously.

"Well . . ." The woman looked uncomfortable, and Bryce veered his furious gaze back to Bronwyn, who had her forehead resting on Kayla's as she and her daughter communed without words. It was such a striking picture that he paused for an instant before launching an immediate attack.

"*This* is the type of irresponsible people you entrust our daughter's care to?" Katrina's eyes widened at his revealing words, and Bryce turned to face the young woman again, ignoring the surprised expression on her face. "Thank you, miss. Your services will no longer be required. Rick, please give the young lady whatever money is owed to her."

"I can pay my *own* babysitter," Bronwyn hissed furiously, but he kept his back to her, ignoring her, while Rick led Katrina out of the room. He turned to face her, and she repeated her claim. "I can pay my own babysitter, damn you!"

"Seeing that you have just lost your low-paying job, I don't think that you're in any position to be stubborn on this issue, Bronwyn." Kayla was glaring up at Bryce furiously, and her scowling little face immediately distracted him.

"Hey there, angel." His voice gentled as he crouched down beside the bed to meet her eyes. "Why so cross?"

"Mummy sleep," she admonished. "Shhh!" He blinked for a startled instant, before lifting his gaze to Bronwyn's shadowed eyes. "It appears that our daughter has a lot more common sense than either of us does." He smiled fondly down at the toddler, who was lovingly stroking her mother's hair. "You're in no condition to argue, Bronwyn. Just do as I say." She gasped at his nerve and was about to protest when he hunkered down in front of Kayla again.

"Hi, sweetheart, do you know who I am?" His eyes were trained on Kayla's perfect little features; she was an enchanting combination of both parents. She had his eyes . . . blue eyes so pale that they sometimes looked almost gray.

"Man," Kayla responded shyly before popping her thumb into her mouth and laying her head on her mother's chest.

"That's right." He nodded. Rick reentered the room silently, and Kayla dragged her thumb out of her mouth long enough to point at him.

"Man," she informed helpfully, and Bryce swiveled his head, caught sight of his brother, and nodded with a grin.

"That's your Uncle Rick." Rick looked startled to hear himself introduced as such, startled and then pleased. He seemed to swell with pride. "I am your daddy . . . Can you say 'daddy'?"

"What do you think you're doing?" Bronwyn was so appalled by his blasé introduction, that her voice came out louder than she had intended. It startled Kayla, who blinked in shock before melting into tears. Bryce looked devastated. He stared at the crying child helplessly, not knowing what to do. Bronwyn, unable to stop herself, continued furiously.

"How can you just announce it to her like that? How can you simply . . ." Kayla cried even harder, and Bryce patted the child's head and cheek helplessly. "Stop ignoring me, damn you, I hate it when you do that!" He looked up then, and when he saw her expression, his face darkened.

"It was you," he seethed. "You made her cry. I thought it was something I'd done, damn you." Bronwyn blinked down at him in amazement before lifting her eyes to Rick's face in shocked realization.

"He can't *hear* me, can he?" she asked Rick, who stood just behind Bryce. The younger man said nothing and merely continued to stare at her levelly. His silver-gray eyes were unnerving in their uncharacteristic iciness.

"Why don't you ask *me* that question?" Bryce asked mockingly, and she returned her gaze to his face, realizing that he had heard her question. She berated herself for being ludicrous. Of course he could hear her. "Ah, but you already know the answer, don't you?" he taunted and she stiffened, feeling like a fool. Kayla had stopped crying and had her head resting on Bronwyn's chest and her thumb back in her mouth. She was eyeing Bryce warily.

"What's your name, angel?" he asked her gently. The child refused to answer and her eyelids grew heavier as she started to slip into a doze.

"Her name's Mikayla," Bronwyn supplied, but he kept his eyes on Kayla's face, ignoring Bronwyn again.

"Go on, tell me your name." He *blatantly* snubbed her. Kayla dragged her thumb out of her mouth and deigned to respond.

"M'kayla." She did not bother to lift her head and barely opened her eyes as she garbled her name the way she always did. It was recognizable enough, but Bryce was staring at the child with a baffled frown. He raised his confused eyes to Bronwyn, and she sighed before repeating the name.

"Mikayla, I named her Mikayla." The frown deepened and something uncomfortably close to loathing settled over his taut, handsome features.

"God*damn* you, Bronwyn," he growled, and she gasped. He didn't like the name? She had named Kayla after him—his second name was Michael. Maybe he thought it was hypocritical of her to name their daughter after him when, as he now claimed, she had deprived him of his child. Bryce looked angry, hurt, and confused at the same time, and he kept glancing at his dozing little daughter and shutting his eyes despairingly. Bronwyn did not understand his reaction.

Rick stepped forward, leveling a resentful glare at Bronwyn that baffled her even further, before laying a calm hand on his agitated brother's shoulder. Bryce looked up and grabbed Rick's hand as if it were a lifeline.

"*Tell* me," he pleaded desperately, and Rick nodded.

"Her name is Mikayla, Bryce," he told his brother gently, with both his mouth and his *hands*.

CHAPTER TWO

"W-why are you doing that?" Bronwyn stammered. Both men ignored her, and Bryce turned back to his sleeping daughter, with his heart in his eyes.

"Mikayla . . ." he murmured, running a gentle finger down the baby's soft cheek. "What a beautiful name."

"What's going on here?" Bronwyn asked in a voice bordering on hysteria, before convulsing into a series of painful coughs. Kayla stirred a little, disturbed by the violent coughing, and Bryce picked the little girl up and cradled her to his chest.

"Give me your flat keys. Rick and Lisa will pack your things." Her eyes were blurry with tears as the coughing tore at her throat and chest. She was unable to respond to the autocratic demand and was appalled when Bryce simply reached for her handbag and tossed it to Rick.

"They're probably in there," he told his brother. The younger man nodded and turned away.

"Wait!" Bronwyn called painfully, trying to get her coughing under control. Bryce handed her a glass of water that she gulped down thankfully. "Why were you using sign language?" she asked urgently, her throat on the verge of giving out. Rick turned back with naked disgust on his face.

"This display of ignorance is an insult to our intelligence, Bronwyn!" he hissed, and her eyes widened with hurt.

"I don't know what's going on here!" Her voice was strained but she hoped she managed to convey her urgency. "Can you hear me, Bryce?"

"I haven't heard much of anything over the last two years, Bronwyn." He shrugged scornfully. "And you know it. *You* did this to me, after all."

"*Me?*" Bronwyn did not know what to react to first: the unbelievable news that her beautiful, strong husband was deaf, or the accusation that *she* was somehow responsible for his condition. It was all too awful to comprehend. "But . . . I . . . *how?*" Rick made an impatient sound at the back of his throat, seemingly sickened by her continued ignorance. He touched his brother's arm to gain his attention. Bryce turned to face him.

"I've asked that girl Katrina where *she* lives." He nodded toward Bronwyn, unable to even say her name. "Some dump downtown. I'll pack a couple of bags for her and Mikayla."

"Pack only a change of clothes for the little one," Bryce ordered, his gaze softening as he looked down into his still-sleeping daughter's pretty face. "If the rags she's wearing right now are any indication, there won't be anything worth keeping. I'll clothe my own child." Bronwyn's eyes stung with tears at that terrible insult; if only he knew how much she had sacrificed and slaved for every single item of clothing the child possessed. She had worked double shifts, bypassed meals, and taken on extra jobs to keep her baby fed and clothed. They may not have been the most expensive clothes, but they were pretty and serviceable enough for an active toddler.

"Pack her toys though," he told Rick. "God knows they're probably not much better than the clothing, but she's bound to have her favorites."

"What do you mean *I* did this to you?" Bronwyn asked, letting the matter of Kayla's wardrobe slide in favor of a much more pressing matter. He didn't respond and she understood that he must have been lip-reading all along. She tugged at his sleeve to get his attention and he directed his arrogant gaze down to her pinched face.

"What do you mean I did this to you?" she repeated, and he frowned before turning away from her, deliberately blocking her out and making her feel about as significant as a fly.

"What are you . . ." She diverted her gaze to Rick when she saw that Bryce was ignoring her. A neat trick that, turning his back on someone when he didn't care to know what he or she was saying. It was certainly effective. "What is he accusing me of?" Rick couldn't ignore her as successfully as Bryce could, but he was definitely doing a good job of trying. He and Bryce were speaking quietly, sometimes lapsing into sign language and cutting her out completely. Feeling muddled, exhausted, and on the verge of hysterical tears, Bronwyn had no clear idea of how to deal with this problem. The situation had just spiraled completely beyond her control and she was too ill to deal with it. She watched as the talking men left the room and took her baby with them and she felt an overwhelming sense of dread. She wanted to snatch her child back and run as fast and as far as she could but all she could do was watch helplessly as the door swung shut behind them.

She covered her face with her hands, feeling as wrung out as a dishcloth. Hot tears seeped through the cracks of her fingers as she allowed herself to weep for everything that she had lost and was still losing. She was so wrapped up in her own misery that the first she knew of another presence in the room was a comforting arm around her narrow shoulders.

"Shhh, it's okay, it's okay . . ." Rick's pretty wife was perched on the side of the bed, her head bowed toward Bronwyn's. "You'll be all right, both you and your beautiful little girl will be absolutely fine. Bryce will take care of you."

"Bryce hates me," Bronwyn negated miserably.

"Bryce could never hate the woman who has given him such a gorgeous daughter," the other woman denied.

"He blames me for what happened to him," Bronwyn groaned. "And I don't even *know* what happened to him! How did he lose his hearing?" She lifted her tear-drenched brown eyes to Lisa's face, and the other woman frowned, her expression thoughtful.

"It was an accident. Rick and I hadn't been dating for long— barely a month since the day he first walked into my bookshop—but we were serious enough that he was talking about introducing me to you guys."

So Rick had met Lisa while Bronwyn was still with Bryce. She remembered how euphoric and secretive he'd been during those few weeks before she had left. She'd even teased him about it over dinner one night and he'd stammered and blushed like a schoolboy. The memory warmed her somewhat, but Lisa's sympathetic voice dragged her back into the horror of the present.

"One night Rick called me to cancel one of our dates because his brother had been in an accident. It was pretty bad. I met Bryce a few weeks later while he was still recovering in the hospital. Rick and I married about four months after the accident, when Bryce was well enough to attend. If I hadn't been two months pregnant at the time, we would have postponed the wedding. Both Rick and Bryce refused to talk about you again. I think Rick was merely following Bryce's lead on that score. He was so completely wrecked by what had happened to his brother that he would have walked over hot coals if he thought that it would make Bryce happy. From the rare bits of information about it that I managed to get out of Rick over the past twenty months of our marriage, I thought that you'd opted out because you couldn't cope with his deafness."

"But I didn't even *know* he was deaf until just now." She coughed painfully and Lisa stroked her hair soothingly.

"Why did you leave him?" Lisa questioned gently.

"I would never willingly have left him. I love him . . . *loved* him." Lisa raised her eyebrows at the telling slip and nodded.

"I know that now. I took one look at you this morning and I knew. So why *did* you leave him?"

"Because he told me to leave. He kicked me out," Bronwyn recalled miserably. "He was unhappy about my pregnancy because we had agreed to wait a few years before starting a family. He accused me of getting pregnant deliberately, of tricking him. It was awful."

"I don't understand." Lisa frowned. "Why would he go off the deep end like that? Surely a pregnancy is something to be celebrated?"

"I don't know," Bronwyn confessed. "I left to give him some time to cool off and went to our house in Knysna. I knew that once he had calmed down enough he would come looking for me. I *never* believed he wouldn't come . . ." Her voice faded away as she remembered the pain, betrayal, and disillusionment she had felt when it became apparent that Bryce would not be coming for her.

"What did you do?" Lisa asked sympathetically.

"I waited. For two weeks I waited. Bryce is usually pretty good about keeping his temper under control, and when he does lose it he usually needs only a couple of hours for his logical thought processes to kick in again. But I'd *never* seen him as angry as he was that night, so I figured that it would take him a little longer than usual to come to his senses." She shrugged helplessly, battling to keep the pain she still felt at the memory from showing. "After a week, I tried calling him. But I was stonewalled. His staff had closed ranks around him. I couldn't reach him or Rick and I didn't know what to do. It felt as if my whole world had imploded." She bowed her head.

"After the initial disbelief and pain, the anger and resentment kicked in. I decided that if he wanted nothing to do with the baby and me, then I wasn't going to make it easy for him to come crawling back. Not that I believed he *would* come back. I suppose I started thinking that way to preserve my pride. I went off the grid—no credit, no bank accounts except the one I already had in my maiden name. The only jobs I was qualified to do didn't exactly keep stellar employee records. I never believed he would actually try to find us." She shook her head dazedly.

"I thought he loved me." It shamed her to admit that now, embarrassed her to confess such a foolish belief in front of this woman who was so obviously confident in her husband's love. "Now he blames me for his deafness, and he's practically accusing me of stealing Kayla from him when he had made it abundantly clear that he had no interest in her!" She heard the bitterness creeping into her voice. "He undoubtedly thinks that the way we've been living is beneath him, but I took good care of my baby. I fed her, clothed her, and loved her after *he* had abandoned us! How dare he waltz back into my life and presume that he'd be the better parent just because he has so much more money than I do!"

"Bryce has kept pretty much to himself in the time since I got married to Rick. He's a difficult man to get to know," Lisa said into the silence that ensued after Bronwyn ran out of steam. "But what I *do* know I like and respect. I can't really reconcile the picture you've just painted with the man I've come to know."

Bronwyn nodded miserably. "I'm sorry," she responded, forcing the words past her tortured throat. "I don't mean to place you in an awkward position. I shouldn't have said those things."

"No, that's not it at all," Lisa hurriedly corrected. "It's just that you each seem so convinced of the other's wrongdoing that there must have been some crossed wires somewhere."

"Hmm." Bronwyn tried to agree, but she was feeling fuzzy again, unable to concentrate.

"Try to get some rest," Lisa suggested gently. "You look done in."

"I didn't . . . would never . . ." She could not complete the thought and was aware of nothing more as she slid into unconsciousness.

~

She looked fragile, like the slightest touch would break her, and how he wanted to *break* her. Bryce glared down at the stranger who was his wife and was eaten up by pure hatred for her. This innocent-looking bitch had destroyed his life and stolen his child. The barely contained violence he felt toward her had been festering for just over two years, and he quite cheerfully would have strangled her in her sleep if it weren't for the fact that their daughter needed her. He watched her labor to breathe and imagined that it sounded hoarse and ragged. He remembered sounds but sometimes wondered if his memory was accurate. For the longest time, despite his unsuccessful attempts to force it out, his most precious memory had been of her voice. Now the memory of the sweet, clear sound of her voice returned unbidden along with the bell-like clarity of her laugh and, lastly, how that lovely voice had sounded during their final argument, thick with tears and entreaties.

She looked so ill. He grimaced, unwilling to feel any compassion for her. If she had worked herself into the ground it was less than she deserved for running out on him, for stealing his child, and for *crippling* him! He lived in a silent world now, the only sounds he heard were mere echoes of memories and her voice . . . always *her* voice.

He had hated her for haunting him, and he hated her still for looking so damned vulnerable, for being ill and weak and nearly defenseless, thereby rendering him impotent to lash out and rail at her the way he had fantasized about doing for so long.

Well, she wouldn't always be sick. He could wait. Revenge, they said, was a dish best served cold. He'd been waiting for two years, so a few more weeks wouldn't make a difference. And how much sweeter the payback would be now that he had her very firmly within his grasp!

∼

Kayla decided that she didn't like scary and noisy helicopters and cried during the entire short, chartered flight from Plettenberg Bay to Camps Bay. Her beleaguered father, who was figuring out that parenthood may not be as fabulous as he had first imagined, battled to keep her calm while Bronwyn, who was feeling the effects of some pretty powerful medication, remained mostly oblivious to it all. Bronwyn was vaguely aware of Bryce frantically trying to shush the child. He made funny faces and played silly little games but Kayla refused to be comforted by someone who was a total stranger to her. She was too small to be belted in but she stubbornly refused to stay in Bryce's lap. Instead she kept trying to crawl over onto her mother's lap, and Bronwyn tried her best to soothe the little girl, but Kayla wasn't too impressed with her limp hugs either.

"*Do* something," Bryce eventually entreated, when Kayla slid from his grasp like a greased pig and melted to the floor in a boneless heap. Once at their feet she wailed pitifully.

"Kayla scairt, mummy, Kayla scairt!" she howled. Bronwyn, thoroughly fed up with the theatrics, reached down and dragged the limp toddler up with as much strength as she could muster.

"*Mikayla*," she managed hoarsely in her toughest, no-nonsense, voice. Kayla was momentarily silenced by Bronwyn's "mummy" voice and her wide blue eyes melted Bronwyn's heart. The poor little thing was understandably scared. Too many changes in too short a time for her. Bronwyn gentled her voice and smiled with what she hoped was cheerful confidence. "It's fine, baby. Sit with your daddy; he'll take care of you." Mikayla glanced over at the swiftly unraveling Bryce with wary speculation in her gaze. Turning to him for protection had evidently not occurred to her.

"Man?" she questioned uncertainly.

"Daddy," Bronwyn corrected tiredly, fading fast. "Go and sit with him." The little girl, clutching her favorite stuffed doll to her chest, took the one small step separating her from Bryce and raised her arms to let it be known that she would allow him to pick her up now. Bryce lifted her into his lap and she curled up against his chest, propping her thumb into her mouth. Huge crocodile tears were streaming down her cheeks. Bronwyn rolled her eyes and leaned back with an exhausted sigh. For a couple of minutes everything was quiet, save for the noisy drone of the chopper. Bronwyn was just settling in for a doze when Bryce spoke, so softly that she could barely hear his voice above all the noise. Not even the headphones she was wearing helped to amplify his voice.

"She's a handful."

Bronwyn opened her eyes and found herself staring straight into his brooding eyes. "Yes." She nodded tiredly. "She tends to be. But she's just frightened right now; this isn't anything that she's used to."

"Tell me about her," he invited, almost reluctantly. It obviously dented his pride having to ask her for anything.

"She's inherited more than just some of your physical traits," Bronwyn said with a smile. "She has a stubborn streak a mile wide and is ferociously independent."

"When did she start walking and talking?"

"She was an early talker." Bronwyn's smile went misty. "She mostly gurgled a lot, babbled incoherently for a while . . ." Bryce was frowning and she stuttered to a halt. "What's wrong?"

"Slow down," he commanded gruffly. "I can't understand a damned thing you're saying!"

Having momentarily forgotten about his deafness, the reminder served as a cruel reality check. She swallowed convulsively, aware of the dry, painful heat in her throat.

"I'm sorry," she whispered before repeating her previous statement as slowly and clearly as she could. Bryce rolled his eyes impatiently.

"I'm deaf, not stupid," he ground out furiously. "Just speak normally; don't babble and don't drawl and keep facing me."

"I'm sorry." She helplessly repeated her apology. She felt hopelessly inadequate. Again, she tried to repeat her previous statement, but she was so nervous by now that she stammered badly. Bryce swore impatiently beneath his breath before deliberately lowering his gaze to Kayla. *That* easily he ended the conversation. The slight was brutally effective and left Bronwyn feeling thoroughly abandoned. She felt like a complete failure and kept her eyes trained on his face, hoping that he would look back up, but he was talking to the still-crying Kayla. He was so absorbed by his daughter that Bronwyn might as well not have been there.

She eventually lowered her gaze to where her hands were curled into tight fists in her lap, and as she desperately fought the urge to cry, she tried to figure out where and how her life had gone so very wrong. She thought back to their first meeting, which had always seemed like something out of a fairy tale to her—Prince Charming meeting Cinderella while she was still in her rags but falling for her anyway.

It had seemed so perfect . . .

∾

He had been, without a doubt, the most handsome man she had ever seen. It was her first day waitressing at the upscale beachfront restaurant in Camps Bay and she could not afford distractions, especially since she had lied about her qualifications to get the job. Fortunately she had managed to bluff her way through the in-house training without looking too incompetent. Since finishing high school six years ago, she hadn't been much good at anything except looking after her ailing grandmother, her only relative. It had been a full-time job, leaving no room in her life for the socializing other women her age enjoyed. Instead, she had spent most of her day in the company of an infirm old woman and any free time she may have had was devoted to her stash of books. It had been a sad and solitary existence for a young woman with such a sunny disposition but Bronwyn had never wished the task away. Her grandmother had raised her without complaint after her parents had died and Bronwyn had loved the old lady fiercely because of that.

They had scraped by, living off her gran's pension and a small trust fund her grandfather had set up for his wife. After her grandmother's death just two months before, the balance of the fund had been spent on the funeral and Bronwyn had been forced to sell their small semi-detached house. Most of the money made from the sale had gone toward settling outstanding hospital bills, with barely enough left over for Bronwyn to pay the deposit on the tiny flat that she was now renting.

So here she was, trying desperately to do well at her new job, but she couldn't take her eyes off the man who had just walked into the restaurant. He was tall, blond, and beautiful, and he was absorbed in the conversation he was having with the lean, dark man beside him. The two men were as opposite as night and day. The blond was big and bulky, almost Nordic in appearance, while the dark one was lean and lithe, with a definite sexy Gallic look to him. They sat down at one of her tables and her mouth went dry. She hurried over, not wanting to keep such important-looking men waiting and thankfully stumbled only once along the way.

"Good morning . . . Uh, hello . . . How may I . . ." She blanked, having already stuffed up the perky greeting that had been drilled into her during training. The men were looking at her expectantly, and she faltered even more beneath the blond man's icy stare. "Your order," she concluded abruptly. "What is it, please?"

The dark man's eyebrows climbed in astonishment, but the blond remained impassive even though Bronwyn, for a fleeting moment, thought that she spotted amusement flashing in those seemingly cold eyes of his.

"Drinks," she continued desperately. "You probably drink. So you probably want some, a lot, I mean . . ." She felt her face going blood red with embarrassment. The dark man was staring at her in complete amazement, with his jaw dropped practically to his chest. The other man though, his jaw was clenched; he looked like he was exerting enormous control over his emotions. She panicked. He was probably angry, probably used to vastly superior service from this restaurant. She floundered again . . . at a complete loss.

"You look thirsty," she murmured, hoping to prompt them into saying something, anything. "And we have plenty of drinks."

"What would you recommend?" the blond asked unexpectedly. His voice was warm and mellifluous and much gentler than she had expected. It seemed completely at odds with the craggy planes of his face, as well as with his tightly controlled expression. His voice flowed over her like warm honey, and she stood staring at him dreamily without being aware of it for the longest time.

"Miss?" the dark man prompted impatiently. "What do you recommend?"

"Uh"—she snapped out of her daze, embarrassingly aware that she had been caught staring at the blond. "Recommend?"

"Drinks," the blond reminded gently.

"Yes of course . . ." She scanned her memory frantically. "Wine . . . we have wine, and of course we have . . . you might like it, because I quite like it, you see?" They didn't seem to see. God, she was being such a socially awkward ditz. She wasn't usually this bad.

"Like what?" the blond asked.

"The . . . um . . . the milkshake. Chocolate especially." The dark man's brows lowered in complete consternation; he really had the most expressive eyebrows.

"You recommend the . . ." He sounded like he was choking, and his face was going an unbecoming shade of red. "The milkshake?"

"I didn't even know they had milkshakes here," the blond said conversationally. "Did you, Pierre?" The other man, Pierre, seemed incapable of replying, and Bronwyn wished the ground would open up and swallow her, she was so humiliated. Milkshake? What was she thinking recommending the milkshake to a pair of men who had doubtless not had one since hitting puberty?

"We have other—" she began miserably but was interrupted by Jake, the manager. Sensing a problem, he had come over to intervene.

"Excuse me, is everything all right here?" he asked politely, sending a surreptitious glare toward the flustered Bronwyn. Bronwyn suspected that he knew she had lied about her previous experience, and it seemed that the owner had hired her against Jake's advice.

Now Jake seemed desperate for her to mess up so that he could have an excuse to fire her. She hung her head and waited miserably for the men to complain. The darker one, Pierre, opened his mouth to say something, but the blond forestalled him.

"No problem at all," he murmured smoothly. "My colleague and I were just having some difficulty deciding what to order." Jake had no option but to retreat, but not before sending a warning glare toward Bronwyn.

"Very well, Mr. Palmer." He practically genuflected as he stepped back. "But if you need anything, please ask for Jake."

"Now why would we do that when we already have an excellent server right here?" the blond, Mr. Palmer, asked smoothly before dismissing Jake with a casual flick of the hand. His colleague gaped at him in disbelief.

"Bryce . . ." Pierre started to say. His name was Bryce! He ignored his friend and refocused his beautiful ice-blue eyes on Bronwyn's flushed face.

"Now where were we?" he asked mildly, his eyes running over her face intently. "Ah, yes . . . I think I'll have the chocolate milk-shake."

"Uh . . ." She gaped at him stupidly. "Uh . . . what?"

"The milkshake, I'll have that. Chocolate of course." She nodded dazedly and scribbled down the order before reluctantly turning her attention to Pierre.

"And for you, sir?" Pierre was staring at his friend in disbelief, before refocusing his attention on Bronwyn. Those previously grim eyes of his were alight with humor.

"What the hell." He had a French accent. She had been so focused on Bryce that she hadn't noticed that before. "I think I'll have that milkshake too!"

CHAPTER THREE

A few hours after arriving in Camps Bay, Bronwyn was still unsettled by the emotions those long ago memories on the chopper had stirred up. She was standing in the conservatory; it was the highest point in the staggered house and had always felt like an eagle's aerie to her. All but one wall, as well as half of the ceiling, was entirely made of glass.

She gazed down at the beautiful, blue Atlantic Ocean with its pristine beaches. To her left was a view of the mountain range, the Twelve Apostles, named after the majestic craggy peaks that loomed above the gorgeous beaches, while the bustling city of Cape Town lay to the right.

The house was exactly as she remembered. Big and beautiful, it was built into the face of the mountain and had panoramic views all around. Bronwyn loved this house, absolutely loved the way it caught the sun and loved the fact that it had *always* felt like home. It still did. She had felt it welcoming her back from the moment she had stepped off the chopper. Bryce had deserted her immediately after their arrival, taking Kayla to introduce her to her new home. Bronwyn had wandered around listlessly before finding herself back in this room—her favorite. Bryce had always complained that she had turned it into a "girlie" room, with comfortably overstuffed furniture, beautiful throw rugs, and anything else that caught her fancy. She had trawled flea markets and out-of-the-way little shops for anything she felt would suit this room, and the result had been an eclectic blend of old and new, a room for all seasons.

He hadn't changed it at all. Everything was still in exactly the same place as it had been when she had left, but the room felt unused, and Bronwyn knew that he hadn't set foot in it over the last two years. The room contained so many memories. They had spent hours in it, night and day; it was the room they had done most of their daily living in, simply talking, often making love, and then arguing fiercely on that last day.

Her eyes flooded with tears and she covered her face with her hands. Kayla had been conceived in this room too. One night, three months or so before their final argument, they had returned home from a party, both of them slightly tipsy. He had looked at her like she was the most beautiful woman in the world and had, indeed, told her that over and over again as he had worshipped her body on one of the rugs in front of the window. They had fallen asleep here, right where she was standing, entangled in each other's arms. They'd been so close it had felt like nothing would ever separate them.

"Bronwyn."

She jumped and swung around, so wrapped up in her memories that it took a few seconds for her to realize that he was no longer the same Bryce who had held her so tenderly that night. He had a sleeping Kayla draped against his chest and looked at a bit of a loss. She felt a combination of anger and regret at the sight of him holding her daughter and possessively reached out for her, but Bryce sent her a quelling look.

"You can barely stand upright. Do you really think you're capable of carrying her without dropping her?" Frustrated by the logic of his words and biting back her protestations only out of concern for her daughter's safety, Bronwyn took a step back.

"It's past her usual nap time," she said, making certain that he was looking at her before she spoke, not wanting a repeat of the incident on the helicopter. "Where can we put her?"

"I have a room prepared for her." He turned away and headed for the stairs, which led down to the second-story bedrooms. Bronwyn tensed when they passed the master bedroom and wondered where *she* would be expected to sleep. He led her to the room that adjoined the master and, with his hands full, he nodded toward the closed door. She obediently opened the door and then gasped when she saw the room. It was a nursery, beautifully decorated in lemon and cream. Toys of every kind were stacked neatly on shelves, and a crib—gorgeously detailed and obviously for a newborn—was positioned close to the large picture window. He carried Kayla to a bigger cot that Bronwyn hadn't immediately noticed. She watched as he tenderly laid his daughter down and covered her with a light-weight downy blanket. He stared at her for the longest time, his hand looking clumsy and huge and infinitely gentle as it stroked the little girl's silky hair.

"Welcome home, Mikayla," he murmured gently before leaning down to place a sweet kiss on her forehead. He raised his head to meet her eyes, and seeing the question in them he shrugged, his face going a little bit red.

"I had the room done a few months after you left. It was that or go stir-crazy. I didn't know if she was a boy or girl, so the colors had to be neutral. She has outgrown just about everything in here but I couldn't imagine . . . couldn't picture how she would look and didn't know how big she would be." His voice broke and he lowered his gaze to the sleeping toddler, his eyes glittering with unshed tears. "*God*, she's so beautiful."

Bronwyn didn't know what to say, didn't know how to respond to this obvious desire he'd had to be a part of his child's life. Why hadn't he come for her if he'd wanted the baby? Why hadn't he taken, or returned, any of her calls? At the same time she couldn't help but feel near hatred toward this clearly conflicted man. He had robbed them of the opportunity to be a real family with his inexplicably cruel actions, and pretty little rooms with expensive toys weren't going to change that fact.

"Bryce." She tugged on his sleeve to get his attention. She wouldn't be swayed by the obvious vulnerability on his face. "I don't know what kind of cruel games you're playing with me. You tossed us away like so much garbage. If you wanted us you would never have done that. I'm sorry that you missed out on the first year and a half of your daughter's life, but you do know that you have only yourself to blame for that, right?" She watched the barb hit home as he flinched at her words. The vulnerability fled from his face to be replaced by fury.

"You should get some rest." His words were icy. "You look exhausted and ill! You're also much too thin. Mikayla needs a healthy mother, not some wraith who can barely lift her."

"Bryce . . . I don't understand. Why do you hate me so much. What have I done to deserve this ridiculous amount of contempt?" It was getting increasingly hard for her to remain upright, but this was important. She was physically weak at the moment, but she was not going to let him walk all over her.

"How dare you ask me that?" he hissed furiously. "How *dare* you, after everything that you've done?"

"I did what you told me to do," she reminded him, her trembling voice as icy as his had been before. "You told me to leave, to get out of your sight! You called me a deceitful, lying bitch and told me that you never wanted to see me again."

"*Just* stop playing the tragic victim," he warned. "The only reason I can stomach having you back in my life is because of Mikayla, but push me too far and I'll make damned sure you never set eyes on her again."

His threat—her worst fear—sent a shiver down her spine, and her throat closed up, shutting her up as effectively as a punch to the jaw would have. Their eyes clashed for a moment, his stormy and furious, hers bleak with terror. Bryce muttered something vile sounding beneath his breath before taking an unexpected step toward her and folding her into his strong arms. His head swooped and he caught her lips in a fiercely tender kiss. Bronwyn gasped in shock, fear, and relief. This felt more like home than the house had. She burrowed closer, wanting the intimacy and affection that she had been missing for so long. Her head tilted back and her mouth opened like a flower beneath his. He groaned, one large hand flat against the small of her back, the other cupping the back of her head. There was an edge of desperation to his kiss, a hunger that had never been present in his lazy, long kisses of the past. His tongue sought and found hers; she felt weak and dizzy with desire. *God* she had missed him so much, enough to allow this moment of weakness, even though she knew it wouldn't solve any of their problems. His hands crept up to cup her face, and his thumbs swept over the silky skin of her cheeks. She had her arms wrapped around his hard, warm body, and her hands splayed against his back. She would have crept into his skin if she could.

He stiffened suddenly before tossing her aside with a vicious curse and glaring down into her dazed face contemptuously. He shook his head grimly before turning on his heel and striding out without another word, leaving her hurt, humiliated, and furious in his wake. Bronwyn wrapped her arms around her shaking body, still utterly devastated by how much he seemed to despise her. There was a time when he had seemed like a dream come true. He had been an enigma but still the most intriguing man she had ever met . . .

~

He had kept *watching* her and making her jumpier than she already was. After slurping down his milkshake with every appearance of complete enjoyment, he had asked her for a meal recommendation, but after the disaster with the drinks, she politely informed him that she highly recommended everything on the menu. He wasn't having that, and, ignoring his impatient friend, he forced her to tell him what her favorite dish on the menu was. She hadn't worked at the restaurant long enough to sample much of the menu and very reluctantly revealed her plebeian tastes by saying that she enjoyed the gourmet brie and bacon burger that they offered. He nodded and ordered said burger. His friend, done with indulging him, ordered something much more in keeping with his sophisticated palate. Bryce went through the same routine with dessert, and Pierre, evidently giving up on him, made his excuses and headed back to whatever glamorous life he led. Bryce remained though, eating his dessert and following it up with coffee. He remained for four hours, the last hour of which had been spent sitting solo at the table toying with dessert, ordering cup after cup of coffee and staring at her. He never smiled and never flirted; he simply *watched* her. Eventually he asked for the bill and when she brought it, he graced her with the slightest of smiles, his serious eyes warm and a bit confused.

"You've never done this before have you?" he asked gently, as if afraid of hurting her feelings, and she flushed painfully before nodding.

"What gave it away?" she joked, feeling like a miserable failure.

"I don't know." He shrugged, his smile widening. "Maybe the way you kept recommending the least expensive items on the menu, despite the fact that it would probably decrease your tip." She was appalled for not realizing that herself and made a mental note to recommend the lobster to every client who asked in the future! She frowned, forcing herself to remember to write that down before giving up and drawing a Post-it booklet from her apron pocket to jot down in capital letters: *REMEMBER LOBSTERS!!!* He was watching her every reaction in complete fascination, and she looked up to find him staring at her again.

"Why do you keep watching me like that?" she asked bluntly, before going even redder, shocked by her own forwardness. His brows lowered as he gave her question some consideration.

"I wasn't aware that I was being so . . . obvious," he murmured. He shook himself out of some kind of reverie before reaching for his wallet and extracting a platinum credit card. It was pretty clear that he had no intention of answering her question. He was a generous, but not overly generous, tipper, and when she returned with his credit card he stood up while pocketing his wallet.

"Thank you . . . *Bronwyn,* is it?" She nodded mutely and he smiled—just the barest tilt at the corners of his mouth—again. "The name suits you." She didn't respond to that, not sure if it was a compliment or not.

He turned to go and then hesitated before turning back to face her.

"How old are you, Bronwyn?"

"Twenty-four."

His expression was inscrutable.

"You seem younger." He shrugged. "I'm twenty-nine."

"Okay?" Why was he telling her this? He was a strange man, but not in a scary way. He seemed so sophisticated, so unlike anyone else she had ever met.

"I'm sorry. It's just that . . ." He seemed to lose track of what he was saying and stood, awkwardly silent for a few seconds. "You just . . . you have . . ." *What?* She had *what?* She ran her tongue over her teeth, afraid that she may have something stuck in them, and then rubbed her nose in case she had a spot on it.

"*Such* amazing eyes," he concluded in a rush.

Huh?

She gaped at him uncomprehendingly for a while, and he went dull-red before clearing his throat and turning away abruptly. He left before she could blink, before she could draw breath, and before she could call him back.

～

It had been nearly a week since their ill-fated kiss and Bryce hadn't spoken to her much since then. He had given her the master bedroom and as with the conservatory, the room had an unlived feel to it. Her wardrobe had been left untouched, but Bryce's clothes were gone; not a tie or even a stray cuff link remained. It was as if he had never shared the same closet space with her. None of her old clothes fit her anymore; they were all a couple of sizes too large. Bronwyn had been dismayed to discover exactly how much weight she had lost over the last couple of years. She had always been slender, so the fact that she had dropped two dress sizes must mean that she looked completely emaciated! No wonder Bryce had said that she looked like a wraith.

She made a concerted effort to eat more, and as Kayla was spending a lot of time with her father, Bronwyn was getting plenty of rest, so much rest that she was getting quite bored. She was sitting in the conservatory, reading an easy (or so the back blurb claimed) guide to South African Sign Language, when she heard Kayla's happy chatter approaching. She tucked the book behind a cushion, not wanting Bryce to know she was trying to learn SASL. Something told her that he would not be happy about it. Any references she had made to his deafness were not well received.

Kayla entered the room in her inimitable way, all happy laughter and incomprehensible speech while Bryce followed her in *his* inimitable way, all scowls and growls when he saw that Bronwyn occupied the conservatory.

"Mummeeeee!" The little girl squealed when she saw Bronwyn, and she clambered into her mother's lap, smelling of sunshine and sea air. She was wearing cute pink dungarees, one of the very many expensive items of clothing her father had purchased for her. He had taken his daughter out shopping, without Bronwyn, the day after their arrival in Camps Bay. He had sent the housekeeper to ask for Kayla's sizes. Bronwyn had felt rather awkward around Celeste, the housekeeper, who had been with them since their wedding just over four years ago, but the elderly woman had welcomed her back with a genuinely warm smile. Bronwyn had written the sizes down and mentally wished him luck with Kayla, who inevitably became a nightmare to handle in any shopping situation. No sooner had they left, than she started worrying about both of them. Bryce might find Kayla more than a handful with his deafness, and Kayla would probably start panicking when she figured out that her mummy was nowhere to be found. Her worrying had come to nothing though, because the two had returned from their shopping spree fast friends and totally inseparable from that point onward. She was a little jealous and resentful at the ease with which Bryce had established a position in her daughter's life. A petty part of her had hoped that Kayla would give him a hard time of it, but her daughter had accepted him without protest and seemed to barely miss Bron at all.

Despite her deep-seated feelings of animosity toward Bryce, Bronwyn tried very hard not to begrudge them this time together, if only for Kayla's sake. The little girl needed Bryce in her life. And Bronwyn had to acknowledge that the toddler, with her boundless energy, would have sapped her last reserves. Now she cuddled the affectionate child lovingly, delaying the moment when she would actually have to look at her grim husband. When she managed to summon up the guts to glance at him, she was surprised by an expression of unguarded vulnerability on his face. The expression was quickly shuttered when he noticed that she was staring at him, and the habitual frown took its place.

"What did you and Daddy do this morning?" she asked Kayla, keeping her eyes trained on his face so that he would not feel excluded.

"We play horsy . . . giddup." The child chortled in remembered glee. She bounced on her mother's lap, and Bronwyn winced as Kayla's shoes dug into her thighs. "Giddup mummy . . . giddup, *giddup!*" Bryce plucked the child from Bronwyn's lap before she could do any damage.

"You're hurting your mummy," he told the child in his carefully modulated voice. He spoke very quietly, and Bronwyn guessed that he had difficulty judging the volume of his voice. He kept it so soft that she strained to hear him sometimes. Not that anything he said was ever directed at her. She guessed that the volume of his voice would grow in proportion to his anger, and he was *perpetually* angry with her. He stared at her thoughtfully for a little while before totally shocking her and sitting down next to her, putting Kayla down to play with the toys that were scattered all over the floor.

"You look much better," he observed, his eyes continuing to run over her face and form. "Not as gaunt, and you're getting some color in your cheeks. How do you feel?"

"Better." She nodded. "Bored." He shocked her by gracing her with the smallest of smiles.

"Yes, you were never one for long periods of inactivity." He nodded. "Have you given any thought to what you want to do once you've recovered?" She stared at him in dismay, having no clue how to answer that question. She hadn't dared think about the future; she had no idea what Bryce wanted from her. Did he expect them to just continue to live together in the same soulless fashion for the next fifty years or so? Because Bronwyn couldn't do that. She absolutely refused to live like this for much longer; she would rather get a divorce. Did *he* want a divorce? For that matter, were they divorced already? She was certain of only two things; he wanted his daughter but he did *not* want Bronwyn.

"I don't . . . what do you mean?"

He frowned. "It wasn't a trick question, Bronwyn," he responded scathingly.

"I'm not sure . . . I suppose I'll find a place to live?"

He didn't like her response. That much was evident from the way he was glowering at her.

"You're not taking Kayla away from me again, Bronwyn. You'll both be staying here. You'd best reconcile yourself to that fact!"

"Staying here as what?" she asked pointedly. A divorce was looking increasingly appealing right now. She had no idea why she hadn't instigated proceedings herself long ago. She supposed she had clung to the remnants of a fairy-tale marriage that had never existed outside of her imagination.

"My wife and my daughter," he responded angrily, his voice rising marginally. "I could do without the wife, but I realize that it's a package deal for now, so I'm willing to suffer your presence in my life again."

"How long do you expect us to continue to live like this?" she pressed. She was trying very hard to keep the emotional strain off her face.

"Live like what? You have it made, Bronwyn, you'll never want for anything, you have everything you need right here. *I'm* the one who will be making the sacrifices, shackled to the wife who crippled me and stole my child from me. I'll be the one saddled with a wife whom I have absolutely no respect for. But I want my daughter, and for now this is the only way that I can have her."

"Oh please, Bryce," she retorted, her face pale with anger and hurt. "You're not quite the prize you think you are. You forget that I'll be trapped in a loveless marriage with a man who kicked me out of the house when I told him I was pregnant with his child. A man who hates me for absolutely no reason at all and who makes no secret of the fact that he doesn't respect me. How on earth do you call that having it made? I'd rather we divorce and try to reach an amicable custody agreement. Kayla and I could live close by and . . ."

"The only other option you have here is if I took her from you, Bronwyn. No compromises. You live here with us, or you leave without her. What's it to be?"

"You can't take her from me . . ." she began helplessly, going ice cold as he pulled the rug out from under her again. Damn him, he held all the cards and he knew it. Her bravado was just empty posturing. She didn't have his resources, and for now she'd have to toe his line until she could find a way out of this mess.

"*Can't* I?" he asked frostily. She floundered beneath his steady gaze, lowering her eyes to where Kayla was happily playing on the floor. "You'd better start thinking about what you want, Bronwyn. Stay or leave. But if you stay, I suggest you start finding ways to make your life here more tolerable."

"But what about . . ." she began before biting her tongue and blushing to her toes. The blush gave her away.

"Sex?" he prompted, and she nodded miserably. "Well, I don't know about yours but *my* sex life is perfectly fine." He shrugged.

"Naturally, I don't expect you to deprive yourself either. If you're concerned that I'll come creeping into your bed one desperate night, don't worry about it. You're the last woman in the world I want to sleep with." His expression was filled with such distaste that Bronwyn's eyes filled with tears of shame. She knuckled them away, infuriated by the display of weakness. His contempt hurt more than she could possibly have imagined. She glanced down at their daughter. The innocently playing little girl remained oblivious to the tension in the room, and Bronwyn was grateful for that. She refocused her attention on Bryce.

"You wanted me the other day," she reminded him defiantly, and he laughed.

"I felt *sorry* for you," he corrected. "Trust me, Bronwyn, the mere thought of touching you makes my skin crawl!" She flinched and struggled desperately to keep her tears at bay and her emotions in check, but one single scalding drop escaped to scorch its way down her cheek. His eyes followed the tear's progress. His jaw clenched, and his expression remained emotionless. He looked like a man under enormous strain. She wiped at the moisture on her face, wanting to be as unemotional as he was but failing dismally when another tear escaped. She averted her face, not wanting to see the scorn in his eyes and pushed herself up as she sought an escape route out of the room. He got up too and stood in front of her, blocking her way to the exit, so she turned away from him and walked to one of the windows, staring blindly out at the magnificent scenery as she fought to control her emotions.

～

He watched her narrow back quiver as she bravely tried to bring herself back under control. *Damn her!* Her tears had always had the power to unman him, but that was something she did not know, something he had never dared reveal to her for fear that she would use them as a weapon against him. But he could tell that Bronwyn hated having him see her tears. He could see her struggling to be strong, but she was so transparent that every devastating emotion showed clearly on her face. The very fact that she was trying so hard to hide any sign of weakness from him made her tears difficult to ignore. He clenched his fists and forced himself to remain where he was, not to give in to the temptation to go and comfort her.

She looked out at the ocean but didn't appear to be admiring the view as she wrapped her slender arms around herself. She seemed so incredibly lonely that it almost physically hurt him not to go to her. But Bryce refused to fall into her trap again; *he* was calling the shots now. The last time he had been so smitten with her that he had barely been able to see straight. He remembered the first time he'd laid eyes on her, how he had stared at her that day, trying to figure out what he found so fascinating about her.

She was tall, about five eleven, but she lacked the grace inherent in a lot of tall women. In fact, on that first day, she had seemed to fall over her feet just about every five minutes. She wasn't even pretty. Her features taken separately were attractive enough, a long straight nose, lush mouth, high arching eyebrows, and the most beautiful, thickly lashed, brown eyes that he had ever seen. Yet when put together in her narrow, oval face, those features just didn't seem to match. Still he had been compelled to stare for hours, drowning every time she shifted those huge, velvet-brown doe eyes of hers to him.

Now he watched her warily, almost wishing that he had never laid eyes on the treacherous bitch. He damned her for looking like a fragile waif with her badly trimmed dark-brown hair curling around her face where it had escaped from its sloppy ponytail. He watched as she straightened her back, coming to some sort of resolution, and turned back to face him. She walked toward him until they were separated by less than a meter.

"I will stay," she said, her beautiful mouth forming the words concisely. It was hell, this lip-reading business. Every time his gaze fell on her full lips, he found himself remembering what they tasted like. "It looks like I have no other choice. When I have completely recuperated and Kayla is settled in, I want to resume my studies." He nodded; one of his objections to her pregnancy had been that she was in the process of obtaining her undergraduate degree in zoology, her ultimate goal to become a veterinarian. He hadn't been comfortable with the idea of her giving that up and maybe one day resenting both him and the baby for having to sacrifice her dreams. He couldn't recall telling her that at the time though but he knew that he hadn't been at his most logical after hearing the news that she was pregnant.

"If this is to be an open marriage," she continued, "I will start seeing other people too. All I ask is that we be as discreet as possible, for Kayla's sake."

She intended to see other men? That thought did not sit too well with him, and he opened his mouth to protest before remembering that it had been his own stupid idea for her not to deprive herself. After all if *he* did not want her, why should she not feel free to find someone who would? Some other guy who would hold her and kiss her? Someone who would be free to wipe away her tears and comfort her? Some other man who would love her and take care of her? Someone who would do what Bryce no longer wanted to do? He nodded, hoping that none of the confusion he was feeling was evident in his eyes or on his face.

"Sounds fair," he agreed smoothly before dropping his gaze pointedly to her bare ring finger. "But open marriage or not, you have to start wearing your wedding rings again."

Bronwyn covered her left hand self-consciously with her right, her own eyes dropping to his strong hands. She had noticed, couldn't help *but* notice, that he still wore his wedding ring, a broad brushed gold and platinum band with a complex Celtic design that had matched her much smaller band.

"I . . . I don't have them," she confessed, and he made an impatient sound at the back of his throat.

"I'm *deaf,* remember?" he prompted sarcastically. "Show me your mouth when you speak!" She raised her face and met his gaze unflinchingly.

"I don't have them."

"You don't have the rings?" he asked in disbelief. "What the hell did you *do* with them?"

"I sold them," she said before fleeing from the room, not wanting to see his reaction to that confession. She would have given anything to hold on to those rings even though they had come to symbolize nothing but lies.

CHAPTER FOUR

Bronwyn hadn't really expected to see the handsome Mr. Palmer again after that disastrous first time, yet there he was, waiting outside the restaurant the following evening after her shift ended. He had looked moody and uncertain, leaning against the wall outside the staff entrance. When she saw him, she hesitated, not sure why he was there.

"Oh . . . sir, are you waiting for someone? Would you like me to deliver a message?" He was frowning down at her in consternation and seemed a little bewildered.

"Have you eaten?" he asked unexpectedly, and her brow wrinkled as she tried to make sense of the bizarre situation.

"Not really." She shook her head.

"Have dinner with me?" The request was so abrupt that it took a few seconds to sink in.

"Uh . . ."

"Look, I know how this must seem," he acknowledged gruffly. "But I assure you, I am not in the habit of lurking around outside restaurants and ambushing the female staff with invitations to dinner. I won't harm you in any way. I'm not some creepy pervert or anything. I just . . . I just . . ."

She waited, watching in absolute fascination as he glowered in frustration and ran an agitated hand through his hair while swearing beneath his breath. He dropped his gaze to the ground as he made a visible effort to gather his scattered wits.

"God," he was muttering to himself. "I sound like a complete psychopath . . ." Her lips curved into a slight smile at the tone of disgusted self-discovery, but she quickly wiped it from her face when he shifted his eyes back to her.

"I had no intention of coming back, but I wanted to see you again."

"Why?"

"I don't *know.*" He sounded so baffled that the smile crept back into her eyes. "Will you have dinner with me?"

"Okay," she said lightly, and his frown deepened. He nodded, pushing himself away from the wall and turning to lead the way before pausing to turn back to her.

"Do you have absolutely no sense of self-preservation?" he growled, and her eyebrows shot up in surprise at his stern tone. "Promise me that after tonight you won't agree to have dinner with any more strange men off the street! It's dangerous. There are all manner of crazies out there. Murderers and rapists and God knows what else. You have to be more careful, Bronwyn. Promise me."

"I promise," she vowed, a little stunned by this unexpected protectiveness from a man she barely knew.

He had smiled in relief and she noticed, for the first time, that he had a rather sexy dimple in his right cheek. "Good. Then let's eat . . ."

~

Bryce had been in an unpredictable mood since she had confessed, earlier that day, to pawning her wedding and engagement rings. Bronwyn eyed her husband nervously across the dinner table. They tended to have late dinners, so Kayla had been fed and put to bed an hour before. She had toyed with the idea of skipping dinner, but she knew that it would be foolish to miss any meals when she was already so weak, and eating in her room would be the coward's way out. Bryce had insisted, soon after her arrival, that they dine together. He seemed to want everyone to think that this was some kind of happy reconciliation. Not that anyone other than the maids had been around to see them together. Rick, Lisa, and their thirteen-month-old baby—Rhys—had resumed their family vacation in Knysna and wouldn't be back in Cape Town for another few days.

Bronwyn was still amazed by how much things had changed since she left. She wondered where Bryce's friends were. Pierre De Coursey, his business partner at DCP Jewellers Inc. and good friend, used to be a regular visitor in their home; she had liked the Frenchman, although she knew he must have wondered what Bryce was doing with a small-town hick like her.

"Where is Pierre?" She got sick of the silence and decided to take the bull by the horns. When she received no response, she looked up to find Bryce contemplating his wineglass. She sighed sadly, immediately realizing her mistake. She waved to catch his attention and he looked up absently. She repeated her question and he frowned.

"You want beer?" he asked in surprise.

"Pierre De Coursey?" She used the Frenchman's full name, hoping that it would help, and watched as Bryce's lips quirked in amusement, causing his dimple to wink briefly. She was a little shocked at the self-deprecating humor she saw in his eyes.

"Sorry, *b*'s and *p*'s, you know? Along with *v*'s and *f*s and *t*'s and *d*'s. It can be a little confusing when there's no context to a comment or conversation. I can get a little lost."

She nodded and dared a slight smile. "What about Pierre?"

"Well he hasn't been around at all since my return. I find this rather strange, since he used to come by most evenings before . . . before . . ." Her voice petered off, and his eyebrows rose.

"Before you ran away?" he inserted smoothly.

"Before I was *driven* away," she corrected, just as smoothly, fed up with being the villain of the piece. His eyebrows raised a notch higher, but he let it slide for once.

"Pierre spends most evenings at home with his family these days."

"His family?" Pierre hadn't been married when she left.

"Yes, he has a wife and son."

"Pierre De Coursey got *married*?" She couldn't quite keep the shock out of her expression.

"Came as a surprise to me too." He grinned unexpectedly and looked so much like his old self that Bronwyn's mouth went dry with longing. "Last year, nearly a full year after you'd left, he quite unexpectedly announced that he was getting married. Admittedly, I had been very much out of commission and not too aware of what was happening in the world around me at the time, but Pierre, who had been a regular and concerned visitor and friend had never even *mentioned* meeting a woman he was serious enough about to marry."

Bronwyn was so busy absorbing the rare and revealing statement about his convalescence after the accident that his comments about Pierre barely registered. To all intents and purposes, it seemed as if Bryce had retreated from the world after his accident and hadn't ventured back into it. He seemed almost reclusive and hardly ever left the house. In fact she could not recall him going to the office once since her return. He and Pierre co-owned an exclusive jewelry company that was renowned for its designer accessories that catered to only the wealthiest members in the most rarefied reaches of society. The company had branches in all the major cities in Europe,

North America, and Asia and had just recently gone public on the stock exchange.

"Alice is fantastic," he was saying. "Just what Pierre needs."

Sidetracked by that, Bronwyn frowned and tuned back in to the conversation.

"Pierre De Coursey married a woman named *Alice?*" Somehow she had always pictured Pierre, when she had even entertained such an absurd notion, as ending up with a woman exotic in both name and looks.

"Yes. She's a nice woman, a bit quiet but sharp as the proverbial tack," he recalled fondly, and Bronwyn forced back a tide of envy at the warmth in his voice.

"How did they meet?" she asked, curious.

"Hospital. Pierre was visiting me and wandered into the wrong ward. Alice had been in an accident too, a really bad one from what I understood. She was unconscious, apparently in a coma, and while every other patient in the room had cards and flowers, Alice had nothing. I don't know, I think Pierre felt a little sorry for her, so he checked in on her every day on his way to visit me and soon learned that she had no family and that she had just moved here from Johannesburg, which meant that she'd had no time to befriend anyone yet. He kept visiting her even after my discharge from the hospital. He brought her flowers and talked to her for months until one day she opened her eyes, smiled, and said, 'It's you.'" Bryce shrugged. "Damned if I know what that meant, but Pierre fell hard and fast. They married a couple of months later, after Alice had convalesced enough to walk down the aisle without aid."

"Oh, what a beautiful story." Bronwyn smiled mistily and Bryce rolled his eyes.

"How like a woman to find it romantic," he scoffed.

"You don't think it's romantic?"

"I think that Pierre just liked feeling needed and enjoyed the idea of having someone almost totally dependent on him. It happens! The love may have come later but initially, in my opinion, that's all it was. Men tend to like it when women arouse our protective instincts; it makes us feel heroic."

"You sound like you're speaking from experience," she couldn't stop herself from pointing out, and he sneered.

"Why the hell do you think I kept coming back to *you?*" She had known it was coming, but she had been unable to prevent herself from rushing into those deep, dark waters. "You made me feel like an all-conquering hero. You kept staring at me with those doe eyes, and I felt like I could take on the world. It's a heady thing, being elevated to near-godlike status like that. I should never have let things go so far. You were a naïve little thing and I took everything you offered, but when we had sex and I learned that you were a virgin, I had no option but to do the right thing, didn't I? Especially since we were so stupid and careless that first time. Even though I wasn't keen on the idea of kids, I didn't want any child of mine growing up without my name."

"What are you trying to say?" She asked softly, glad for once that he could not hear the emotion in her voice but unable to hide the tears sparkling in her eyes. "That our marriage was based on a lie?"

"No lie." He shrugged. "Well, okay, maybe a lie by omission. I never told you *why* I was proposing."

"I thought . . ." *that you loved me.* She couldn't bring herself to say the words, and her voice faded into nothing.

"I know what you thought, but I felt it was best to allow you to continue believing in your happily-ever-after fairy tale." There was absolutely nothing she could say in response to that, and she stared at him through her misty eyes. He broke eye contact first and raised his glass to his lips, taking a hearty slurp from it. For a second she was almost certain his hand was trembling, but he quickly lowered it and raised his gaze to meet hers once again. There was nothing but disdain in that stare, and she knew that she had imagined the slight trace of vulnerability. "Would you like to meet Alice? I'm sure the two of you will get along."

Surprised by the sudden change in subject and the unexpected gentleness in his voice, she nodded helplessly. She had lost contact with all of the friends she had made at university. She had tried contacting a few of them since her return. Of course, most of them had moved on to their postgraduate studies, a few had left the city to continue their studies elsewhere, but the ones who had remained had shown no real desire to resume their friendships with her. If she could befriend Pierre's wife, it would go a long way toward staving off the crushing loneliness she was starting to feel in this house.

"I'd like that." She lowered her eyes to her plate, lifting her knife and fork in an attempt to pretend that nothing was amiss, but the violent trembling in her hands made a liar of her, and she had no choice but to put the utensils back down. She really should not be this devastated by the knowledge that everything she had initially believed about her marriage was a lie. Like her belief that Bryce had married her because he loved her when he had *never* loved her. His revelations should hold no surprise, not after the way he'd treated her two years ago. Still his words had hurt so much more than they should have; it felt like she had been punched in the stomach, and the pain was unrelenting.

"I'll invite them to dinner tomorrow night. Pierre and I have business to discuss anyway," he said softly, and she nodded, lowering her head even more, petrified that he would see her tears. She stared blurrily down at her plate but was barely able to see its contents. To her absolute horror she felt the scalding tears overflowing and watched as they dripped into her plate. With an agonized sound, she hurriedly got to her feet, scrubbing at her face in the process.

"I . . . excuse . . ." She caught a brief look at his grim face, and unable to stand it anymore, she fled, hearing his muffled curse on her way out. There was a horrible silence, followed by an equally horrible crash as Bryce apparently flung something against a wall. The sound of breaking glass spurred her on and she was up the stairs and into her room like a shot. Thankfully the violent noise had not awoken Kayla, and Bronwyn curled up into a small ball in the center of her bed, leaving the lights off, needing the dark to lick her gaping wounds in private.

~

She had awakened in his arms. Bronwyn smiled in contentment and snuggled closer. His strong arms tightened around her and he kissed the top of her head almost reverently. They had been seeing each other for only a month but the chemistry between them had been so potent that it had not taken much for Bronwyn to forget all her grandmother's warnings about men and their "salacious appetites." In fact she thought she had been particularly strong in not giving in much sooner; Bryce was a *very* persuasive kisser, and tonight it hadn't taken much for them to fall into bed together. It had been her first time, and Bryce had been a little shocked at the discovery. He had been excruciatingly gentle and incredibly thorough in making sure that she was completely satisfied. He hadn't left an inch of her body unexplored. Now she was limp, sated, and wondering when they would be able to do it again. She moved her thigh experimentally but still found him disappointingly unprepared for a second round.

"Give me a second," he groaned. "You wore me out, damn it. I need to regain my strength!"

"You just can't keep up with me, can you?" She purred teasingly and he growled before flipping her onto her back, pinning her down, and kissing her thoroughly. She felt him stir against her and grinned against his lips.

"Now that's more like it," she murmured encouragingly, and he grinned, lifting his head to look down at her. The grin faded abruptly and his eyes went silver with desire and something deeper, something so achingly tender it made Bronwyn's heart melt.

"I can't remember my life before you," he said wonderingly. "I can't remember *me* without *you*. I never want to let you go. Tell me you'll marry me . . . please?"

"Bryce?" she whispered uncertainly.

"Bronwyn Kirkland, will you marry me?" he asked almost desperately. She was so overwhelmed by his words that she could do nothing but nod.

"Yes, *yes*, Bryce, I love you so much," she managed to whisper, her voice thick with tears of joy.

"Shhh . . . don't cry . . ." he soothed as he slid gently into her welcoming body. "No more tears. We're going to be so happy together."

She awoke in his arms, feeling both warm and protected. Bronwyn felt a dizzying sense of déjà vu as she struggled to find her bearings. She couldn't believe that she had fallen asleep after the emotional turmoil at dinner—she had been so certain that her tumultuous thoughts would keep her awake. She had her face pressed to his chest and she could feel his heart beating steadily beneath her cheek.

"Bryce?" she whispered tentatively, not sure where her dreams ended and real life began. Maybe she was just now waking up after their first time together and everything in between had been nothing but a vivid dream. He didn't stir and she moved restlessly against him, feeling his arms tighten possessively around her. His large hands started stroking her back leisurely and she burrowed closer, reveling in the comfort and not quite ready to relinquish it yet. She still wasn't certain if this was a dream or real, but she didn't care anymore; she was in Bryce's arms exactly where she belonged.

His warm hands crept beneath the thin cotton blouse she was wearing until his dry palms found the soft, naked skin of her slender back. She sucked in a breath at the electrifying contact and arched toward him with a slight moan. It felt like *forever* since he had touched her last. Her hands crept up over his broad chest, feeling the heat of his skin through the thin material of his T-shirt. She looked up, trying to see his face in the dark, but she could see nothing except the gleam of his eyes.

"Bryce . . ." she murmured dreamily, half-asleep and still lost in the memory of her dream. She lifted a hand to his face. She loved the feel of his stubbled jaw beneath her hand. He made a slight sound and abruptly lowered his head to capture her soft, surprised lips with his hard and demanding mouth. The kiss was a lot more ruthless than she had anticipated; she had been expecting gentleness, not this almost violent caress. Still it was *Bryce*, her beloved Bryce, and she would deny him nothing. His kiss softened and became almost desperate as he leaned into her and over her, until she was flat on her back and he was cradled between her spread thighs. He loomed above her, not once relinquishing contact with her soft mouth, and she moaned as she wrapped her arms tightly around his neck, not wanting to let him go *ever* again.

He eventually came up for air and fumbled with the buttons of her blouse, while she tugged at his T-shirt and dragged it over his head before he had managed even half of the buttons. Losing patience, he ripped the fragile garment apart, sending mother-of-pearl buttons flying everywhere. Bronwyn giggled and Bryce stilled abruptly.

"I've missed your laughter . . ." The sound of his sexy, smoky voice startled her into complete wakefulness. "I always loved your laugh." He sounded so wistful that Bronwyn wished she could see his face. She raised a curious hand to his mouth but he leaned back, denying her the contact.

"Bryce what . . ." she started to say, but he cursed softly before leaning to the side and switching on the bedside lamp. The unwelcome present immediately forced its way into the bedroom as Bronwyn found herself staring up into the rough-hewn features of an older, harsher Bryce than the one she'd just dreamed about. This was not the man she had fallen in love with; this man was battle scarred and hated her more than she had ever believed possible.

"I want to see you," he muttered harshly. "When you speak, I want to know what you're saying! When you laugh, I want to see your eyes light up, and when I make you come"—his voice lowered sexily—"I want to see you scream even if I can't hear it."

"I don't think . . ." she began uncertainly, preferring to make love with him in the dark, where she could fool herself into believing that he was the old Bryce, the one who had pretended to love her, even if he now claimed that he never had. A shaft of agony pierced through her as she recalled his confession at dinner, and she tried to move away from him but he would not permit it. He pinned her down, his eyes boring into hers, so that she was unable to hide her pain from him. His brows lowered into an intimidating frown, and she flinched, wondering what scathing remark he had in store for her this time.

"You were crying at dinner," he said almost accusingly.

"What do you expect?" she asked bitterly. "You can't keep cutting me without spilling my blood, Bryce."

"Such drama." He grinned caustically. "Don't cry again, it irritates me!" The demand was so ridiculously petulant that she gaped at him in astonishment. He took advantage of her open mouth and swooped in for another hungry kiss.

"I want you," he groaned, grinding against her so that she would have no trouble mistaking his meaning. "I want to make love with you." He raised his head to look down at her, trying to gauge her receptiveness.

"Only it's not 'making love,' is it?" she asked bitterly. "Without love it's nothing more than a cheap screw." He made a dismayed little sound and covered her mouth with his own before she could say anything more. Bronwyn soon forgot everything as his mouth wove a seductive spell over her. His wicked fingers seemed to be everywhere at the same time, and his mouth soon followed.

He paused when he reached her braless breasts and he stared at them for a long moment. Bronwyn squirmed uncomfortably as she fought the desire to fold her arms over her petite assets. She had always been self-conscious about her small breasts, but Bryce had always loved them. Now he was staring at them almost analytically, and she found herself flushing to the roots of her hair.

"They haven't changed," he murmured, almost reluctantly raising his eyes to meet hers. "I expected them to be different . . . you know, after Mikayla?"

"I couldn't breastfeed her." She shrugged. "I was ill for a while after the birth, and by the time I was well enough, she was on the bottle and my milk had dried up." His eyes darkened.

"Ill?" Not wanting to discuss that right now, Bronwyn distracted him the only way she knew how, she arched her back until her nipples brushed his naked chest. She hissed as they made contact with the hot, silky flesh that was lightly dusted with soft, golden hair. He groaned at the contact and lowered his eyes back down to her breasts; they were barely a handful—creamy little mounds with raspberry-red tips. His breath caught on a sob of pure desire, and he bent down and did what she was aching for him to do: he took one of the distended tips into his mouth. She squealed, nearly coming off the bed at the electric jolt that swept through her body, and he raised his head to grin at her.

"They're still as sensitive as I rem—" He was cut off when she lifted impatient hands and pulled his head back down, forcing him to focus on the task at hand. He laughed wickedly and proceeded to give her what she wanted with as much enthusiasm as she was taking it.

Soon they were both completely naked, and Bryce paused above her, his arms planted on either side of her head as he held himself aloft. He stared down into her face with an intensity that unnerved her, before reaching over to the nightstand and fumbling open a drawer to yank out a condom. For a painful moment, Bronwyn wondered why he had a handy stash of condoms in the drawer, before he spoke again, immediately distracting her.

"Still such innocence in those eyes, such trust, they still stare at me with such adoration," he muttered, half to himself as he dragged on the condom. "How can your eyes tell such *lies?*" Shocked by the near hatred in his voice, Bronwyn gasped in horror as she recognized that this act of sex, if completed, would be another cruel means of hurting her, just another weapon to use against her. Before she had a chance to formulate any kind of protest, he entered her with a gentleness that belied his harsh words and took what she had so heedlessly and freely offered just moments ago. She was so well-primed for it that despite everything, she moaned and her slender thighs clenched around his hips. Her long legs wrapped around his waist as she welcomed him back into her body. He had gone completely still, and she opened her eyes to see him staring down at her triumphantly. Her eyes filled with tears and he glared down at her.

"Don't you *dare*," he warned darkly. "Don't cry." She couldn't help it, tears overflowed even as she shoved herself up against him. He groaned and met her lunge with one of his own.

"Don't cry."

Bronwyn found herself whimpering desperately in time with his thrusts, even while her tears continued to flow and her heart continued to break.

"Please don't. Please don't," he continued to almost beg, kissing the tears away. His tenderness acted as a balm to her ravaged soul and worked to end the weeping as nothing else could have. "My beautiful, Bronwyn . . ."

Her body arched as the sensations heightened and he reached down between their bodies to find her sensitive little clitoris. His long, clever thumb rubbed across the excited nubbin and that, combined with his thickness inside of her, sent her hurtling over the edge of reason. Her breath hitched in her chest and her head tilted back while her entire body convulsed and clenched around him. She screamed as the powerful orgasm swept through her, and Bryce half-laughed incredulously.

He couldn't take his eyes off her. So absorbed was he in her climax that his own took him completely by surprise. He shouted hoarsely as his entire body bucked and he jerked once, twice before with another shout—her name—he poured himself into her with a broken sob. His eyes closed as his brain shut down and his body went limp. He stirred himself only to remove the condom before flopping down beside her again, dropping a heavy arm over her waist.

"I miss your breathless little sounds." He broke the silence five minutes later, after their heartbeats and breathing had returned to normal, just as Bronwyn was starting to feel awkward and wondering *now what?* "Those half-formed gasping little words, *God* they used to turn me on more than you can imagine." She lifted her head from his chest to stare at him.

"You never mentioned that before," she pointed out, and he smiled.

"Because I *knew* that if I'd said anything you would immediately have felt self-conscious about it." His reminiscent smile became a wicked grin. "And I didn't want you tensing up at crucial moments."

"Yet you feel comfortable enough telling me about it now?" she asked, curious, and he snorted.

"I can't *hear* them anymore," he pointed out, and she tensed. "So getting self-conscious about any sounds you produce while we're making love is a little pointless."

"Are you going to tell me what happened to you, Bryce?" she asked faintly, and it was his turn to tense up. "Or are you *never* going to afford me the opportunity to defend myself?"

"You were there," he reminded grimly, and she frowned irritably.

"*Why* do you keep saying that? What do you mean I was 'there'?" she asked angrily. "Where the hell was I?"

"There when I had my goddamned accident!" he snapped before launching himself out of bed and stalking around the bedroom angrily, looking for his clothing. She leaped out as well and walked around his back until she was facing him again. She was stark naked, but she no longer cared about anything except getting to the bottom of this strange accusation.

"I was *not* there when you had your accident!" she retorted indignantly.

"I saw you," he forced the words out between clenched teeth.

"What?" She was completely baffled now. "Saw me where? Bryce I don't even know *when* you had your accident. Please just tell me what happened!"

"It burns me to have to tell you something that you already know, Bronwyn," he gritted. "You're playing me for a fool and I don't like it!" He moved to step around her but she put her hands up against his broad chest to stop him. He felt about as immovable as a block of granite.

"Please, just . . . just . . ." Her eyes begged him when words failed her.

"I went after you that night, when you raced out of here like a bat out of hell," he said so quietly that his lips barely moved. "As you *knew* that I would. You were going so fast that I was terrified you would get into an accident." His lips twisted at that bit of irony. "It took me a few minutes to get my car out, so by the time I headed out in the direction you had gone, you'd disappeared. I was frantic and wasn't paying attention to anything around me. I was so focused on trying to spot your car that I didn't see the couple crossing the road until it was almost too late. I swerved to avoid them and the car rolled. I was drifting in and out of consciousness, trapped in the car, when I saw you standing there amongst the crowd, staring at me with nothing but ice-cold contempt on your face . . . you heartless *bitch!*" He hissed viciously. "You turned around and walked away without so much as a backward glance.

"I wasn't even surprised when I woke up three days later in Intensive Care to be informed that you hadn't even bothered to visit or call. I couldn't have cared *less* if I never saw you again but for the fact that you were having my baby. You were having my baby and you had simply disappeared off the face of the earth. Is it any wonder I hate you? Not only is my accident your fault, but you walked away from me when I was at my most vulnerable, when I needed you most, and you took my daughter along with you!"

Bronwyn's face was ashen with shock at his story. She ached to think of the agony he must have gone through in that hospital, wondering about his baby, but she was also filled to the brim with fury and offense that he *dared* to think she could do something so awful as walk away from him while he lay injured and bleeding. Not to mention his ridiculous statement that the accident had been her fault when he had caused the entire sorry situation.

"I concede," she began quietly, with barely repressed sarcasm, "that maybe the accident was my fault because for some crazy reason I saw fit to flee after you drove me out of the house right when *I* needed *you* most. But I absolutely refuse to listen to this nonsense about me standing impassively by the side of the road while you lay bleeding and trapped in a car. Or, worse, walking away while you were still *in* the car!

"I didn't know that you'd been in an accident until the day you walked into my hospital room. I would never have stood there watching you suffer, and if I had known you were in the hospital, no force in heaven or hell would have kept me away from your bedside, because, even though you had treated me like something to be scraped off the bottom of your boot, I still loved you so damned much!" He started to say something but she held up her hand.

"No. You've had your turn; it's only fair I get a chance to defend myself against this . . . this *insult!* I did not think you would immediately come chasing after me—you were so irrationally angry that I knew you needed time to calm down. I headed straight for the beach house in Knysna. I stopped only for brief bathroom breaks and drove the distance in just under five and a half hours. I was confident that once you had time to calm down and think, you would change your mind about the baby."

"I *saw* you," he maintained, clearly not believing her. "Saw you with my own eyes!"

"You were sliding in and out of consciousness; you were in shock and in pain . . ." she pointed out reasonably. "You don't think that maybe you were delirious as well? Seeing things that were not there?"

He frowned and shook his head.

"No, of course not," she scoffed. "Not Bryce Palmer, he *never* makes mistakes."

"God damn you," he growled. "I know what I saw . . . you were standing there looking impassive and completely uncaring."

"This?" She waved her hand back and forth between their naked bodies. "This thing that just happened between us? It was a mistake that shouldn't be repeated. I should never have let you touch me, but you got me in a moment of complete weakness. That ends now. I won't allow a man who just hours ago said I made his skin crawl use me like this again. Now, if you'll excuse me, I need a shower," she informed him unsteadily. There was really nothing she could say or do right now to prove that she hadn't been there that day. She didn't know if she'd ever be able to convince him that she hadn't been there. He seemed so convinced.

That a man she had once thought loved her could believe something so unspeakable about her was incredibly painful. Bryce was completely wrapped up in his thoughts and did not even seem to notice when she left the room. Bronwyn escaped to the en suite bathroom and locked the door securely behind her, afraid that he would come in and bombard her with yet more reasons he did not believe her. She ran the shower as hot as she could stand it but shivered beneath the relentless spray. God, if he had spent the last two years believing something so awful about her, it was no wonder he hated her so much. It was an obstacle that could not easily be overcome because he had it firmly in his head that she had betrayed him in the worst possible way by leaving him literally broken and bleeding.

She knew how her stubborn ass of a husband's mind worked. To his way of thinking, all of his sins were now superseded by her "unforgivable betrayal." How very *convenient* for him. It made complete sense that he would believe something like this about her. It was easier for him to blame her and hate her rather than deal with the fact that due to his own thoughtless actions he had lost his wife, his child, and his hearing all on the same night. Unfortunately he didn't doubt what he had seen that night, and while Bronwyn could understand why his mind had fabricated this bizarre coping mechanism, she couldn't forgive it.

She hunched over and clasped her arms around her midriff, afraid that she would be sick. She swallowed down the nausea and leaned back against the tiles of the shower stall, sliding down against the wall until she was sitting on the floor with her knees raised to her chest. She had her face buried in her knees and her arms covering her head.

She did not know how long she sat there shivering, unable to get warm, unable to even cry as she tried to deal with the shock of knowing how very much her husband despised her. The needle-like spray suddenly stopped and Bronwyn raised her head hesitantly, a bit disorientated by the sudden cessation of water. She looked up to find Bryce standing at the entrance of the shower stall and was baffled by his unexpected appearance.

"But I locked the door," she murmured in a small voice that he might not have caught if he'd had his hearing.

"You forgot to lock the other door," he pointed out quietly, able to read her lips despite the steam, and she groaned, remembering that the luxurious bathroom was shared by two bedrooms. "Come on, Bron . . . you need to dry off. You'll make yourself sick again." She noticed, for the first time, that he had a huge, fluffy, white bath towel draped over his hands. She nodded but didn't move, and Bryce shocked her by stepping into the wet stall, uncaring of the fact that he wore socks and was dressed in clean boxer shorts and a T-shirt. He hunkered down in front of her and draped the bath towel around her shoulders, helping her up in the process.

"You've been in here for nearly an hour," he informed her grimly. She tilted her face to his, still shivering violently.

"I . . . I c-couldn't get warm," she stuttered, and he frowned, evidently not catching that, but probably understanding the gist of it. He wrapped his arms around her and dragged her nude, wet body to his. He held her so tightly and so closely that the trembling abated almost immediately. He led her out of the shower stall and unlocked the door, leading her back into the master bedroom. He gently steered her toward the bed and seated her on the edge, kneeling in front of her as he patted her dry with the fluffy towel.

"You're wet," she observed inanely, noting the dampness of his T-shirt and shorts while she tried not to stare at his muscular naked legs. He had showered as well, if his damp hair was anything to go by. He caught her words because he was looking directly at her when she said them and shrugged in response.

"I'll dry," he dismissed. She noticed that it was still dark outside and grimaced. She checked the time on the alarm clock on her bedside pedestal; it was just after three thirty.

"Why did you come to my room tonight?" she asked hoarsely, and even though she was looking right at him when she asked it, he did not respond. Instead he lowered his eyes and continued to pat her dry. He left her briefly to pad to the bathroom and returned moments later with a smaller towel for her hair.

"We'll have to dry this," he was muttering. "You've been so sick; I don't think it would be wise for you to sleep with wet hair. Where is your dryer?" She pointed to her dresser and he picked her up, ignoring the jerky movement of protest she made. He deposited her on the padded seat in front of the dressing table, and Bronwyn was confronted by her own haggard reflection. She looked a sight; her face was gaunt and unnaturally pale, and her eyes looked feverishly bright and overly large. The towel was still draped around her shoulders, but it had fallen open to reveal the thin body beneath. To Bronwyn's own eyes she looked too thin, and she wondered how Bryce had been able to bring himself to touch her when she looked like this. He switched on the machine and started drying her hair, running his fingers through it with a rough tenderness. She blinked in surprise and sluggishly raised her hands in an attempt to take the blow dryer from him.

"I can do it," she protested. He lifted the machine out of her reach and watched her in the mirror until she dropped her arms in resignation. He grunted in satisfaction and went back to the task of drying her hair.

When it was dry enough to suit him, he ran a brush through the dark, silky mass and then tied it back with one of the hair ties lying scattered on the dressing table. He picked her up again and deposited her back onto the unmade bed, tucking her under the covers and tossing the towel aside before climbing in beside her and dragging her stiff body close to his. She lay with her head on his chest, listening to his heart beat steadily beneath her ear and wondering what this was all about. He remained silent though and eventually Bronwyn relaxed enough to drift off to sleep again.

CHAPTER FIVE

B ronwyn cautiously opened her eyes to a sunlit bedroom. There was no sign of Bryce, and instinct told her that it was way after midday. She heard Kayla's joyful laughter outside, and she guessed the little girl was in the swimming pool, probably with her father, who was diligently teaching her how to swim. Bryce had had a child-proof fence built around the pool sometime during her absence, another one of those preparations he'd made in anticipation of a child he'd had no idea if he'd ever meet.

Bronwyn sat up shakily, feeling refreshed yet strangely hollow. She felt like someone who'd had a long and desperately needed sleep after the death of a loved one, only to wake up to the discovery that even though life would go on, it would be forever marred by the tragedy of loss. She could not remember the last time she had slept so soundly, possibly that last night before leaving Bryce two years ago; she certainly had not had much peace of mind since then. She got up and made her way to the bathroom, trying not to think of the night before. She wasn't sure what any of it had signified and definitely wasn't sure where it left her and Bryce.

She made her way downstairs a little over half an hour later, wearing a pair of faded jeans and an old T-shirt. The clothes were from her old wardrobe and were too baggy on her. Bronwyn resolved to eat even more, still feeling incredibly unattractive because of her thinness.

When she reached the living room, she stood at the open patio doors staring out at the pair in the water for the longest time, feeling ambivalent about the obvious enjoyment they seemed to find in each other's company. She felt a little left out and again bitter toward Bryce for allowing this to happen to them. She was about to turn away and head in search of something to eat when Bryce glanced up and caught sight of her. She could not see his expression because of the sun's glare off the water, but he went strangely still before heading toward the side of the pool and depositing a protesting Kayla on the paving before heaving himself out alongside her.

"Daddy more swim . . ." the child was protesting, but he was watching Bronwyn and did not see her display of temper. Bronwyn watched in amazement as the little girl impatiently patted her father on his leg and made a clumsy sign that Bronwyn knew signified "daddy" or "father." Bronwyn was familiar with it because she had been meaning to teach her daughter the word in sign language. Bryce looked down at his precocious offspring and grinned when she said "daddy" with one of her chubby hands again before making swimming gestures.

"Later, baby," he laughingly promised, picking her up and depositing her on his wide, bronzed shoulders. "First we'll have some lunch with your mummy." The child looked up and noticed Bronwyn for the first time. The delight on her little face warmed Bronwyn's heart. Bryce had pretty much monopolized the little girl's time since their arrival eleven days ago. And while he sometimes seemed at a loss as to how to deal with Kayla, he was muddling through without asking Bronwyn for any assistance. It concerned her that he seemed so able around the child. She worried that he might start to wonder why he needed Bronwyn around at all. Now that she was feeling healthier, she vowed to spend more time with the little girl whom she had missed so much. She wouldn't allow Bryce to usurp her so completely any longer.

Bryce made his way toward her, and she stepped onto the patio, relishing the feel of the hot, early autumn sun on her face. She picked up a bright-pink beach towel adorned with characters from Disney's *Finding Nemo* cartoon and held it up as he deposited the happily chattering little girl into Bronwyn's arms. She wrapped the towel around Kayla and hugged her small body close. Her daughter was bubbling on about swimming, her daddy, and various other concerns that were of great importance to any nearly nineteen-month-old little girl. Bronwyn nodded and made the appropriate noises, but she was preoccupied with Bryce, whose eyes were sweeping over her from top to bottom, making her feel naked and vulnerable.

"How do you feel?" he asked quietly, and she shrugged, managing a slight smile.

"Well rested."

He nodded at her reply but seemed at a loss for words.

"I hope you're hungry. You're just in time for lunch," he said, gesturing toward the glass-and-wrought-iron patio table situated close to the huge stone barbeque at the other end of the large patio. Celeste was just laying out what looked like a delicious lunch. The older woman, always one of few words, flashed them a smile and retreated with a nod.

"I'm famished." She nodded and headed toward the table, depositing a still-prattling Kayla into her high chair and placing the provided plastic bowl and plastic spoon onto the surface in front of the toddler.

"She's a messy eater," Bryce pointed out with a wince, and Bronwyn grinned, realizing that he must have discovered that particular trait the hard way. Most of Kayla's meals seemed to wind up all over herself and anybody else in the general vicinity, but the little girl obdurately refused to allow anybody to feed her, insisting that she could do it herself. It was a stubborn streak that she had inherited from her father, and Bronwyn wished that she had been there to witness that particular battle of wills firsthand. It must have been a novelty for Bryce to discover someone as hardheaded as himself, especially someone as tiny as Mikayla.

"I know." Bronwyn smiled. "She rejects any attempt to help feed her. I usually give her extra portions in the hopes that she manages to get as much of it into her mouth as she does all over everything else. But sometimes I have to take the bull by the horns and feed her myself anyway, despite her fervent protests."

"She is also inordinately fond of ice cream," he pointed out with a grimace, seeming to recall something particularly unpleasant.

"I'm guessing you discovered one of her favorite pastimes?"

"Finger painting?" He nodded and she laughed.

"Unfortunately ice cream, especially chocolate, seems to be her favorite medium," Bronwyn said solemnly.

"I thought Celeste would quit after Kayla demonstrated her talent on the kitchen walls, but luckily she seems to have the patience of a saint."

"I hope that you reprimanded Kayla?" Bronwyn asked with a frown, and he shook his head.

"She seemed so proud of her painting," he responded, and Bronwyn sighed before shaking her head.

"She's testing you," she informed. "She knows better than to mess on the walls, she wouldn't dare do it at ho—" She halted, knowing that the word *home* would be a mistake and not wanting to destroy the fragile peace between them. "She wouldn't have done that in our old flat. She wants to see how much she'll be able to get away with here. You've got to be firm with her, Bryce. Don't let her take advantage of you."

"I wouldn't know how to go about reprimanding her," he offered quietly. "I haven't had much practice at this fatherhood business. I want her to like me." Judging from the pained look on his face, it grated to admit as much and she bit her lip, unsure how to respond without rekindling hostilities.

"I can guarantee," she began reluctantly, not really wanting to help him with this but knowing that it was in Kayla's best interests, "that she *loves* you already, Bryce. She won't like it if you raise your voice to her, she may even shed a few fake little tears, but she'll get over it. You're as much of an authority figure to her as I am now, and she has to get used to that. We're here to teach her right from wrong. If we don't she'll become a spoiled brat. And while a bit of spoiling never hurt anyone, I would not want her to become intolerable." He was paying close attention to her mouth, and Bronwyn was careful to enunciate clearly and slowly.

"It makes sense, I suppose," he said. "I'll try to be a little less indulgent, but it's still such a treat for me to give her things and spoil her a bit."

"That's understandable." Bronwyn nodded. "You'll get over it soon enough, once the novelty wears off and she becomes bratty."

"She'll never be *that* bratty." He grinned before becoming quite serious. "You did a good job with her, Bron."

"Uh . . ." The compliment was as unexpected as it was flattering, and Bronwyn had no idea how to respond to it. "Thank you." She could not read his mood at all and wondered if she could trust what seemed to be an armed and uneasy truce. She bent her head and focused on her food. The cook had prepared a light lunch of crispy fried filleted hake—a delicious Cape game fish—herbed baby potatoes, and steamed fresh vegetables. Her mouth fairly watered at the sight of it. She checked Kayla's bowl and was gratified to note that the little girl's vegetables had been mashed into manageable chunks. Kayla had already started digging in with her chubby little fingers, and Bryce groaned when she proceeded to lift her fist to her mouth and suck the food off it.

"Mummy." She picked up a piece of fish between two grubby fingers and held it up to her mother. "Hmm nice . . . Mummy . . ."

"I already have food, Kayla. See?" she pointed out, lifting a fork with some fish speared onto the tines. Kayla dropped the fish back into her bowl and lifted her plastic spoon and attempted to imitate her mother. When the fish kept falling back into the bowl, she glared and tossed the spoon aside in frustration before resorting to using her hands again. Bronwyn put aside her own utensils and lifted the plastic spoon, firmly placing it back into her daughter's hands.

"Use the spoon, Mikayla," she ordered firmly, but the little girl shook her head mutinously.

"No 'poon, Mummy," the child protested, tossing it aside again the moment her mother let her hand go.

"Kayla, I'm not going to tell you again," Bronwyn warned, picking the spoon up and wrapping the child's stubborn fingers around it. Bryce watched the little power play unfold in fascination. Kayla, knowing how far she could push her mother, sulkily held on to the spoon and clumsily rooted around her bowl, messing about rather than actually attempting to eat. Bronwyn ignored the recalcitrant child and quite deliberately went back to her own lunch.

Kayla was now scooping up spoonfuls of food and placing it in little mounds on the tray of the high chair in front of her. Bronwyn finished off the last of her fish and sighed before dragging a wet wipe from the container Celeste had thoughtfully left within easy reach and wiping Kayla's face and hands clean. She ignored the way the child tried to evade her attempts and after giving her face a thorough wipe, Bron lifted the squirming toddler out of the high chair and into her own lap. She grabbed Kayla's bowl and spoon and very determinedly began spooning food into the protesting child's mouth.

"No, Mummy, *no*! No!" Kayla was sobbing hysterically and working herself up into a fine little tantrum. Bronwyn could feel it in the way her small body was tensing up more and more. "Kayla no want! Kayla no like!"

"Kayla, you *will* eat your food!" Bronwyn managed in her sternest voice. The child's determined squirming was rapidly tiring her mother out, and Bronwyn knew that she would have to give up the fight soon. She lifted the spoon to Kayla's mouth, and the baby kept her mouth tightly shut, turning her head away.

"*Mikayla!*" The unfamiliar sound of Bryce's raised voice shocked both mother and child into momentary stillness. Kayla's eyes swallowed her face when they encountered her father's stern countenance. His voice softened on his next words. "Listen to your mummy."

The child obediently opened her mouth to the proffered spoon, her large blue eyes never wavering from her father's face. She took in bite after bite until she had emptied her bowl, and when she was done, she begged to be let down. Bronwyn helped her down and watched with a helpless smile of sheer adoration as Kayla toddled over to her father and crawled into his lap, curling herself up and tucking her thumb into her mouth. Bryce's face reflected a mixture of surprise, aching vulnerability, and confusion as he wrapped his arms around the sleepy little girl. He lifted his awestruck eyes to Bronwyn's smiling face.

"She always gets a little peevish when she's tired," Bronwyn informed, watching as Kayla's eyelids drooped more and more until she was fast asleep.

"I'm hesitant about raising my voice to her," he admitted quietly.

"I find it difficult to judge exactly how loud I'm actually being. I don't want to terrify her. Sometimes I worry that . . ."

He left the sentence hanging and dropped his eyes down to his daughter's sleeping face. Bronwyn waited, hoping that he would finish what he had been about to say, sensing that he had been about to reveal something deeply personal. He didn't say anything further though, and it left her wondering about the insecurity she had heard in his voice.

"Bron . . ." he said after a long silence. He kept his gaze trained on Kayla's sleeping face. "About last night?" Bronwyn tensed, and she lowered her eyes to the ice-cold glass of mango juice in her hands.

"I just . . . I never meant . . ." He paused again, and the silence grated on her nerves until she could stand it no more. His beautiful blue eyes at last rose to meet hers.

"Look, Bryce," she said, breaking the silence, hoping that her face reflected the resolution that she could hear in her voice. "I *know* how much you hate me. In fact, believing what you do about me, I can even understand *why* you feel the way you do. Anybody who would so cold-bloodedly desert their spouse at the scene of an accident is certainly someone who deserves no forgiveness."

"You're . . ."

"I'm not even going to try to defend myself anymore," she said firmly, interrupting whatever he'd been about to say. "There's really no point, is there? You've hated me for so long I don't think I'll ever be able to change your mind. All I ask is that you put this . . . this *contempt* you have for me aside for Kayla's sake. Hate me if you must. I think I can almost live with it now that I know you never really loved me, but try to be less obvious about it." His eyes narrowed as he assessed her face; there was another lengthy silence as he considered her words before shrugging.

"I have a couple of questions," he murmured, and she bit her lip before nodding. "How long were you at the beach house?" Whatever she had expected, that certainly wasn't it. She blinked a couple of times before shrugging.

"A couple of weeks," she managed softly.

"So, if your story is to be believed . . ."

She resisted the overwhelming urge to reach over and slap him for the blatant sarcasm in his voice.

". . . You went there directly after leaving here, to *wait* for me, right?"

"Why don't we just agree to let this matter go?" she asked, not in the mood to defend herself against any more of his crazy accusations.

"No." He shrugged her request aside nonchalantly. "So, how is it that you never once heard about my accident? Apparently it was in all the papers and had news coverage on radio, television, and the Internet. Are you telling me you missed all of that?"

"Do really think that I spent my days watching the telly and listening to music?" she asked in exasperation. "I could barely drag myself out of bed and into the shower most days. I was ill from the morning sickness, exhausted, scared, and every day that passed without word from you sent me deeper into depressed isolation. So yes, I'm telling you I *missed all of that!*"

His eyes flickered and she thought she caught a glimmer of uncertainty in them before they went icy with disdain again. She shook her head.

"When are Rick and Lisa due back from their holiday?"

"Saturday," he replied shortly before continuing on with the original conversation. "So after it became painfully self-evident that I would *not* be coming for you, what did you do then?" Not caring for the mockery in his eyes and voice and fed up with his determination to disbelieve every little thing she said, Bronwyn got up shakily and rounded the table, reaching out possessively to take her daughter from his arms.

"I'll put her to bed," she told him without meeting his eyes.

"Your story is full of holes, Bronwyn, you know that," he murmured almost gently. "I'd be willing to move on if you'd only admit to being at the scene of my accident." She lifted blazingly furious eyes to his.

"It would be so terribly convenient for you if I admitted to that, wouldn't it, Bryce?" she asked angrily. "That way you wouldn't have to feel any guilt about driving your pregnant wife out into the streets. No guilt about leaving her to fend for herself while she was so ill she was terrified she would lose your baby. You wouldn't have to be accountable for anything that has happened since the night I left. Well, you can go to *hell* because I refuse to give you that satisfaction."

Bronwyn turned away angrily and carried Kayla back into the house. She headed straight for the baby's room and after tucking her in, stood beside the cot and watched the baby sleep, her heart absolutely overflowing with love for the innocent child.

"You're worth everything, my darling," she whispered, leaning over to kiss her short, silky curls. When she straightened up and turned around, Bryce was standing in the doorway, still wearing nothing but his board shorts. She frowned resentfully, annoyed that a deaf man could move so silently, and moved to pass him. He barely shifted, crowding her abominably as she tried to squeeze through the doorway and into the hall. She flushed crimson when she inadvertently brushed against his muscular naked chest. She frowned up at him, making sure he was looking at her before she spoke.

"Get out of my way," she demanded, and he grinned lazily.

"Glad to see you're getting your fire back, babe . . ."

"*Don't* call me that," she reprimanded, and he grinned.

"You never complained before." She went an even brighter red as she recalled the very rare instances during which he had used the endearment in the past—*always* in the most intimate of circumstances and very rarely outside of bed. He had used it now just to rattle her—she could see it in his eyes. She pursed her lips and pushed her way past him. He grabbed her wrist, just as she thought she'd managed to escape.

"Pierre and Alice are coming around for dinner," he informed her idly, ignoring the way she tugged furiously, trying to get loose. "Try not to embarrass me with any more lies or insincere shows of concern while they're here." She gasped at the sharp stab of pain at his casual cruelty.

"Bryce, I'm really starting to *hate* you," she stated conversationally, and he raised his brows lazily.

"*Are* you?" He smiled. "That's a shame. I did so enjoy being worshipped by you."

"I never worshipped you, you arrogant bastard!" she managed furiously. "I *loved* you. More than you could ever comprehend." His grip slackened and she tugged herself free. "I now see that you never deserved that love!" He seemed unable to respond, merely keeping his level gaze on her emotional face. She made a despairing little sound in the back of her throat and turned to walk away.

"Bronwyn," he called after her, and she stopped, her back going rigid as she braced herself for another blow. "If you loved me you would never have left me."

"I didn't leave you, you jackass," she muttered beneath her breath, knowing that he could not see the denial while she stood with her back to him.

"You would never have driven off without giving me the chance to apologize . . ." His voice was closer, and she knew that he had come up right behind her. "You would have stayed to hear me grovel and beg your forgiveness, because if you *loved* me, you would have known

me well enough to appreciate that an apology would not be far off."
His hands came to rest on her narrow shoulders, and she flinched as
she felt the warmth of his flesh through the thin cotton of her T-shirt.
She turned around slowly and lifted her eyes to meet his.

"I *knew* that," she admitted. "I left to give you some space to
clear your head and to give myself time to gather my own confused
thoughts. I knew you'd come and that's the reason I waited and
waited and *waited* at that damned beach house! I knew you would
come . . . only you never did.

"When I eventually concluded that maybe you really wanted
nothing to do with us, I called your office to talk about child support
and was quite bluntly informed that—Mr. Palmer did not want to
speak to me or hear from me ever again—You weren't answering your
cell phone, and nobody was answering at the house." She watched
as his eyes hardened and his hands fell away.

"My God, can't you ever stop lying?" he muttered in frustration.
"I could buy into *maybe* being mistaken about seeing you at the scene
of my accident. I can even try to believe that maybe you hadn't seen
a single newspaper article, television report, or heard any radio news,
but none of my people would *ever* have said those words to you!"

"Oh, believe what you want, Bryce," she responded wearily and
turned away. She was so sick of defending herself to him.

"Oh no you don't." He caught her arm in a bruising grip to
prevent her from walking away. "I spent *two* years looking for you,
Bronwyn. Why would I have told my staff to stonewall you when I
was trying so hard to find you? So you are not going to try to make
me feel guilty about something that I never authorized, something
that would never have happened, not in a million years!" She shook
her head and stepped back, jerking her arm violently out of his tight
grip before deciding to make use of some of the SASL that she had
learned and using her hands rather eloquently to say something *quite*

unmistakable. For a second he was taken aback, and he blinked a couple of times before bursting into laughter, the sound so natural and spontaneous that it took her completely by surprise.

"You didn't just tell me to . . ." He trailed off before saying the obscenity, and she jutted her jaw stubbornly, refusing to be charmed by his genuine amusement.

"So what if I did?" she asked defiantly. His eyes were still brimming with laughter as he shrugged.

"Nothing, I'm just impressed with your extensive knowledge of SASL." He shrugged and she went bright red.

"Not that extensive," she told him self-consciously. "It was the first thing I learned because I knew that it would probably come in handy in most of my dealings with you."

"Good call," he complimented, and she cleared her throat before moving away from him without another word and retreating to her bedroom.

CHAPTER SIX

Alice De Coursey was not all what Bronwyn had been expecting. The woman was a couple of years older than Bronwyn, about thirty, and so tiny that she made Bronwyn feel like a giant by comparison. She could not have been more than five feet tall and had a small, perfectly proportioned body. She had soft brown eyes shielded by silly, little round glasses and she was almost pretty in a wholesome way, with freckles splattered across her nose and an endearingly mischievous grin. Her shoulder-length, uncontrollably frizzy, sandy-brown corkscrew curls gave her a kind of Raggedy-Ann appeal. She was certainly *not* the drop-dead-gorgeous woman Bronwyn had expected a beautiful individual like Pierre De Coursey to fall for. She walked with a slight limp and still had faint scars on her upper arms and a slightly longer, more pronounced one on her round, firm jaw.

Her intimidatingly gorgeous husband doted on her. In fact every time Pierre looked at her, his eyes positively glowed with love. He lit up when she smiled and beamed whenever she laughed. It was a revelation for Bronwyn to see the previously austere Pierre so transparently in love. The man who had terrified her when she'd first met him now laughed freely, told silly jokes, and changed *nappies*! Their baby boy, Tristan, was about five months old and had a sweet, placid temperament. He had his father's pitch-black hair and his mum's large brown eyes. Kayla was quite excited to see the baby and meet new people, but she fell asleep half an hour after the couple's arrival.

"She's such a beautiful little girl," Alice was telling Bronwyn after the latter had put Kayla to bed. "Such a little livewire . . ." Bronwyn laughed.

"That's a polite way of phrasing it," she told the woman. "She's hell on wheels. When she started toddling, she was an unstoppable force. You wait until Tristan gets to that age; you'll be running yourself ragged. I'm just happy we managed to get her off to bed with so little fuss tonight."

Alice laughed and Bronwyn smiled, really liking the other woman. She had feared that Alice De Coursey would be an unbearable snob, the way Pierre sometimes tended to be, but not only was she *not* a snob, she had somehow managed to destarch Pierre in many ways. The man was definitely a lot more relaxed and a great deal more pleasant to spend time with. He was fluent in SASL, and he and Bryce were engaged in what looked like a serious conversation. Alice followed her eyes and smiled. She leaned conspiratorially close to Bronwyn.

"Pierre was *very* relieved when he heard you were back."

Bronwyn frowned, that came as a surprise to her; she had always believed that Pierre did not care much for her. In fact he had barely spoken to her after arriving for dinner, leading Bronwyn to assume that he had heard the same story about her as Rick. "From what I understand, Bryce became something of a recluse after you left. He hardly ever leaves the house; he works from home, never goes into the office, and leaves it to Pierre to run the more social end of the business." Bronwyn bit her lip and watched as her husband laughed at something Pierre said, the joke silent and just between the two of them.

"Where did Pierre learn to sign?" she asked quietly, admiring the fluent, graceful gestures of Pierre's hands.

"He used to drive me to my physiotherapy sessions after I had recovered from the accident enough to start strengthening my weak leg, and they happened to have SASL classes at the same clinic, which fortunately coincided with my visits. Pierre saw it as an opportunity to kill two birds with one stone, so to speak."

"I would like to learn," Bronwyn confided softly. "Could you give me the address of this place?"

Alice smiled. "Of course." She nodded. "I'll even go with you if you'd like."

Bronwyn smiled gratefully before nodding. "I'd really like that."

~

"Did you enjoy your evening?" Bryce asked in an indulgent voice that grated on Bronwyn's nerves, after the other couple's departure. They were standing on the front step watching the taillights on the De Coursey car grow more distant as it made its way down the steep, winding drive leading from the Palmer home back down to the main road.

"Yes." She replied abruptly. "Alice is fantastic. I really like her."

"I knew you would," he confirmed, still looking and sounding like an indulgent father. For some reason Bronwyn felt like slapping the self-satisfied smirk off his face. Did he have to look so damned *smug*?

"Yes of course." She looked straight up at him, her eyes gleaming angrily. "And, as we all know by now; you're always right." He couldn't hear the venom in her voice, but he could certainly see it in her eyes and he took the tiniest step back.

"What the hell is wrong now?" he growled furiously.

"Nothing," she hissed. "I'm tired . . . I'm going to bed."

"Oh come on," he fumed. "You're not going to do this to me. You're not going to play this game."

"I'm *not* playing any games. I'm too tired for games." She turned away and headed back indoors. He followed her inside and caught her elbow to halt her progress. She tried to tug her arm away, but his grip, while gentle, was unrelenting.

"What's going on?" he asked on a whisper. "Did Alice or Pierre do or say something to offend you?"

"No," she shook her head abruptly. "No, of course not."

"So then it's me?" he stated matter-of-factly.

"Is it ever anyone else?" she muttered snidely beneath her breath, but he couldn't read her lips because she ducked her head as she said it. She tried to wriggle her arm and glared up at him when he wouldn't release her.

"You're hurting me!" she stated as clearly as she could, and he let her go abruptly.

"I'm sorry." His immediate release and apology took her by surprise, and she felt a little guilty when she saw a flare of genuine remorse in his eyes. "I didn't mean to hurt you."

"You didn't," she admitted. "But I'm tired and I have nothing more to say to you tonight."

"You think you can dismiss me and expect me to obey like a whipped dog?" he sneered, taking hold of her elbow again and giving her a gentle shake to emphasize his point.

"No, I expect you to respect my wishes," she told him tiredly, all of the fight leaving her. Her arm hung limply in his grip. He sighed and took hold of her other elbow before running his hands caressingly up her arms.

"Tell me why you're angry with me," he coaxed, and his large hands moved up to cup her narrow face gently. His thumbs traced the outline of her trembling lips, and he leaned toward her, his lips almost touching hers.

"I want to be with you again tonight," he whispered hoarsely, and she flinched.

"No." She shook her head firmly. He frowned and stepped back, releasing her abruptly.

"Why not?" he asked coldly.

"How can you even ask me that? I told you, last night was a mistake. And do you really think I want to get back into bed with the man who said I made his skin crawl?" she asked.

"Look, I was an ass when I said that, okay?" he admitted, throwing up his hands in surrender. "I'm sorry. It was a blatant lie expressly designed to hurt you as much as possible. It was that or admit that you were right about me wanting you the other day." She continued to stare stonily up at him, knowing that he was repudiating his words now because he wanted her back in his bed.

"I won't beg," he warned.

"I wasn't expecting you to," she muttered, and he frowned uncertainly.

"What?" When she refused to repeat the words he hadn't caught, he swore angrily and turned away from her. "I hate this! I want to know your every word. I want to hear my daughter's laughter. I want so many things." She softened a little at the helpless frustration in his voice and took a step toward him. She rested a tentative hand on his rigid shoulder and stepped around to face him. He shrugged off her hand and glared at her.

"*Don't*," he warned dangerously, and her brow lowered in confusion.

"Don't what?"

"Don't you dare pity me." His voice was as hard as granite, belying the vulnerability she had heard just seconds before. "I don't want or need your pity!"

"Trust me, the last thing I feel for you is pity," she told him, but he must have missed the words because his confused frown deepened before he swore in irritation.

"Just go to bed, Bron," he muttered tiredly as he brushed by her. Bronwyn watched his broad back as he retreated. He turned a corner and she heard a door slamming in the distance as he shut himself into his study.

Bronwyn stood there for the longest time, valiantly fighting back her tears of frustration. She did not know this bruised, battered, and embittered man as the Bryce she had adored and married within weeks of meeting him, but there was still something so compelling about him. He reminded her of a badly wounded lion, confused and exhausted but unable to stop fighting.

She swallowed down the incredible pain of realization, recognition, and resignation. God help her, she still loved Bryce. She had always loved Bryce. She loved him, hated him, and resented him all at the same time. Yet the only other certainty she had in life besides Kayla's love was the knowledge that Bryce hated her more than she had ever thought possible, and she did not know how she was going to shield her vulnerable heart from the agony that he was so very capable of inflicting on her.

～

"Where are you going?" Bryce did nothing to hide the deep suspicion in his eyes late the following morning as he took in Bronwyn's attire. They were in the living room, where Bryce had been glaring down at his laptop screen before she'd distracted him with her presence. She was wearing a pair of designer black slacks, one of the pieces that she had left behind, combined with a pretty silk turquoise top. Despite the fact that the clothes were still a little baggy on her,

Bronwyn thought the combination looked charming. Especially with her dark hair falling in lustrous waves to her narrow shoulders and her lips tinted with shell-pink lipstick. She had even taken on a healthy, light-golden sheen after spending some time out in the sun the day before. For the first time in a long while she was relatively happy with the way she looked.

"Out to lunch, with Alice," she informed casually, taking a seat opposite his. "Will you be okay with Kayla? She's in the kitchen with Celeste at the moment. They're baking a cake."

"Of course I'll be okay with Kayla," he dismissed before continuing. "When was this lunch thing decided?" he asked highhandedly, and she laughed at the autocratic question.

"Not that it's any of your business, but this was *decided* after dinner last night."

He frowned, missing her sarcasm.

"I don't remember you making this arrangement," he said, clearly trying to recall the evening before.

"Well you and Pierre were having your little powwow." She shrugged lightly. "What did you expect Alice and I to do? Sit around quietly and wait for our husbands to rejoin us? We talked, hit it off, and befriended each other. This is what friends *do*. We get together, have lunch, and go shopping . . ."

"You're not well enough to venture out yet," he said authoritatively. "Alice can come around here for lunch. I'll SMS Pierre immediately and arrange it." He whipped his mobile phone out of his jeans pocket, and Bronwyn stayed his hand by placing her smaller one over it.

"No." She shook her head decisively, and he frowned.

"But . . ."

"I'm meeting Alice for lunch," she reiterated.

"I don't like it."

"Well that's just too bad, isn't it?" She was getting annoyed with his arrogance and her glare told him so.

"How are you getting there?" She frowned and lifted the set of car keys she was holding.

"I'm taking the Jeep," she responded. The Jeep was one of the five cars he owned. Bronwyn had never seen the sense in anyone having more than one car, but Bryce loved his cars. She had already noted that his beloved metallic blue Maserati was gone, and she guessed that it must have been the one he'd been driving when he had his accident.

"I didn't give you permission to use the Jeep," he retaliated smugly, and she bit her lip.

"You've never been selfish with your things; I didn't think you'd mind," she said uncertainly.

"I gave you a car as a wedding present. What happened to it?" he gritted, his eyes narrowing as he reminded her of the beautiful sporty BMW. She flushed as she struggled to respond to that question.

"What do you think happened to it? I sold it," she whispered softly, defiance in her eyes. She had loved that car, but she had sold it before selling her wedding rings. She had clung to her marriage, her love for Bryce, and the rings that had symbolized both, for as long as she possibly could. The corners of his lips curled downward and she lowered her eyes, not wanting to see the contempt he had for her reflected on his face.

"Why?" he asked quietly. The question threw her. She had expected yet another one of his scathing set downs.

"I needed the money," she confessed huskily. "I was seven months pregnant and I had no place to live. Up till then, I'd been staying in cheap hotels until the money I had in my personal bank account dried up." The money in her personal account had been hers, money earned during her short-lived waitressing career, and that had been left over from her grandmother's trust fund. It had lasted longer than expected after she had scrimped and saved, going without a lot of things in order to keep a roof over her head. She had worked three separate jobs, until she had been forced to concede that she wasn't doing herself or her unborn baby much good. So eventually she'd had to sell her car and put some of the money down as a deposit on the small flat that she and Kayla had been still living in when Rick found her again. The money from the car and the rings had kept her comfortably afloat for nearly a year. The added income from work had been used for food and rent. The car and rings had paid for the extras and had helped with the medical bills as well as with feeding and clothing Kayla.

"It took me that long to grasp that our marriage was well and truly over," she admitted shamefully. "It took four long months before I—at long last—accepted that I couldn't continue living my life in limbo. I needed a place to stay, someplace that would be good for both the baby and me. I also knew that I would need medical care soon and some sort of financial cushion for a month or so after giving birth. I didn't want to abandon Kayla for work mere days after giving birth to her. I wanted to spend some time with her." He stared at her in silence for a long time, and she wet her lips nervously, not really knowing what to expect. Not even sure that he'd caught half of what she'd said. She had spoken a little too quickly, without really giving any thought to his deafness.

"I expected you to use the money in our mutual account, or to use your credit card. I was hoping that you would because it would have helped me track you down. I nearly went crazy wondering how the hell you were taking care of yourself. Why didn't you use the money, Bronwyn?" he asked hoarsely, clearly staggered by her words. "Surely your health and the baby's welfare meant more than your stubborn pride?"

She blinked at him in mute shock.

"I used my own money, Bryce," she repeated with a shrug, knowing that the money had been a pittance compared to what he had. But at least it had been *hers*. "In my old account."

"What account?" he asked blankly, and she frowned.

"The account I had before we married," she said quietly.

"You still *had* that account?" He practically exploded, and she winced, understanding how that must look to him. "After two years of marriage, you still had a bank account in your maiden name? What the hell was that about, Bronwyn? Your escape clause?"

"Hardly," she scoffed. "It barely had enough in it to see me through the first month. I just never got around to closing it, that's all. And besides, you have no right to get all self-righteous with me over it. *You* had cut me off so completely I'd assumed—"

"What? That I'd be happy to let you and the baby starve to death or wind up homeless?" he interrupted fiercely, and her mouth opened and then closed again as she tried to gather her thoughts. Yes, she should probably have used the money. When she thought back to all the unnecessary suffering that she had endured, it seemed stupid now, but at the time she'd been trying to prove a point.

"Bryce," she tried to find a way to explain her decision to him and drew a complete blank. "After four months of constant and inexplicable rejection, I gave up on trying to reach you. By that point I didn't think that you deserved to have the baby or me in your life. I wanted to move on and couldn't do so with *your* money. I needed to do it on my own, without being beholden to the man who had made it clear that he didn't want anything to do with us. I didn't feel entitled to your money after making that decision."

"You didn't feel entitled to it?" Bryce latched onto those words, obviously dismissing the rest of what she had said. "To the *father* of your child's money? I don't even know how to respond to that,

Bronwyn. You may not have felt entitled to it, but Kayla certainly was, and *is*, entitled to it. You could have set aside your pettiness and considered her in all of this!"

"Oh please just *stop* throwing Kayla in my face. I did everything I could for her. I gave her the best I could afford after you kicked us out. How was I supposed to know you'd have this turnaround where the baby was concerned? As far as I knew, you didn't want her and didn't think that she was entitled to anything you had. She didn't want for *anything*. Her clothes may not have had designer tags and her toys may have been secondhand, but my baby was well loved and well taken care of. Don't you dare imply anything else!" More interminably silent staring from him, but she refused to lower her eyes, refused to be intimidated or cowed by him. Instead she met his inscrutable gaze head-on, with chin tilted defiantly, eyes sparking, and fists clenched. She looked like a feral cat ready to defend herself and her baby against any and all threats.

"What time are you meeting Alice?" The question threw her completely, and she blinked in astonishment, surprised and relieved that he had let it drop. She checked her watch.

"In about half an hour," she told him.

"You *will* come back?"

Not understanding the question, she merely stared at him confusedly for a few moments.

"What?"

"You won't run off again?" he rephrased, and she reeled in shock at the depth of vulnerability and insecurity his question had revealed.

"Uh . . . n-no. Mikayla . . ." was all she managed, and he nodded shortly, realizing that she would never leave without her daughter.

"If not for Mikayla . . ." He seemed to ask the question before he could stop himself, and in doing so, clearly revealed a lot more than he had ever intended to reveal. "Would you come back?" She hesitated, her eyes lowered as she pondered the question, and seeing the uncertainty on her face, Bryce made a slight movement with his hand.

"Forget it," he snapped, before she could even think about formulating a response. "It was a stupid question, and it's really not that important. As long as you don't leave with my daughter, I don't give a damn what you do." Somehow the words sounded hollow and untrue, ringing with bravado and not much conviction. They avoided each other's eyes—each afraid of the truth they might spy in the other's gaze.

"I have to go," she muttered evasively, getting up from the chair. He jumped up too and caught her arm to halt her progress.

"Wait." She stood quietly in his grasp, her eyes searching his harsh features warily. He looked moody and uncertain, not at all sure of what he wanted to say or even why he'd halted her progress.

"I don't want you to go by yourself," he said, almost reluctantly. "I want one of the security team to go with." Bronwyn frowned at that. She had always hated the discreet security detail that had followed them just about everywhere after they had first gotten married and had complained about it so much that he had cut her personal detail down to one supposedly unobtrusive guard to keep her happy. Bronwyn had agreed to the compromise because the one guy had been better than a team, but she had never felt comfortable with what she had always felt was a blatant display of wealth.

"Bryce, I don't want to have some gorilla following me around all afternoon," she snapped, and his lips tightened.

"I'll ask Cal to take care of the matter personally." Cal was his head of security and Bronwyn had always liked the quiet man who read Shakespearean sonnets in his spare time. She hadn't really seen him since her return. She was relieved to learn that he still worked for Bryce since she had feared that she might have gotten him into trouble after instructing him to take that fateful night off two years ago. She had wanted a private and romantic evening with her husband and had dismissed the entire staff. She knew that it was probably one of the only reasons she had been able to disappear so completely. Cal had left only a skeleton staff on duty that night. Her personal guard, not expecting her to leave the house that night, had also been given the night off.

"I'm glad Cal still works for you," she said, all the heat fleeing from her voice and expression.

"He's been acting as my personal guard," Bryce said before making an odd sound in the back of his throat. "You still have my numbers right?" he continued hesitantly, and she nodded again. "If you need anything, or if you feel ill, call me."

"Bryce." She smiled reassuringly up into his eyes. "I'm fine, but in the unlikely event of that status quo changing, I'll be sure to give you a call." His eyes frosted over.

"Don't mock me, Bronwyn," he said coldly, and she shook her head, alarmed that he had misread her humor.

"I wasn't," she assured gently, lifting her hand to cup his jaw. "I'll be fine, but I promise to call you if I feel ill." He stepped away from her soft hand, leaving it hovering in midair. He continued to look down at her for a few long moments.

"I'll tell Cal to meet you in the garage. Let him do the driving," he said bossily before swivelling on his heel and leaving the room. Bronwyn sighed despondently and stared after him for one long, wistful moment before straightening her shoulders and leaving too.

～

Alice met her at the restaurant entrance with a warm hug and a smile. Her mischievously sparkling eyes traveled past Bronwyn's shoulder to where Cal stood hovering in the background, before tossing a conspiratorial glance back over her own narrow shoulder. When Bronwyn saw a large man, similarly dressed in black suit and dark glasses standing a little off to the side, desperately striving to look "unobtrusive" behind Alice, she laughed in genuine amusement.

"All the cool kids have one these days," Alice wisecracked cheerfully, her expression so comical that it set Bronwyn off again.

"Where's Tristan?" Bronwyn asked Alice after their initial warm greetings.

"I told Pierre that this was a ladies' afternoon and as such he had to take Tristan to the office with him." She grinned. "He was a bit reluctant. He loves having the baby around, but Tristan has this nasty habit of chewing important documents. Pierre still shudders every time he thinks of a certain document that got gummed just minutes before he had to hand it back to the legal department. The way he tells it, he had no option but to give it back as is. He made no comment about the drool and as such none of the legal team had the courage to say anything either. They merely retyped everything before sending it off." She laughed conspiratorially.

"According to Pierre it was 'damned embarrassing.'" She imitated her husband's voice and accent perfectly, and Bronwyn's grin widened appreciatively. "Apparently he has an important meeting today, but I hardly ever get time to myself, so while he may grumble, he doesn't really mind. In fact, he'll never admit it but he gets a total thrill out of having his son to himself for part of the day."

"Well, I still feel a bit guilty about leaving Bryce with Kayla," Bronwyn admitted. "He's been remarkable with her, but I feel like he's been doing all the work."

"So?" Alice interrupted coldly. "You have been doing all the work for the last two years, and you've paid for it with your health. It's time for Bryce to put in some hours."

"But . . ."

"And you can't tell me he's not enjoying this time with her. He's getting to know his daughter, and from what I could see last night, he's totally in love with her."

Bronwyn nodded with slight smile.

"So no more guilt; just enjoy yourself. As far as I can tell, you haven't had too much fun over the last two years."

Bronwyn's smile faded, and Alice shrugged, the gesture so Gallic, it could only have rubbed off on her from her husband.

"I know nothing about your situation, Bronwyn," she said quietly. "But Pierre's version of events, definitely gleaned from his friend, was so one-sided that I'd always vowed to reserve judgment until I met you. And there seems to be a whole lot that Bryce left out when he told Pierre his story. I mean, he had certainly never told Pierre that you were pregnant. I can't tell you how shocked Pierre was when he learned that you were back in Bryce's life and with a *child!*"

Bronwyn blinked stupidly at that. Pierre hadn't known about her pregnancy? She had a sudden vivid flashback of Rick in her room at the hospital. It hadn't really sunk in at the time; she had been frightened, panicky, and floating on a medicated cloud, but her brother-in-law had looked startled at Bryce's first mention of a child. How could Bryce not have told Rick or Pierre about their baby? Had he told his "crack" team of private investigators? It was a bizarre detail to leave out. If he really wanted to find her, why wouldn't he have told anybody about her pregnancy? Surely it would have made her search easier. Granted, some instinct had urged her to use her maternal grandmother's maiden name over the last two years, just in case Bryce decided that he wanted her baby and not her. It had been bothersome because she'd had to keep changing doctors and clinics; nobody would have believed her "forgotten ID" story twice.

"Bronwyn?" Alice's voice seemed to come from a great distance away, and Bronwyn had a hard time focusing on Alice again. "Are you okay?"

"Why wouldn't he have told Pierre or Rick about the baby?" she mused aloud, and Alice frowned

"That's a good question," Alice murmured. "But one that only Bryce can provide the answer to." Bronwyn nodded absently but found it hard to focus on anything else for the rest of the afternoon. She enrolled in the sign language classes after lunch. The clinic offered afternoon and evening classes, and Bronwyn opted to attend a day class once a week. She and Alice also arranged a standing lunch date on the day that she would attend the class.

"So every Tuesday? Same time and place?" the other woman double-checked as they said their good-byes a couple of hours later. "And next time, let's keep the husbands out of the conversation!"

"I'm sorry if I seemed a little distracted," Bron apologized quietly. "It's just . . ."

"Forget it, you and Bryce obviously still have a great deal to work out."

CHAPTER SEVEN

The house was in chaos when Bronwyn returned home half an hour later. Kayla was screaming her head off in the den while Bryce held her writhing little body in his arms as he frantically tried to soothe her. Celeste stood to the side, wringing her hands nervously, a concerned look on her plain face.

"Oh my God! What's going on here?" Kayla's crying worsened when she heard her mother's voice. She managed to pull herself out of her father's arms and launched herself toward her mother, her unsteady gait nearly sending her off balance.

"Mummy! Kayla *ouch*! Kayla ouch, Mummy!" Bronwyn sank to her knees, and her heart dropped like a stone when she registered the genuine fear and pain on her little girl's face. As the child crept into her mother's open arms and snuggled against her chest, Bronwyn allowed her furious eyes to meet Bryce's. His face had closed up like a shutter, a remote look in his eyes as he stood watching them, his hands thrust into his trouser pockets.

"What did you *do* to her?" she hissed, her maternal instincts on full alert. "I trusted you to look after her and I come back to this?" Kayla had stopped her hysterical sobbing and was hiccupping into Bronwyn's chest, her tense little body relaxing as she clung to the familiar comfort her mother represented. Bryce's shadowed eyes revealed absolutely no emotion; his clenched jaw the only visible sign of his tension. She got up, Kayla in her arms, and advanced toward him, a stalking lioness intent on protecting her cub.

"What happened here?"

His eyes remained level but he refused to say a word.

"Bryce, answer me! She *never* cries like this unless she's hurt. How did she get hurt?"

His eyes flickered a little, as he cast an involuntary look down at the little girl who was staring up at him with huge, tear-drenched blue eyes. Her thumb was propped in her mouth and her breath still hitched. Bronwyn glanced over her daughter's little body, doing a damage assessment. Her eyes detected no visible signs of injury until she reached one plump little bare foot. Her big toe was bleeding and looked somewhat swollen. Bronwyn made a soft sound of dismay and lifted the foot to inspect it more closely. Fortunately the damage seemed minimal, and judging from Kayla's ever-lessening sniffles, the immediate shock of pain had worn off already. As the haze of panic dissipated, Bronwyn began to recognize that the damage *she* had done by storming blindly into the fray may have been a lot worse than the injury to Kayla's toe. She had shown an appalling lack of trust by assuming Bryce had been responsible for the toddler's injury, and she was beginning to feel like an overprotective fool.

"Bryce," she began hesitantly, taking a step toward where he stood. He was as still and remote as a statue. He ignored her and swung on his heel to leave the room abruptly. Bronwyn made a dismayed little sound, and Kayla, her pain mostly forgotten already, dragged her thumb from her mouth to add her own opinion.

"Daddy go bye-bye," she observed solemnly before resting her head on Bronwyn's shoulder and sticking her thumb back into her mouth.

"Yes," Bronwyn whispered, burying her face in her daughter's silky curls. "Daddy's gone away." But that wasn't entirely true; he hadn't left the house, she had heard his study door slam and knew that he was probably brooding in there. She knew that she would have to get to the bottom of things sooner rather than later and also had the sinking feeling that she was the one who would have to make serious amends. She glanced over at the appalled Celeste and nodded down at the drowsy little girl in her arms.

"I'll take care of her toe," she said hoarsely, and Celeste mumbled that she'd be in the kitchen. Bronwyn fussed over Kayla for a while, her mind on Bryce while she kissed the toe of her now-giggling baby all better and placed a cute *Finding Nemo* Band-Aid on the tiny cut. Kayla's eyelids started to droop after half an hour of cuddling and playing with her mother—it was way past time for her afternoon nap. Bronwyn carried her to the housekeeper in the kitchen.

"Celeste, would you mind . . ." She left the question unfinished, and Celeste nodded immediately and bustled forward to take an unprotesting Kayla into her arms. Bronwyn dropped an affectionate kiss on the sleepy child's forehead before hurrying out of the room toward Bryce's study. With each heavy step she took, she felt more and more like Daniel preparing to beard the lion's den. When she reached the ominously shut study door, she paused to listen but couldn't hear a sound coming from behind the door. She cautiously knocked on the solid wood before berating herself for her thoughtless action. Now she faced an unfamiliar dilemma: did she just enter? Or did she wait until he eventually came out on his own? She regarded the suddenly insurmountable obstacle of the door cautiously before deciding to take the bull by the horns and open the door.

Bryce sat behind his huge desk, with his elbows resting on the gleaming wooden surface and his face buried in his hands. His large shoulders were shaking slightly. He looked terribly vulnerable, and in that moment Bronwyn felt like a voyeur of the worst kind. She cleared her throat to alert him of her presence and then swore softly beneath her breath when she realized that the gesture was as futile as her knock had been.

"Bryce . . ." Again she swore, feeling like a complete idiot, and hesitantly took a few steps toward him, lifting her hand to his shoulder in the process. He leaped out of the chair like a scalded cat and swore furiously. He glared at her, looking a bit shaken and a lot furious.

"*Don't* sneak up on me," he berated hoarsely.

"I didn't," she protested, shocked by the near violence of his reaction. "I knocked but . . ."

"You knocked?" His voice dripped with derision. "I can't *hear*, damn it!"

"Well, what was I supposed to do, then?" she responded defensively.

"There's a doorbell," he informed, calming down marginally, and she stared at him in confusion.

"A doorbell? But how . . ." her question trailed off when he pointed toward the lamp on his desk.

"The lamp is rigged to flicker when the bell rings. It works for both the front door and the study door. Two flickers for outside, one for inside."

"Oh. That's quite clever," she murmured, impressed by the ingenious device and feeling like a complete idiot for not realizing sooner that the flickering lights that she had absently noticed intermittently since her return were not the result of an electrical fault as she had assumed.

"Clever, yes." He smiled humorlessly and practically sneered the words. "It's a common-enough device for the deaf. There are so many ways to make our lives as convenient as possible, clever little toys that light up and vibrate, tablet computers and smart phones with face-to-face call capabilities, SMSes and various other little gadgets designed to ease my life. Yet not one of these clever little toys would ever be able to alert me to the fact that my little girl is standing right behind me, trying to get my attention, not one of them could prevent me from turning around and treading on her before I'm able to stop myself." *Oh God!* After her initial panic at finding Kayla in floods of tears and obvious pain, she had suspected that it might be something like this. Of course it was an accident, something that Bryce would tear himself up over, a situation that she had worsened with her stupid overreaction. His eyes were tormented, and she swallowed back a sob as she cupped his jaw in her slender hands.

"Bryce," she whispered, her eyes liquid with regret and sympathy. He saw nothing but the sympathy and mistook it for pity. He jerked away from her and turned his back on her.

"No," she moaned softly, not willing to allow him to close himself off when he was clearly in pain. She stepped around him and forced him to meet her eyes.

"Mikayla and I are going to have to learn not to sneak up on you then," she told him firmly. "You are not at fault here, Bryce, it was an accident!"

"You've changed your tune rather quickly," he mocked, and she flushed.

"I overreacted," she conceded. "I'm sorry. I shouldn't have gone off the deep end like that. I know that you would never intentionally hurt our daughter."

"Intentionally or not, I did hurt her," he pointed out harshly. "And I can't promise that it won't happen again in the future. And she—she's frightened of me now. I don't think . . ."

"She's a baby, Bryce," Bron pointed out firmly. "She was shocked and in pain, but she'll soon forget. Children are resilient and have a much larger capacity for forgiveness than we do. She has also learned her lesson, and I doubt she'll be coming up behind you without warning you in some way in the future. One thing about your daughter"—she smiled fondly—"she's a fast learner!"

"She was crying so much," he remembered in a shaken voice. "I couldn't make her stop! Her little face was so sad and confused. I felt like a *monster*."

She took a step closer to him, her heart going out to him.

"Oh, Bryce," she began, not sure how to make this better. "I'm so sorry."

"I don't need your pity," he snarled, as defensive and dangerous as a wounded animal. Bronwyn blinked, his abrupt mood swing throwing her completely off guard.

"I don't *pity* you," she denied, placing one tentative hand on his forearm, but he shrugged her off and signed something at her, glaring wildly while he did.

"I don't understand," she said helplessly, and he responded with another mutinous flurry of sign that left her completely adrift. His eyes were burning with anger and some other emotion that she could not define.

"Bryce, please . . ." she begged, not sure why it mattered to her that she comfort him. "Don't shut me out like this." He said something else, again with his hands, and then quite abruptly turned his back on her. Once again shutting her out as completely as he could. She sobbed a little before lifting a clenched fist to her lips and biting down on her knuckles, not sure how to deal with this. She stared at his broad, stiff back through burning eyes. She refused to let him do this.

Bryce had *always* been much too good at shutting her out. After a bad day at work, he used to closet himself in his study and refuse to speak to her about it until after it was resolved. She had never told him how much that had hurt her, and the *one* time she had dared mention it, he had quite condescendingly informed her that she wouldn't understand anyway and not to worry about it. That had made her so furious, but she had let it slide. She had let a lot of things slide back then, in an effort not to upset Bryce. But she wasn't that silly, spineless girl anymore, and she was determined not to let him shut her out again, not this time. Not when it was so important to their future as a functioning family. She threw back her shoulders resolutely before stepping around him again to meet his glare with a ferocious one of her own. She chose to ignore the scorching anger in his eyes.

"I won't allow you to turn your back on me this time, Bryce. And I refuse to leave until you acknowledge me and we talk about this!" she told him resolutely, and his lips tightened as he signed something particularly vicious looking back at her.

"I don't *know* what you're saying," Bronwyn all but screamed in frustration, and he smiled, a feral showing of teeth that bore no resemblance to his normally beautiful smile. He signed again and quite abruptly grabbed her upper arms and kissed her. *Hard!* His tongue forced its way into the tender interior of her mouth, assaulting and insulting rather than caressing and loving. There was nothing remotely affectionate in the embrace, nothing but contempt and anger.

"I *said*," he told her scornfully, when he lifted his head to end the vile kiss. "That since you refuse to leave, you might as well make yourself useful!"

God, what on Earth had made her think she could deal with this man on an equal footing? Whenever she tried, he moved the goalposts and left her floundering. She couldn't take him on and win; she couldn't even hope to try. More fool her, for thinking that she could.

"Not so eager to stick around now, are you?" he taunted when she took a step back. "Then again, you never were any good at seeing things through, were you? Important things like your studies and our marriage."

"You're the one who abandoned our marriage, Bryce. And then you compounded your sins by believing, and *telling*, the most despicable lies about me!"

"Will you ever stop singing this same pathetic tune over and over again? Your self-righteous indignation does not sit well with me, Bronwyn. This air of injured dignity is wearing thin and getting on my nerves."

"Since we're apparently 'forced' to make a life together, don't you think we should try to set our differences aside and be a family?"

"Then *let's* be a family Bronwyn," he muttered smoothly. "Let's be man and wife." He took hold of her thin upper arms again and dragged her toward him, securing her lips in another kiss. This time the kiss contained all the elements the former had lacked—heat, sensation, and desire. Bronwyn moaned in despair, but his mouth captured the desolate little sound and swallowed it hungrily. His lips were soft but insistent against hers; they opened her mouth with the skill that she had always been unable to resist, and his tongue flowed in, skilfully subduing any protest she may have made. But Bronwyn was beyond protest, hadn't even *thought* of protesting. She knew that this wouldn't solve any of their problems—would probably worsen them if anything—but she had always melted at the first sign of tenderness from him, and this mocking kiss was so humiliatingly tender.

His hands moved up to cup her face, thumbs caressing her jaw as he coaxed her to open up a little more, to respond despite herself and, God help her, did she respond. She kissed him back, parried with his tongue, and ran restless, seeking hands over his shoulders, his neck, and his face. He made a satisfied little sound when her questing hands burrowed beneath his T-shirt and found the silky hot skin beneath the cotton. Somehow, together, they managed to rid him of the T-shirt without once losing contact. Her blouse soon followed suit. Before she knew it, the rest of their clothes were off, and they were skin-to-skin, with nothing between them but a fine sheen of sweat. He closed his hands around her waist and lifted her up. Bronwyn immediately knew what he wanted and obliged him by wrapping her long legs around his waist and her arms around his neck.

He staggered toward his desk, her weight throwing him a tad off balance, but his mouth never lost contact with hers. There was a terrible clatter as he swept stationery from the surface of the desk, nearly sending his computer monitor toppling over the side in the process. He lifted his lips from hers as he laid her down on the desk and plunged into her in the same fluid motion.

Someone sobbed in relief. Bronwyn didn't know which of them it was, but she suspected it was Bryce. He rested there for a while, bearing her down with his weight. He felt big, hot, and hard inside of her and showered her face with worshipful little kisses as he began to move. Her legs had fallen away from his waist and now dangled over the edge of the desk with her thighs spread wide to accommodate his powerful thrusts. His hands were flat against the desk on either side of her head as he focused all of his formidable attention on their mutual pleasure.

He was starting to groan, and his long, smooth strokes were becoming choppier and less controlled. Bronwyn drew her legs up and wrapped them around his waist again, lifting her bottom from the desk to allow him easier and deeper access. He lowered his head to her breasts, licking, sucking, and kissing them hungrily. One of his hands dropped down to where their bodies were joined and he touched her in a way that had always driven her wild. This time was no exception—she grunted in surprise, breathing his name, before squealing with pleasure as she shuddered, then shuddered again and fell apart all around him.

He moaned, moving his hands to her slender hips to hold her steady as he focused fiercely on her contorted face. Sweat was beading on his brow as he slammed into her. Bronwyn, who was just descending from her climax, tensed up again as yet another powerful orgasm crept up on her.

Bryce's back arched and he lifted her clear off the desk with his frantic plunges. He held her close as he shuddered violently and poured himself into her, as they came simultaneously. They cried out their pleasure and desperately clung to each other as the world receded. Bryce collapsed onto her and she briefly bore his full weight before he braced his hands on the desk and relieved her of some of the burden. His eyes were searching her face almost desperately, and Bronwyn wasn't sure what he was hoping to find.

He kissed her sweetly and the part of him that was still buried deep inside of her pulsed lazily in reaction to the gentle caress. Bronwyn gasped as she felt the movement and wondered if they could do it again so soon after the mind-shattering bliss of just minutes before. But he ended the kiss abruptly and lifted himself off and out of her without any warning. The suddenness of the separation left her feeling ridiculously vulnerable. He swore, his face darkening with anger.

"I didn't use any protection." She flinched at the reminder of how much he would loathe getting her pregnant again. But after the last time, getting pregnant by Bryce wasn't exactly high on *her* to-do list either.

"I'm on the pill," she admitted huskily. "I asked the doctor for a prescription last week during my checkup." She flinched when he laughed scathingly.

"Do forgive me if I choose to doubt you, my dear. We both know how very unreliable you are when it comes to taking care of the birth control," he mocked, and she trembled violently at the derision in his voice and the contempt on his face. He gave her one last piercing stare before dropping the matter.

"Did I hurt you?" he asked almost impersonally as he hunted around for his boxers. Her reply obviously held little interest for him because he had his back to her. She didn't bother responding but sat up, humiliated by the position she found herself in—laid out on his desk, naked, and spread out for *his* pleasure. She was covered in a mixture of their perspiration and other fluids and smelled of sex and sweat. She felt used and cheap and her cheeks burned with mortification. He couldn't have made his disdain for her any clearer, and Bronwyn was disgusted with herself for falling into his arms so easily every time. She was a little shell-shocked by her unforgivable stupidity and could barely gather her scattered thoughts. She just wanted out of the room and away from Bryce but for some reason she couldn't seem to figure out how to do that.

She stood up and crossed one arm over her naked breasts and used the other hand to cup the wispy triangle of curls at the juncture of her thighs in a classic pose of feminine shame.

When Bryce looked up and saw her he was struck as still as a statue. Her tear-filled eyes were darting frantically around the room, searching for her scattered clothing. He had dragged on his boxers by now and urgently started hunting for her things, hating the trapped and desperate look in her eyes. He eventually found her blouse and handed it to her, but she didn't move. She looked almost catatonic and Bryce swallowed down an irrational surge of panic. He helped her into the blouse and buttoned it clumsily, but she looked even more vulnerable with only her lower half exposed. She ducked her head and hid her face behind her heavy fall of hair. He hunted around but couldn't seem to find her panties. Instead he turned up a dainty bra and her creased trousers. Deciding that the latter would do, he helped her into them, hunkering down to physically lift her feet, one at a time, into the trouser legs. The position brought his face level with the fine curls at her center, but her very nakedness made her seem even more defenceless and in need of his protection.

He eventually managed to get her all zipped and buttoned up, and when he looked into her face he saw that her lips were moving and the tears that had been threatening had spilled over. He gripped her arms urgently, hating the sight of her tears. He focused on her lips and was able to discern that she was saying the same thing over and over again.

You keep punishing me . . .

Bryce acknowledged that fact to himself. He *did* keep punishing her, but what she didn't know was that he was punishing himself as well. He hated seeing her like this, and he hated the guilt that burned away at his insides like acid with every reluctant tear that she shed. He kept telling himself that she deserved it but it was getting so damned hard to keep convincing himself of that fact. He lifted a hand to her face but she flinched away from him and he glowered, hating the reaction. He had never physically hurt her, he had always taken great care *not* to hurt her, and seeing her flinch away from him like he was the monster he so dreaded becoming, had the same visceral effect on him as a punch to the gut. He gingerly wrapped his arms around her and tugged her against his chest. She was as stiff as a board and refused to relax in his embrace. Eventually realizing that she was probably emotionally drained, he lifted her into his arms and rather awkwardly managed to open the door and carry her upstairs to her bedroom. Thankfully, Celeste and Kayla were nowhere in sight. He placed her onto the soft bed and knelt in front of her, trying to catch her eyes.

"If you'd just *admit* it," he said. She lifted her dull eyes to his, seeming to register his presence at last and frowned in confusion.

"Admit what?" She looked confused, and he gritted his teeth as he tried to maintain his temper.

"Admit that you were at the scene of my accident and that you lied about trying to reach me. I could try to forgive you and we could start rebuilding our relationship. Just be honest, Bronwyn." She sighed tiredly, defeat weighing heavily on her shoulders. She shifted her eyes again and shrugged, looking like someone who just wanted to be left alone and would do anything to achieve that end.

"If that's what you want, Bryce, then I confess to being guilty of everything that you accused me of. I stood beside that road and watched you suffer before walking away. I never tried to contact you; I preferred to struggle along with no money, no home, and rapidly deteriorating health.

"I didn't try, and fail, to reach you just after Kayla was born either, when I was so ill I could barely hold the phone, when I was terrified I would die and she would be left alone. I clung to my stubborn pride and quite selfishly never *once* thought about what was best for you or our daughter." She shaped the words so clearly, he had absolutely no difficulty understanding her. It was what he had wanted, what he believed to be true, a wholesale admission of guilt, but it did not sit well with him and it certainly didn't *feel* right. He wasn't quite sure how to proceed from here and gently pushed her down until she was lying back on the bed.

"You need to rest," he said as gently as he could, but he was an inaccurate judge of his own tone of voice at the best of times, and from the way she flinched, he suspected that his words had emerged a lot harsher than he had intended. Still she obeyed him and lay unresisting, looking utterly drained of any desire to fight him anymore. He tugged the covers up over her unmoving body and kissed her forehead tenderly before standing up. He hovered uncertainly, feeling faintly ridiculous in nothing but his black cotton boxers.

"Try to get some sleep. Don't worry about Kayla. I'll see to her dinner and get her to bed . . ." He seemed to be rambling now and Bronwyn was confused by his uncertainty. "I'll bring her up to say good night later. Things will get better now, Bron," he vowed in an awkward rush, but Bronwyn refused to acknowledge his impulsive promise. "You'll see. They'll get better."

～

Well, things certainly *felt* better when she woke up the following morning. She felt warm and cherished and soon realized that it was because she was being cradled in Bryce's arms with her back pressed to his warm chest. It was only the second time she found herself waking up beside him since her return, and after the events of the last twenty-four hours, she felt more than a little ambivalent about his presence in her bed. He had one arm wrapped around her waist with his hand cradled between her breasts, and the other arm was tucked beneath her head. One of his muscled thighs was squeezed between her own slender thighs. Against her better judgment, Bronwyn felt safe, secure, and almost cherished. She felt his warm and steady breath feathering against the vulnerable nape of her neck, and she fought back a little shiver of pleasure. She slowly became aware of the fact that they were both naked—and vaguely recalled Bryce brusquely helping her out of her clothes sometime during the night. The scorching hot length of his erection was pressing up against the small of her back. She immediately tensed.

"Relax." His voice sounded like the contented purr of a cat and had the exact opposite effect of relaxing her. "I'm not going to jump you this morning. We need to talk."

"I have nothing to say to you," she responded mutinously, safe in the knowledge that he could not hear her or see her lips.

"What did you say?" he surprised her by demanding, and she tensed even further. He turned her resisting body to face him as if she weighed no more than a feather, but she kept her gaze glued to his jaw. "I know you said something . . . I could feel the vibration in your chest!"

"I asked what you wanted to talk about," she lied, meeting his eyes. He looked unconvinced, and his eyes seethed with frustration, but he tamped it down determinedly.

"Us . . ."

"I thought we'd said all that needed saying last night," she responded. "I'm a liar and you're the victim of my vindictive and cruel nature." He chose to ignore her sarcasm.

"I want to know what you meant last night when you said that you were terrified that you would die," he probed softly, watching her face carefully. They were lying so close together that it was difficult to conceal the smallest emotion from him.

"There were complications." She shrugged casually. "It was a difficult pregnancy, worsened by the fact that I was . . . malnourished." How humiliating it was to admit that. She lowered her eyes again, embarrassed by her inability to take care of herself. "I was underweight and weak by the time I went into labor. It was a long, intense labor, and because my body had been deprived of the vitamins it needed during the pregnancy, it was ill-equipped to deal with the . . . trauma . . . of an extended labor. There was some tearing, I lost a lot of blood and went into shock. I remember them asking for the name and number of my next of kin right after Kayla was born." She felt moisture on her cheeks and was appalled to discover that she was crying silently. God, she was *so* sick of crying all the time, but it was so difficult to recall the fear and absolute loneliness of that moment without succumbing to emotion. "I was so scared. I just wanted to hold my baby. I wanted to be sure that she was okay. The doctors all looked so grim behind their masks; they told me that she was fine but nobody would show me." She felt a rough thumb wiping away the tears on her cheeks and shut her eyes at the gruff gentleness. She swallowed bravely before continuing. "One of the last things I remember before everything went dark was begging to see my baby, and then a doctor calling my name and swearing. I remember him swearing because he sounded so angry and so concerned that he reminded me of you. For a split second I thought it *was* you! And I was so *happy* . . ." She could feel him trembling now, as if chilled to the bone, but for some reason she couldn't seem to stop the flow of words. He had asked, he had wanted to know, and she was *not* going to sugar coat it for him. She cleared her throat hoarsely before continuing.

"They told me my heart stopped . . . twice. Of course, I don't remember it at all. I just woke up to the sound of Kayla's crying. It took so much strength to turn my head but . . ." She smiled radiantly up into his face, her tears blinding her to his expression. "She was the most beautiful thing I'd ever seen. So perfect and so healthy, and in that moment I knew that I would do *anything* to keep her safe!"

"Bronwyn . . ." Bryce's throat was tight with emotion, and he struggled to get the words out. "Why didn't you . . ."

"Call you?" She completed the question and gazed at him levelly. "Perhaps I was stubborn . . . or stupid? Maybe I didn't love Kayla enough to want the best for her?" He didn't want her truth, he had forced her into uttering the only major lie she had ever told him, and she would be *damned* if she ever tried to convince him of the facts again. She was tired of defending herself to a man who refused to see the truth. Well, now the truth was something that Bryce would have to discover for himself. She had given up on it and on him.

"I'm so sorry," he whispered painfully, his own eyes shimmering with what could only be tears. "God, I'm so sorry you had to go through that on your own."

Bryce wasn't quite able to process everything he had just learned without wanting to howl in agony at the horror of it all. Her *heart* had stopped for God's sake! She had *died* and he hadn't even known about it. His beautiful, fragile Bronwyn had nearly been snatched from him forever and the knowledge was eating him up alive. His own suffering seemed almost immaterial when measured against the cripplingly painful facts that she had just revealed and yet he couldn't help thinking that if she had just stayed, come back, called him— *anything*—he could have protected her, kept her safe from harm. He ignored the shrill voice screeching at him in the back of his mind, *Who would have kept her safe from you?*

"You said the nurse asked you for your next of kin's contact details. Why didn't you give them my number?" he asked gruffly.

"Oh, now why on earth would I do that?" Bronwyn asked flippantly. "I much preferred the thought of leaving Kayla an orphan."

His brow lowered threateningly. You didn't have to be able to hear to recognize such blatant sarcasm.

"Bron, now's not the time for facetiousness!"

"Well," she blinked up at him innocently, forming her words carefully so that there would be no misunderstanding. "I'm just telling you what I believe you want to know, since it has become rather self-evident that the truth gets rejected when it doesn't suit you. What I don't get is how on earth you could marry a woman you have such a low opinion of. By now we've established that I'm foolish, fickle, cruel, and selfish! God knows what you saw in me in the first place. You must be an *appalling* judge of character." She disentangled herself from his arms and jumped out of bed, uncaring of her nudity. She just wanted to get away from him.

"Where are you going?" he asked, sounding panicky.

"Shower," was her succinct reply.

"But we haven't finished our talk . . ."

"I've said all I have to say on that particular subject." She waved her hand dismissively and turned toward the en suite.

"Bron," his voice was gruff with some indefinable emotion, and she turned to face him. He stared at her for a long moment, looking completely lost for words, before shaking his head.

"Rick and Lisa got back from their holiday last night, and I thought it would be nice to have them come by for the afternoon. I'd like Rick to get to know Kayla, and I think that you and Lisa might get along." She nodded in response, part of her looking forward to seeing Rick again and the other part remembering his cold-bloodedness at the hospital when she had been ill and defenseless. She *was* looking forward to spending more time with his new wife though; the woman had been very kind to her in the brief moments they had shared.

"That'll be nice," she murmured before turning back toward the bathroom, and this time he let her go without protest.

CHAPTER EIGHT

Rick, Lisa, and Rhys arrived just after one o'clock. The couple was holding hands and looked tanned, healthy, and happy. Rick's greeting of Bronwyn was strained; merely a curt nod before he grinned at his older brother and immediately struck up a conversation in SASL, rather rudely excluding both Bronwyn and Lisa. The other woman shared a wry smile with Bronwyn before clasping her hand warmly and planting a totally unexpected kiss on her cheek.

"You look so much better than the last time I saw you," she said with a friendly smile.

"Rest and sunshine will do that," Bron responded easily before stepping back and giving Lisa an all-encompassing once-over.

"I don't remember much about you, beyond your kindness that day, but I have to say, you're looking very good too." She snuck a glance over to her expansively signing brother-in-law. "I'm happy the whole . . . situation with Bryce and I didn't ruin your holiday!" Lisa shook her head with a smile.

"Rick was a bit withdrawn for a while, but Rhys and I soon dragged him out of it." She nodded down at the sleeping baby in his stroller and grinned good-naturedly.

"Oh, I'm so relieved to hear that." Bronwyn couldn't help but respond to Lisa's warm personality. The woman was absolutely lovely. She could see how Rick fell for her so quickly.

"So where is your beautiful little girl?" Lisa sent a questioning glance around the sunny patio as if expecting Kayla to pop out from some nook at any moment.

"Poor little thing. Bryce was preparing her for your impending visit all morning and while she has no idea what cousins, aunts, and uncles are—I think she's expecting some exotic form of animal—she kept chattering on about it throughout her lunch. She wore herself out and drifted off to sleep almost immediately after completing her meal. It's for the best; she gets cranky if she doesn't have her afternoon nap. She'll be up again in an hour or two." She glanced over to where Bryce and Rick were still immersed in conversation and frowned.

"Can *you* understand sign language?" she asked quietly, and Lisa's eyes became pools of liquid sympathy.

"A little. Rick has been teaching me," she admitted softly.

"What are they talking about?" Bron wondered wistfully, and Lisa squeezed her hand again.

"I think Rick is telling Bryce about his shark cage dive." She shuddered at the unpleasant recollection.

"Oh dear . . . Rick *still* does stuff like that?"

"Apparently it was the first time he's ever gone shark cage diving. He loved it but told me that he doubts he'll do it again, now that he's experienced it. I should hope not. It gives me jitters whenever I think of him down there with all those huge great whites circling the flimsy little cage he considers protection!"

"He'll settle down a bit now that he's married with a child, I suspect," Bron stated confidently.

"*Sure* he will." Lisa rolled her eyes. "Or maybe he'll simply drag Rhys and me along with him. Back when we were dating, before I got pregnant, he did a brilliant job of talking me into doing the crazy stuff with him! In fact I'm pretty sure getting pregnant so soon was my body's defence mechanism kicking in to save me from Death by Crazy."

"*No*," Bron gasped, unable to picture the sweet, bookish-looking woman participating in some of the extreme sports Rick commonly did for fun.

"Well let's see: bungee jumping, parasailing, parachuting, hang-gliding." She ticked off her fingers as she itemized. "Navigating in some crazy off-road race, white-water rafting . . . these are just a *few* of the insane things I found myself roped into doing back then."

"Ballet recitals, operas, poetry readings, symphony orchestras, shopping for *really* old furniture," Rick interjected.

"Antiques," Lisa inserted smoothly, smiling affectionately as her husband came over to join them.

". . . Art exhibitions," Rick continued to recite as if she hadn't interrupted, dropping an arm around his wife's narrow shoulders and angling himself so that Bryce was able to lip-read what he was saying. "These are just a few of the really boring things *I* have found myself participating in since getting married."

Lisa snorted and rolled her eyes again.

"At least *I* don't have a thing for jumping off high mountains and out of perfectly good planes," she scoffed, and he grinned before dropping a quick kiss on her lips and whispering something in her ear.

Bronwyn watched them enviously and unconsciously found herself raising her eyes to Bryce's face. She was startled to see that he was studying her intently, and she lowered her gaze quickly but he came over to stand beside her. They stood side by side for a couple of moments, not touching, watching the younger couple whispering and giggling with each other. Bronwyn nearly jumped out of her skin when she felt the first tentative, wholly unexpected touch of his large hand in the small of her back. Her eyes flew to his impassive profile, but he kept his eyes straight ahead, watching his brother and Lisa with a slight smile playing about his lips.

His hand moved up hesitantly, until it was in the nape of her neck, beneath the thick fall of her hair and the heat of his skin singed the delicate flesh of her vulnerable neck. He massaged her soft skin gently before clearing his throat to get the younger couple's attention; they jumped apart guiltily, grinning like kids.

"Ready to eat?" Bryce asked quietly before turning toward the patio table that was laden with delicious food and fruit. He kept a possessive hand on Bronwyn as he led her toward the table and let her go long enough to pull out a chair for her. Bronwyn glanced up at him warily before accepting the seat. He used to do things like that for her all the time in the past, unconscious acts like opening doors, helping her into coats, seating her. It was an old-world chivalry that Bronwyn had found completely charming. He hadn't done anything like it since her return, and Bronwyn realized with a pang that it was one of the small details she had forgotten, yet subconsciously missed, about him. She nodded her thanks, wondering what was behind the sudden courtesy. His hand unexpectedly lowered to her cheek and his thumb stroked her flesh briefly, but he moved away before she had any chance to react to the unexpected caress.

Baffled, Bronwyn's eyes followed his progress as he sat opposite her, next to Lisa, leaving Rick no option but to sit beside Bronwyn. Rick largely ignored her in favor of his brother and wife, leaving Bronwyn feeling snubbed and ridiculously hurt. She *knew* why he was behaving the way he was, knew that he was merely being loyal to his brother, whom he felt had been treated unfairly. Yet Bronwyn still couldn't help but feel almost betrayed by Rick's blatant display of hostility. By the time they were halfway through the meal, Lisa was glaring daggers at her husband, and Bryce was looking almost as strained as Bronwyn felt. Rick was either oblivious to the tension he was creating or—more than likely—ignoring it.

"Bronwyn," Bryce's quiet voice interrupted Rick's animated description of some of the more exotic sights he and Lisa had been treated to during their "and baby makes three honeymoon," as he had so delightfully described the holiday. "You're not eating . . ."

Bronwyn looked down at her barely touched meal and shrugged helplessly, a bit thrown by the abrupt shift in topic.

"I'm not that hungry," she responded with a strained smile. "And I was wrapped up in Rick's story."

"You should eat," Bryce prompted. "You're still too thin . . ."

Bronwyn snapped, instantly and utterly fed up with everything. The ridiculous untruths he believed about her, Rick's hostility, and her own weakness in both body and spirit.

"It's always something with you, isn't it?" she hissed furiously. "I wasn't well spoken enough, pretty enough, graceful enough, educated enough . . . I was never good enough for you. I doubt I'll *ever* be good enough. No wonder you jumped at the opportunity to get rid of me," she reflected bitterly. "All you needed was an excuse, and I very conveniently provided you with one when I got pregnant. And then, to add insult to injury, you came up with that *ridiculous* . . ." She stopped abruptly, remembering her resolve to let him muddle through the facts and find the truth for himself. She shook her head furiously, turning to a gaping Rick.

"And as for *you* . . . How dare you sit there judging me with nothing but the so-called facts your stupid brother gave you to go on?" She was so furious, hurt, and frustrated that she couldn't stop herself from clenching her fist and punching him on his arm. He winced and angled his chair away from her. "I thought you were smarter and fairer than that, Rick!" She got up and turned to face

Lisa, who was staring up at her with an approving grin playing about her lips.

"I'm sorry," she whispered, her eyes burning with the tears she refused to shed. "Please excuse me . . ."

Lisa nodded and Bronwyn turned to flee, leaving absolute silence in her wake.

"Well," Lisa drawled into the shocked silence. "I think she's a little angry, don't you?"

"Stop it, Lisa," Rick grunted irritably. "This is none of your—"

"Don't say it," she warned direly. "Don't even *think* about saying it!"

Rick wisely shut up.

"Your behavior was atrocious, and I was so ashamed of you."

"Lisa, you don't know—"

"She claims that she tried to call me," Bryce interrupted the squabbling couple quietly, and Rick frowned.

"What?"

"Before having Kayla, as little as a week after leaving me and then again after she gave birth." He knew enough to read between the lines of her sarcastic responses of that morning. "She said she tried to call me. She said she tried my cell phone, but of course that was wrecked in the accident. She also professes to have tried the house but you'd given Celeste and the staff time off while I was recuperating. But then she also says that she tried to contact the office and was stonewalled by my people."

Rick gaped at him.

"Bronwyn tried to contact you?"

"So she claims." Bryce shrugged, trying to disguise his unease behind the careless movement. "My staff would not have given her the run-around, not unless I'd given specific instructions to that effect. Something I could not have done while laid up in hospital.

So she has to be lying. But why the hell does she keep telling the same lie, over and over again?"

"Bryce," Rick looked aghast. "You did give an order to that effect."

"*What?*" Bryce leaped to his feet at the outrageousness of the remark. "What in God's name are you talking about?"

"It was the same night as your accident. Pierre, Cooper"— Cooper had been Bryce's personal assistant at the time, a young and ambitious self-starter who had since moved on to bigger and better things—"and I were all there. You had just gotten out of surgery and you were still groggy, but when I asked you where Bronwyn was, you were very adamant that you did *not* want to see her or hear from her ever again. You were in so much pain and the fact that I had to write down everything I said was adding to your emotional strain. I knew that something pretty awful must have happened between the two of you. The mere fact that she wasn't at the hospital was testament enough of that, but I still figured the words were bluster and that you two would work things out, so I shrugged them off."

Bryce's face revealed absolutely no emotion as he got up from the table and dug his cell phone out of his pocket.

"Call Pierre and ask him if he knows of any calls Bronwyn may have made to my office while I was recuperating."

"Bryce . . ." Rick began.

"Just *do* it, Rick!" The younger man nodded and dialed. Bryce watched his brother's face as he spoke with Pierre, unable to read his lips while he had the phone up against his ear. He kept picturing Bronwyn's tormented face as she had flung her bitter words at him. He hadn't been able to read half of what she'd said to him, but he had gotten the gist of it. She actually believed he didn't think she was good enough for him? Where the hell had she gotten a demented idea like *that*? He was still mulling over the question when Rick disconnected his call and looked up. Bryce watched his younger brother's expression closely, anxious to know what Pierre had revealed. When Rick first spoke, Bryce was so intent on watching his brother's eyes that he missed the first few words and impatiently signed for him to start again.

"Pierre doesn't know of any calls Bron may have placed to the office," Rick began, and Bryce felt an overwhelming surge of despair battling with an equally large dose of anger at himself for almost believing the treacherous little bitch! Rick was still talking and it took all of Bryce's concentration to focus on his brother's lips again. ". . . *Does* remember you categorically stating that you wanted nothing more to do with her. Like me, he didn't take the words seriously, so he placed no such order on your behalf. Pierre thinks that Cooper may not have dismissed your words as lightly. After all, Pierre is your friend and partner, and I'm your brother, and unlike Cooper we had no jobs on the line." Bryce said nothing, merely stared at his brother thoughtfully for the longest time. The anger and despair was forgotten as a terrible feeling of sinking panic rapidly settled over him, and he frantically tried to figure out what to do next.

"Rick," he said out loud, as carefully and concisely as he could, not wanting his brother to misunderstand his next words in the slightest way. "I want you to find Cooper. I want to know if she's lying about this because . . . because . . ." He couldn't bear to utter the words. His eyes slid away from Rick's, and he found himself meeting Lisa's gaze. He saw that her lips were moving and he automatically focused on them.

". . . If she's telling the truth about trying to call you, she may well be telling the truth about everything else, right?" He hid a wince as Lisa verbalized the words he had been unable to speak, and his eyes shut in horror at the mere idea of such an atrocity. *God*, how could he live with himself if his terrible treatment of her since her return had been unjustified? He met Rick's gaze, wondering if the misery and overwhelming dread he felt were evident in his eyes.

"She also said that she *wasn't* there when I had my accident. That she didn't leave me to . . ." He couldn't even bring himself to say it, realizing now how ridiculous it was to believe that his soft-hearted wife would ever leave him, or anyone else for that matter, injured and alone at the scene of an accident. He sat down on the closest chair with a thump, feeling bewildered and sick to his stomach.

"Oh my *God*," he groaned. "Oh my God! I was so determined to blame her for this, but what if I was wrong, Rick? Do you know what that means? The things she went through on her own . . . how she struggled to make a decent life for Kayla and herself. She nearly *died* having our baby, and I wasn't there for her. Even if she's lying about everything, there's just no excuse for letting her go through all of that on her own!" His brother put a firm hand on his shoulder, forcing Bryce to look up to meet his gaze.

"Calm down, Bryce, you tried to find her, remember? Even believing what you did about her, you still tried your damnedest to find her. Let's just figure out what the truth is before you start with the self-recriminations."

Bryce covered his face with his hands, not sure what to do next, feeling helpless and completely lost. It was a feeling he was all-too familiar with since losing his hearing, but it wasn't a feeling he would ever learn to live with. He got up abruptly, his head swimming with chaotic thoughts, his objective clear.

"I have to talk with her." His eyes blindly sought out his brother and sister-in-law. "I . . . excuse me." He saw Rick start to sign something but Lisa reached out and stayed his brother's hands before nodding encouragingly at Bryce.

⁓

She was on the nursery floor, playing with an active Kayla, who looked refreshed after her afternoon nap. Bronwyn had her back to the door and didn't see him at first. In fact, it was Kayla who alerted her to his presence. The little girl saw him hovering in the doorway, and her whole face lit up as she squealed excitedly.

"Daddy!" She toddled toward him, her chubby arms outstretched. Bryce smiled at the little girl as he swept her up into his arms, keeping his eyes on Bronwyn's slender back, noting how it tensed, before she squared her shoulders and stood up to face him. Bryce was trying to handle the little girl's effusive chatter and watch Bronwyn's face at the same time. Eventually he gave up on trying to follow Kayla's confusing baby talk and focused entirely on Bronwyn, nodding now and then to keep Kayla happy.

"Are you okay?" he asked her quietly, noting the stubborn tilt of her jaw and the unshed tears in her luminous eyes. He felt like an absolute bastard driving her to the brink of tears . . . *again*!

"I'm fine." She nodded, folding her arms defensively over her chest.

"I . . ." he began, but Kayla was bouncing up and down, demanding that he play horsey with her. He kissed the little girl, before going to the door and hollering for Rick, immediately quieting Kayla, who looked up at him uncertainly, wondering if her daddy was mad at her. Bryce grinned down at her reassuringly, making airplane noises and flying her around the room for a few moments, before Rick came panting up the stairs.

"What?" he asked urgently.

"Kayla . . ." Bryce planted an affectionate kiss on his daughter's silky cheek. "This is your Uncle Rick!"

"Unca?" The girl wondered doubtfully.

"Yes and he likes to play horsey!" Rick, who had been grinning foolishly down at the little girl, abruptly stopped smiling and met his brother's eyes in horror.

"Unca, horsey?" the little girl asked excitedly.

"You want to play horsey with Uncle Rick while Mummy and Daddy talk?" Bryce asked gently, knowing that she wouldn't understand anything but "play horsey" and "Uncle Rick."

"Uh, Bryce . . ." Rick began while back-pedaling frantically; he stopped abruptly when Kayla bestowed her most radiantly trusting smile on him and held out her arms.

"Horsey, Unca Wick?" she asked coyly, and Rick swallowed visibly before stepping forward and lifting the little girl from her father's arms.

"What an accomplished little flirt you already are." He chuckled before meeting Bryce's eyes.

"You're going to have your hands full with this one, in twelve or so years' time, big brother." Bryce grinned halfheartedly and shrugged.

"I'll cross that bridge when I come to it. Please keep her busy, Rick. Bron and I need to—"

"Say no more," Rick interrupted cheerfully while Kayla tugged at his hair and shirt, impatient to be off. "Come along, Kayla, let's go and meet your cousin and your auntie Lisa. She loves to play horsey too!" He carried the friendly little girl, who seemed to have forgotten all about her parents at the prospect of playing with exciting new people, out of the room and left Bronwyn and Bryce to contemplate each other quietly for a few moments.

"What's the problem this time, Bryce?" Bronwyn asked with what appeared to be sarcasm, if her face was any indication. "I'm so sorry I stormed out and ruined your perfect little party."

"The night you left," he began quietly, trying to keep his voice level and calm, not wanting to come across as accusatory or angry. "After my accident, Bron, I *swear* I saw you in the crowd and, even though I knew that I was the one who had driven you out of the house in the first place, in my mind, abandoning me there was completely unforgivable. I know that my reaction to your pregnancy was cruel and unwarranted, but despite that, you were my wife, the person I depended on the most, the woman who claimed to love me, and you *left* me there! It made no sense to me and it hurt so damned much. It also gave me an excuse to hate you because feeling anything other than that was just too . . ." He broke off awkwardly, aware of her frown and her confusion.

"Bryce, I wasn't . . ." she began but he held up a hand.

"Please . . . I . . . let me speak." He shut his eyes painfully. "I remember it so vividly; I looked up and saw you standing there on the fringe of the gathering crowd. You looked cold, remote, and so beautiful. You were wearing the dress that I loved. Remember? The little black one with the floaty skirt. I tried to call you, but my voice wouldn't work. I now know that I was shouting at the top of my lungs." He grinned feebly. "I just couldn't hear myself. Do you understand why it's been so difficult to let go of that image? How I can't ever get the memory of you turning your back and walking away from me out of my mind?"

Bronwyn stared up into his dark and tormented face. She knew how much it must have cost him to come up here and reveal how much he been hurt by her perceived actions that night. She sighed; so much for letting him muddle through it on his own. She couldn't, not when he had just presented her with the means to refute his repulsive accusation.

"Bryce." Her throat caught, and she inhaled deeply as she fought back the ever-present urge to cry. "I have something to show you." She led him into the master bedroom and toward the huge walk-in closet that housed her old wardrobe. She opened the door and rifled through the contents briefly before lifting a padded hanger with a flimsy scrap of black chiffon hanging from it.

"This dress?" she asked gently, and he winced as if the dress brought back cripplingly painful memories. He nodded. She shut her eyes tightly as she fought for composure, so did not see the slight movement he made toward her before stopping himself.

"Bryce," she murmured unsteadily, opening her eyes again. "I was wearing a pair of jeans and a T-shirt when I left that night. I left with nothing but the clothes on my back. This dress . . . it's been hanging here for the last two years." Bryce shifted his gaze to the dress and shook his head, unable to believe that he had gotten something so very crucial to the well-being of their relationship so totally *wrong*. He took the dress from her and ran the flimsy material gently through his large hands.

"Rick could have packed . . ." he began, but she touched his hand to get his attention and shook her head slowly, keeping her eyes level.

"Why don't you ask Rick? I'm sure he'd remember a dress like this among the endless amounts of toddler-proof wear he packed for me." She nibbled at her lower lip. "I left on a Tuesday night, remember?"

He nodded.

"This is a cocktail dress, Bryce," she pointed out. "Were we at a party that night?"

He hesitated before responding.

"No. You called me at the office and told me you were cooking a special meal because you had something exciting to tell me . . ."

His voice broke and he was trembling from head to foot. Bronwyn was the one who remained rock-steady for a change, while Bryce looked like he was on the verge of tears. "I came home and found you wearing your tattered blue jeans and one of those T-shirts you'd bought in the Seychelles. You said that you didn't feel like dressing up for dinner."

"So you changed your clothes and we had a picnic in the conservatory. After dinner I told you I was pregnant and you . . ."

He swallowed painfully.

"I reacted in the worst possible way," he grated. "I told you to leave and you did."

"Wearing the same jeans and T-shirt that I'd been wearing all evening," she finished. His face contorted savagely, and he flung the dress aside with a vicious curse. Bronwyn flinched at the sudden movement, unable to gauge his mood, not sure if he believed her or not. He brushed past her abruptly to slam his way into the en suite, and she was shocked to hear the sound of violent retching coming from behind the closed door. She hovered outside, unsure if she should venture in or wait for him to come back out. She had just made up her mind to go in, when the ghastly sounds stopped and she heard the toilet flush, followed by the sounds of water running and gargling.

He opened the door slowly, and she found herself staring up at him warily. He looked awful, hollow-eyed, hunted, and like he had aged ten years in the last ten minutes. He couldn't *quite* bring himself to meet her eyes.

"I . . ." he began. "I don't know . . ." He raised a violently trembling hand toward her but checked the movement abruptly, his hand falling limply back to his side.

"Bryce . . ." she murmured uncertainly, but he shook his head abruptly, lifting his eyes to her face, and Bronwyn was horrified by the depth of self-loathing she saw in his tortured gaze. It was mingled with overwhelming regret and something akin to fear and desperation.

"God, how you must *hate* me," he murmured.

"I don't think . . ." But it was too late, he turned away before she could say anything more and exited the room abruptly. Bronwyn felt ridiculously deflated by the anticlimactic end to such an intense conversation. That Bryce believed her was no longer in doubt, but he now seemed wholly unable to deal with his own culpability in the failure of their relationship.

∿

"Don't bother finding Cooper," Bryce growled upon stepping out onto the sunny patio where his brother, sister-in-law, and the two toddlers were happily playing. They, all four, came to an abrupt halt at the sound of his gruff voice. Lisa and Rick looked concerned, Rhys started crying, and Kayla merely looked happy to see him, as always. While Lisa picked Rhys up for a cuddle, Kayla babbled on incoherently but Bryce couldn't focus and was unable to tell what the child was trying to communicate. It was difficult enough to understand her under normal circumstances, but the emotional turmoil he was in right now made it damned near impossible to make out what she was trying to say to him. He nodded and smiled blindly down at her, before switching his gaze to Rick.

"Why not?" his brother asked when their gazes met.

"She's telling the truth," Bryce bit off tautly, the knowledge still tearing him apart.

"How do you know?"

"A dress." Bryce shook his head in shattered disbelief. "I was *so* sure of what I'd seen that night, I could remember every single detail of the accident scene down to the dress she was wearing as she stood there watching me scream her name." He fought back the urge to laugh like a maniac, knowing that it would send him careening off the edge of reason. "Only she wasn't wearing a dress the night she left me, Rick. I should have known that because I now remember thinking how damned sexy she looked in those jeans, just moments before everything went to hell. Not the cocktail dress I'd been remembering her in for the last two years but a pair of *jeans* and a T-shirt. Oh God . . . oh my *God!*" He saw Rick go pale and knew that he had to look equally pasty-faced. The younger man blasphemed shakily.

"So now what, Bryce?"

Bryce shook his head helplessly at his brother's question.

"Now I give her everything she wants because that's the least of what she deserves."

"What if she wants a divorce?"

It was the one thing Bryce had been trying not to think about, and he flinched from the question.

"I wouldn't blame her." Bryce's eyes fell to his happily bubbling daughter, who was trying to share her stuffed toys with a still-crying Rhys. "But I'm not sure what I'll do if she asks for one."

∽

Bronwyn came down about an hour later to find Rick and Lisa in the conservatory with Kayla and Rhys. The children were playing together contentedly. There was no sign of Bryce. Rick hopped to his feet agitatedly when he saw her enter the room and immediately apologized.

"I was unforgivably rude and needlessly cruel, Bron," he muttered, shoving his hands into the back pockets of his jeans. "I'm so sorry. I know I hurt you, but . . . damn it, Bron, he's my brother and he was so *damaged* and so completely changed by something we all thought was your fault. It just felt like too large an obstacle to overcome!"

"Technically it was my fault," she pointed out grimly. "He came after me that night, and if not for that he would not have had his accident."

"No, it was *his* fault and he admits as much. If he hadn't been such an absolute bastard about your pregnancy, none of it would have happened. I'm so sorry, Bronwyn."

"Ricky." She sighed wearily, not sure why she felt the need to comfort him but wanting to set his mind at ease nonetheless. "You were being loyal to your brother. It was his word against mine. You did what you thought was right."

"What do you plan to do now?" Rick asked after an awkward pause. He was unable to look her in the eye, and she knew how hard the truth must have hit him. Knowing how unjustly he and Bryce had treated her would not sit comfortably with someone who had such an innate sense of fairness. She knew that it would eat at him for a while and that their relationship might never go back to the way it was before.

"What do you mean?" she asked tiredly.

"Well, my brother is pretty torn up about this, Bron."

She laughed grimly at his words, cutting him off.

"Yes, and it's always about *him* isn't it?" she asked bitterly.

"No, it's just . . ." Rick trailed off awkwardly, not sure what to say. "Will you leave him?"

"He doesn't really want *me*, you know? He wants Kayla. I'm just excess baggage." She shrugged.

"He'll give you just about anything you ask for right now," Rick pointed out.

"Is that so? Well then, where is he? Maybe it's time I start making my demands. While his guilt lasts . . ."

"Bronwyn, you're being—" he began, but Lisa, who had been keeping the children occupied, interrupted whatever he'd been about to say.

"Bryce is in his study," she informed quietly, absently picking Kayla up and handing her over to Rick while she lifted Rhys into her arms. Bronwyn nodded her thanks and dropped a loving kiss on her daughter's head before turning on her heel and heading out of the room.

~

She didn't ring the doorbell; she wanted an honest reaction from him and did not want to give him time to mask whatever he was feeling. So she strode in confidently and then halted before she'd gotten more than two steps into the room, suddenly unsure of her decision.

He sat behind his huge desk, with his head in his hands in almost exactly the same pose as the day before but he looked so incredibly lost and alone that, for a moment, she was unsure of what her next move should be. He must have sensed her presence because he looked up unexpectedly, pinning her to the spot with his tormented gaze. It said a lot for the changed status of their relationship that he did not immediately fly off the handle because of her supposed "intrusion" into his lair.

"I can't fix this," he admitted bleakly. His voice was quivering in a way that would have killed his pride if he had been able to hear it. "I don't know how to." He looked strangely defenseless with his messy hair and his disheveled clothing, but she steeled herself against his vulnerability. While she was happy that he now knew the truth, the simple fact of the matter was that she couldn't trust him with her heart. It had *never* been safe with him, but she hadn't known it until he had so ruthlessly rejected her two years ago. Yes, he was now filled with regret about the mistake he had made immediately following his accident, but he still had no explanations or apologies for the behavior that had driven her out in the first place.

She did not know what to say to him, did not know what she wanted from him anymore. Just the day before she had idealistically and unrealistically imagined that if they tried to get along, their relationship would improve and they could build on that. Of course, they both had Kayla's best interests at heart and wanted to provide stability for her, but Bronwyn deserved better than a second-rate marriage, with them staying together only for the sake of their daughter. Right now Bronwyn also honestly believed that Kayla would be better off if their marriage was severed sooner rather than later. It was better than raising their baby in an atmosphere of mistrust.

After all, this was the man who had thought nothing of kicking her out of their home after discovering that she was pregnant with his baby. The same man who had left her to fend for herself when she was at her weakest. He had also accused her of the most heinous of acts and no amount of guilt now could make up for his many sins. Any relationship that they tried to salvage from this wreckage of a marriage would be based on a foundation of guilt and misguided obligation.

"I don't think it *can* be fixed anymore, Bryce," she said reluctantly, moving toward his desk and sitting down in the huge leather chair across from him. He flinched and averted his face briefly before turning his head to look at her once more.

"So what do you want to do?" he asked tonelessly.

"I don't know," she admitted helplessly. "I think we would all be better off if we, you and I, were no longer together. Let's face it, after two years of separation, the next logical step is a mere formality."

"You want to leave," he said matter-of-factly. "Again."

"I didn't exactly *want* to leave the last time, Bryce," she reminded him pointedly. She was small-minded enough to enjoy seeing the barb hit home. "I just don't think this situation can be redeemed. Too much has been said and done to go back." He scrubbed a tired hand over his face before tilting his head back and shutting his eyes. After a few moments of silence, he opened his eyes and looked back at her with his piercing eyes.

"What do you plan to do after you leave?"

"I'm going back to university to finish my studies."

"Won't it be difficult to be a full-time student when you're a single parent again?" Her mouth gaped in surprise at the wholly unexpected question.

"Correct me if I'm wrong, but I assumed that I was no longer a single parent." His eyes flickered with something akin to relief, and Bronwyn's surprise very quickly turned to horrified comprehension. "You thought I was taking her away from you?" He nodded in response to her shocked question.

"Whatever you may have done to deserve it, Bryce, I won't deny you your right to be a father to Kayla. Even though you once tossed away that privilege as cavalierly as you would a pair of old socks." Another direct hit. "And don't get me wrong here; I am not doing it for you! Kayla needs you in her life." He nodded again, this time more confidently.

"So you want to finish your studies?" he prompted after clearing his throat awkwardly.

"I'll have to find a decent place to live and a job to pay for—"

"That won't be necessary," he inserted hurriedly. "The job, I mean. I'll pay for your studies."

"The only money I'll ever want from you will go toward the upbringing of your daughter, Bryce. I can take care of myself!"

"This from the woman who was practically on her last legs when we found her? You will not run yourself into the ground again. I can, and will, take care of you."

"I am not your property; you have no right to speak to me as if I were," she said, seething, and he swore in frustration.

"Okay, can we compromise on this?" he asked meekly after what looked like a colossal effort to rein in his temper. "I have a suggestion." She waited silently for him to continue, her arms folded defiantly over her chest as she prepared for battle.

"You and Kayla stay here." He lifted a silencing hand as she started to protest. "No, wait, just listen. You and Kayla stay here, and that way, she and I would be able to see each other all the time. You find that job to pay for your studies, and you'll have built-in babysitters for Kayla in both Celeste and me. You won't be run off your feet, studying, working a part-time job, and caring for a demanding toddler. You also won't have to worry about rent and food."

"What's in this for you?" she asked suspiciously.

"Like I said, unrestricted access to my daughter," was his simple response. "And enough time to get to know her better."

"What about us? Our marriage?" She broached the subject warily, and he averted his eyes down to his clenched hands again.

"Well there *is* no more marriage, is there?" he droned tonelessly. "This house is big enough for us to live completely separate lives. We could work out some kind of schedule, times you may need certain areas of the house to yourself. Please don't reject the idea out of hand just because it came from me. It makes sense and you won't be killing yourself trying to make ends meet. I won't interfere with your life at all."

"What about your work?" she asked when his eyes were on her again.

"I work mostly from home these days." He shrugged and she hesitated, her mind busily going over every angle of his plan. "I do plan to spend some more time in the office in the future, but we have an excellent in-house day-care facility, so she'll never be too far from me."

"This can't be a permanent arrangement," she said after a long pause, knowing that she was compromising way too much. Her instincts were screaming at her to move out, but she kept thinking of Kayla and how much she adored her father. "And if I'm staying here, I'll want to pay rent," she cautioned, and he dipped his head in acquiescence.

"I know it can't be permanent, but it'll give you time to arrange your future; it will give *me* time to get to know Kayla and vice versa. You can pay a reasonable amount for rent, and the amount will include food and utilities. But if you're paying rent, you won't be able to pay for your tuition and books, so I'd like to give you a student loan, low interest, which you can pay off in your own time," he hurried on when it looked like she was about to protest. "It's a better deal than you'd get from any bank, Bronwyn. No strings attached. Once you've finished your studies and are settled into your new career, you'll be better equipped to move out, and Kayla will be old enough to understand."

"Bryce, that will take years." She was aghast at the thought of living in limbo for so long. But still, it was an awfully tempting suggestion, and Bronwyn knew she'd be a fool to turn it down when she had so few other options. But things were starting to get sticky again, too many ties and way too many complications. "We have to move on with our lives."

"And so we shall. We'll just be sharing a house, Bron . . . nothing else. This works out to everyone's advantage, and it's best for Kayla."

"We'll have to . . ." She cleared her throat, not really wanting to be the one to mention the inevitable. "We'll have to start proceedings."

"Proceedings?" He looked confused.

"*Divorce* proceedings," she clarified, and he very quickly averted his face, shielding his eyes from her.

"Yes, of course." He nodded before lifting his eyes to her face again.

"It will be awkward once we start seeing other people, Bryce." She decided to be the one to bite the bullet and speak the inescapable words. He cleared his throat uncomfortably before nodding again.

"I just ask that we both practice some discretion when it comes to that. Any . . . uh . . . any liaisons you . . . *we* see fit to start will have to be conducted outside of the home. For Kayla's sake, of course. Anything else would confuse her."

"That sounds reasonable," she agreed, even while nervousness ate away at her stomach. She wasn't sure that she *was* doing the right thing. Sure, she was taking the easy way out, but apprehension kept niggling away at the back of her mind. She got up gracefully and looked down at him for a long moment. "This marriage was probably never meant to be, Bryce. We were always too different." He averted his gaze, saying nothing in response, and Bronwyn sighed before turning away and heading toward the door.

"We were good together once." The words sounded torn from him, and she turned around to face him again.

"For a very brief time, so long ago that it seems like a dream now," she reflected, her eyes misty. She dipped her chin at him before leaving.

Bryce watched her go before slumping back into his chair and kneading his temples with his fists. God, how the hell had this happened? How could he have gotten everything so wrong? He thought back to that terrible night and fought the painful memories, but they were relentlessly flooding back.

CHAPTER NINE

That night, two years ago, Bryce had leaned against the door-frame and watched as Bronwyn, unaware of his presence, flitted happily around the kitchen. She had her back to the door and her sweet little behind, deliciously molded by the faded fabric of her jeans, had wriggled energetically to the beat of the lively salsa tune coming from the iPod speakers on the kitchen counter. She clearly thought she was alone in the house. It was something she did quite often: dismissed the servants to surprise him with a meal that she had lovingly prepared. He would be lying if he didn't admit to loving these moments of intimate domesticity. Eventually, he found the temptation of that cute little butt too much to resist. He crept up behind her to grab her hips and draw her back against him. She squealed in delight before turning in his grasp and throwing her arms around his neck. His own arms crept around her slender waist and they danced together sexily for a while. He started nuzzling her neck before she laughed and pulled herself out of his embrace.

"Silly man, stop distracting me," she chided, bracing her hands on his chest. "Dinner will be spoiled if I allow you to lead me into temptation."

"I can give dinner a miss," he growled as he reached for her again, but she giggled happily and danced out of his reach.

"But *I* can't," she laughed. "I'm starving. Why don't you go and shower off the day's grit and grime while I finish up in here?"

"God, you make it sound like I work on a construction site." He smiled down at her, indicating his disheveled gray suit.

"Hmm, I'd like that," she murmured as she eyed his tall, broad form critically. "It'd certainly help with all the flab."

"*Flab?*" He pretended to be outraged but was completely confident that he sported no flab or excess weight of any kind. She laughed again and wrapped her arms around his waist before stretching up to drop a sweet kiss on his mouth.

"I love you," she told him, and he smiled back. He loved it when she said those words to him, and he felt such overwhelming tenderness in return that it nearly brought him to his knees. He brushed her silky brown hair from her forehead and planted a kiss on her soft skin.

"My Bronwyn," he whispered against her forehead, tugging at the ponytail she had secured in the nape of her neck and dragging her head back for a proper kiss. When it ended he was aching with desire, and she looked a little dazed.

"Get dinner done, woman, before I head straight for dessert," he growled as his eyes dipped to the small breasts straining at her light-blue T-shirt so that she could not mistake his meaning. She wasn't wearing a bra—she hardly ever did when she was at home—her breasts didn't need the support, and he could see her nipples tenting the soft fabric. The sight made him hotter than hell, and he had to force himself to move away from her. After two years of marriage, he was constantly surprised by how much he still wanted her.

He eagerly rushed through his shower, and by the time he entered the conservatory, she had laid out a picnic beside one of the floor-to-ceiling plate-glass windows, the one with the ocean view. He'd never seen her look more beautiful, and again his stomach tightened with that feeling of tenderness. She was sitting on a blanket that she had spread out on the floor, and he dropped down next to her. He reached for the bottle of red wine that she'd placed within easy reach and frowned when he noticed that there was only one glass.

"You're not having any wine?" he asked, and she shook her head. Her beautiful eyes tangled with his, and he frowned as he tried to read the emotion in them. He could usually read her pretty easily, but her eyes were a mystery tonight and it unsettled him a bit.

"I'm having water tonight."

"Are you still worried about your reaction to that glass of wine at Pierre's party last week?" he asked in concern, referring to her dizzy spell. He'd attributed it to overwork and a bad vintage.

"That's not it." She smiled cryptically while her small fingers worried the edge of the blanket. Bryce tried to puzzle through her odd behavior as he poured his own drink.

"So tell me this news that you're so excited about," he prompted, referring to her giddy phone call to his office that afternoon.

"After we've eaten," she said quietly, and his eyes dipped to the Mediterranean feast that she had laid out before them. She had prepared seed loaf, feta cheese, and black olives as appetizers, along with fresh vegetables and dolmades with hummus, complemented by aubergine and tzatziki dips and falafels in pita. She lifted an olive to his lips, and he opened up, sucking at the tips of her fingers as he accepted the tangy fruit into his mouth. He returned the favor, and they had the rest of their meal in a similar fashion, laughing and murmuring intimacies as they fed each other. By the end of the meal, she was leaning back against his chest, with her head nestled in the nook between his jaw and collarbone. They quietly watched the sun drop into the ocean and turn the horizon into a painter's palette of red, orange, crimson, and scarlet.

He had his arm draped over her shoulder and across her breasts, and she was toying with his long and capable fingers. Bryce reveled in the closeness, wondering, not for the first time, how the hell he had gotten so lucky. He felt utterly at peace; they belonged together. They were like two halves of a whole. God knows he had never believed that such an utterly clichéd thought would ever cross his mind, but there it was; she was his other half and he could spend the rest of his life with just her by his side. They were a perfect unit. He shut his eyes to the sunset and tightened his arm around her slender frame. She lifted his hand to her lips and pressed a kiss into his broad palm.

"Bryce," she murmured quietly, and he made a slight sound to let her know that she had his attention. "I'm pregnant."

Their new living arrangements were not as bad as Bronwyn had feared they would be. Bryce pretty much kept his word, and she hardly ever saw him around the house and would have sworn that she and Kayla were alone in the house if not for the little girl's constant references to her daddy and what fun they had while Mummy was at work or at school. She had been back at university for nearly a month; luckily her late enrollment for the first semester in March had been easily accepted, and she had been allowed to resume her studies with very little fuss. It was about six weeks since she and Bryce had made their deal, and Bronwyn was starting to relax and enjoy the freedom of movement that she now had. She worked part-time in a bookshop. It was a job that Lisa, a bookshop proprietor herself, had told her about. Most of Bronwyn's lectures were over by one in the afternoon, so she worked from about two to six every day, leaving her with enough time to enjoy her evenings with Kayla. It was so quiet in the esoteric bookshop that she often had time to study. She also had weekends off because the shop's owner was older and didn't like having the business open on weekends. The pay was good, the work was easy, and the hours were ideal; she could have kissed Lisa when the other woman told her about it. Bronwyn also loved the challenge of studying again; she hadn't even known how much she missed it until she had gone back. Exercising and expanding her brain after such an extended period of nothing but "mummy duty" felt wonderful!

She was making new friends at school, and she spent a lot of time with Lisa and Alice as well as with Lisa's cousin, Theresa. The latter was a year older than Bronwyn's twenty-eight and had a six-month-old baby girl. They (unimaginatively) called themselves the "Mummy Club" and spent most Saturdays actively avoiding mummy duty by leaving the babies with their husbands and escaping for a well-deserved girls' day out. They were all busy women: Lisa had her shop, Alice was a chef, and both Theresa and Bronwyn had just started studying again, Theresa only part-time because of the new baby.

Bronwyn was actually starting to enjoy her life again, despite the unusual situation at home. Soon she started noticing that one of her professors, a man in his mid-thirties, appeared to be taking more than the usual interest in her. She didn't quite know how to react to that fact. It had been so long since she'd felt even remotely attractive that the male interest, while flattering, was a little unnerving. It also felt so *wrong* to even be talking to a man who was so obviously attracted to her while she was still married to Bryce. It made her wonder about the divorce. She had assumed that Bryce would start proceedings, but she hadn't heard a peep about it from him. She wasn't sure if he was expecting *her* to do it or if he was content to let things stay as they were for the moment. The uncertainty was driving her mad, so she took it upon herself to speak to some of the law students about her options. Being young and overly ambitious, most of them advised her to "take him for everything she could get," but one young man had thoughtfully given her his father's number after informing her that his parent was a divorce lawyer. He also cautioned her to tread carefully when there were custody matters to consider.

She hadn't used the number yet and wasn't sure if she should or even if she *could*. The thought of finally ending her marriage, even if it could only be described as such in the loosest possible terms, was not a pleasant one. Not when she still cared for her husband, more than he probably deserved.

The ambiguity of her feelings reached even greater heights when her professor, Raymond Mayfair, acted on his interest in her and asked her out. Bronwyn battled with the decision for a while before accepting his invitation. She made sure to warn him that nothing would ever happen between them while she was married. He graciously accepted her terms and told her that he just wanted to spend time with her.

That night she deliberately sought Bryce out for the first time in more than two months and found him hiding out in the den and watching television with the sound turned down. For some reason, the den, with all its audio visual equipment, was the last place she'd expected to find him. An ignorant assumption, she acknowledged, since his deafness didn't prevent him from watching television or enjoying music with heavier beats. He sat in an easy chair and the only parts of him that were visible to her were the back of his head and his right hand, which was hanging over the arm of the chair with a glass of amber-colored liquid dangling from his fingers.

At first, she was so preoccupied by the fact that she had found him after half an hour of searching that what he was watching did not register with her. Then she glanced up and found herself riveted by her own smiling face on the huge flat-screen television. The camera angle changed to include Bryce in the shot; he was leaning toward her, his mouth to her ear as he whispered something intimate enough to make her blush. It was their wedding DVD with the sound turned down. She was dressed in a beautiful white concoction that had cost the earth but that Bryce had paid for, and he looked gorgeous in a stylish black tuxedo. They both looked so young and happy and were wrapped up in each other to the exclusion of everyone else. She watched as he fast-forwarded through Rick's best man speech and resumed playing when the focus was back on them.

She took a step backward, feeling like she was intruding on yet another moment that she knew he would not want her to witness. Her back hit the door and her fingers fumbled with the handle but her eyes remained glued to the screen. He hit the pause button, and she panicked, thinking that he was about to get up, but he merely leaned forward, his attention still focused on the screen. She shifted her stricken gaze to the larger-than-life frozen image of her beaming face. She looked radiant and so hopelessly in love. The room was absolutely silent, and she was achingly aware of how loud the pounding of her heart sounded to her own ears and of how ragged her breathing had become.

After a seemingly interminable amount of time had passed, she succeeded in getting a decent grip on the door handle and managed to slip out without him ever knowing that she had been there. But the haunting image of Bryce in that silent room watching that video stayed with her all evening. She didn't understand why he had dug up that old thing. It served only to emphasize how catastrophically they had failed as a couple.

She still needed to talk with him; she couldn't go out with Raymond without telling Bryce about it first. It was the decent thing to do. So she waited another couple of hours until she heard him prowling around in the kitchen. She ventured boldly into the spacious room and stepped immediately into his line of vision, not wanting to startle him. He was just turning away from the huge double-door refrigerator with some sandwich ingredients stacked precariously in his arms and stilled abruptly at the sight of her. The abrupt cessation of movement unsettled the food and dislodged a tomato, which rolled from the top of the armload and landed on the floor between them with a soft plop. Bronwyn winced and they both stared down at the mess the unfortunate tomato had made on the tiled floor. They looked up at the same time and their gazes met uncertainly.

"I'm sorry, I didn't mean to startle you," she apologized, both verbally and in the sign language that she was still trying to learn in her free time. Because of school, her lessons had had to be moved to Saturdays before her usual get-together with the other ladies. His eyes dropped to her busy hands and narrowed sharply as they took in the graceful movements of her fingers.

"It's okay," he said out loud, shrugging slightly. He didn't mention the sign language she had used, and she was both relieved and somewhat disappointed by that. He brushed by her and headed toward the large wooden island in the middle of the kitchen to drop the ingredients on the black marble–topped surface, while Bronwyn used a damp paper towel to wipe up the mess on the floor. When she was done, she rounded the island to face him again while he busily went about constructing an imaginative sandwich. He kept his eyes on his task and Bronwyn sighed in frustration before waving her hand beneath his eyes to get his attention. Finally, reluctantly, he looked up to face her.

"I have to talk to you about something," she half signed, half spoke, and he nodded warily. "I need you to watch Kayla tomorrow night." Something akin to relief flickered in his eyes, and he smiled slowly, nodding again.

"Of course." His eyes dropped back to his sandwich. "I know that you have to start studying, mid-terms can't be that far off." Bronwyn groaned, this was going to be more difficult than she had originally anticipated. She waved her hand beneath his eyes again.

"Bryce," she began when she had his attention again. "I have a date." She said the words aloud, choosing not to sign them, and his eyes remained fixed on her lips for such a long time that she began to wonder if he might have misunderstood her. His large hands were resting on the wooden surface of the island, his sloppy sandwich teetering unsteadily between them, and as she dropped her eyes, wondering if she should repeat the statement, she noticed them curling into huge fists and knew that he had not misunderstood or misread her lips. He was trying to figure out how to deal with her words.

"You're married," he reminded, almost absently, his voice sounding strangely hoarse. She raised her eyes to his face again and was startled to see how strained and pale he looked.

"We're not married, Bryce," she whispered. "Not really. Not for a long time now. You know that. You said it yourself; there *is* no marriage. We're separated and merely sharing a house."

"Who . . ." He began to frame a question but then simply turned the one word into a question. "Who?"

"One of my professors. He's a nice man, decent."

"How *decent* can he be if he dates his students?" Bryce hissed furiously.

"I'm not a child, Bryce, and Raymond is only two years older than you are. It's hardly unethical for us to go out on a perfectly harmless date."

"I don't think you should do this," he began, but she held up a silencing hand.

"I didn't come to you for your blessing, Bryce," she told him firmly. "I felt that telling you would be the right thing to do, because we *are* still legally bound. Yes, we have a child together and we're sharing a house, but our marriage, if we can call it that anymore, is over. I want to move on with my life, and the only way either of us can do that is if we get a divorce. So if you won't start the proceedings, then I will. I'll be seeing an attorney as soon as possible." He lowered his gaze back to his sandwich.

"It's probably better that way," he agreed quietly. "If you need me to watch Kayla tomorrow night, I will." He raised his enigmatic eyes back to hers and she smiled gently.

"One more thing, Bryce," she said tentatively. "I don't want a security guy hovering in the background while I'm out tomorrow night. So I'm dismissing Paul early. Please clear it with Cal." Poor Paul would probably be relieved to have the time off. Her life was pretty mundane, and while he was too professional to ever show it, she suspected that he was bored out of his mind for the most part.

"Fine," he gritted after a long pause, clearly not happy with that idea but acquiescing when he realized that she wasn't going to budge on the matter.

"In fact, I would prefer it if Paul didn't come to campus or work with me. It's a waste of your resources. I'm perfectly safe, and I would just feel more comfortable without him constantly hovering in the background." She knew that she was pushing it and that Bryce wasn't likely to budge on this, but she really felt like a pretentious freak with a bodyguard constantly dogging her steps. It made her feel completely conspicuous.

"Bronwyn, I take your and Kayla's safety very seriously," he said darkly.

"Look, of course I want Kayla to be safe, and I absolutely agree on the issue of security for her, but I'm not quite in the same boat. I'm your all-but-estranged wife. Not quite the prime target for kidnappers."

"Prospective kidnappers don't know the intimate details of our marriage, Bron," he pointed out reasonably. "You're living with me, you're the mother of my child, and you're a target. End of story. Paul stays."

"Well, can you at least give me some time to myself on Monday then? I have something to take care of." While she *had* just informed him she would be seeing an attorney, she didn't want Bryce hearing about it from the hired help before she had a chance to tell him about it in person. That wasn't the way she wanted him to learn the news.

"What?" he asked suspiciously.

"Bryce, I don't ask you for much, just grant me this one request and allow me to cling to the illusion that I still have some semblance of privacy in my life."

"Only on Monday?" he clarified reluctantly, and she nodded. "Very well, I'll inform Cal."

"Thank you," she said, and he inclined his head curtly before turning away from her and heading to the refrigerator, his rigid back telling her that he wanted her gone by the time he turned back. Bronwyn wasted no time in beating a hasty retreat. She headed to the nursery to watch Kayla sleep and silently mourned the loss of the life she could never have with the man she so desperately loved.

∽

Bryce wanted to break something, wanted to hurt someone, preferably the smarmy bastard who had ingratiated himself to Bryce's *wife!* *God*, this was so much worse than he'd imagined. Bronwyn was moving on with her life and seeing other people. What if she let this guy, this *Raymond*, touch her or, worse, make love to her? His stomach rebelled at the thought, and he picked up his half-made sandwich and tossed it into the trashcan.

He pressed the heels of his hands to his eyes and frantically tried to figure out what to do, how to make this right, but he didn't know how. He no longer had any control over his own life. Everything was sliding so swiftly downhill that he knew it was only a matter of time before it all ended. Bronwyn didn't see herself as his wife anymore. She wanted nothing to do with him, and who could blame her? After the way he had behaved, it was nothing less than he deserved. He could threaten her with a custody battle, but he didn't have it in him to do that to her or Kayla.

After all those months of self-righteous anger and believing *he* was the wronged one, while his Bronwyn suffered unimaginable horrors on her own, he now had to face up to the fact that he had brought all of this upon himself. Blackmailing Bronwyn to stay with him, after everything else that he had done wrong, would in no way, shape, or form restore his self-respect. He had to let her go; she deserved to be happy and it was obvious that he couldn't make her happy, that he had very *rarely* made her happy. That was his failure, his shame, and his cross to bear, and he would no longer have her share that burden.

∾

"What the hell do you mean, you're *pregnant*? What about your studies and the mutual decision we made when we first got married? We were going to wait, Bronwyn, remember? Just tell me you're joking." The fury he had felt that night scorched its way through his body and obliterated his ability to think rationally. He moved away from her and jumped to his feet to glower down at her. She had looked so confused and hurt that for a moment he nearly softened, nearly took her into his arms to comfort her. But then those two words echoed their way through his brain again and his white-hot, bitter anger reasserted itself. The sense of betrayal left an acrid taste in his mouth.

"I know that it's sooner than we'd planned," she said softly, trying to maintain an even tone of voice. "But this is the reality of our situation now and it can't be changed. We're having a baby . . . a *baby*, Bryce. Don't you understand how wonderful that is?"

"I can't believe you did this. I can't believe you would stoop to this," he gritted out bitterly. "This was supposed to be a joint decision. I'm not ready for this, Bronwyn. I don't *want* a kid, damn it!"

"But it's our *baby* . . . we made it together," she protested, and he could hear the pain and confusion in her voice but just couldn't keep the venom out of his own, knowing that if he allowed her to see through his anger to his own pain and confusion, she would think that what she had done was okay, and he was too furious with her to allow her to think that yet.

"You mean *you* made it, without my consent." He could barely look at her. He didn't want to see her tears—he hated her tears—but he could hear them in her gasp and in her voice when she spoke.

"I don't know why you're being like this," she cried. "I didn't plan this, it just happened. Our birth control failed. I asked the doctor and he said that if I'd had a stomach virus or anything like that it could provide a window of opportunity. And you know that I was sick a couple of days before your company party three months ago." Damn her, she was trying to cover her tracks. He strode out of the conservatory and downstairs into their en suite, while she trotted behind him, still trying to tell him about a stomach bug that she had had three months ago. How the hell could she expect him to remember something like that, anyway? He pushed back the niggling voice that told him he *did* remember it and that he had pampered her ridiculously while she had been sick. Instead, he convinced himself that he couldn't recall whatever insignificant bug she was referring to. He opened the medicine chest and yanked out her birth-control pills.

"*What are you doing?*" She sounded scared and appalled as she watched him count the pills in the box. His eyes clouded over with a haze of red when he realized that the numbers were right.

"God, have you been chucking pills down the drain every night?" he wondered out loud, hating himself even as he asked the question.

"You *know* I wouldn't do that," she defended urgently.

"Is that so? I obviously don't know you as well as I thought I did, do I?"

"Of course you *know* me, Bryce." she laid a tentative hand on his rigid forearm, and his flesh burned beneath the contact. He yanked his arm away and turned away from her. His eyes flooded with tears, he needed time to think, but he couldn't think with her standing in the same room, not when she was crying, not when *he* was the one responsible for her tears.

"Get out of here," he whispered harshly, wanting her out of the room, not wanting her to hear or see how much he ached to take her into his arms.

"What?"

"Get the hell out," he snarled, bracing himself before turning to face her. He *barely* kept himself from flinching when he saw her tears. "Go *now*." She uttered a low cry and whirled from the room, fleeing as quickly as she could. Bryce finally allowed himself to break, sinking back against a tiled wall as his legs gave out and sliding down to the floor. He clasped his head in his hands and shook uncontrollably as he tried to imagine his life from this point on.

CHAPTER TEN

Bryce had to go in to the office the following morning—the day of Bronwyn's Big Date. He hadn't done so in months, but he and Pierre had an urgent meeting with a very important client and the man had requested Bryce's presence. As he was the business's CFO and Vice President of Marketing, Bryce knew that it was time to pick up the reins of his life again. He had responsibilities to Pierre, their employees, their clients, and to himself. It was time but it was just unfortunate *timing*. Celeste was down with the flu, Bronwyn had a test, also her all-important *date* was that night, and Bryce wasn't about to bail on this fatherhood business just because things got a little sticky. He hadn't even told Bronwyn about this meeting, but he figured that she had coped with much worse crises over the past couple of years, so he could deal with this one all on his own.

That meant taking Kayla into the office and she was in a terrible mood. He dressed her in her prettiest pink frock, promising her all kinds of treats if she just did this one thing for Daddy today. He didn't need his hearing to know that she was muttering a whole lot of "Kayla no want tos" into his hair as he tied the laces on the tiny red sneakers she'd *insisted* on wearing with the girly little dress. He'd relented on the shoes because he was getting pretty sick of trying to reason with her. Bad parenting, he knew, but it was a matter of picking his battles, and he was running late. He was also terrified of losing his temper with her while there was no one else around and wanted to get out of the house and to the office as soon as humanly possible.

By the time Cal—who also acted as his driver these days—parked the car in the underground parking lot of the huge building in Central Cape Town, which hosted DCP Jewellers Inc., he was exhausted and feeling more than a little harassed. Petulant, angry tears were seeping down his daughter's rosy cheeks, and he could more than imagine her nagging crying. He knew her well enough by now to know when she was acting up and when she was just being difficult.

"Kayla." He hoped his voice was firm enough. "Stop crying. You're going meet some nice, new friends." She was shaking her head in response to his promise, and he could read her lips well enough to understand that she didn't want "new fwends." He groaned and dropped a kiss on one wet, chubby cheek.

"Of course you want new friends." His plan was to drop her off at the company's day-care center. Quite a few of the young executives who were present stopped in their tracks to stare as he made his way through reception. He nodded at them abruptly, not caring for the open-mouthed shock they were all displaying but knowing that his presence, especially with a toddler in tow, would fuel gossip for months to come. They were naturally curious because not many of them had seen him since his accident; also God only knew how much noise Kayla was making. Pierre loomed in front of him and grinned as his eyes dropped to the fractious child on Bryce's hip.

"Hello, Mikayla," he smiled down at her, signing so that Bryce could catch what he was saying. "Why so grumpy?" He reached over and tried to tug the resisting child into his arms. Kayla refused to go, burying her wet face against Bryce's neck and tightening her small, surprisingly strong arms around his shoulders. Bryce met Pierre's amused eyes and groaned.

"A little help, if you please?"

"Hey, mine isn't old enough to throw tantrums yet." Pierre shrugged, dropping his hands into his trouser pockets and rocking back on his heels. "I have *no* idea how to deal with this."

"I'm taking her to the nursery but she's going to hate me for deserting her," Bryce informed as he hugged the crying child closer.

"By the time you fetch her again, she'll be having so much fun, she'll cry when you try to take her home."

"God, this parenting business is tough," Bryce muttered. "I don't know how the hell Bronwyn coped on her own for two years."

"That's why Mother's Day is so much bigger than Father's Day will ever be," Pierre quipped. "I'm off to the Mezzanine Conference Room; meet you there in ten minutes?"

"Sure," Bryce agreed. Naturally, that was easier said than done. Kayla stubbornly clung to his leg when he set her down in the nursery, and he and one of the nursery school teachers tried desperately to bribe and cajole her into letting go. Twenty minutes later, exhausted and rumpled, Bryce made his way into the Mezzanine Conference Room, troubled that he'd had to leave his crying and begging daughter behind and wondering how often Bronwyn had had to go through the same ordeal over the past two years. How difficult it must have been for her, especially being able to *hear* Kayla's begging and crying, when she turned to walk away.

His first big business meeting outside of his home, after the accident, was not as tough as he'd expected it to be, largely due to the sign language interpreter Pierre had thoughtfully employed. The same woman would be Bryce's new assistant and would ease his transition back into the office. He still intended to spend a lot more time at home than before the accident, but the meeting made him realize just how much he'd missed being in the thick of things and at the heart of the deal.

~

Bronwyn could barely focus on what Raymond was saying; her mind kept straying back to the lonely image of Bryce sitting in front of that television with her image frozen on-screen. There was something so stark, sad, and desolate about the memory that it ate her up inside every time she thought about it.

"You seem preoccupied." Raymond's gentle voice intruded on her thoughts, and Bronwyn was startled back to the present and the man sitting opposite her. He really was a nice man, tall, lean, and almost handsome, with dark eyes, slightly thinning black hair, and a warm smile. Bronwyn really liked him but not enough to seriously consider dating him.

"I think this was a mistake," she mumbled, and he frowned. "It's too soon. It just doesn't feel right for me to be out with you." He smiled in understanding.

"I was wondering where your mind was," he said.

"Maybe . . ." she began, and he covered one of her helplessly fluttering hands with his own.

"Some other time?" he completed, and she nodded gratefully. "That's okay. I can wait until you're ready."

The crazy thing was Bronwyn wasn't sure if she would *ever* be ready. Despite everything that had happened, she still loved Bryce, and she didn't know how to stop. While his past behavior had been unforgivable, it had also been completely out of character. How could the man who now loved his daughter so unreservedly have rejected the idea of Bronwyn's pregnancy in the first place? It made no sense. And yet, while she was confused and conflicted, she still couldn't forget about or forgive those two years that she had struggled to keep both herself and her baby alive and safe. She loved him and yet she resented him for abandoning them so completely. And there was just no way she could reconcile those two conflicting feelings in any kind of emotionally satisfying manner.

"Thank you for understanding, Raymond."

He shrugged.

"I can't say I'm not disappointed, Bronwyn. I would still like to get to know you better and spend time with you. I hope I get that chance."

"You're a really nice man, Raymond," she responded. "But I shouldn't have come out with you. I'm still married, and while my husband may not be perfect, he's the father of my child and at one point, he was my whole life. I don't know what I'm doing here. I can't make any promises, you understand?"

"I understand." He smiled again, squeezing her hand in reassurance. "I hope you know that I'm here, as a friend. If you need a shoulder to cry on or someone to listen, I'm always here."

"Thank you," she whispered, trying desperately to blink back her tears at his graceful acceptance of the situation.

~

Bryce, who sat alone in the darkened den, was startled when the unmistakable flash of headlights coming up the drive disturbed the unrelenting dark. He jumped up and stepped out onto the wide balcony that overlooked the driveway, knowing that he would not be spotted in the dark. It was Bronwyn, home a lot sooner than he had expected. She was standing beside the car, her head bent over her bag as she fumbled for her house keys. He frowned, making a mental note to talk to her about her carelessness. She really should have her keys out before she got out of her car; they had the best security money could buy, and there were guards all over the property, but he still didn't want her taking unnecessary risks. He could see her clearly in the light that was spilling from the front porch, and his stomach clenched at how beautiful she looked in the pale blue wraparound skirt that molded to her long legs with every move she made. Her white top dipped low enough to show off her modest cleavage and it set his blood boiling. She looked too provocative, too bloody *tempting*! He was sure that the pervert professor could not possibly have kept his hands to himself.

Burning up with the need to know if that bastard had laid his grubby paws on her, he made his way downstairs, sure he would be able to read her expression and know if she had let the man touch her. He just needed to *know* . . .

◇

"How was your date?" The deep voice, sounding so unexpectedly from behind her, made Bronwyn jump in shock. She was busy setting the alarm and botched up the code when he startled her. She took a deep steadying breath and quickly reentered the correct code before turning to face him.

"It was fine," she murmured, knowing it was too dark for him to read her lips; she used her hands as well.

"When did you get so good at signing?" he asked huskily, stepping into the small pool of light in the hall and neatly trapping her between his body and the door.

"All those times I met Alice for lunch? Before going back to university? We were going to the same center Pierre went to for *his* sign language lessons. I go mostly on Saturdays now."

"Why?" She shrugged awkwardly, trying to step back when he took a small step forward but finding herself with no place to go when her back hit the door. He was so close she could feel his body heat and smell his wonderfully clean scent.

"I don't know," she said quietly. "I wanted to be able to talk to you." He very gently lifted his thumb and forefinger to her chin and used it to tilt her face up to his.

"I didn't catch that," he whispered. She repeated her previous statement and his eyes darkened.

"You wanted to talk to me? Despite the way I've treated you?" There was a *world* of vulnerability in his voice, and Bronwyn tried not to let it disarm her.

"I know how it feels to have no one to talk to," she said, closing her eyes to hide her pain from him.

"Oh *God*, sweetheart . . . Bron . . ." The anguish in his voice undid her, and she found herself unable to resist when he lowered his head and rested his forehead against hers. His warm breath washed over her face, her lips, and she shuddered before going up onto her toes and brushing his mouth with hers. He went so still that she thought he would shatter, but when she moved her small hands up to cup his face, his breath escaped on a strangled sob. He tentatively wrapped his strong arms around her slender body to gather her close and responded to her sweet kiss with unbelievable tenderness and reverence. The kiss did not last long; it was over before it properly began, and Bryce took a step back, lifting a hand to gently palm one of her cheeks, his eyes bright with some inscrutable emotion. Bronwyn tilted her face into his hand and lifted her own much smaller hand to cover his. They stood that way for what seemed like an eternity but what was, in reality, only a few seconds before Bronwyn stepped around him. She left without a word, unable to find the right words, not even sure if there *were* words for what she was feeling.

~

Bryce groaned the following morning, when his boisterous twenty-one-month-old daughter bounced her way onto his bed at some ungodly hour. One sharp little knee narrowly missed his groin to land painfully on his abdomen, causing him to curse softly under his breath as he doubled over in pain.

"Kayla, honey, why don't you go find your mummy? It's her day off today." He caught her to stop her bouncing and planted a quick kiss on her soft cheek. She giggled at the feel of his stubble.

"Tickley." She formed the word clearly as she rubbed her cheek squeamishly.

"Go and wake Mummy up, sweetheart; Daddy's trying to sleep. I'll give you some sweeties if you go to your mummy!" He cajoled.

"See fishies." He frowned at that bit of information, wondering what the hell he was missing in translation. He often had trouble with voiced and unvoiced consonants, but he doubted very much that she meant "vishies," so the word *had* to be "fishies," which confused the hell out of him.

"What?"

"Fishies, Daddy, see *fishies*!" She made a squirmy, fishlike movement with one of her plump hands. Okay, so he definitely hadn't misread the "fishies."

"Where's your mummy?" He kept her still when it became obvious that she wanted to bounce again.

"There," she pointed to his bedroom door, the dimple she'd inherited from him deepening as her smile widened. He looked up to find Bronwyn standing in the open doorway. Well that certainly explained how Kayla had gotten into his room; she wasn't tall enough to open doors yet. Bronwyn was leaning against the doorjamb with her arms folded over her chest and her eyebrows raised.

"Don't think I missed that blatant bit of bribery just now," she said, and he groaned.

"C'mon, Bron, you know the weekends are your domain. I didn't want to rob you of any time with our precious little *angel*. It wouldn't be fair to you," he quickly smooth-talked, but she wasn't having any of it and he could practically hear her *hah!* Their high-strung "angel" of a daughter had escaped his grip and was jumping on the bouncy mattress again, her curls flying as she chanted, "Fishies, fishies" with every bounce. Bryce grimaced as he read her lips.

"What's all this about 'fishies'?" he asked, feeling ridiculous as he said the word. He glanced up and caught Bronwyn staring at his naked chest. She blushed when he caught her staring and took a few seconds to gather her thoughts before responding.

"Uh . . . I'm taking her to the aquarium today and was wondering if you'd like to join us." He blinked up at her, wondering if he had read that right.

"What?"

She repeated the question, using her eloquent hands this time, and he blinked again, more than a little shocked by the unexpected invitation. Her blush deepened and she started to say that he didn't have to if he didn't want to, but he quickly brushed that aside before she changed her mind completely.

"Sure! I've never been! That would be great! Kayla will love it!" He knew he was speaking in exclamations but he didn't want any misunderstanding. "Give me ten minutes and we can head off." He jumped out of bed, forgetting that he was wearing nothing but skin and quickly grabbed a sheet to preserve modesty when he felt a breeze on areas best kept covered in the presence of his little girl and his estranged wife. Tucking the sheet in at his waist, he grabbed Kayla while she was in midjump and hugged her to his chest, twirling her around for a couple of seconds. "We're going to see the fishies, baby!"

He dropped a kiss on the toddler's cheek before setting her down, where she tottered dizzily before plonking down onto her butt. She laughed happily after the dizziness passed and held up her arms to him for another round.

"Not now, sweetie. I have to shower and then we're going to see all the pretty fishies."

"Nebo?" she asked worriedly, and he grinned at the thought of the Disney movie that she insisted on watching at *least* five times a week, with her daddy of course! Bryce was thankful for the subtitle option on DVDs and never thought he'd be the type to recite the dialogue of a cartoon movie word for word in his lifetime.

"Yes, Nemo too," he promised. "I'll be quick," he told Bron on his way out.

"No rush." She smiled. "I still have to get Kayla ready. We can leave in about half an hour."

Bronwyn watched him leave, his broad tanned back rippling with muscles, the sheet molding his tight behind much too lovingly. Her mouth went dry as she recalled that flash of nudity; he was so gorgeous that it was a real shame to cover it up. She grinned as she recalled his near schoolboy giddiness at her impulsive invitation. She hadn't seen him that lighthearted and ecstatic in, well, *ever* really. Even before her pregnancy when they had been happy together, there had always been this reserve in him, a darkness that he had tried to keep hidden from her. She had always believed that it would only be a matter of time before he confided in her but then she had gotten pregnant and they had run out of time. She sighed at the dark turn of her thoughts; it was too bright and beautiful an autumn day to dwell on the past.

"Come on, Kayla, time to get dressed." She held out her hand to the toddler who happily made her way over, still chattering excitedly about "Nebo" and "fishies."

∼

The Two Oceans Aquarium was based at the V&A Waterfront in Cape Town. It was teeming not only with marine life but with children, teens, students, and noisy families. Bryce and Bronwyn, as a young couple with an energetic toddler, blended in completely. For once the ubiquitous Cal and his team had been told to remain very much in the background. Bryce had commanded them to remain outside, despite Cal's obvious uneasiness with the high security risk such a busy place posed. Bryce had even chosen to drive them himself—a rarity these days—while the security team had remained a discreet distance behind them.

Now Bronwyn was achingly aware of how much like a normal family they must look amidst the tide of humanity. Kayla was up on Bryce's shoulders, and her little feet frantically paddled against his chest every time she wanted him to stop and let her down so that she could investigate something closer. She had loved the touch pool, where she got to stroke and touch all manner of tide-pool life: fish, starfish, and even a small octopus. She had squealed with every new sensation under her fingertips. Their little girl was nothing if not adventurous, and unlike a lot of the other children her age who backed off squealing and crying, she kept coming forward to touch something new. Of course, the highlight for her was the display of clownfish. The beautiful exhibit had actually been named "Nemos." Bryce had guided her into the little bubble beneath the display, which had afforded her a 360-degree view of the tank. She had squealed and clapped in delight when she found herself surrounded by so many "Nemos." It had been very difficult getting her back out to give other children a chance but she hadn't had time to sulk with so much to see and do.

Bronwyn sensed that, despite his laughter, something was not quite right with Bryce. He seemed jumpy and sweat beaded his upper lip. She often caught him looking around frantically when she was farther away from him and then almost noticeably sagging in relief when he caught sight of her. At first she was confused by his uncharacteristic lack of composure, but then she caught the way he shrank away anytime someone brushed by him or got too close. With startling clarity, she recognized that her husband, who had once seemed so strong and infallible, feared the milling crowd of people around them. She even suspected that he was mildly agoraphobic. It explained why he had confined himself to the house these past couple of years, why he rarely ventured out, and why he preferred having Pierre or Rick come by to see him at home. This once social creature had been cut off from the world in more ways than she had known. It said a lot for how much her invitation must have meant to him, if he was willing to brave *this* for a day out with her and Kayla.

She made her way to his side and firmly slid her hand into his. His startled gaze met hers, and when he saw the understanding glimmering there, his eyes shone with gratitude.

"Do you want to go home?" she asked, and he hesitated before shaking his head.

"I'm okay . . . now." He lifted their clasped hands gratefully.

Neither openly acknowledged the situation again, but she rarely left his side after that and he seemed less tense. He appeared to be genuinely enjoying himself by the time they reached the underwater tunnel that led them through a multitude of manta rays, barracudas, tuna, and ragged-toothed sharks. The display was so awesome that even Kayla went quiet as she took in the strange, beautiful blue world that surrounded her. Her little hands were clasped together under her father's jaw and Bronwyn watched as she started to droop more and more until her head was resting on top of Bryce's and she was fast asleep.

"Hold still," she urged, digging out the digital camera and taking yet another picture of father and daughter. He grinned before taking the camera from her and stopping a passing tourist, asking the man to take their picture. He shifted Kayla so that she was cradled in his right arm, her head resting on the curve of his shoulder and her arm draped around his neck, and he hauled Bronwyn against his left side, wrapping his arm around her waist and holding her close.

"Smile, sweetheart," he urged into her ear, and she was startled into obeying. The tourist took three pictures in quick succession before handing the camera back to Bryce.

"You have a great-looking family, mate," he said in a thick Aussie accent before handing back the camera and heading off with a wave.

When they left the aquarium, Bryce pushed Kayla's cart while Bronwyn tucked her hand into the crook of his elbow to maintain contact. Cal and his team were taking their brief to remain discreet so seriously that Bronwyn didn't even see them. Bryce led the way toward one of the many restaurants dotting the waterfront, a Greek place that served fabulous food, and they sat down at a table beneath one of the umbrellas out in the early autumn sunshine. They were quiet for a while, watching the world go by, until Bryce broke the silence.

"Thank you."

She lifted surprised eyes to his solemn face. "For?"

"Earlier." He cleared his throat and she watched his Adam's apple bob sexily as he swallowed. "Thank you for earlier. Crowds are . . . difficult for me. Ever since the accident I can't stand being in large crowds. It's so bizarre. There I am with all these people around me and I *know* there should be noise, voices, footsteps, and laughter, but instead there's nothing. It's like being in a huge void, until I'm jostled and then it feels like being ambushed because I didn't see or hear it coming. After the accident I was so paranoid, I kept wondering who was behind me, kept *imagining* someone was there, and I'd turn around so quickly that I'd startle everyone around me, only there'd be no one there, but I'd immediately get the same feeling and turn again. I knew that it would only be a matter of time before it would get to the point where I'd just keep turning round and round and round until I went insane. So before that could happen I . . ."

"You shut yourself in," she completed, and he nodded.

"It's crazy, I know," he confessed, and she smiled with a shake of her head, covering his lightly trembling hand with her own.

"No, it's not. You lost one of your senses, Bryce. Naturally there'd be physical, mental, and emotional repercussions. I read that people go through the stages of grief after losing their hearing. Did you . . . did you *talk* to anyone after the accident?"

"You mean a psychiatrist?" he clarified dryly. "I was seeing one for nearly a year; it's because of him that I was able to even *contemplate* coming out today. I was so much worse immediately after the accident and I very stubbornly refused to talk to anyone. Yes, I was in denial and furious that something like this could have happened to me, but I shoved it aside because I had something bigger to take care of. I was adamant that talking to shrinks could wait. But Pierre and Rick kind of forced my hand. They blackmailed me into seeing someone."

"How?" she asked, curious. One thing she knew about her stubborn husband was that when he made up his mind about something, it was very difficult to get him to change it again. He cleared his throat and gulped down a healthy mouthful of white wine.

"At the time, my *sole* purpose was to find you," he admitted. "But I was so incapacitated and the only two people I trusted to help me with that were Rick and Pierre. They had private detectives working on it and because of my antisocial phobias, they were the ones who dealt with those detectives. They threatened to stop acting as liaisons between the detectives and me if I didn't see someone. I couldn't let that happen, and since I knew I wouldn't be able to deal with the detectives myself, I had no choice but to comply with their demands. I resented the hell out of them for imposing that ultimatum, but in the end, Bron, they saved my sanity." They remained silent for a while after that, while Bronwyn thought about everything that he had revealed.

"And the . . . the deafness is permanent?" She asked the question that she had been too scared to broach before and winced at the immense of amount of pain that darkened his eyes. "There's nothing they can do about it?"

"To put it in the simplest of terms, I suffered major nerve damage in both ears. I hit my head so hard that the doctors told me I was *lucky* that deafness was my only major, lasting injury. *Lucky*, can you believe that?" His voice rang with outrage at the memory, and he shut his eyes briefly before shaking his head and meeting her eyes again. "They told me that the damage to my right ear is less catastrophic and said that an operation might restore *some* of the function."

"It didn't work?" she asked sympathetically, aching for him. What he had done to her was unforgivable, but he had paid in spades for it already, and she found herself unable to hate or resent him any longer. She just felt numb and confused.

"I didn't have the operation," He shrugged and she blinked. Stunned by that information.

"What? Why?"

"It seemed pointless." His jaw was set, and while she longed to prompt him for more information, she sensed that he wouldn't be receptive to any more questions. She sighed, his stubbornness and uncommunicativeness merely serving to remind her of why she felt their marriage no longer stood a chance of working. Yes, he had paid for his unforgivable and baffling reaction to her pregnancy, but they had so many other insurmountable problems.

169

"I'm sorry that this happened to you, Bryce," she said earnestly. "I'm so sorry."

"I'm not the only one who suffered, Bron." For the first time since it happened, he was brushing it off because there was so much more he needed to know about what had happened to her during those lost years. "After you left the hospital, what happened? Where did you go? Who took care of you?"

"I really don't want to talk about this," she began hesitantly.

"Please." The single, softly spoken word undid her more than any other could have, and she lowered her eyes to her peacefully sleeping daughter before lifting them back to Bryce.

"Thanks to selling the car, I had enough money for a few months' rent and food. Luckily Kayla was a healthy baby, and I didn't have to worry about extra doctor's bills."

"What about you? How were *you* after her birth?"

"We coped, Bryce," she said. "I stayed home for a month and a half and my next-door neighbor, Linda, would often drop by to do some of the cooking for me. The first few times I went out job-hunting, Linda babysat Kayla for me. Eventually I got the job in Plettenberg Bay, where I ran into Rick and Lisa, and the rest is history." The censorious glint in his eyes told her what he thought of the huge gaps in her story.

"Where did Kayla stay while you were at work?"

"Linda usually took care of her but Linda was elderly, and she . . . she died just before Rick found me. I got sick soon after her death, and the day I ran into Rick was my first day back at work. I hadn't found a replacement for Linda and had to hire a babysitter for the day." Her situation had been utterly desperate. Heartbroken over her friend's death, broke, and sick, she was at her wits' end. If Rick had *not* found her that day, she didn't know what she would have done. Odds were she would have lost her job that day anyway as she had been making too many mistakes.

Bryce didn't need her to spell it out to understand how bad the situation had been, and a grim silence settled over them while they contemplated their roast lamb and potatoes, appetites lost.

"How was your health after her birth, Bron?" he asked again, alerting her to the fact that he had noticed her earlier evasiveness on that matter.

"It was . . . I wasn't . . ."

He maintained steady eye contact, and she bit her bottom lip before shrugging and giving him the brutal, unvarnished truth. "I was often sick. I was weak after giving birth and didn't get enough rest after taking Kayla home from the hospital. I was up at all hours, feeding and changing her, and then I was back at work. I never fully recovered and couldn't afford health care for myself since all of my money was assigned to buying food and clothes for Kayla. I ate leftovers at work whenever I could and the odd sandwich when I couldn't. It sounds worse than it was, Bryce."

"So when you got the flu . . ." He left the statement unfinished and she nodded.

"Yes, it raged out of control because my immune system had taken such a beating in the past. The day Rick found me, the only reason I was at work was because Gerhard would have given my job to someone else if I'd missed one more day, and I wasn't getting paid for staying at home. I couldn't afford the doctor and had been fending off the flu with cheap over-the-counter stuff."

"Bron," he began.

"I know it was irresponsible, Bryce. I know that I had a baby to take care of and I could have gotten seriously ill or worse—"

"You *were* seriously ill," he interrupted, but she continued as if there hadn't been an interruption.

"But I was taking care of her the only way I knew how; I was keeping her fed, healthy, and happy. I needed to work, you understand?

I'd made arrangements in case anything happened to me; I made sure that the authorities would know to call you, for Kayla's sake. I wouldn't have left her alone. I knew that you'd take her if I wasn't part of the package. I knew that you'd love her and take care of her." He seemed at a loss and frowned down at his plate before sighing tiredly and scrubbing his hands over his face.

"God," he groaned wearily. "How did we ever get to this point?" He reached over and stroked one long finger down the side of her face. "Eat, sweetheart. I never want you to go hungry again."

"I'm . . ."

"Please?" She couldn't resist the naked pleading on his face, and she smiled before nodding and lifting her fork, her appetite restored. He remained quiet for a while longer, breaking the silence to tell her an amusing story about taking Kayla into the office the previous day. He peppered the story with wry humor, and she found herself laughing more than she'd laughed in a long time. Eventually they started talking about other things—university and work—and for a short while, it felt as companionable and comfortable as it had been in the past.

CHAPTER ELEVEN

Is she asleep?" Bryce asked when Bronwyn joined him in the den after putting Kayla down for the night. She nodded in response to the question and tried not to let the intimate domesticity of the scene unnerve her too much. He was sprawled on one of the huge comfortable sofas that Bronwyn had begged him to buy when she had first seen it, four years ago.

"Yes, she was still going on about 'Nebo' when she dropped off." He smiled faintly at that.

"I don't think she's going to forget about today too quickly," he murmured, fingering the rim of the glass of scotch he had poured for himself, indicating a glass of red wine on the little table beside the sofa. "Wine?"

Not wanting to refuse and end the comfortable atmosphere between them just yet, she nodded and curled up on the opposite end of the large sofa, tucking her feet beneath her.

"Wouldn't it be wonderful if today turned out to be her first real memory?" He smiled faintly at her dreamy question.

"It would be a happy one for all of us," he agreed. He tilted his head to look at her appraisingly, and she met his eyes with a laugh.

"What?"

"What's your first memory?" he asked, and she giggled.

"Chasing a butterfly around our backyard, tripping over the puppy and falling down, *hard*. According to my Gran, I was three when it happened. She remembered because it was at my birthday party and I made such a fuss because I thought I'd hurt the dog. Apparently I insisted that we take him to the 'doggy doctor'!"

His eyes crinkled at the corners.

"What about you?" she asked him, still smiling at her own memory. "What was your first memory?" The smile faded from his eyes to be replaced by a somber frown as he shrugged.

"I don't remember."

She laughed at that. "It's your first *memory*. By its very definition you should remember it." He looked uncomfortable and refused to meet her eyes. Realizing that something was wrong, she tried to catch his eye.

"Bryce?" she prompted, waving her hand to get his attention and not expecting much in the line of a response from him. If this followed the old pattern of their marriage, he would freeze her out and retreat back behind the walls that seemed to have been specifically designed to keep her out. It amazed her now, how little she actually knew of the man and merely brought home the fact how much was still wrong, how much would *always* be wrong, with their relationship. She was just resigning herself to watching him get up and leave when he unexpectedly spoke, still not looking at her.

"My first memory is of my father. He's shouting at me and angry because I'd accidentally dropped his wristwatch into a toilet bowl. Can't really blame him—it's a gold watch. Of course, I wasn't aware of the significance of that at the time. I was three as well. I know because that was the same day I broke my arm . . . so there are records of the date," he said it almost absently, and Bronwyn's brow furrowed.

"How did you break your arm?" she asked, but he wasn't looking at her and didn't see the question. She reached over and in a gesture similar to the one he'd used on her the previous night, gently tilted his jaw so that he was looking at her. She repeated the question and he seemed to shake himself out of his reverie, but when he spoke again, his voice was so horribly empty.

"He was very angry," he said with a shrug.

"Your *father* broke your arm?" She needed clarity on this point and wasn't sure she understood. He nodded abruptly before draining his glass.

"I'm exhausted," he muttered gruffly. "I was wondering, would you and Kayla like to go to the beach with me tomorrow? I'll fix a picnic lunch. Unless you've moved your ladies' get-together to tomorrow? Since you missed it today?"

"A couple of the others had other plans this weekend as well, so we decided not to meet until next week. Anyway, the beach sounds nice," she agreed absently, not really paying attention, her mind on what he had just revealed. He smiled before getting up abruptly.

"Great." He sounded pleased. "It'll be an early-ish start. I think eight o'clock should do it." He turned to head out of the door, then hesitated and turned back to her. He leaned over her.

"Thank you for today, Bron," he said sincerely, bending down to drop an unexpectedly sweet kiss onto her opened mouth. "I'll see you in the morning."

"No, wait. Bryce . . ." But he was already striding away, leaving her to fret over the unexpected information he had divulged about his father. Had it been an accident? Or deliberate? The latter possibility left her cold and unable to fall asleep for the longest time.

Bronwyn woke to the conspiratorial sound of whispering just outside her door, and a bleary-eyed look at her bedside clock told that her it was seven thirty a.m. She groaned at the thought of getting Kayla up and ready in time for Bryce's early start. She was exhausted after an uneasy night's sleep. She cleared her throat and frowned when the whispering outside her door continued. She pushed herself up when the door handle turned slowly and braced for an energetic wake-up call similar to the one Bryce had received the day before. She leaned forward when nothing happened; the whispering continued for a few more moments before her daughter's dimpled face appeared around the door. When the little girl caught sight of her mother, she gasped and abruptly jerked back out of sight.

"Mummy not *sleep!*" Bronwyn heard the toddler hiss frantically before she was shushed by an unmistakeable, deep voice that always managed to send delicious shivers down her spine. Intrigued now, Bronwyn leaned even farther forward, wondering what they were up to. After another few moments of whispered exchanges, Kayla stepped around the door, already dressed in a pair of pink denim dungarees, a yellow-and-pink T-shirt, and her favorite pair of red squeak sneakers. In her hands she solemnly clasped a handful of multicolored autumn flowers, which Bronwyn recognized from the garden outside.

"Hello, Mummy." She grinned.

"Good morning, sweetheart. What do you have there?" The little girl solemnly handed her the flowers before leaning up on tiptoes to kiss her mother on the cheek.

"Happy Mummy day," the little girl said carefully in a well-rehearsed way.

"Mummy's day? But . . ." She glanced up to see Bryce standing in the doorway with a tray clasped in his hands, her eyes huge and vulnerable in her face as she tried to figure out what on earth was going on here. "Bryce, it's not . . ."

"Yes it is. You've missed out on two, so Kayla and I are making up for lost time." He placed the tray in her lap and removed the flowers from her numb fingers to place them in the empty vase on the tray, before moving the vase to her nightstand. He dropped a kiss on her cheek. "Happy Mother's Day, Bronwyn."

Kayla solemnly held up a small gift-wrapped box, and when Bronwyn opened it she frowned in confusion.

"What's this?" It was an electronic beeper-like device nestled in a custom-molded Styrofoam cushion.

"The smart key to your new car," he informed with a slight smile, and her eyes widened when she turned the small device over and spotted the prominent BMW logo on the other side of the key.

"Bryce, this is too much," she protested helplessly.

"This is nowhere near *enough*," he interrupted gruffly. "Nothing I do can ever be enough."

"I don't know what to say," she said, unable to read his mood and not sure how to react.

"You don't have to say anything." He grinned, flashing a dimple identical to his daughter's and looking just as mischievous as the toddler. "Just enjoy the car. It's not quite as sporty as the last one you had; I wanted something bigger and safer because of Kayla."

"But when did you . . ." She couldn't seem to gather her thoughts, and his smile widened.

"I started shopping when you told me about how you were forced to sell the last one. It was delivered yesterday, but the visit to the aquarium kind of distracted me. I figured you must be sick of that Jeep by now. I know you're not a fan of it." She nodded dumbly in response to that observation, still staring blankly down at the key in her hand. Bored with the lack of attention, Kayla started tugging at her father's hand. He glanced down at her and signed something to her that Bronwyn didn't quite catch. Whatever it was seemed to satisfy the little girl because she grudgingly settled down

"Take your time getting ready," he told her. "Kayla and I will be downstairs packing our picnic. It's going to be a beautiful day; sunny, with blue skies and not a single cloud on the horizon."

~

His prediction proved accurate; it *was* a beautiful day, the most perfect day Bronwyn had ever spent with Bryce. After leading them down to Bronwyn's gorgeous, sleek, new silver sedan, he told her that she would be doing the driving. He had only Cal on security and—always a consummate professional—the man was keeping such a low profile that Bronwyn was barely aware of him in the discreet black sedan parked a few meters away from them.

A little nervous about test-driving the new car in front of one of the worst backseat drivers that she had ever met, she tried to demur. Unfortunately, he wouldn't have it, and after strapping Kayla into the baby seat that was already installed in the back, he made quite a show of settling in on the passenger side. Bronwyn rolled her eyes and headed for the driver's side, prepared for a day's worth of male condescension from him.

She was rather pleasantly surprised that he valiantly refrained from commenting when she had problems starting the keyless car. He kept a bright smile glued to his face when she ground the clutch and the car lurched forward and limped out of the driveway. She sent a nervous glance at his profile after she had *finally* managed to get them down to Main Street and could tell that his smile was beginning to fray at the edges after less than five minutes in the car. She bit back an irreverent chuckle before pulling the car over to the shoulder of the road. He glanced over at her in alarm and she smiled at him sweetly.

"Do you want to drive?" she invited, and he grinned sheepishly.

"No, you're doing fine. I'm sorry if I seem tense. It's just that since the accident I've been a bit nervous in cars. That's why I have Cal do most of my driving these days."

"Well, I don't know where we're going, so it's better if you do the driving today," she said reasonably. "I'll take over if you get tired or something." He shook his head placidly.

"I'll be okay," he assured her. "It doesn't really matter if I'm driving or not, I'm still uneasy in a car," he grudgingly explained, and she could see how much it cost him to reveal that weakness to her. "I'll give you directions."

"Fine, but keep the wincing down to a minimum, mister," she warned. "You've always been a terrible backseat driver."

"What do you mean?" He looked so genuinely baffled that she snorted in exasperation and restarted the car.

Following his directions and ignoring his occasional grimaces and harshly indrawn breaths, she drove them safely to Boulder's Beach where Bryce spent most of the morning trying to keep Kayla away from the penguins. Bronwyn laughed helplessly at their antics. Kayla turned it into a game, running from her father while she tried to pet one of the many wild penguins that fearlessly waddled around on the beach, completely ignoring his warnings that they would bite. At around twelve, when it was too hot to remain on the beach, they packed up and he directed her to the wine lands of Stellenbosch. Bronwyn was becoming more confident in her handling of the car and was grinding the gears less often, which in turn meant a more relaxed Bryce. They had a picnic lunch in one of the beautiful privately owned vineyards in the picturesque Stellenbosch.

"It's so beautiful here," Bronwyn observed dreamily as she tilted her head back to enjoy the sun filtering through the leaves of the giant oak tree that they were picnicking beneath. They were sitting up on a hill that overlooked a vast vineyard. The vines were starting to go vivid shades of orange and red and made the entire valley look like it was aflame in the afternoon sunshine. "And peaceful. How did you know about this place?"

"The family of a business acquaintance of mine owns this vineyard. I cleared this with him."

"Anybody I know?" she asked, tucking her feet beneath her and rummaging through the picnic basket that he had settled on the blanket.

"I don't know," He shrugged. "Cord Strachan?"

"As in Strachan Diamonds?" Her eyes widened. The Strachan family was one of South Africa's wealthiest and most influential families. They controlled a huge chunk of the diamond mining industry in the country and the latest generation provided a rich source of fodder for local and international gossip columnists.

"They supply most of our rough diamonds." He nodded. "I remembered that Cord mentioned this place over one of our business lunches a couple of years ago." *Before* his accident, of course; any socializing had been done before his accident. The reminder saddened Bronwyn and the awkward silence that followed was entirely her fault. Luckily Kayla demanded attention and distracted them with her antics. Bryce kept the little girl entertained with silly games all through lunch, as Kayla had the natural tendency of a toddler to grow bored very easily. Eventually, after a companionable lunch, Bryce packed them all back into the car and directed her to drive the short distance to a small town called Klapmuts and there introduced them to a place Bronwyn had never known existed.

She stood in an enclosed tropical garden and gazed in awe at the hundreds of butterflies that fluttered around her. It was like watching a garden of wildflowers take flight, and Bronwyn could do nothing but stand and stare, her eyes filling with tears as their wings kissed her face and hair. Kayla was just as entranced. She was in her father's arms and reached out one chubby hand to try and capture the delicate creatures as they flitted by.

"Oh my God," Bronwyn breathed, lifting a trembling hand to her mouth. "Oh my God, Bryce . . ." He couldn't hear her of course; he couldn't even see what she was saying as his attention was focused on the fragile creatures that were haphazardly darting from flower to flower and person to person. How dare he make this so difficult for her? Just when she had decided to contact the divorce lawyer, he did something so wonderfully tender and so unbelievably sweet. He knew that she loved butterflies, that she had always loved them. She had countless earrings, chains, charms, printed skirts, and blouses with butterflies scattered all over them. It would be so easy to believe that he had planned this day out of some manipulative need to keep her complacent. But when she looked up she found herself charmed by the arresting picture he made with his head tilted back and his eyes closed. He was lost in his own world, enjoying the sensation of the delicate butterfly wings brushing against his face, and Bronwyn instinctively knew that he had done this to make her happy. She stood on her toes to drop an impulsive kiss on his cheek and startled him into opening his eyes. He looked down at her quizzically.

"This is perfect," she told him, and his eyes warmed. "Thank you."

He dropped an arm over her slender shoulders and gave her a quick, little one-armed hug.

"I saw an advertisement for this place last winter and I knew that you'd like it." *Last winter?* At least six months before her return? He had learned about this place and thought of her. Not with any hatred or resentment it seemed. Instead he had thought about something that would make her happy. It was startling to know that he hadn't always thought of her in anger over the last couple of years, and Bronwyn wasn't sure how to process that information.

~

They got home shortly before eight, and Kayla was once again drooping in exhaustion. Bryce took her from Bronwyn's arms.

"I'll put her to bed," he offered.

"Bryce, you've been taking care of her all week, I should—"

"And you've been taking care of her on your own for years. This is the least I can do," he interrupted, and she protested no further. She knew that he needed to make up for the past but that wasn't what she wanted from him anymore. They had to think of the future and ensure that it was a happy one for all of them. Bronwyn just couldn't live with his secrets any longer. And she was only human, so she still felt so much anger and bitterness toward him for misjudging her so horribly.

She went upstairs to take a hot shower, and when she headed toward the study later, she ran into Bryce as he was coming from the kitchen with a glass of fruit juice in his hand.

"Hitting the books?" His deep, quiet voice sent a little tremor of awareness shivering up her spine. She shoved back the unwanted frisson of sexual awareness and forced herself to smile.

"I'm doing research on an assignment due in a couple of weeks," she explained.

"Well, don't overtax yourself," he advised before heading upstairs. She saluted his back sarcastically.

"Yes sir," she said smartly before rolling her eyes at her own childishness and continuing on her way to the study. She didn't get much done before the rigors of the weekend caught up with her and her eyes drifted shut.

She came awake with a start when she felt strong arms encircling her and lifting her up.

"Wha . . . I was just taking a catnap," she protested groggily, somehow managing to speak clearly enough for him to read her lips.

"You've been in here for nearly four hours, and judging from the computer screen, you've done all of five minutes' worth of work. That wasn't a catnap, babe; you were completely out."

"Just *so* tired," she murmured incoherently before snuggling up to his warm, strong, and *naked* chest. He must have been in bed until some instinct had told him to check on her.

"It's okay," he soothed into her hair. "Sleep, sweetheart." She sighed contentedly, burrowed closer, and was asleep seconds after he'd deposited her in bed.

It was still dark when she woke up, but the room was filling with the eerie gray light of the impending dawn. She soon recognized that she was in Bryce's room, in his bed, and wrapped in his arms. He lay spooning her, his knees tucked into the crook of hers, one strong arm snaked under her head and the other draped over her torso. His large hand was possessively spread over her abdomen. Bronwyn tried not to think about how incredibly right this felt and focused on extricating herself from his hold. She moved experimentally, but his arms flexed and his hand gently exerted a little bit more pressure on her stomach. She relaxed until she felt the tension seeping out of his arms and heard his breathing regulate again. Once she was sure he was still asleep, she subtly tried to move away again, but his reaction was the same as before. She sighed quietly and stilled her movements, wondering why he hadn't taken her to her own bed. She was still wearing the tank top she had donned after her shower the night before, but her sweatpants were missing. He must have removed them to make her more comfortable. This left her wearing only her tiny silk bikini panties, and judging from the expanse of hot, smooth male flesh pressed up against her back, Bryce wasn't wearing much more than a pair of boxers.

She groaned softly, knowing that she should try harder to remove herself from his arms, but it felt so good to be held by him that she was tempted to stay where she was. She carefully laid her hand over his where it rested low on her stomach and gently tried to lift it. His hand quite unexpectedly curled around hers and she jumped in response to the touch.

"I just wanted to hold you." His voice rumbled in her ear. His hand briefly tightened around her smaller hand for a few seconds longer before he let her go and removed his arm from around her waist. He shifted away from her, giving her the space to leave if she so desired. Bronwyn hesitated for a brief moment, impulsively turning around to face him. She could barely make out his expression in the predawn light, and against her better judgment she reached out a hand to touch his stubbled jaw. His own hand lifted to trap her against the bristly surface of his skin. Her palm brushed against the lower edge of his sensuous lips.

"If you don't leave now, Bronwyn . . ." He left the rest of the desperately whispered warning unspoken, and Bronwyn closed her eyes briefly, praying for the strength to get up and walk away. She steeled herself and gently dragged her hand out from under his.

"Wait," he whispered urgently, and she hesitated. He moved closer, bracing himself on one elbow to look down at her. "I'm sorry, I have to do this." Before she could react, his mouth found hers in an achingly sweet yet infinitely hungry kiss.

"So sorry," he apologized again, when he lifted his mouth to stare down into her face tenderly before dropping back down to claim her lips again. His kiss was tender and loving and, as a result, Bronwyn found herself helplessly responding to it. Her lips opened up and welcomed him in and his tongue happily accepted the invitation, gently courting and coaxing hers.

His hands moved down the slim column of her neck, to her shoulders, stroking every centimeter of silky skin he encountered. His lips followed his hands down. She felt his hot, moist breath on her sensitive skin as he worked his way down, kissing every inch of available skin. She cried out when she felt his breath on one tautly beaded nipple through the thin cotton material of her top. His mouth moved over the nipple and he very deliberately breathed onto the bud through the cotton. The material sensuously abraded the sensitive peak, while his fingers fluttered up and down the small slope of her breast, circling, taunting but not quite touching the eager tip. Bronwyn sobbed desperately as she wondered how he had gotten her so hot, so *fast*. He glanced up into her face, over the small mound of the breast, and grinned almost satanically. He hovered for an endless moment before bending his head and drawing the tight nub of her nipple, cotton and all, deeply into his hot, wet mouth. At the same time he buried his free hand between her legs and found the other eager nubbin desperate for his touch through her silky underwear.

It was like being jolted by a huge bolt of lightning; she screamed and arched off the bed as she climaxed unexpectedly and with ferocious force. Her back bowed and she remained taut for what seemed like an eternity, as the spasms went on and on, while he drew her nipple deeper and deeper into his mouth. He had one hand cupped in the nape of her neck with the other still buried between her legs and kept them there even after she went completely boneless and collapsed back onto the bed. He lifted his head to chuckle hoarsely.

"You're so bloody gorgeous," he whispered as he gave her one final stroke with his long finger before moving his hand to rest on her heaving stomach. She barely heard him over the thunderous crashing of her heart. She could hardly move and she was only just aware of him dragging her top off and tossing it aside. He went back to work, kissing her skin, licking, sucking, and nipping reverently. Bronwyn tried to regain her equilibrium but it was an impossible task when Bryce was so determinedly keeping her off-kilter.

He was patient and undemanding and Bronwyn sighed dreamily, feeling ridiculously relaxed after her massive orgasm, while his sweeping hands and loving mouth continued to do deliciously wicked things to her. Gradually, his relentless patience started to have an undeniable effect on her. Her nipples had beaded back into tight, hard nuggets, and her breathing became more and more ragged as he kissed and caressed his way over her entire body, front and back. Her panties had long since disappeared, and she became sharply aware of that fact when his lips found their way to her flat stomach. His tongue swirled in and around the dent of her belly button, and she helplessly shifted her hips, encouraging him to move even lower. She was amazed by how quickly he had managed to get her so incredibly aroused again after her earlier climax.

All thought fled her mind when his talented mouth found the moist core of her femininity, and she shuddered violently with every stroke of his tongue. She barely had time to brace herself before a second, even bigger climax had her writhing around in ecstatic agony. He managed to still her helplessly thrusting hips between his large hands as he continued to lave her with his incredibly clever tongue.

"*Stop*," she whispered, unable to tolerate the overwhelming sensations for much longer, but of course he could not hear her and continued to relentlessly coax the almost painfully pleasurable response from her. He made her come again and again until Bronwyn, so overly sensitive after her repeated orgasms, had to pull at his hair to make him stop.

Bryce dragged himself up over her body and braced himself above her to stare down into her sweaty face. His eyes were smiling down into hers and he looked justifiably smug.

"Wow," she whispered after her climactic shudders eventually stopped. It was light enough now for him to read her lips, and his smile widened into a grin. She glanced down between their bodies and noticed that his boxers had disappeared and that he was still *very* aroused. She comprehended how incredibly one-sided this entire experience had been, and she reached down to touch him. He hissed when her fingers closed around him and groaned when she stroked his hard, hot length lazily.

"No," he whispered, when she tried to guide him to her and she frowned up at him. "I don't think it would be a good idea."

"Why not?" she asked in confusion.

"Because you'll hate me if we do."

"No," she denied. "I won't. I'm not that unfair, Bryce. We both want this. *I* want this. Please." He was helplessly thrusting himself against her hand and she once again tried to bring him to her.

"No, sweetheart," he managed tightly. "Just your hand. We don't have to go further than that. Just your hand is fine."

"*No*," she protested again. Why wouldn't he make love to her? Her hand loosened and he groaned before reaching down and tightening his own hand over hers.

"Don't let go," he begged hoarsely.

"Bryce, please make love to me." He groaned again and let go of her hand. She released him, her hands moving up to stroke and caress the rest of his body instead.

"I'm sorry," he apologized. "I never meant for any of this to happen. I just wanted to hold you."

"I know," she appeased, kissing his chest and neck lovingly before raising her head to meet his eyes. "It's okay."

"No," he whispered quietly. "No, it's not." He hovered for a moment before, with a growl of brutal self-denial, he dragged himself out of her arms and off the bed all in one swift movement. He stood at the side of the bed, gloriously naked and painfully aroused, to stare at her for a heartbeat before turning away and heading toward the en suite. Bronwyn watched the door close gently behind him and an instant later, heard the shower going on. She turned her face into the pillow with an anguished sob and wondered at the amount of self-control it must have taken for him to get up and leave her. She was tempted to join him in the shower, but she knew that he believed he had done the right thing. She could not undermine the sacrifice he had just made by stepping into that shower with him.

She dragged herself out of the warm bed and to her own room. Knowing that she would get no more sleep that morning, she showered as well and tried not to think about how difficult it would be to get through the day ahead.

CHAPTER TWELVE

Getting through the day really *was* a lot harder than she had anticipated once she remembered her appointment with the lawyer that afternoon. She was so tempted to let it slide, especially after the wonderful weekend the Palmer family had just enjoyed, but she couldn't keep leaving things up in the air like this. The weekend and the incident between her and Bryce that morning had complicated matters, but it hadn't really changed the big picture. The marriage was over, and it had been over for a very long time. It was with a heavy heart that she kept her appointment after her morning lectures and started the divorce proceedings. Jason Goodson, her attorney, had been a bit dismayed to discover that despite Bryce's sizeable assets, Bronwyn wanted nothing from him other than continued child support and joint custody. Goodson had tried to dissuade her from this course of action, but she had remained firm in her decision until he'd had no choice but to accept his client's wishes.

Getting through the rest of the afternoon was hell. Nothing seemed to go right, she couldn't concentrate enough to get any studying done, and the bookshop was even quieter than usual. It offered no distraction from her inner turmoil. To top off a truly miserable day, after she finished work she discovered that she had a flat tire on her brand-spanking-new car. To make matters even worse, her cellphone battery had died and she didn't have her charger. Of all days to have given Paul the day off, this was the one time she could actually have used his help. Sobbing with frustration, she returned to the shop to call the Automobile Association and then waited nearly half an hour for them to arrive. Luckily, she had discovered the flat tire before leaving work and could safely wait for the AA inside the shop. By the time they had fixed the tire, she was nearly an hour late and the autumn sun had already disappeared behind the mountain. When she got home it was to find Bryce in the kitchen feeding a happily chattering Kayla. The toddler was intent on redistributing clumps of mashed potatoes from her bowl to her chubby fists and onto her hair. Bryce looked up when Bronwyn entered his field of vision, and his indulgent smile immediately faded.

"Where the *hell* have you been?" he asked in a controlled voice, his face dark with tightly leashed anger. "I've been going out of my mind with worry."

"I had a flat tire," she explained tiredly, dropping her bag onto the kitchen table and sitting down next to Kayla, picking up a damp cloth to wipe the food from the little girl's face and hair. "The AA guys thought it may have been a slow puncture that I picked up on one of the gravel roads yesterday."

"I've been sending message after message and getting *zero* response from you," he growled, still in that frighteningly controlled voice.

"Well, my battery died." She shrugged, doggedly wiping the smudges from Kayla's face despite the child's frantically shaking head. "I'm sorry."

He swore, startling both her and Kayla, before handing the toddler's spoon to Bronwyn and stalking from the kitchen.

"Daddy go 'way!" Kayla informed redundantly, waving happily at the door through which her father had disappeared. Bronwyn sighed and dropped a kiss onto the child's silky curls, grimacing when her lips met a clump of cold food.

"You need a bath, little girl," she groaned, overcome with exhaustion at the mere thought of it, when all she wanted was to soak her own weary bones. "Want a bubble bath with Mummy?"

Kayla grinned and nodded happily, starting to sing a tuneless song occasionally peppered with words like "mummy," "bath," "happy," "bubbles," and "play"; the rest was complete gibberish. Bronwyn laughed as she carried the child up to the master bath, wishing Bryce could hear the charming little ditty.

They were soon happily settled in the huge round tub and immersed in fragrant warm water. Kayla was on Bronwyn's lap and both of them were enjoying the massive amount of bubbles in the tub when Bryce walked in. He halted at the door, visibly surprised to see his wife and child sporting foam bubble caps and beards. Bronwyn yelped, feeling like an idiot for not locking the door, but she had been so preoccupied with Kayla that she hadn't even thought about it.

"Daddy," the child squealed, happy to see him as always. "Baf?"

"Uh . . . not right now, sweetheart." He shook his head regretfully, raising a wicked eyebrow at Bronwyn. "Although I would *love* to." She rolled her eyes at the pathetic attempt at a leer and he chuckled.

"Sorry, Bron, I thought you were giving her a bath. I didn't know you were in the tub with her. I'll talk to you later." He turned to leave.

"Daddy no go!" Kayla demanded, fiercely unhappy that her father was about to leave. Bronwyn groaned and buried her face between the child's fragile shoulder blades, then looked up to meet his amused eyes.

"You might as well stay; she'll be insufferable if you don't," Bronwyn said. He nodded, lowering the lid on the commode and sitting down, leaning forward with his elbows resting on his denim-clad thighs and his hands loosely clasped between his knees. Happy that her daddy was watching, Kayla launched into full show-off mode. She decorated her mother's face and hair with more bubbles before dragging a plastic doll into the water and starting a chatty tea party with it. Soon she was totally absorbed in her game, and Bryce shifted his beautiful eyes from child to disconcerted mother.

"I didn't mean to lose my temper earlier," he murmured.

"I know." She shrugged, shampooing Kayla's hair while the child continued to play. "You were worried. I'm sorry."

"I was imagining all the worst scenarios," he admitted, lowering his eyes to his hands. "I was on the verge of calling the police. I'd already decided I would once I'd finished feeding Kayla." Because his eyes weren't on her, she chose not to respond to that.

"I regret this morning too," he said after a prolonged silence interrupted only by Kayla's happy chatter. This time he *did* raise his eyes to her face. He looked both uncomfortable and sincere.

"I know," she said again. "But even though I couldn't really see it this morning, you did the right thing by leaving."

"It nearly killed me," he admitted gruffly.

"I know it wasn't easy." She nodded. "But thank you. I'm sorry for pressuring you to stay. It would only have led to even bigger regrets." She grabbed the showerhead and started to rinse Kayla's hair. The child squirmed irritably when it interfered with her game.

"Kayla, sit still." Her mother's tone brooked no argument. Kayla stopped moving and sulkily leaned back against Bronwyn's chest. Bryce watched the two of them with a slightly dazed smile on his lips, and Bronwyn frowned, unable to interpret the expression on his face.

"You're both so beautiful," he whispered, sounding awed and humbled. He looked so possessively proud that Bronwyn squirmed uncomfortably.

"Bryce."

He didn't see her lips form his name. Instead he reached for a small towel and draped it over Kayla's hair, knotting it turban-style around her head. He reached for another, bigger towel and opened it up, patiently waiting for Bronwyn to finish soaping and rinsing their daughter before kneeling beside the tub to reach for the squirming toddler. His white T-shirt immediately got drenched when he wrapped the small child in the towel. He picked her up before nodding down at Bronwyn, who immediately sank down beneath the rapidly dissipating bubbles.

"I'll take it from here; you enjoy the rest of your bath," he urged, and she smiled gratefully, watching his tall, well-built form as he retreated from the bathroom.

"Oh God," she moaned, burying her face in her wet hands. This was going to be so difficult. She straightened her narrow shoulders resolutely before finishing her bath and heading off to find her husband. He was in Kayla's room, reading the sleepy little girl a bedtime story. Bronwyn watched silently from the doorway, unseen by both father and daughter until eventually Kayla fell asleep. Bryce stopped reading and leaned down to drop a kiss on Kayla's baby-soft cheek.

"Good night, angel," he murmured, so quietly Bronwyn nearly missed it. When he got up and turned around, he seemed unsurprised to find her standing in the doorway. She came forward and dropped her own good-night kiss on Kayla's cheek before straightening to meet his gaze unflinchingly.

"We need to talk," she said, and he nodded. She led the way out of the room and downstairs to the living room. She couldn't do this in the conservatory, not where they had shared so many experiences, both good and bad. He headed straight to the drinks cabinet and poured two glasses of neat scotch, seeming to realize that they would need it. He handed her one of the heavy, crystal glasses and gestured toward two comfortable chairs.

"Shall we?"

She nodded, sitting down opposite him and taking a nervous sip of the fiery liquid that swirled so prettily in the glass. She coughed and he grinned.

"Still can't hold your liquor, I see," he teased.

"Bryce, I filed for a divorce today," she said very quickly. His grin faded, and he went as white as a sheet. His eyes dropped to his glass and he lifted it to his lips with a somewhat shaky hand before downing the contents in one gulp.

"I see."

"I want nothing from you," she continued hastily when his eyes lifted to meet hers again. "Just what we discussed before: child support and joint custody." He got up and headed back to the drinks cabinet. He refilled his glass, doubling the amount this time. When he sat back down, he said nothing, merely drank down half of the liquor with a slight shudder.

"Say something," she urged.

"Nothing more to say." He shrugged. "Nothing more to *do* really, except sit here and get very, very drunk."

"Bryce," she admonished, but he didn't see her lips form his name because he was up once again, refilling his glass. When he returned to his seat this time, he brought the decanter with him and held it up to her with a questioning tilt of his head.

"You want some?" He invited, indicating toward her barely touched alcohol.

"Bryce we need to talk."

He laughed rudely, sounding anything but amused.

"About what, goddamn it?" His voice rose and she jumped in fright. "You always want to talk but nothing much ever gets said! You want a divorce, you want child support, and you want joint custody? Fine, they're yours. I'll throw in the house in Knysna and a few million too! How does that sound?"

"I don't want those things."

"Of course you don't," he sneered. "You're too good for my money, for my apologies, and for my love, aren't you?"

That *did* it! Bronwyn jumped up and, before she really had time to think about her actions, tossed the rest of her drink into his sneering face. She waited for him to blink the stinging alcohol from his eyes before she laid into him.

"*What* apologies? *What* love?" She both signed and screamed at him. "So far I haven't heard a word of apology from you. Not for tossing me out or for misjudging me. And you haven't once, not once since our wedding, since before our wedding for that matter, told me that you love me! In fact you did the polar opposite of that; you told me that you married me out of duty, that you'd never loved me. Are you telling me *different* now, Bryce? Make up your damned mind because I'm getting sick of your multiple personality disorder."

"Bronwyn . . ."

"No! You have the utter *gall* to tell me that nothing much ever gets said." She was still using hands and mouth to make it absolutely clear how she felt. She didn't want him to miss a single word. "Well whose fault is that, Bryce? You've never really opened up to me. Trying to learn anything at all about you is like extracting blood from a stone. I was happy with our marriage before I left, but after being on my own for two years and really thinking about it, I recognized how completely screwed up our relationship was. It was all give from me and nothing but take from you. You hide yourself so completely from me that I wonder if the man I fell in love with ever really existed. So, you're right, the time for talking is over. I'll stay in this house as per our agreement but this divorce will happen."

"Why are you suddenly so desperate for a divorce?" he asked suspiciously. "Is it that professor? Are you leaving me for him?"

"How can I leave you when we're not even together?" she asked in exasperation. She was frustrated that none of her words seemed to be sinking in "And *no*, I don't want a divorce because of Raymond. I doubt I'll see him again outside of school. And just because *you've* played away during this marriage doesn't mean that I will." He looked completely confounded by her words and signaled for her to repeat them, evidently thinking he'd misread her words. When she repeated what she'd said, his jaw dropped to his chest as he stared at her in obvious shock.

"What the hell are you talking about?" he asked. He was still sitting down, insouciantly sipping at his scotch, even though the alcohol she had tossed on him had drenched his head and shoulders. Bronwyn was still standing and glowering down at him. "I haven't 'played away' as you so eloquently put it."

"You're the one who told me that your sex life was 'just fine,' remember? What else was I supposed to gather from that statement?" He choked on a sip of scotch and coughed for a few minutes before eventually blinking rapidly to clear his eyes and stare at her stupidly again.

"Bronwyn . . . I was in an accident. I spent six months convalescing, a year in therapy, and the rest of the time actively avoiding crowds. I went out only once, and that was to a surprise party for Theresa De Lucci just a couple of weeks before we found you again. When do you think I had time to shag other women?"

"You said . . ." Okay, so maybe he'd lied.

"I was trying to save face. You were asking me about sex and all I could think about was getting you naked and beneath me again. Hardly something I wanted to advertise when I was still so angry with you."

"But the condoms?"

"What?"

"In the pedestal drawer," she elaborated, and his lips twitched.

"Rick and Lisa have used that room in the past and while they did the responsible thing in purchasing condoms, they never really got around to using them, and she got pregnant faster than you could blink." He stared levelly up at her for a beat before grinning wickedly. "Were you jealous, Bron?"

Damn him!

"Not at all." She kept her face expressionless but couldn't quite hide the betraying flush from him. "I just thought you were a hypocrite for getting weird about Raymond when you'd all but admitted to sleeping with other women. It doesn't matter anymore anyway. The divorce still stands." Her words brought the reality of their situation back to him and he sobered immediately. "I want to pick up the pieces of my life and move on. I just can't be happy living like this."

He stood up, towering above her, and his eyes bored desperately into hers.

"We can be a family, Bronwyn," he urged, holding out an imploring hand. "This weekend proved that."

"No, all this weekend proved is that you still have secrets that you refuse to share with me. And it will always be that way, won't it, Bryce? You will always close off some part of yourself from me. I've never really known you and I doubt that I ever will."

"Sweetheart, please," he groaned.

"Don't call me that," she said. She just felt tired and defeated. He stood there, hand still outstretched and looking miserable, with alcohol dripping from his hair and into his eyes. For a very brief moment she felt herself softening.

"I know that I've been an utter bastard," he admitted.

"Yes."

His admission strengthened her resolve.

"I'm sorry . . . ?"

"Is that a question? Or an actual apology?"

He hesitated briefly and she rolled her eyes. "Get back to me when you know for sure." She swept from the room, and Bryce stared at the door for a long time after she'd left.

Now that this whole divorce thing was becoming a palpable fact, he admitted to himself that he wasn't quite so willing to roll over and give her everything that she asked for. He wanted his wife and child but he was a broken man, both physically and emotionally, and it hardly seemed fair to saddle her with his innumerable problems after everything that he had already put her through. Yet he knew that without her he'd go back to being the empty husk he'd been after she'd left. He sighed and corrected the thought, after he'd *driven* her away. Two years ago he had been careless with the most precious thing in his world and had lost it as a result. He wished that there were some way to regain her trust and reconcile with her, but in his heart he didn't think he deserved that much anymore.

"You still with us, Bronwyn?" Bronwyn blinked when a slender hand was waved in front of her face and she saw that the four other women sitting at the restaurant table were staring at her expectantly. They had been discussing Theresa's marriage renewal ceremony, which was coming up later in the year. The other women were excitedly exchanging ideas for the event.

"Sorry, I missed that," she muttered, and Alice snorted.

"You've missed large chunks of the conversation from what I could tell," the other woman said with raised eyebrows. "What's going on with you? You checked out of this conversation before it even started."

"I'm divorcing Bryce," Bronwyn told them after taking a fortifying sip of alcohol. It had been a difficult week. She and Bryce had barely spoken since Monday even though he had tried to approach her on numerous occasions. She'd spent her time actively avoiding him and felt like a rank coward because of it.

"Seriously?" Lisa looked stunned by the information, and the other women were all staring at her sympathetically.

"Yes. I've spoken to a lawyer."

"But I thought things were getting better." Lisa looked devastated by the information, and Bronwyn sighed quietly before shaking her head.

"No, the plan has always been to get a divorce. We're living together because it's convenient right now and less stressful for Kayla, but as soon as I graduate and find a job I'm leaving."

"But that will take years." Theresa unknowingly echoed the words Bronwyn had spoken to Bryce when he'd first suggested his house-sharing idea to her.

"Yes and it does bother me. I really don't want to take advantage of Bryce's generosity . . ."

"Oh *bullcrap*," Theresa cut her off with what for her was uncharacteristically strong language. "You're the mother of his child and you spent the first year and a half of Kayla's life struggling to take care of her at the cost of your own health. So don't you *dare* feel bad about accepting the aid that you're entitled to receive from the father of your child. It's the very least he can do." The other women stared at Theresa in surprise, and she looked a little uncomfortable before shrugging. "It's something I feel strongly about." Bronwyn smiled before nodding her agreement.

"You're right, Theresa, but Bryce has suffered too. He missed the first year and a half of Kayla's life, and he had that accident while following me and we all know how that ended."

"All things that could have been avoided if he'd acted less like an arse after he discovered that you were pregnant," Lisa pointed out reasonably.

"Yes, what married man reacts like that to the news that he's going to be a father, anyway?" Alice added her two cents worth. "I like Bryce but seriously, that was a jerk move."

"I think that everything will seem a lot less complicated after a couple of drinks," Roberta Richmond, who had joined their group for the first time that night, suggested with a decisive nod. She wasn't quite up to speed on the Bronwyn and Bryce situation, but she showed her solidarity by ordering a round of drinks—even though she kept herself restricted to nonalcoholic cocktails. The woman, at twenty-six, was a couple of years younger than Bronwyn and was a friend of Theresa's. Apparently they had met at some football thing that Sandro, Theresa's husband, attended regularly. The tomboyish young woman was now the only single, childless member of their group. Theresa had informed them before inviting Bobbi—as she preferred to be called—that the other woman had very few female friends. Bronwyn liked her positive energy. She was a good addition to their little group.

They spent the rest of the day tossing back cocktails, and, in an effort to cheer her up, the other women started offering Bronwyn all kinds of increasingly bawdy advice on how she could bounce back from her divorce. One of them suggested Bronwyn hook up with a male stripper, which actually made very little sense, but they weren't very sensible by that point.

"I guarantee a male stripper would know what to do between the sheets." Lisa nodded knowingly.

"Please, like you'd know," Theresa scoffed.

"I heard they are mostly gay," Bronwyn ventured.

"No way." Alice looked disappointed by the very idea.

"We should do some research," Bobbi mused, licking the salt off her margarita glass. "Find a stripper and ask him if he's gay."

"Where are we going to find a stripper?" Bronwyn asked, curious, more than a little tipsy.

"I know a place," the very shy and straitlaced Theresa, of *all* people, volunteered.

"Stop it," Lisa gasped, scandalized. "You do *not!*"

"I do," Theresa maintained smugly. "I saw a documentary about it last week."

"Well, what are we waiting for then?" Alice asked eagerly. "Let's go find us some strippers!"

~

Bryce always positioned himself in a room that would get hit by any car headlights whenever he knew Bronwyn was going to be out late. That way he could be certain she was home safely before heading to bed. He would never be able to sleep if he knew she was still out. He always worried about whether she was safe when she was out late with her bunch of gal pals. Unfortunately the women were all quite adamant that security not be present at their gatherings, but the men had collectively agreed to always have at least one guy incognito and keeping an eye on them. Still, it didn't prevent Bryce from getting stressed out every time it got a little too close to midnight on these girlie Saturdays. Right now it was *after* midnight and the responses he'd received to the frantic SMSes he'd sent to both Rick and Pierre—whose guy had security detail that night—had been pretty similar: *Chill out bro, they're fine* and *Relax! I've checked. There's nothing to worry about.* He supposed he would have to be content with that.

At long last, close to one in the morning, the headlights swept up the drive, and he leaped up from the sofa in the den and headed to the front door, fury mixed with the relief he felt.

Strangely enough the headlights were sweeping back down the drive just as he got to the front door, and he was still trying to figure out what that meant when the door swung open. His wife staggered, that was the only word he could think of to describe her movement, into the foyer. Her face lit up when she saw him, and he blinked in surprise until the fumes hit him.

"You're *drunk!*" he accused in disbelief. That explained the headlights; she had probably come home by taxi. She said something that he didn't quite catch, and he imagined that she was probably slurring her words. She held her hand up, thumb and forefinger an inch apart, and he shook his head. "*More* than a little, Bronwyn. Where the hell have you been?" She winced and rubbed her ears and spoke again, and he caught enough of her words to comprehend that he'd probably used a little too much volume on the question. He took a deep, calming breath like his speech therapist had taught him to and repeated the question in what he hoped was a quieter voice. It was always hard to judge when he was feeling this riled up.

". . .With girls."

He caught just the tail end of that, but it was enough.

"You've been out with 'the girls' before but never till nearly one in the morning," he said, seething.

You're not my dad! she signed sloppily before trying to weave her way past him. She lacked the necessary coordination though and instead walked right into him. Bryce grabbed her upper arms and steadied her. She smiled blindingly up at him before quite unexpectedly running her hands over his bare forearms and then up over his biceps. He was so distracted by her touch that for a second he didn't know that she was speaking. Her eyes had glazed over with familiar desire, and she seemed to be talking more to herself than him. He tried to focus on her lips and not on his burgeoning erection, but it still took a few moments before any of what she was saying sank in.

"*Stripper?*" Okay, this time he knew he was bellowing. "What stripper?" To his utter disappointment, she stopped her seductive stroking of his skin and frowned up at him. She lifted one of her hands from his arm and raised a forefinger to her lips in the universal *shushing* gesture.

"What stripper?" he asked again, in what he knew was a whisper, and she rolled her eyes.

"Massive Marvin," she informed him helpfully, but then removed her other hand from his overheated skin to say the rest in clumsy sign language. *But he's not that massive. You're much bigger than he is . . .* She paused thoughtfully while she ran her eyes over his body and then switched back to words. "Much bigger, all over!" Right. That last gesture was not exactly standard sign language but accompanied by the look she directed downward it was quite unmistakable and *very* flattering. He felt his face heating and his body hardening even more. He watched as her eyebrows sprang almost all the way to her hairline as she recognized what was happening to him. She raised her glassy eyes to his once more and licked her lips hungrily. *God,* he knew that look. She wanted him as much as he wanted her, but she was so drunk that he knew it would be wrong to act on their mutual need right then.

Sleeping with her while she was wasted was *not* part of his reconciliation plan. Okay, he still had no real idea what the hell his reconciliation plan was, but he was pretty sure that sleeping with her right now would not be the best first step.

"He's gay," she said. Her lips formed the words clearly enough, and he frowned in confusion at the non sequitur.

"What?" he asked. She was so bloody enchanting like this, but at the same time utterly confounding.

"Massive Marvin. He's gay."

"And that disappointed you?" he asked levelly, trying not to sound jealous at the thought of his wife ogling some other guy. Of course, he had no idea if he succeeded or not, but he hoped that he managed to sound as neutral as he was pretending to be.

"No, it was more of a scientific experiment." Her eyes were on his lower lip, and he wondered what the hell she found so fascinating about it.

"Going to a strip club was a scientific experiment?" He knew that he sounded like a complete idiot, but he wasn't sure he was following this weird conversation correctly. He kept feeling like he was missing something.

"You have such a gorgeous mouth." She totally threw him with that one. "Much better than Massive Marvin's."

"Are you going to compare me to this Massive Marvin guy all night?" he asked resentfully, feeling ridiculous even saying the stupid name.

"No . . . not fair, he'd lose." She went up on her toes and completely slammed him by kissing him. Her arms crept around his neck, and her body was flush against his. He could feel every single curve of her body through their clothes. His arms went around her waist and his hands cupped her firm butt and lifted her until he could feel her feminine heat against his aching hardness. God, it felt amazing having her in his arms again. It would be so easy to strip her naked, push her up against the wall, and . . .

Whoa there, buddy! He lifted his head and his hands, raising them up with his palms out in a gesture of surrender, and wondered, with the slightest hint of hysteria, why *he* was always the one calling a halt to things. One day he was going to give her what she so desperately wanted and to hell with the consequences. But, he conceded wryly as he looked down into her frustrated face, that day was not today. She was weaving on the spot and if not for the fact that she still had her arms tightly wrapped around his neck, she would probably have fallen.

"Babe, you can't keep torturing me like this," he could feel the hoarseness in his throat and wondered if he'd managed to get the words out loudly enough for her to hear. "Come on, let's get you to bed." Her expression brightened at the word "bed," and Bryce rolled his eyes, dragging her arms away from his neck and assisting her up to her room. After another frustrating battle in her bedroom, where she seemed to have grown at least six extra arms and put them to good use, he thankfully managed to get her into bed.

He stared grimly down at his passed-out wife, his body hard, aching, and heavy with suppressed lust. He couldn't live like this anymore; it was enough to test a saint, and he was no bloody saint. He shook his head in disgust before heading for his usual cold shower.

CHAPTER THIRTEEN

When Bronwyn joined them in the sunny kitchen for breakfast the following morning, she was wearing a gigantic pair of sunglasses and moving gingerly, with the caution of someone nursing a hell of a headache. She was dressed in a faded shirt and an ugly pair of sweat pants that had seen better days. Her hair was a complete mess. She tried to swallow down her nausea when Bryce gestured toward a pile of pancakes with a raised eyebrow.

"Coffee," she grunted as she sat down carefully in the chair immediately to Bryce's right. His lips twitched as he poured some of the hot, dark brew into a mug and placed it on the table in front of her. Kayla was staring at her mother curiously.

"Mummy sick?" she asked worriedly, and Bronwyn shook her head before wincing as the movement set off the annoying little drummer gremlins that seemed to have taken up residence in her brain.

"I'm okay, sweetie." Her voice was hoarse and she cleared her throat self-consciously before smiling reassuringly at her little girl. Satisfied with her answer, Kayla went back to playing with her food and singing her off-key little ditty.

Bronwyn flinched at the noise before daring to glance up at Bryce, who was still watching her quietly. She remembered embarrassing bits and pieces of what had happened after she had returned home the night before and didn't quite know what to say to him this morning.

"You know, Bron," he said, breaking the awkward silence between them, and she looked up a little too quickly at the sound of his voice. She bit back a groan and looked at him fully, bracing herself for his censure.

"Yes?" she prompted when he remained silent a little too long.

"I'm all for it if you want to use me for . . ." He glanced over at Kayla before lowering his voice. "*S-e-x*, as long as we come to some sort mutual of agreement over it. No more of this coming-on-to-me-in-a-moment-of-weakness crap. At least that way we both know exactly where we stand, and I won't feel like an utter bastard when I act on these mixed signals that you're sending."

"I'm so . . ."

He made a rude sound, cutting off her apology.

"Don't. Just *don't* apologize. I don't think I can handle it right now."

"Bryce, I think that I should move out. Not far from here, close enough for you to have access to Kayla. You'll still have her when I'm at school of course, and she could have a sleepover here at least once a week. I've been thinking about it . . ."

"Clearly."

". . . and it's a workable solution," she continued, ignoring his sarcastic little interruption. "One that would suit our lifestyles."

"And how can you afford a place of your own on the salary you're earning?" He looked shell-shocked by her words, but Bronwyn refused to allow her resolve to weaken. Theresa's vehement words the night before had made her think that maybe she *did* deserve something more than this warped arrangement that he had suggested.

"Well, you'll have to pay for it," she told him resolutely, and his eyes narrowed. "You will pay for my new place, my studies, and child support. I think that it's the least you can do. I don't want hundreds of thousands or half of your company or any other kind of payday, but it would be stupid of me not to ask for your support until after I've finished my studies."

"I don't want you to move out," he said grimly.

"I know, but if I don't move out, we'll keep repeating the same cycle. I don't *want* to want you, Bryce. But I do, and if I stay here we *will* wind up in bed together again and that'll be a huge step backward for us. For me."

"Bronwyn, what will it take to convince you that I don't want to lose you, or Kayla? That I honestly want to save our marriage?"

"Bryce, there's nothing left to save," she said with a bitter smile. "Yes, I'm physically attracted to you, but we can't base a marriage on that alone."

"That's all you feel for me? Physical attraction?" he asked hoarsely.

"Yes," she lied, happy that the sunglasses hid her eyes from him.

"What about Kayla?" he asked.

"Kayla will be fine; we'll *all* be fine, Bryce."

"Bronwyn." His voice dropped to an urgent whisper, rife with despair. "Please, don't do this. Give us a chance. I know that I've done horrible things and behaved reprehensibly, but . . ." She held up her hands, hating to see him beg and knowing that if she allowed it to continue, she would cave.

"Bryce, you've hurt me and I'm finding it . . . a little difficult to move on from that." She removed her sunglasses, grimacing a bit as the bright light burned into her retinas, but she wanted him to see the truth in her eyes. "I'm trying to forgive you, but I'm only human, and the mistakes you made were enormous. Try seeing it from my point of view. Try to imagine how it felt to be so completely rejected for getting pregnant. Imagine how lost I felt when you didn't call, when you refused to take my calls, when you seemed to reject me at every turn." He opened his mouth to say something but after a quick, painful breath closed it again, and he allowed her to speak. "You've made some cruel comments about the clothes and toys Kayla had when you found us again. But every single cent I made went into keeping her clean, clothed, fed, happy, and healthy. It was a huge responsibility that I had to bear by myself. You weren't there, Bryce. It was just me and I had to make the best I could of our situation.

"And then, when you found us again, you behaved like *you* were the wronged one! Your deafness was somehow *my* fault and I had 'abandoned' you at the scene of an accident." She could hear the stark bitterness in her own voice and knew that it had to be visible in her eyes and on her face. She was still so very *furious* at the unjustness of those particular indictments. "Do you not see how unforgivable those accusations were? How insurmountable these problems are? And now *you* want us to be a family, *you* don't want a divorce, and you expect me to somehow be grateful for that? You expect me to forget all the pain you've inflicted? Well, I can't do it, Bryce. I wish I could, but since I have no idea what set you off in the first place, how on earth am I supposed to trust you not to go off the deep end again? What if I inadvertently trigger your rejection button again? I can't live with the uncertainty. I don't want to and I refuse to allow my daughter to experience the same pain and confusion.

"I know I've said it before, but I'm also heartily sick of your secretiveness, Bryce. This situation has made me recognize how much you've kept from me. You're completely closed off and that's not something that's only recently developed. I've come to discover that you've always kept things from me and I don't even *care* what those secrets are anymore."

It was a long speech and it had been difficult to maintain her focus and keep facing him so that he could catch all of it. She had tried to intersperse it with as much sign language as she could, but she still couldn't be sure that he had caught all of it. The hangover headache had quite happily invited a tension headache to join the wild party in her brain, and the pain was becoming almost unbearable.

"I was trying to protect you," he confessed after a long silence, and Bronwyn cast an eye over to her daughter, who was starting to watch her parents with a worried frown, not as oblivious to the tension as they had hoped. Bronwyn cast a reassuring smile at Kayla. Not quite sure what to make of that last statement.

"You and the baby," he said. "I wanted to protect you."

"Protect us from *what*, Bryce?" she asked, combining the spoken words with broken sign language to convey her frustration. Every little bit that he so begrudgingly revealed made her recognize how very much he was still keeping hidden from her. She'd seen only the very tip of this iceberg, and she was astounded by her own former ignorance. How had she never recognized the magnitude of this problem? She had been so blinded by her love and happiness that she'd never known what an unhappy and troubled man her husband was. She had been so naïve and stupid.

"From what?" she asked again, and he shook his head helplessly. "Why did you react that way to the news of my pregnancy?"

He sighed deeply and the sound seemed torn from the depths of his chest. His eyes were stark with unhappiness and fear. He shook his head again before pushing himself up and dropping a kiss on top Kayla's head. The little girl managed to smear some scrambled eggs across his cheek but he didn't seem to notice as he straightened up to look at Bronwyn again. The naked vulnerability on his face tore at her heart and she bit the inside of her cheek to prevent herself from blurting out something stupid. Something like she loved him or that she would stay. She felt like she would do anything to wipe that look of utter isolation and agony from his eyes.

"I'll get my assistant to look into viable homes for you. Once we've compiled a list of possibilities, you can decide which one suits you best." He turned and walked out of the room, leaving Bronwyn feeling wrung out and deflated by the hollow victory.

Bryce waited until he was safely back behind the closed door of his study before bending at the waist and inhaling deeply as the consequences of his promise hit him like a freight train. She was going to leave him and he was going to let her because she deserved her freedom, because it was cruel to saddle a vibrant and affectionate woman like her with an emotionally crippled husband, and most importantly because he still didn't know how to explain his actions on that long-ago night.

~

A *baby*, Jesus God, he had thought. He wasn't ready to be a father! He would be terrible at it. He would be like his *own* father—abusive, mean, and absent in both heart and soul. He couldn't have a child yet, not until Bronwyn healed him some more. Over the last couple of years, she had been a balm to his restless and damaged spirit. In time, her gentle calm and kindness would have spread to him, would have seeped into his soul and made him the kind of man that he longed to be. He would have been ready to be a father then and responsible for a brand-new life. And yet she was pregnant *now* . . . she had his baby inside of her at this very moment. His breath hitched on a sob as he saw her in his mind's eye, getting rounder, softer, her breasts growing full and heavy with milk. He saw her giving birth, saw their baby: angry, red, naked, and crying and loved it with all his heart. He wanted that life with his entire being.

Not just the two of them but the *three* of them: A family.

Yes, he wanted that life badly, and with Bronwyn by his side, he was almost certain that he could have it. He wasn't his father. He had practically raised Rick without harming a hair on his head, so why would he be any different with his own children? God, Bron probably hated him so much right now, but he would try to explain it to her. Maybe he could *finally* tell her about his father and she would understand. She wouldn't think he was a monster just because one had sired him. She would forgive him. She *had* to. Surely she loved him enough to forgive him?

He was already back on his feet and ready to go talk to her when he heard the engine of her BMW roar to life, followed by the unmistakable sound of tires squealing in the driveway. His stomach clenched and his heart just about stopped.

"No . . . nonononononono . . ." The litany sounded like a prayer as he lurched from the room. He heard a screech as she battled with the clutch and then the throaty purr as the car obeyed her commands and sprang to life. He was just out of the front door when the car went hurtling out of the driveway. "God, please . . ." he begged as he turned back and palmed his own set of keys from the table in the hall before diving for the Maserati that he had left parked in the front. She wasn't a good driver, and she usually battled with the curves on the steep, winding road. He followed her at a distance, careful not to spook her; he could see her taillights a few bends down and knew he would be able to catch up to her in his faster car. He only prayed that she didn't misjudge a curve and get hurt. God, he would die if she were injured or if the baby got hurt. She would *never* forgive him if anything happened to the baby, would never believe that he wanted it as much as she did but had just been too damned cowardly to admit it. He wanted them safe. He wanted them with him. He would give anything in the world to take back the last half an hour. He was petrified that when he managed to catch up with her, she wouldn't want him anymore, wouldn't *love* him anymore!

He couldn't live without her love. All that stupid overwhelming tenderness he had told himself he felt for her, how the hell had he not recognized it for what it was? The road was leveling out when it happened—a young couple, hand in hand, stepped into his path. They were so absorbed in each other that they didn't see him coming. He swerved to avoid them and went off the road. He had just enough time to feel gratitude that he had left the steep curves behind him before the car flipped and rolled several times. He was briefly aware of feeling excruciating pain everywhere, and his last thoughts before he passed out were regret that he might never see his baby and absolute terror that he might never hold Bronwyn again.

When next he opened his eyes, it was to profound silence. He gradually came to understand that he was hanging upside down and held suspended by his seat belt. He blinked at the gathering crowd outside the car and the first face he saw clearly was hers. He smiled, relieved that she had come back but puzzled by the complete lack of emotion on her face.

"Bronwyn." He felt his lips form the word but couldn't hear it. It was incredibly quiet; he hadn't expected an accident scene to be this deathly silent. He tried again, called her name, and felt his throat tighten and hoarsen as he kept calling and calling without once uttering a sound. She didn't move, she merely watched him, and he went cold with dread. She *hated* him.

God, he had known that she would eventually hate him . . . he had *always* known it. He had spent the past two years waiting for her to fall out of love with him. He wasn't good enough for her love. Some part of him had always known that the son of a monster didn't deserve such a glorious creature's love.

Still, he begged and pleaded with her to come to him. God, she was so lovely, he adored her in that dress, he always had. But she had ignored him. She had turned around, walked away, and left him in pain and in silence.

~

Five days after Bronwyn's devastating announcement, Kayla was sitting in a patch of late autumn sunshine in the conservatory with her daddy and happily playing house with her dolls and tea sets. She was dressed in a pink princess costume and those ubiquitous red sneakers that she so loved. Bryce had brought his laptop upstairs and was sitting on the heated tile floor next to her, enjoying the sunshine as he read and replied to his most urgent e-mails. He stopped occasionally to take a sip of imaginary tea from a dainty plastic cup, smacking his lips every time, which inevitably sent his daughter into paroxysms of giggles. He loved watching her laugh. She looked exactly like her mother when she laughed so unreservedly. Bronwyn used to laugh like that; she'd put her entire body into it as the laughter worked its way out from her belly. He couldn't remember the last time she had laughed like that and felt a pang of regret at the loss. It had always been such a joy to see and hear her laughing, and he often wondered if Kayla's laughter sounded anything like her mother's.

He watched Kayla play and contemplated his previous fears that he would hurt her the way his father had hurt him. The thought of anybody, including himself, harming her in any way was repellent and raised every protective instinct he had. Something that had once seemed so inevitable had become a complete nonevent. He hadn't expected to trust himself around her, had thought that he would need constant supervision, someone to keep an eye on him and make sure he didn't hurt her. But from the moment he had first laid eyes on her all he had wanted was to spend time with her, get to know her, spoil her, and love her.

She amused him, baffled him at times, and even angered him on the odd occasion, but the only time he had physically hurt her had been by accident. It was an incident that still weighed heavily on his mind because of his reprehensible behavior toward Bronwyn afterward. He sighed heavily. Kayla toddled over to wrap her arms around his throat and plant a moist kiss on his cheek.

"Daddy sad." She had learned to speak to him only when he was facing her, and he saw her sweet words clearly.

"No, baby, I'm happy to be with you," he reassured her, and she smiled brightly.

Love Daddy, she signed clumsily, and his heart simply melted. He kept it together as he signed *I love you* back at her. That satisfied her, and she went back to her dolls. Bryce swallowed the lump in his throat and blinked the scorching moisture from his eyes. It had been two weeks since Bronwyn had told him that she wanted to move out, and tomorrow he would be taking her to look at the flats that he had personally selected. The divorce papers had been delivered earlier in the week, and he had shoved them into one of his desk drawers rather than put his signature on them. He knew that he was running from the inevitable, but he felt such an overwhelming sense of panic every time he thought about those papers that he often found himself on the verge of hyperventilating. He could feel the panic rising even now and set aside his laptop to focus on Kayla, hoping to tamp down the anxiety.

∼

Bronwyn walked into the conservatory, where Celeste had told her she would find Kayla and Bryce and froze in surprise at the sight that met her eyes when she entered the room. Bryce was sitting quietly while Kayla bustled around him, draping him in material. Bronwyn recognized the burnt orange throw from the sofa, the shell pink pashmina that she had left on one of the chairs the night before, a couple of bright-red curtain cords, and a couple of frilly doilies that Bronwyn had stowed away ages ago. The pashmina was draped over his shoulders, the throw over his lap, the doilies adorned his shoulders, and the cords were decorating his wrists like bracelets. Kayla took a step back and tilted her head contemplatively before nodding. She reached for her shiny plastic tiara and with the matching clip-on earrings and placed them on his head and ears.

"How do I look?" she heard Bryce rumble from beneath the elaborate draping, and for a moment Bronwyn thought the question was aimed at her before she realized that he hadn't seen her yet. It was Kayla's opinion that he sought.

"Pwetty," the little girl replied, her curls bouncing with her assertive nod.

"So, can I have some tea now?"

"Of course." The little girl sounded so adult that Bronwyn bit back a giggle, unutterably charmed by the scene in front of her. She proceeded to pour her imaginary tea into a plastic cup and balanced it on a matching saucer before handing it to her father. She followed it up with a bigger plate of very real biscuits. Bryce made appreciative sounds as he munched and "sipped" and Kayla imitated him, chatting in her mostly unintelligible language all the while.

Bronwyn stepped farther into the room, startling both of them simultaneously. Kayla hurled herself at her mother for a hug, and Bryce tugged at one of the clip-on earrings in embarrassment, going bright red at being caught playing dress-up. He gave up with a sheepish shrug when he saw Bronwyn's amused smile, and a reluctant grin tugged at his lips.

"You're early," he pointed out, and Bronwyn jiggled Kayla on her hip, bussing the little girl's cheek before responding.

"We had some plumbing issues and had to close shop early. It may take a few days to sort out. So I may not be working on Monday either if they don't fix the problem over the weekend." She kicked off her shoes and let Kayla down when the little girl wriggled impatiently. Bronwyn sank down on the floor beside Bryce while Kayla fixed the earring he had tried to remove earlier.

"Daddy pwetty," Kayla announced proudly as she tugged a doily back in place on one of her father's broad shoulders before dropping down into his lap and resting her head on the same shoulder she had just redecorated. Her thumb immediately went into her mouth.

"*Very* pretty," Bronwyn agreed with a smirk, and Bryce rolled his eyes.

"We're princesses," he explained, and she laughed.

"Very fetching," she complimented. Kayla repeated the word "fetching" around her thumb before pointing to the plate of biscuits with her free hand. Bryce reached for the plate and held it up to Bronwyn, who picked up a chocolate chip biscuit with a smile.

"I'd *love* some tea," Bronwyn prompted, and when Kayla lifted her head to give him a pointed look, he sighed and "poured" a cup of tea. The cup looked ridiculously tiny in his hand as he daintily held it up.

"Thank you." Bronwyn nodded politely as she accepted the offering. "So this is what you do every day?"

He snorted and nodded toward the closed laptop on the floor beside him.

"I *was* trying to get some work done, but this was just so much more diverting," he confessed with a charming grin.

"You were always so easily distracted from work," she reminisced. "Like the time you flew me to Mauritius for a long weekend, completely forgetting about that important conference call you had on the Monday."

"I have no regrets." He shrugged. "That was a hell of a weekend." They had spent most of it naked on a private beach.

"Pierre was furious with you," she recalled.

"He got over it. Besides, we were newlyweds, he understood."

"We'd been married for more than a year," she corrected.

"Your point being?"

"Do you remember that street performer who followed us from the marketplace back to the hotel?" she asked, and his eyes lit up with laughter at the memory.

"He wouldn't stop his horrendous serenading the entire walk back."

"You begged him to stop, bribed him, and offered to put his unborn children through university," she said, giggling.

"I don't think he understood my high-school French," Bryce laughed.

"He was awful!" they both said in unison before lapsing into an awkward silence.

"We had *some* good times, didn't we?" he asked after a few minutes.

"The best times," she agreed.

"Don't you think . . ."

"Bryce." She stopped what he'd been about to say with a slight shake of her head, and his voice faded. He cleared his throat, shifting the weight of his now-dozing daughter until she rested more comfortably against his chest.

"So, you're free tomorrow?"

She nodded in answer to his question.

"Well, I've selected a few flats for you to view tomorrow. I'll shift the appointments to the morning, so you can have the afternoon free."

"Thank you." There was really nothing more to be said after that.

Of course, each place he drove her to was more extravagant than the next. Accommodation in Camps Bay didn't come cheaply, and judging by the sizes of the so-called townhouses he took her to, none of the places would range anywhere under eight figures. Since they were remaining in the area, he'd told Cal that he wouldn't be needed, and for the first time the family found themselves completely alone. It was an almost novel sensation for Bronwyn, who had gotten so used to the silent, hovering presence of the security guys that she felt inordinately exposed without them at first. But she soon got caught up in the whole flat-hunting experience

"Bryce," she finally spoke up when she found herself standing in the living room of the third mini mansion he had taken her to. "These places are all much too big."

He frowned at that and shook his head.

"I chose them because they all have both ocean and mountain views," he explained quietly. "I know how much you love both. And this one has a patio and garden. You enjoy gardening. You haven't had much time for it recently, but at least you'll have the option. The next place on the list has a garden *and* a secure playground for Kayla. The pool is fenced in and there is ample room for a pet if you ever decide to get that dog you've always wanted." She hadn't known that he had personally researched every place that he was showing her. She had assumed that he would pass the task off onto his assistant, but the level of care and consideration he'd put into this task, despite his clear reluctance to have them move out, was touching. She didn't know what to say and swallowed heavily before turning away to shakily caution Kayla not to run too fast as the little girl careened from empty room to room.

"The master bedroom will get the sunrise in the morning," he continued after clearing his throat awkwardly. "And the living room gets the sunset. I thought you'd like that."

"You didn't have to go to so much trouble, Bryce. I know that you don't want us to leave. I didn't expect you to put so much work into this."

"If you really have to leave me again, Bron, I want to know that you're safe, happy, and well taken care of. This is the only way I know to ensure that." She bit her lip uncertainly and he rewarded her with a grim smile before showing her the rest of the spectacular flat. By the time twelve o'clock rolled by, he'd shown her seven places, each one less than five minutes' drive away from his house. He clearly meant to keep them close by.

"I chose this one because I thought you'd like this," he told her as he led her to the second floor of the last place. It was an enormous duplex with panoramic views, a garden, a huge kitchen, four rooms, three and a half bathrooms, and a second-floor balcony that opened up from the main bedroom and overlooked the ocean.

He opened a door on the second floor and stood aside to let her enter, and Bronwyn's breath was sucked out of her body at the emotional sucker punch he'd just dealt her. It was a small, beautiful conservatory. Two walls and half of the ceiling were made entirely of glass, one side facing the ocean and the other the mountain. It was absolutely beautiful. Her eyes flooded with tears as she realized that Bryce had chosen this place because he knew how much she would miss their conservatory when she moved out of the house.

"Do you like it?" he asked, standing behind her as she automatically walked toward the window overlooking the aquamarine ocean.

"It's beautiful," she whispered hoarsely, blinking back tears, before realizing that he couldn't see her lips. She nodded, keeping her back to him.

"I knew you would." His voice sounded empty and she turned to see him reach for his cell phone and tap out a message to someone. Once he'd completed it, he looked up at her with shadowed eyes.

"I've contacted the estate agent to let her know that I'll be making an offer on this place."

"But . . ."

"It has a garden, views, a fully equipped kitchen, a fenced-in pool, it's close to the stores and schools, and of course you'll have your own security detail. It also has this . . ." He indicated one of the floor-to-ceiling glass walls. "It's perfect for you."

She nodded miserably, watching Kayla tug at her father's trouser leg as she tried to show him something that she had spotted through the window. Bryce looked down at his daughter before dutifully following her as she tugged him toward whatever had caught her attention. Bronwyn furtively swiped at a few errant tears and moved over to join them at the window. Her heart, already irretrievably broken, had just crumbled into a million tiny shards and the sharp little fragments were tearing her apart.

"Ready to go?" he asked after a few minutes of fawning over Kayla, and she nodded when he looked up at her. He hoisted Kayla up onto his hip and rested his free hand in the small of Bronwyn's back as he guided her ahead of him.

She expected him to drive them directly back to the house but instead he detoured down to the beachside restaurants that dotted the Camps Bay coastline, stopping outside one of the smaller places. Bronwyn gasped when she recognized it and her eyes flew to his profile. Why was he bringing her here?

"I thought we could grab some lunch," he explained, throwing her an enigmatic look before unbuckling his seat belt and climbing out of the safe-as-houses Audi that he now preferred driving.

He rounded the bonnet of the car and held the passenger door open for her. She unbuckled her own belt and reluctantly got out of the car. He had Kayla out of her car seat before Bronwyn could react, and he once again placed his hand in the small of her back in order to gently steer her toward the familiar restaurant.

"Bryce." She resisted and looked up at him with pleading eyes. "I don't want to eat here."

"I've already made a reservation and every other place will be packed at lunchtime on a Saturday. Besides, Kayla will get cranky if she doesn't get her lunch soon." Bronwyn cast a skeptical eye over her brightly smiling daughter, who was happily hugging Broccoli, her well-worn green-haired little ragdoll.

"Are you hungry, Kayla?" he asked, and Kayla nodded sunnily.

"Hungwy," she replied, and Bronwyn, realizing that she was outnumbered, bit back any further protests and reluctantly entered the restaurant where she had first laid eyes on him so long ago.

CHAPTER FOURTEEN

The restaurant was the same as she remembered it. Of course, the staff was different but the menu and décor—but for a few small changes here and there—transported her back to a less complicated time. Bryce whispered something into their server's ear and sure enough, they were led to the same table that he had been seated at on that first day. A high chair was promptly provided for Kayla, and after taking their drink orders, the server bustled off and left them to stare silently at each other. Kayla was excited by the new surroundings and picked up her toy cell phone to tell her cousin "Wees" about it.

"Why did you bring us here?" Bronwyn broke the silence with a defeated little sigh, and he shrugged.

"I was feeling nostalgic." No. This had definitely been a deliberate decision that had very little to do with nostalgia. When he had agreed to her moving out, she had thought that he was beginning to accept her decision to get a divorce. This move, however, seemed to be the opening salvo of a counterattack.

The server returned with their drinks and for their meal orders. Neither of them had even glanced at the menu, but Bronwyn knew it by heart and ordered steamed chicken and vegetables for Kayla and chicken Marsala with mashed potatoes for herself. Bryce kept his eyes pinned to hers as he directed his order to the hovering server.

"I'll have the milkshake. Chocolate. And the Brie and bacon burger." The young man, clearly a much better server than she had ever been, reconfirmed their orders before leaving.

"Bryce, I'm not sure what you're hoping to achieve here but . . ."

"You were standing over at that table when I first saw you." He pointed toward a nearby table and she blinked over at it. "You had this look of utter panic on your face. I'd been to this restaurant several times before and knew that if you were serving at that table, then you were probably working this whole section. That's why I requested this table."

"You *requested* this table?" She gaped at him in disbelief, absently picking up Kayla's bright-pink toy phone when she dropped it on the table and handing it back to her so that she could continue her make-believe conversation. Bronwyn had always assumed that he'd been placed at one of her tables by chance.

"I did. I noticed you almost immediately and then simply couldn't look away." Yes, she remembered that disturbingly intense stare. She'd been even more of a klutz as a result of it. "I was riveted, charmed, confused, and *fascinated*. Unequivocally and helplessly fascinated." He gazed off into the distance, lost in his memories. The harsh lines of his face had softened, and a sweet, wistful smile flirted with the corners of his lips.

"I barely heard a word Pierre said and categorically dominated your time by calling you over for the smallest little thing," he recalled.

"I didn't mind," she confessed, allowing the sweetness of the memory to claim her as well. "I was equally fascinated. I barely remembered that poor Pierre was there half of the time."

"You were the most entrancing thing I'd ever seen," he said, his voice gruff, and she shook her head dismissively.

"Hardly."

"You *still* are, Bronwyn." He brushed aside her automatic

protest. "You're not some boring, conventional beauty, true. And yeah, you tend to be a little clumsy at times. But you're unusual, interesting, and to *me* you're just so indescribably gorgeous. I never thought that I deserved you. You were too good for the likes of me." She didn't understand that sentiment at all. He was heartbreakingly handsome and she was painfully plain. He came from a background of wealth and privilege while her family had been as poor as church mice. He had been Oxford educated with a master's degree in business while she had barely made it through high school. It had been a classic Cinderella tale, and Bronwyn had been the one to feel inadequate when compared to him.

"I should have left you alone," he was saying, his low voice alive with misery and his eyes filled with such profound sadness that Bronwyn felt her eyes tearing up in response. "I *tried* to leave you alone after that day, but I just couldn't stay away from you. I had to see you again. You were so sweet and gentle and every time I was with you . . . I felt . . ." His voice had gone so quiet that she could barely hear him, and the last word was almost silent, but she could have sworn he said *cleansed*. He'd felt *cleansed* when he was with her? It was such an odd choice of words that she knew she must have been mistaken, but what else could it have been?

His voice had faded away completely now and he wasn't speaking anymore, merely staring down at the place setting in front of him. His large hands were curled into fists on the tabletop, and Bronwyn reached over to cover them with her own hands. The gesture brought his eyes back up to hers and she was startled see *moisture* sparkling in them.

"I should have stayed away from you," he repeated. "But I couldn't. I *can't*. You're my light, Bronwyn. You're my love. I'm so lost without you. I've always been so *lost* without you."

"Bryce."

He shook himself and glanced over at their perceptive daughter, who had stopped playing and was watching them with wide and worried eyes. She looked on the verge of tears.

"I'm sorry. I shouldn't have started this conversation with Kayla around." He forced a smile for the little girl's sake and dragged his hands out from under hers. She watched as he brusquely wiped at his eyes and put on a cheerful front for their daughter.

She kept stealing glances at him, wondering at the unfamiliar man that he'd allowed her to catch a glimpse of today. That was what she had wanted—*demanded*—from him. Honesty. And he had just given her a huge chunk of honesty. But whatever his truth was, she now knew that it was devastating, and she was certain that whatever it was had been responsible for his painful reaction to her pregnancy. Some truly awful thoughts were starting to form in the back of her mind, but her suspicions were so ugly that she forced them back down and dismissed them as impossible.

She watched as he gently teased and played with their daughter and forced herself to remember the day that she'd told him about her pregnancy. He had reacted in a near-violent explosion of emotions, accusations, and . . . fear. She recalled the look in his eyes and now understood that he had been absolutely *terrified* by her news. She was completely staggered by this unexpected new insight into the confusing events of that night.

"Protect us from what?" she asked, but he was playing with Kayla and didn't see her question. She waved her hand to get his attention, and he blinked up at her, his too-long hair flopping over one eye in the process. That errant lock of hair made him look so boyish and vulnerable that she felt a lump forming in her throat. She unthinkingly reached over and brushed the hair out of his eyes with gentle fingers. He leaned into her touch, but she withdrew her hand almost immediately.

"A couple of weeks ago you said that you wanted to protect us from something." She went back to what was foremost on her mind, absently rubbing her fingers—still tingling from the brief contact with his skin—on her denim-clad thigh. "Protect us from what?" He sighed harshly.

"Let's talk about this when we get home. I was stupid to think this could be the place for that discussion," he deflected cryptically, and her brow furrowed in frustration. She was sick of the diversions and delays. The conversations that started but never seemed to finish. She picked at her food after it arrived and made sure that Kayla ate hers with as little mess as possible. The little glances she sent Bryce's way revealed that he was merely toying with his food as well.

"Do you remember our first date?" he asked her, and she smiled at the memory.

"How could I forget?" she said, recalling. "You showed up here at the end of my shift, asked me out, and spent the rest of the evening lecturing me about crime and safety."

He snorted.

"We *also* talked for hours about our favorite movies, music, and books," he reminded.

"Yes. And all the time you kept staring at my mouth." She hadn't meant to say that, and when his gaze—which had already been fixed on her mouth—went blistering hot at her words, her breath quickened and the residual tingling in her fingertips spread like wildfire through her body before gathering in the sensitized tips of her breasts. Her bra felt uncomfortably tight, and she could feel the blood slowly inching into her cheeks.

"You wouldn't believe the fantasies I was weaving around that mouth," he said absently, licking his lips as if he could taste said mouth on his tongue. "And those mile-high legs of yours. God, I could picture them wrapped around my waist or thrown over my shoulders . . ." Both scenarios had come to fruition the first time he'd gotten her into bed.

Her breathing quickened even more as she remembered that particular night—he had been insatiable and so very creative. God, she missed him in her bed . . . in her body. She shook herself, tossing a guilty glance at her daughter, who now had her toy phone pushed up against the side of Broccoli's head so that the doll could "speak" to Rhys as well. The girl caught her eye and smiled.

"Firsty, Mummy . . ." Bronwyn sneaked a little peek over at Bryce and could see that his own cheeks had gone a dull red, his pupils were dilated, and his breathing was labored. She recognized the signs of his arousal immediately and knew from the way he shifted in his seat that his jeans were getting a little snug in the crotch area. God, this wasn't helping their cause. She had to control herself. She couldn't seem to keep her hands off him for the most part, and it wasn't doing either of them any good. She looked away from him, trying very hard to ignore what was happening to both of them, and smiled down at her daughter, who was starting to look a little grumpy at being ignored.

"Okay, sweetie," she placated. "Do you want water or some juice?"

"Duce," Kayla demanded, and glared defiantly back when Bronwyn leveled a reprimanding stare at her. Her rebellious lower lip started quivering before she sighed dramatically and gave in. "Peese. Duce peese."

"Good girl." Bryce, who seemed to have gotten a modicum of control over his body, praised her in a hoarse voice. He flagged the server over and nodded at Kayla. When she understood what her father wanted her to do, her tiny chest puffed up with pride, and she smiled winningly up at the younger man.

"Duce peese."

The server grinned.

"Orange or apple?" He wisely gave her only two choices, and she opted for the apple.

When the man trotted away, Bryce looked meaningfully over at Bronwyn.

"You know that I'm as hard as a steel pipe for you right now, don't you?"

"*Bryce*," she squeaked, tossing a scandalized look over at Kayla. The little girl was oblivious to them and craning her neck to see where her new friend—the server—had gone.

"And it's always been that way between us. From the very beginning," he pointed out, ignoring her shock. "That's another thing I never told you. While I was riveted, charmed, fascinated, and all of that, I was also turned on beyond belief. Aside from not wanting to leave when Pierre did, my body didn't give me much choice in the matter. I was pretty much incapable of standing upright without shocking every damned person in here that day. Every time I thought I had it under control, you'd smile or something and I'd go to instant attention again. I had a terminal case of wood for most of the first year of our marriage as you know . . . but in those first few months it was damned near impossible to control. I was like a horny teenager with you."

"I never quite understood what you saw in me," she admitted on a whisper, and he sighed quietly.

"Bronwyn, I don't know how much clearer I can make this, so listen up. To me . . . You. Are. Stunning. Sometimes I can't stare at you for too long because it almost physically hurts me to look at you. It's crazy, my chest tightens and burns to the point of actual pain until I remind myself to breathe." He smiled bittersweetly. "That has happened more often than I care to reveal. You're so lovely that something as fundamental as breathing becomes damned near impossible around you."

She searched his harsh face for any sign of deception, but his strong jaw was clenched, his eyes almost hard, and she knew that it couldn't have been easy for him to reveal that particular tidbit to her. She really affected him that strongly.

"You've stolen my breath on numerous occasions too, you know," she confessed, reaching over to stroke his jaw. The server chose that moment to return with Kayla's apple juice, and Bronwyn's hand dropped down to the table, where she started toying with her dessert spoon.

She thanked the server for the juice and reached into the baby bag for Kayla's sippy cup. After transferring the juice from the glass into the cup, she screwed the top on tightly and gave it to Kayla, who was not very happy about having the grown-up glass confiscated.

She refused to take her juice from the sippy cup, and Bronwyn gave her a sip of the leftover juice in the glass. She refused again and tried to take the glass from her mother. When Bronwyn moved the glass a safe distance away from her, she started kicking up a fuss. She was showing all the telltale signs of a toddler in desperate need of a nap and on the verge of a tantrum. Bronwyn had only to glance over at Bryce before he summoned the server over for the bill. Their conversation was put on immediate hold as their parental roles took precedence.

They packed up and left the restaurant pretty quickly, and as he drove them home, with a crying Kayla strapped into her car seat, Bronwyn felt a pang of regret over yet another unfinished conversation.

～

Bryce found Bronwyn in the conservatory a few hours later, sitting on the sofa with her legs tucked beneath her and a glass of wine in her hand. She was staring pensively out as the sun dropped gracefully into the ocean and set the horizon on fire. It was a beautiful sunset, but if Bronwyn's somber face was anything to go by, she wasn't fully appreciating the sun's last hurrah as it fled from the night. She was running one elegant finger round and round the rim of her wineglass, her restlessness betrayed by the swift, repetitive movement.

Bryce glanced down at the sheaf of papers he held in his hand and shut his eyes as he sent an uncharacteristic and desperate prayer to a God he hadn't really acknowledged since he was a boy. He was all out of options here. He had no choice but to give her what she wanted.

"Bronwyn," he murmured, and she jumped, nearly spilling the wine. She blinked up at him as if surprised to see him standing there. She self-consciously tucked an errant strand of brown hair behind her ear.

"Bryce, you startled me." He sat down next to her and turned to face her.

"Sorry about that," he apologized. "I just wanted to give you these." He handed over half of the papers he was holding, and she put the glass onto a side table to take hold of the documents. She stared blankly down at the big, bold words at the top of the first sheet.

"That was fast," she murmured. He reached over and angled her jaw upward, and she realized that he hadn't been able to read her lips. She repeated the three words, keeping her face determinedly neutral.

"I had them drawn up last week. I gambled on the fact that I knew you well enough to guess which place you'd go for."

"Why bother showing me the other places then?" she asked, and Bryce shrugged. Yes, he'd been confident she would go for the last place, but he had wanted her to have choices and . . . he had wanted to spend time with her.

His first instinct was to cling to his reticence, but all her accusations of secrecy were valid. He *had* kept things from her—important things that would probably have made a big difference to their marriage. But if he wanted any kind of future with her, he would have to let go of his fear of appearing weak and vulnerable in her eyes and keep her "in the loop," so to speak. And if that meant keeping her up to date on the minutia of his every fleeting thought, then so be it.

"I wanted the choice to be yours. You may have hated that last one. I didn't want to presume too much."

"And yet you went ahead and drew up the necessary paperwork?" she asked with an incredulous little shake of her head.

"I like to be prepared," he muttered, abashed. "All you have to do is sign these and the flat will be yours. Finances have been taken care of." *Naturally.*

"Still you could have taken me to three or four places instead of eight."

He sighed and bit the bullet.

"I also wanted to spend some time with you and Kayla," he confessed. He could see the shock in her eyes and wondered if it was a result of his words or the fact that he'd actually said them out loud. He watched her luscious lips form an *o* and took a deep breath before rushing in to the next bit of this ordeal.

"I wanted to spend some time with you before I gave you these," he said, holding out a second sheaf of papers. He had a moment's hesitation when she reached for them and tightened his grip when she tried to take them. After a brief tug of war, he reluctantly released the papers and stepped back. He tried to gauge her reaction, but her usually open face had closed up and revealed not a single emotion as she read the top of the first page. He was breathing in uneven gasps, and he counted slowly to twenty, then thirty, as he tried to regulate his breathing.

She looked up at him and the impact of her devastated gaze hit him like a two-ton truck. She said nothing for the longest time, and when she spoke her words nearly sent him to his knees in agony.

Thank you, she signed.

Bryce nodded before turning and walking away.

∾

Bronwyn stared at the signed divorce decree in her hands for the longest time and now understood that the restaurant hadn't been a counterattack, it had been a farewell. For an endless age shock kept her numb, but by agonizingly slow degrees feeling returned. She felt . . . raw. Her entire body felt like an open, festering wound. She sat perfectly still, afraid to move because even the simple act of blinking was *excruciating*. When she allowed herself the luxury of crying, it wasn't a cathartic act meant to heal. Instead the tears lodged in her throat and scalded her skin like acid.

She had gotten what she had asked for. Her marriage was over.

∾

Hours later she found herself staring at the front door of the only place she could think of to go. She rang the doorbell, and after several minutes a disheveled-looking Rick opened the door. He blinked down at her in confusion.

"Bron?"

At the sound of his voice the fragile control she'd managed to exert over her emotions shattered, and she burst into tears and launched herself into his arms. He folded her into his embrace and murmured soothing little sounds into her hair. "What's this now? Shhh, sweetheart, it's okay. It's okay." He was drawing her farther into the house. And after a few long minutes of inconsolable weeping, Bronwyn surfaced enough to take in her surroundings.

She was sitting on a sofa, curled up against Rick's bare chest, which was now slick with her tears. Lisa was sitting on her other side, patting her back comfortingly.

"I'm sorry," she whispered, her voice hoarse after her extended bout of crying. "You were asleep. I wasn't thinking of the time." They were both dressed for bed. Rick in loose pajama bottoms and Lisa in a tank top and shorts. A quick glance up at the clock on the wall told her that it was nearly midnight.

"Don't worry about it," Rick dismissed. "Tell us what happened. You didn't drive here in this state did you?"

She blinked in confusion, trying to gather her thoughts.

"No. No, of course not. Cal brought me." She vaguely recalled waking the man up and remembered the concerned glances he kept directing at her via the rear-view mirror. Lisa held up a box of tissues, and Bronwyn gratefully took one and blew her nose.

"Is Kayla okay?" Rick asked urgently.

"Yes, she's fine. She's with B-Bryce." She stumbled over his name and almost lost it again. "He signed the p-papers," she told them, and Lisa's eyes immediately went soft and sympathetic. Rick merely looked confused.

"What papers?" he asked.

"The d-divorce papers," she whispered, and Lisa hugged her fiercely.

"Aaah God." Rick sounded pained.

"I'm so sorry, Bronwyn," Lisa said.

"I thought this was what you wanted." Rick's confusion was obvious, and Bronwyn glanced up into his bewildered face.

"It's for the best," she said. "But it still hurts, Rick. It hurts so much. I never stopped loving your brother. I just can't . . . *live* with him anymore. Do you understand?"

Rick sighed and nodded slowly.

"Yeah, I get it. Bron . . ." he said gruffly. "I love you like a sister and while I failed you for a while there, I still want you to be happy. I get that you don't think you can be happy with Bryce anymore. His behavior was . . . inexplicable. But I hope you understand that I have to go and make sure that he's okay. You stay here with Lisa, all right?"

"Yes. This can't be easy on him." She was grateful that Bryce would have someone there for him. This wasn't what he had wanted. He had done it for her because he thought that it would make *her* happy. "You'll need these." She handed over her house keys and the electronic gate remote. Rick nodded and—after one last hug and kiss for Bronwyn—left the room to get dressed. He returned briefly to let them know he was leaving, and then it was just Lisa and Bronwyn. Lisa took control of the situation, shepherding Bron into the kitchen and pouring some sweet tea down her throat. Bronwyn just couldn't seem to stop the endless flow of tears.

"I didn't expect it to be this hard," Bron confessed after Lisa led her to a spare bedroom.

"I know," Lisa responded quietly. "I can't even imagine how this must feel, Bron." Bronwyn laughed half hysterically.

"I think the only one right now who has any idea how I feel is Bryce. Can you believe that? Our marriage is over and all I can think is that Bryce would understand how I'm feeling. That I can talk to him about this. It's so messed up . . . I had to leave the house before I sought him out for comfort. I'm just a walking disaster, Lisa."

⁓

After aimlessly wandering around the huge house like a lost little boy, Bryce eventually found himself standing in the nursery. That was where he discovered a modicum of peace. He dropped into a rocking chair and watched his precious daughter sleep. He didn't know how long he sat there, leaning forward with his elbows resting on his knees and his fists folded one over the other. He had his mouth pressed into his knuckles in an effort to keep from uttering the despairing cry that had been lodged in his throat since he'd handed over those papers all those hours ago.

So absorbed was he in his thoughts that he remained unaware of the third presence that had entered the room until he felt a warm hand cupping the exposed nape of his neck. He jumped, but the hand squeezed his neck reassuringly, and the familiar scent of Rick's aftershave immediately dampened his fight-or-flight instincts.

He got up and followed Rick out of the room into the well-lit den. His brother walked over to the liquor cabinet and poured a couple of whiskeys before coming back and handing a glass over to Bryce. The scene reminded him of the one weeks ago when Bronwyn had told him that she'd filed for a divorce, and he forced away the sharp stab of pain as he sat down in the same chair he had occupied that night.

They sat quietly for a while, sipping their drinks before Rick set his aside to sign something.

Bron is with Lisa. Bryce nodded an acknowledgment.

I know. Cal SMSed me and told me where he was taking her.

There was another long period where they merely sat and sipped their drinks.

You okay? Rick's concern was reflected in his gray eyes and Bryce shrugged.

No. The sign was curt.

I'm sorry, Bryce.

Why? Not your fault.

You know what I mean. Bryce sighed and nodded.

It was inevitable. I don't deserve her trust. Not after what I did.

236

Why did you react that way to her pregnancy? Rick asked, and Bryce stared at the proud and strong man sitting across from him. But all he saw was an earnest young boy with freckles on his nose and a gap-toothed grin, a boy whom Bryce had once protected with every fiber of his being. Bryce had suffered bruises, broken bones, and bloody noses for that kid and given half the chance would do so again. Their father had never touched Rick—had never gotten the chance—and as a result Rick was a well-adjusted man who had never known the evil that Bryce had grown up with.

He had never wanted Rick to know about it, had kept it from him all these years, but as he stared at his brother he acknowledged that Rick no longer needed his protection and right now Bryce needed to talk about the past.

"I thought that I'd . . . be like our father," he said aloud. Rick said nothing, merely kept his gray eyes steady on Bryce's. It gave Bryce the courage to continue. "I thought that I would be a danger to the baby, or Bron." Not by a flicker of an eyelash did Rick betray any emotion as Bryce's story came pouring out. Bryce dropped his eyes, trained his gaze on his glass, and spoke for what seemed like hours. When he risked a glance up at his brother after the words had trickled to a stop, Rick was leaning forward in his chair, with both hands clasped tightly around his glass. His skin was ashen and his eyes gleaming with suppressed emotion.

"Why didn't you tell me this before?" he asked.

"I wanted to protect you from that knowledge."

"Protecting me when I was a kid, sure . . . I get that. Protecting me now? Not so much."

"I didn't want to stain your childhood memories with the truth."

"You couldn't possibly have done that, since most of my memories involve you and the fun we had . . ." His eyes went distant, and Bryce watched his mouth form a foul word. "All those so-called sports injuries? He did that?" Bryce nodded, and Rick swore again. "*Sonofabitch!* Shit, Bryce . . . I'm so bloody sorry."

"Not your fault." Bryce shrugged.

"How many of those knocks did you take for me?"

"It's not important, and this is why I didn't want you to know. I didn't want you to blame yourself. I made a decision to protect you and I did. End of story."

"Why didn't you tell Bron about this?"

"Tell her what? That I allowed a dictatorial bastard to use me as a punching bag? That I may turn into the same dictatorial bastard and use my fists on her and Kayla someday? She's a hell of a lot better off without me." The words burned like acid but they had to be said.

"Why do you think you'd hurt Bron or Kayla?" Rick asked him, and Bryce could feel himself growling at his brother's deliberate ignorance.

"It's in my blood."

"Yeah? It's in my blood too. Think I'd ever harm a hair on Lisa's or Rhys's head?" Bryce blinked stupidly, completely thrown by Rick's question. It wasn't something that had ever occurred to him.

"Of course not."

"Why not? He was my father too." He watched Rick's chest heave as the younger man sighed heavily. "Bryce, you have to talk to a therapist about this. You have to see that you would never physically harm your wife and child."

"Ex-wife . . ." *God.*

"You have naturally protective instincts, Bryce," Rick was saying, while Bryce still reeled from the emotional impact of the words "ex" and "wife" in relation to Bronwyn. "You . . ."

"Enough," he whispered. "Enough, Rick. Please."

Rick stopped talking but he didn't make a move to leave, merely got up to refill their drinks and sat down again. He was clearly content to remain sitting for however long Bryce did. Comforted by his younger brother's stoic presence, Bryce sat immersed in his thoughts for a while longer.

CHAPTER FIFTEEN

Money certainly made life a lot easier, Bronwyn reflected as she watched the movers bring in the last of her newly acquired furniture. Relocating from Bryce's house into her new home should have taken a lot longer than it actually had, but with money to grease the wheels, packing up an old life and organizing a new one took less than two weeks.

She was moved in to her new "home" before she could blink, and all that was left was the unpacking. She tried to turn it in to an adventure for Kayla, who was being surly and uncommunicative.

"Isn't this a pretty room, Kayla?" she asked, injecting bright enthusiasm into her voice, but Kayla wasn't having any of that.

"No."

"Come on, baby, it's very pretty," Bronwyn maintained patiently. "You have a princess bed. Isn't that great?"

"No. I go home." She had only recently stopped referring to herself in the third person.

"This is our *new* home." Bronwyn smiled sunnily and Kayla glared at her, her little lip protruding rebelliously. Bronwyn felt awful to have moved her again so soon, especially since Bryce had become such an important fixture in her life.

"I want Daddy!" She stamped her foot and Bronwyn's smile slipped a bit.

"You'll see Daddy tomorrow," she explained. "Tonight we'll sleep in our new home. We can have ice cream. Do you want ice cream, sweetie?"

"No."

"Of course you do." Bronwyn couldn't help but smile a little at the stubbornness. "Chocolate ice cream. Your favorite."

"I no like ice kweem," she blatantly lied.

"Hey, Bron, where do you want this box?" Lisa was lugging a medium-size box of photos, and Bronwyn directed her toward the study. Lisa, Theresa, Bobbi, and Alice were all helping with her move and had decided to stick around for one of their Saturday ladies' nights afterward. Bronwyn welcomed the show of support and the company. She knew that they didn't want her to be alone on her first evening in the new place.

"Do you want to help me unpack your clothes?" she asked Kayla. "You can tell me where to put everything. That'll be fun."

"No."

Bronwyn sighed. She was heartsick and tired. She hadn't seen much of Bryce since the night he'd handed her the divorce papers. He had had his attorney contact hers to tell her that he would be giving her a monthly allowance to spend or not spend however she saw fit, and that he would pay to furnish the flat. Bronwyn had tried to refuse but had been told that the money had already been transferred into her bank account and what she did with it was her business. She had decided to give in gracefully and accept the generous alimony.

"Why don't you show Broccoli our new house?" she asked. Despite the mutinous set of her face, the little girl picked up her well-worn little doll—one of the few toys she still had from their life in Plettenberg Bay—and trudged off.

"You okay?" Theresa asked, coming up to stand beside Bronwyn. Bronwyn glanced over at the pretty woman and shook her head.

"Not really." Her voice wobbled slightly. "I feel like such an awful parent right now. She'd just gotten used to the other house, and here I am, uprooting her again."

"Children are resilient." Theresa put a comforting arm around her shoulder and gave her a reassuring squeeze. "You'll both be fine."

"I wish I could be so sure." Bronwyn stifled a sigh before pasting a determined smile on her face. "Still, there's no use in worrying about it right now. Too much to do."

Theresa smiled sympathetically.

"Bronwyn, it's okay to be emotional about all of this, you know? I can kind of relate to what you're going through. Sandro and I are happy now but we've had some . . . *extremely* difficult times in the past." That news surprised Bronwyn. On the few occasions that she'd seen the couple together they had seemed completely devoted to each other. It was hard to believe that they hadn't always been the perfect couple. "So anytime you need to talk, or just a shoulder to cry on, I'm there for you."

"That means a lot," Bronwyn whispered, hugging the other woman gratefully. "Thank you."

After her friends had left later that night and Bronwyn was alone with her thoughts and her sleeping daughter, she sat down in the darkened conservatory and sadly looked around the still-chaotic room. The place felt alien and a little cold. Even though she had often complained about Bryce's security team being a blatant invasion of her privacy, she felt a lot safer knowing that Paul had been assigned as the head of her security detail. The man was now in charge of the team that would take care of security for this separate household. It was comforting to know that they were just outside if she needed them. Her cell phone beeped and she dragged it out of her jeans pocket.

You settle in ok? A smiled tugged at her lips. It was from Bryce.

All good. A bit messy still.

Kayla ok?

Grumpy. She misses you.

☹ *I miss her. You too.*

She didn't know how to respond to that. She missed him like crazy but telling him that would definitely send a mixed message.

It's late. I'm off to bed. It was abrupt but she didn't want to be charmed by him. She didn't want to encourage him. They both needed to move on. No matter how painful and difficult it was for them.

Right. I'll see you 2m. G'nite.

She held the phone to her chest for a few long moments before eventually dragging herself up and to bed.

∼

The bell jingling above the shop door jarred Bronwyn from her thoughts. She'd been staring down at her notes for about half an hour without actually absorbing any information and—despite it being nearly closing time—a customer would be a welcome distraction. She put what she hoped was a bright, welcoming smile on her face as she raised her eyes. The smile immediately withered when she saw who was standing there.

Bryce met her eyes with a brief nod before walking farther into the shop. Bronwyn pushed herself halfway out of her chair and then hovered uncertainly between standing and sitting, a puzzled frown on her face. He was supposed to have Kayla today, but there was no sign of the child.

"Bryce?" He didn't see her question and continued his browsing, picking up a book here and there and reading the back-cover blurbs before replacing them on the shelves. She made her way to him and tapped him on the shoulder. He turned to face her with a polite smile on his face. Baffled by his odd behavior, she frowned and used sign language to ask him what he was doing there.

"Well, I wanted to learn how to balance my chakras." He held up a book. His smile remained bland and polite. "And I've been thinking of buying some healing crystals or something."

"Where's Kayla?" she asked worriedly.

"I had to go in to the office this afternoon for an emergency meeting and instead of dropping her off at the day-care center, I thought she'd enjoy spending some time with Rhys since it is Lisa's day off. When I swung by to pick her up a couple of hours later, she wasn't ready to stop playing. Lisa suggested I let her stay for dinner. So I found myself at loose ends and thought you might like to grab some dinner."

"I don't think . . ." God, she was tempted. But their divorce had just been finalized and it seemed like a step in the wrong direction. They had fallen into a comfortable routine over the two and a half weeks since she had moved in to her new place. She dropped Kayla off at his house after breakfast in the mornings on her way to campus, and he brought her home before dinner every night. Kayla stayed over at his house on Friday nights, and Bryce returned her to her mother late Saturday afternoons. Bronwyn had her for the remainder of the weekend. They were coolly friendly when they spoke, and those brief moments in the mornings and evenings when Kayla was handed from one parent to the other were the only times they saw each other. He sent her the occasional SMS during the day, but that was it. It had been a bit of an adjustment for all of them.

"I think we should try to be friends at least," he said. "For Kayla's sake. It's just dinner."

"It's never *just* dinner with us, Bryce," she pointed out.

"Please?" His beautiful blue eyes mutely pleaded with hers, and Bronwyn had another fleeting moment of doubt before doing what she had wanted to all along. She told herself that she was doing it for Kayla's sake—it was important for the little girl to have parents who got along—but she knew that she was lying to herself. She couldn't resist the idea of spending time alone with him. He was her weakness, and while spending more time with him wouldn't help her overcome that weakness, it certainly did a good job of keeping the part of her that craved his company satisfied. It didn't seem to matter how counterproductive it was.

"Okay," she consented, determinedly squelching the screeching protests in the back of her mind. She glanced around the empty shop. "I'll close up and we can get going."

"*Gino's?*" Bronwyn smiled radiantly up at Bryce, all the tension that had built up during the drive dissipating. She had followed Bryce's car to the tiny family-run restaurant in Green Point and had laughed out loud when she recognized the familiar route. Gino's had been her favorite restaurant back when they had first started dating. She had insisted on going Dutch in those early days and had often suggested Gino's because of its affordability. The food was good and the atmosphere warm and cozy. They had stopped coming here after their engagement, and Bronwyn had all but forgotten it existed. She was surprised that Bryce remembered it.

"I thought that you'd like it," Bryce informed, his voice quiet, before glancing over at Cal, who was hovering behind them as usual, his eagle eyes sharply assessing the streets around them. The silent signal Bryce sent his way was acknowledged with a curt nod as Cal spun on his heel and headed back to the car.

Bryce put a confident hand in the small of Bronwyn's back and led her inside the little restaurant. The place was the same as it had always been—noisy, chaotic, and filled with laughing people. A young server led them to an intimate corner in the back and handed them the well-worn leather-bound menus with a smile.

"I'll be back in a few minutes for your drink orders," she said perkily after lighting the ubiquitous candle in the center of the round table. It was pretty gloomy in their corner, and Bronwyn worried about Bryce's ability to lip-read in the bad light.

Do you need a little more light? she signed, and he shook his head.

"I can see you fine." He smiled, his eyes running over her face like a silent caress.

"Oh." She blushed, his blatantly sensual look making her feel more than a little hot under the collar. There were a few moments of silence before Bryce spoke.

"Are you enjoying the new place?" he asked.

"Of course." She said. "Kayla's still having problems sleeping at night though."

"It's confusing for her. She'll get used to the new routine soon." His smile was bittersweet. The server came back for their drink orders, and after they had ordered, Bryce refocused his attention on her. "What about you? How are you adjusting to your new lifestyle?"

"It's not that much different from life in Plett. Aside from the fact that we have money, of course, and I don't *really* have to work and I no longer worry about Kayla when I'm away from her." She laughed self-deprecatingly before shaking her head. "Okay, it's a *lot* different from our life in Plett. Anyway, I miss her, of course, but I know that she's with you and that she's safe." She was half signing every other sentence, still concerned with the lighting in the place.

"Do you?" he murmured, his eyes intent on her lips.

"Of course," she dismissed airily. "I don't know if I've said it before, Bryce, but you're great with her."

"I didn't think I would be," he admitted awkwardly, shifting uncomfortably in his seat. "Being around kids is . . . *was* way out of my comfort zone. I enjoy them but I don't always feel . . ."

He hesitated and she leaned forward intently, sensing that he was considering his next words very carefully.

"Confident around them," he completed, his voice kind of fading away on the last word. Baffled, she stared at him for a long moment before shaking her head.

"I'm not quite sure I understand what you mean when you use the word 'confident,'" she said bluntly. "Confident in your ability to take care of them, you mean?"

"That, and I don't trust myself not to lose my temper around them." Again she could see how difficult that was for him to admit, and she knew that she had to tread very carefully here.

"Kayla does like to test my patience," she said with a fond smile. "And I have lost my temper with her on a few occasions, but it's all about how you handle the situation, and quite frankly, Bryce, you're a pushover when it comes to her. She knows that she can get away with way more than she ever could with me."

The server returned with their drinks and asked if they were ready to order. They both darted guilty glances down at the menu—they hadn't even thought about food yet. Recognizing their looks, the girl laughed and promised to return in a couple of minutes. After they had taken care of the business of ordering, Bronwyn turned expectant eyes on him, waiting for him to pick up where he had left off.

Bryce took what looked like a fortifying sip of his red wine before raising his eyes to meet hers.

"You were right when you accused me of keeping stuff from you during our marriage," he said, surprising her by steering the conversation into a completely different direction. "Stuff I felt that you didn't need to know. Stuff I thought you'd see as weakness. Stuff that I was too embarrassed to tell you. I once told you that you made me feel like an all-conquering hero, that you made me feel like I could take on the world. It really was a heady feeling, Bron. I enjoyed being your 'hero,' the 'prince' who had swept you off your feet.

"I never expected to find a woman who made me feel like a hero instead of the villain I'd always believed myself to be. So, instead of telling you everything you needed to know about me, I allowed you to think that I was this *perfect* man. I spent two years trying to maintain that illusion and trying to live up to the inaccurate impression you had of me. When something went wrong at the office, I bottled it up and kept it from you. I closeted myself away to work it out alone rather than allow my frustration with whatever problem I had to spill over into our lives."

"Bryce." She was a little stunned by his revelations and tried to gather her thoughts before responding. "I never expected you to be this *perfect* heroic husband. I fell in love with a man, not a superhero."

"You didn't know the real man, Bron," he said heavily. "And that's why I had to sign those papers. I wanted to give you a chance to get to know me. Flaws and all. I wanted us to have a fresh start, to go back to the beginning. I wanted this dinner to be a new beginning for us."

"So, let me get this straight, you agreed to a divorce because you wanted us to start *dating* again?" she asked incredulously. Not quite sure she had understood him correctly.

"Basically . . . yes," he confirmed, and Bronwyn felt like the top of her head was about to blow off. She actually lifted a hand to her face, almost certain that steam was billowing from her nose and ears like she was some maddened cartoon character. Unfortunately their server chose that moment to return, and Bronwyn waited impatiently while the woman offloaded the piping-hot, aromatic bowls of pasta and crispy garlic bread onto the table in front of them. As soon as the server left, Bronwyn turned her frowning gaze back on the uncomfortable-looking man sitting across from her.

"And did you really think, after the emotional turmoil of the last few months, that I'd be on board with this scheme of yours?" she asked, trying extremely hard to rein in her temper, unable to believe the absolute arrogance of the man. "And what's this? Phase One of some big reconciliation plot?"

"There is no such thing," he said quietly. "I was just *hoping* you'd understand what motivated me."

"You wanted to start a new, honest relationship by deceiving me into coming out to dinner with you? I mean, what is this if not luring me here under false pretences? I'm not quite feeling the honesty here, Bryce," she pointed out sarcastically. He had the grace to look repentant.

"I didn't say it would be an easy habit to break, Bron," he said uneasily, and she swallowed down the irreverent giggle that wanted to burble from her lips. For some unfathomable reason, she was both irritated and oddly charmed by his flagrant presumption. She felt so many conflicting emotions that she wasn't quite sure how to approach this crazy new spanner that he had tossed into the works. Part of her wanted to move on and rebuild her life without him in it, a larger part *wanted* to know why he had such a low opinion of himself. She wanted to know why he thought he was a villain. She didn't for a second believe that the man she had fallen in love with had never existed, but it disturbed her that *he* clearly thought that. Still, they couldn't keep going around in circles like this. It wasn't doing either of them any good.

Bryce, I don't know if I can go another round with you, she signed sadly. *It's so exhausting.*

"For now, let's try to enjoy our dinner," he suggested. "Nothing more, nothing less. Just dinner. Okay?"

She hesitated for a long moment before nodding with a resigned little sigh.

"Okay. Just dinner."

The rest of the evening wasn't as strained as Bronwyn had expected it to be after that outrageous conversation. Bryce kept her entertained with his tales of Kayla's daytime antics. He didn't touch on the controversial subject of dating again, but it remained there between them, the huge elephant sitting at the table with them.

The wind was howling when they left the restaurant a couple of hours later, and a combination of rain and hail was viciously pelting down on Cal who dashed over to meet them when they paused under the eaves of the restaurant. The huge black umbrella that Cal held up over his head was being buffeted by the wind, and Bronwyn didn't have high hopes for its survival. It was mid-June and winter—which had been late in arriving—was gleefully showing off its jagged teeth. Cape Town was notorious for its terrible winter storms, and this one, which had arrived without much warning, looked like it was going to be one of the bad ones. They quickly decided that bringing Kayla home from Rick and Lisa's place in such bad weather wasn't a good idea, and they ducked back into the restaurant for a few minutes while Bronwyn called Lisa to ask if Kayla could sleep over. The other woman readily agreed with their decision and put the sleepy little girl on the line to say good night to her parents. Kayla sounded happy enough but Bronwyn was naturally worried, as Kayla had never spent a night away from either of her parents before. After a few more minutes of reassurance, Bronwyn hung up and met Bryce's concerned gaze.

"You okay?" he asked, and she nodded, blinking back the sheen of tears. Kayla's first overnight stay away from her parents was a big deal, and Bronwyn felt more than a little emotional about it.

"She'll be fine." Bryce gave her a self-conscious one-armed hug. Bronwyn was touched by his masculine awkwardness at the sight of her tears, and she gave him a wobbly smile as he led her back outside. Once again they hesitated under the eaves, where poor Cal had been left waiting.

I don't want you to drive home in this weather, he signed urgently. Bronwyn stared out at the deluge and tended to agree with him. She definitely didn't fancy driving in this downpour. The near gale-force winds didn't help matters. She bit her lip as she stared out at their cars parked by the sidewalk. Unfortunately Bryce had dismissed Paul before they'd even left the bookshop, stating that he and Cal would ensure that Bronwyn got home safely.

Cal can drive you. I'll follow, he signed authoritatively, and she shook her head. She didn't like that suggestion at all, not with Bryce being an uneasy driver himself, but she knew that protesting for that reason wouldn't sit too well with his pride.

"Bronwyn, you can't mean to argue with me on this matter," he said aloud. "I know you don't want to drive in this weather."

We can all go in your car, she decided. *Paul can pick mine up in the morning.*

He looked a little stunned by that decision but agreed quickly as if he were afraid that she would change her mind.

Cal—who was proficient in sign language and had been

following the conversation—looked relieved that they had made up their minds and ushered them toward Bryce's sleek car.

"Do you think my car will be okay here?" she asked Cal worriedly as he held the car door open for them.

"Don't worry about it, ma'am, I'll have one of my guys pick it up tonight," he assured her.

"I don't want to inconvenience anybody, and this weather is atrocious."

"It's our job," Cal said with a polite smile. "We'll take care of it." Realizing that he wasn't going to bend on the matter, Bronwyn ducked her head and climbed into the back of the car; Bryce followed, his bulk taking up most of the space in the backseat. Bronwyn immediately felt boxed in, but he seemed to be aware of how uncomfortable she was, so he kept to his side of the car. Despite his attempts not to crowd her, Bronwyn was still hyperaware of his larger-than-life presence. Naturally conversation was severely limited because of the lack of light, and she tried not to squirm during the short drive from the restaurant to her new home.

She unthinkingly tried to start a conversation to alleviate the awkwardness but was immediately aware of the futility of the gesture. The words died in her throat before they had even properly formed. That left her to toy with the buckle of her seat belt, and after a few minutes of restless fidgeting, she jumped when his warm hand closed over her fingers.

He didn't say anything, merely lifted her hand to his lips and dropped a sweet kiss onto her sensitive palm. Her breath caught as she tried to see his face in the gloom, but she couldn't see anything other than the whites of his eyes. He squeezed her hand reassuringly before dropping it gently into her lap.

When they arrived at her townhouse, Cal asked her to open the electronic gates and slid the car to a smooth stop right at the front door. He dashed out to open the door on her side, and as she ducked beneath the umbrella he held up for her, she heard the other door open and saw that Bryce had exited the car as well. Before she could utter a word of protest, he had rounded the car and dismissed Cal, taking the umbrella from the other man and walking her to the front door himself. When they reached the lit porch, she turned to him with a nervous smile.

"Thanks for dinner," she said quickly, not sure what else to say really. He continued to look down at her, his handsome face and hair wet from the lashing rain. He really wasn't getting much protection from the large umbrella, focusing his attention on keeping her dry instead.

"I'm sorry if you thought I was being deceptive tonight, Bron," he said after a few long moments of silence. "That wasn't my intention."

She sighed softly.

"You definitely need a little more practice in the full-disclosure department," she conceded. He looked confused and realizing that he hadn't quite understood her, she repeated the statement—to the best of her ability—in sign language. The shadows that were lurking in his eyes cleared up at her words, and she was moved by the hope that bloomed on his face. Yes, he had gone about this the wrong way by foolishly using Kayla as a platform to launch his crazy campaign for reconciliation from, but she had to admit that she was intrigued. More than that, she couldn't deny that she had been profoundly affected by the vulnerability and shocking lack of self-confidence that he had revealed earlier. His words were hard to ignore and impossible to forget.

"I guess I'm just a sucker for punishment," she said aloud, and judging by the smile that lit up his face, he could read *that* without a problem. "I'm going to Pierre's birthday party on Saturday, and since Alice told me that you'll be there too, we might as well go together."

"I'd like that." His voice was thick with barely restrained excitement, and Bronwyn found that lack of cool quite sweet.

"We can work out the details later." She smiled.

"I'll fetch Kayla from Rick and Lisa's place in the morning and bring her home at the usual time," he said after an awkward pause.

"That works."

"Great."

"Okay . . ."

They stood there for an endless moment leaning toward each other, oblivious to the storm raging all around them. She stared at his mouth, knowing that it was foolish of her to want to kiss him so badly. If nothing else it was premature. Especially since this fledgling relationship that they were trying to build from scratch wasn't ready for any kind of physical intimacy yet. But Bronwyn ached for it so desperately that she could almost taste him on her lips. His head lowered, hers tilted back, and the world slowed down and . . . stopped. Her senses were so incredibly heightened that she could almost count each individual drop of rain as it hit his face and beaded in his hair and on his long eyelashes. His lips had just *barely* brushed against hers when the wind caught the umbrella and ripped it from his loosened grip, flipping it inside out in the process. They jerked apart abruptly, both flustered and breathing heavily. Reality shoved its way between them and quite literally dumped a shock-load of icy water all over them both. Bronwyn shuddered when she felt the freezing rain dripping down the back of her neck where the collar of her coat gaped a bit.

"You should get inside before you catch a cold," he urged, ushering her toward the door, and she nodded numbly. She messed up the security code a couple of times before he gently pushed her aside and did it for her with hands that trembled only marginally less than hers. Once he had the door opened, he turned to her, caught her face in his cold, wet hands, and kissed her unceremoniously. There was no finesse to the kiss at all, just raw passion, and Bronwyn was left feeling a little dazed and unsteady on her feet when he released her seconds later.

"Good night," he said gruffly, jerking the collar of his soaked coat to protect his already wet neck from the rain and turning to walk back to the car. She stood in the doorway and watched as he gestured at Cal to remain in the car before he climbed into the passenger seat and shut the door in one smooth movement. The car remained standing there after that, and she knew that he wouldn't leave until she stepped inside and shut the door. She waved at the dark figure in the front of the car before stepping back and shutting the door. As she watched the car head back down her driveway, she sighed and for once tried *not* to dwell on the definite mistakes that she had made tonight.

She really was a fool when it came to her relationship with Bryce. She made the same stupid blunders over and over again, but tonight she had seen something in him that had never been there before. She had seen resolution in his eyes as well as an unfamiliar mix of determination and vulnerability. The man she'd been married to would never have let her catch so much as a glimpse of that susceptibility before. It gave her hope.

~

"Hi." Bryce looked almost shy when he brought Kayla home the following evening. The little girl threw herself at Bronwyn and they reconciled like two people who had been separated for months instead of a mere day, showering each other with exaggerated hugs and kisses.

After a long and exuberant greeting, Kayla ran off to her room to check if her toys had missed her too, leaving her parents to stare at each other nervously.

"Hey." Bronwyn returned his greeting and pushed her hands into the back pockets of her jeans as she rocked back and forth on her heels. It had been raining incessantly since the night before, and Bron stared out at the dismal weather over Bryce's shoulder. He was still standing on the porch, as was his habit when he dropped Kayla off. He never came inside.

"It's freezing out there," Bronwyn observed inanely. "Do you want a hot drink?" His eyes lit up at the invitation and he nodded quickly. He turned and signed his intentions to stay at Cal, who was waiting in the car. The other man nodded and sent back an "okay" sign.

"You've done a lot with the place in such a short time," he said, looking around the homey kitchen as he sat down at the island. He watched as she bustled around the large room, preparing a pot of tea. She sat down across from him a few minutes later with the pot of tea steeping between them.

To keep her hands busy and her anxiousness at bay, she poured his tea, automatically making it the way he liked it.

"Do I make you nervous?" he asked, and her hands stopped their restless movements as she considered his frank question. How like Bryce to cut to the chase.

"No," she replied. "*You* don't but the situation does. Don't you feel the same way?"

He took a sip of his tea as he considered her question and placed his dainty teacup carefully back into its saucer before replying.

"I'm bloody terrified," he admitted with a disarming grin. "Terrified of saying or doing the wrong thing. Last night is a perfect example of me screwing things up without meaning to." The smile faded and his eyes darkened. "Our entire *marriage* was an example of me screwing up without meaning to."

She honestly had no idea what to say in response to that and was relieved when Kayla came running back into the kitchen with Broccoli clutched to her chest. They were both grateful for the interruption and focused their attention on the little girl, who was talking a mile a minute. After a few minutes of fussing over the child, Bronwyn tapped Bryce on his shoulder to get his attention.

"Do you want to stay for dinner?"

"I'd like that very much," he said.

"We're ordering pizza," she warned in case he was expecting some miraculous home-cooked meal after she'd spent all day at school and work.

"No problem." He whipped out his phone. "I'll let Cal know that I'll be staying a while. He and Paul can order takeout for dinner too."

She nodded as she sent Kayla to the refrigerator for the magnetized pizza menu that she kept low enough for the child to reach.

~

"I can't remember the last time I had pizza," Bryce said, leaning back against the sofa with a contented groan. "That was delicious."

They were all in the living room, where they had enjoyed an impromptu picnic on the heated carpet. Kayla liked the novelty of eating on the floor and constantly crawled from her mother's lap to her father's lap, loving the undivided attention from her doting parents. She was currently sitting on her mother's lap and Bronwyn could feel the child's head getting heavier and heavier as she started to doze off. It was getting close to her bedtime.

"Bath time, munchkin," Bron whispered into her ear.

"No baf, Mummy," the child protested sleepily.

"Yes bath, Kayla."

The little girl was grubby and her face was covered in pizza stains. The child pushed herself up and heaved a long-suffering sigh that nearly had Bronwyn in stitches when she heard it.

"Daddy baf I?" she asked, probably knowing that her dad would go easy on her. Bronwyn raised a questioning brow at Bryce, who nodded, his gaze tender as he smiled at the little girl.

"Come on then," he invited, holding his arms out to her. She toddled into them and he hugged her close for a long moment, shutting his eyes as he inhaled her baby scent. "Love you, sweetheart."

Bronwyn's heart turned to mush as she watched them. She turned away and busied herself cleaning up the dinner debris as she struggled to keep the waterworks at bay. She kept her back to them as Kayla led him out of the living room and upstairs to the bathroom. She left them to it for about ten minutes while she fiddled about in the kitchen, before she followed them upstairs.

Bryce was already toweling off a chatty Kayla by the time Bronwyn joined them. He smiled up at her as she entered his field of vision; the look on his face was so warm and unaffected that Bronwyn couldn't help but smile back.

"That was a fast bath," she said quietly, and he shrugged.

"I used the hand shower," he muttered. "She's asleep on her feet as it is. I thought hosing her down would be more efficient in this case."

He picked Kayla up and carried her to her girlie bedroom.

"She's had a busy day," he explained, dragging a pretty pink nightgown over Kayla's head. There was a nervous quality to his constant stream of chatter that Bronwyn found endearing. "We went to the South African Museum this morning. She had a blast, loved the animal and bird exhibits. I had to stop by the office after that so she hung out with her day-care buddies for a couple of hours before lunch. You had fun with your friends, didn't you, Kayla?" She nodded sleepily, and he grinned as he lifted her onto her bed and tucked her in.

They spent a few minutes reading the little girl's favorite nursery rhymes in tandem, which turned out to be an entertaining and unique experience for all three of them. In fact, Bronwyn and Bryce were enjoying the experience so much that they didn't notice that Kayla had fallen asleep. It was Bryce who first discerned that Kayla was sleeping, and he shushed Bronwyn, who was really getting into her Mother Goose impression. They crept out of the child's room and paused at the doorway to watch her sleeping for a few minutes.

"At least I managed to get something right, huh?" Bryce said, his voice brimming with pride, and Bronwyn tilted her head back to meet his eyes.

You got a lot right, Bryce, she signed, and he grimaced—his eyes dull with disbelief—before turning away and heading back downstairs. She followed him, her gaze fixed on the tense set of his broad shoulders.

"I guess I'll be going," he said once she had joined him at the foot of the stairs.

"No," she shook her head. "We have to have an uninterrupted talk, Bryce. I'm open to the idea of a fresh start because I still love you. I've never stopped loving you, even when you were being a total arse. I just didn't think the situation was healthy for us or for Kayla. I felt like our marriage was doomed because I couldn't see us growing as a couple or as a family when we still had so many unresolved issues between us. You want another chance? Then we're going to do this properly. No more secrets."

CHAPTER SIXTEEN

Bryce watched her slender back as she led the way back into the living room, and swallowed nervously. This was what he had been dreading from practically the moment he'd first met her. He had tried his best to avoid this "talk" and had destroyed his marriage in the process. It was time to take a leap of faith and believe that if she still loved him despite his past cruelty, she could love him enough to overlook even his inherent cravenness. After everything that he had put her through, she more than deserved the truth. He just hoped that he was strong enough to face the consequences if she wanted nothing to do with him afterward.

She stopped walking and he was so wrapped up in his anxiety that he crashed right into her. They both lost their balance and his hands encircled her upper arms to steady her. For a few breathless moments he had her lithe body plastered right up against his, her back to his front, and his body responded with embarrassing predictability. He released her almost immediately and put a decent distance between them, hoping that she hadn't felt him hardening against the curve of her firm little behind.

Focus, Bryce! he snapped at himself, drawing in a shuddering breath. He moved past her and headed directly to the sofa. He dropped down and folded an ankle over his knee in an uncomfortable attempt to hide his erection from her. The damned thing had no sense of occasion and even the gravitas of the situation wasn't doing much to tamp things down.

Bronwyn sat down in a chair across from him and stared at him unsmilingly for a few long seconds. That look was more than enough to bring his body back under control. He wasn't sure how they were supposed to start this conversation and waited to take his cues from her. When she continued to just stare at him, he started to feel uncomfortable and shifted restlessly in his seat. When had she perfected that damned soul-piercing icy stare? It hadn't been a part of her "irate spouse" repertoire in the past.

"Well," he said uncomfortably. He was used to silence but he found himself wanting to fill in this particular conversational void with inane words, hoping that it would prompt some kind of response from her. "Well . . ."

She said nothing, her usually expressive face completely devoid of emotion. She wasn't going to make this easy on him . . . and really, why should she? He had once told her that he couldn't fix the damage he had wrought—but quite honestly he hadn't even tried. He could see that now. He hadn't tried because he hadn't felt like he'd deserved to try. Well he was done with being crippled by fear. He could fix it—he *would* fix it. He just had to take the damned leap.

∼

"When we first met . . ." He broke the silence, and Bronwyn made a relieved little sound at the back of her throat. She was grateful that he had ended the interminable silence even though she hadn't really expected him to start the conversation without some kind of prompt from her. "You were the most enchanting thing that I'd ever seen. You so obviously weren't coping with that job, you looked harassed and you were so horrified when Pierre and I sat down at one of your tables."

"You weren't supposed to notice that," she interjected dryly and then nearly kicked herself for interrupting him. He laughed softly in response to her words.

"I noticed all right," he said with a reminiscent little smile. "Your beautiful eyes aren't very good at hiding your emotions, sweetheart. You were so fascinating. Quite possibly the worst waitress I've ever had." She bit her tongue at that one, but his grin widened at the look on her face. "See? You didn't like that. Your eyes don't lie. Pierre couldn't understand my fascination, and I, in turn, couldn't understand how he wasn't seeing the most bewitching creature in the world. Like I said before, I just couldn't stay away from you. I kept going back, and the more time I spent with you, the more time I *wanted* to spend with you. The main reason I proposed—contrary to some of the cruel things I've said about it—was because I couldn't imagine my life without you by my side. You loved me. You had told me so many times and I so *desperately* wanted to say it back, but I couldn't. I was so happy with you but I didn't think that I *knew* how to love. I wanted you to teach me. I wanted you to make me a better person."

"I don't understand," she shook her head.

"I know, I'm sorry. I'm not doing a very good job of this." He cleared his throat. "Do you remember the conversation we had that evening after we returned from the aquarium?" She nodded and watched him swallow painfully before throwing back his shoulders like someone preparing himself for battle. He seemed unable to meet her eyes and kept his gaze fixed on the wall behind her.

"You asked me what my first memory was," he said dully. "What I told you, about my father, when he broke my arm—what he did wasn't an accident. It wasn't the first time he'd hurt me, just the first time I remembered it. And I certainly remember every damned time it happened after that."

"Oh my God . . ."

He didn't see her words. He still wouldn't look at her as he continued to speak in a terrifying dead voice. She had unconsciously brought both hands up to her mouth in shock. A part of her had been expecting to hear something like this, but now that he was saying the words, she couldn't quite believe them.

"After Richard was born," he never called his brother Richard, but for some reason the formality suited the gravity of the conversation, and Bronwyn didn't question it. "I had to do everything in my power to deflect the old man's temper and blows onto me. He never laid one filthy finger on my little brother. I wouldn't let him. I tried to ensure that Rick remained unaffected by the whole sordid mess. If the mean-spirited bastard had lived longer, I may not have been able to shelter Rick as much, but I was thirteen when he died. Rick was ten and still young enough to genuinely mourn our father. Our mother was just a withdrawn shell of a woman who died a few months before my eighteenth birthday. She died mere months after being diagnosed with ovarian cancer. She didn't even try to fight it. It was like she'd just given up on life. She'd checked out mentally and emotionally after my father's accident anyway. *I* was the one who raised Rick, *I* took care of him and made sure that he was fed and properly clothed."

"But I thought your family was rich," she murmured dazedly, but because he still seemed unable to meet her eyes, he didn't see her words and she waved a little to get his attention before signing them.

"Money doesn't stop an abuser from being abusive. My mother could have obtained the means to take us and leave, but she wasn't emotionally strong enough to make that decision. He had her completely cowed, and sometimes I hate her memory even more than I do his. She allowed him to hurt me, to hurt her, and if I hadn't been there to prevent it, she would have allowed him to hurt Rick as well, and I can't forgive that." He shuddered at the thought, and his eyes drifted back to the wall. "We were his perfect family. He had beaten us into submission, and yet he *always* found more reasons to hit my mother and me.

"But like I said, he *never* got his grubby fists on my brother." His words were fierce and shaking with outraged pride. "I was a pretty big kid, and the one time I confronted him was just before he died. He went after Rick but I stood up to him, chest to chest, and he backed off." Bronwyn could picture it, a scared young boy protecting his little brother by bravely facing down a monstrous man, and she had to curl her hands into tight little fists to keep from crying out at the heartbreaking images that were forming in her head.

"He hit me only once more after that and then he died, in a freak yachting accident. God, I hated him and that hate festered in me. The beatings I took, the verbal abuse he heaped on me, it all stayed with me and twisted me inside. My mother was pitiful, she couldn't love us and she was terrified of her own shadow. Rick, I was his big brother, he was duty-bound to love me. Nobody had ever just loved *me* . . . until you. But I didn't have faith in your love. I believed that you wouldn't feel the same way about me if you knew about how I'd let him hit me and learned about what an absolute coward I was. How could you possibly respect me once you understood how I had crawled to get away from him? How I had begged and pleaded with him not to hurt me, how I had pissed myself in fear and pain—more than once . . ." His voice broke on those last words, and she watched his face contort as he fought to control his emotions.

She was a lost cause. Her face was streaming with tears, and she reached for him but he flinched away and got up to pace to the window. He didn't want her to touch him, and she wept for the lonely, hurt child he had been and for the emotionally distant and psychologically scarred man that he had become. He was sharing what he felt were his most shameful secrets, and it broke her heart that he thought this was *his* shame and not that of the pathetic excuse of a man who had fathered him.

"I never felt like I deserved you," he said, keeping his rigid back to her. "But like I told you before, I just couldn't stay away from you after that first meeting. I kept making and breaking promises with myself just to spend time with you. When I proposed to you, I thought that I could manage the relationship; that I could keep your love for myself without tainting you, without hurting you. God, what a miserable job I did of that." He started pacing in front of the window, prowling back and forth like a restless lion and shoving his hands into the pockets of his tailored trousers.

"The night you told me you were pregnant . . ." He stopped moving and grimaced as if the memory pained him as much as it did her. He allowed himself a quick, haunted glance at her before turning away again. "I went off the deep end, Bron. I panicked. I couldn't be a father, not with my history. What if I hit our baby, what if I started hitting you? My mother always told me that my father never *touched* her until after I was born. She never said as much, but she made me feel like the catalyst to all that violence! What if I was the same? What if our baby's birth triggered the same reaction in me? What if I hurt you? I c-couldn't stand that thought, Bron. But then I ended up hurting you anyway, didn't I? I hurt you with my wild accusations and the irrational and stupid things that I said. Words can be even more painful than fists, I knew that, but I still couldn't seem to stop myself! I didn't even *believe* the crap I was saying. And I honestly did think that you would end up hating me for getting you pregnant in the middle of your studies, that you would grow to resent me." He shook his head and sat down opposite her again.

"This is going to sound like some lame, stupid excuse, but that night, when I told you to leave, I wanted to give myself time to think and to breathe. I *never* meant for you to leave the house, Bron, just the room. I calmed down almost immediately and realized what a fool I was being. I didn't know what kind of father I'd be, but I figured that with you by my side I could possibly be okay. I'd taken care of Rick practically from the moment he was born, without once hurting him, and the thought of raising a hand to you is so abhorrent that it sickens me. I stopped thinking of us as a couple and started imagining what it would be like to be a family. The thought of anyone, especially me, hurting you or Kayla is unbearable, but how do I *know* something won't set me off someday? How can you ever trust me around her, knowing what you do about me now?"

Bronwyn had her hands pressed over her mouth again as she tried to muffle her sobs, but she was wholly incapable of preventing the tears from flowing down her cheeks. She was a mess. She wanted to go to him but she knew he would not permit it, not until after he had said his piece. Yes, the emotional wound had been lanced, but the pus that had been festering away beneath the surface for so long had to drain before the healing process could begin.

"I'd just made up my mind to tell you everything," he continued in the same rambling, disorganized way that had characterized his entire monologue up till now. He was bouncing between the past and the present—just stating his thoughts as they popped into his head. "I heard your car starting up and I panicked, I was so sure that you would hurt yourself. I immediately gave chase and had my accident. Thinking I saw you there, I think it was the only way I could cope with having driven you away. I think that my subconscious had to have you betray me, because it gave me an excuse to tell myself that I hated you. I needed that excuse because knowing that I was to blame both for your leaving as well as for my deafness would have sent me even further off the deep end.

"But I never stopped looking for you, Bron, and it wasn't just about finding the baby. I think that part of me always knew that you would never have done what I accused you of doing, so I had to find you to be sure you were both okay. I was so ashamed of my behavior that I even withheld the news of your pregnancy from Rick and Pierre. What I'd done was completely inexcusable, and both Pierre and Rick would have had no qualms about letting me know that." He raised his eyes to hers and winced when he saw her tears. His jaw clenched and his hands curled into tight fists before he lowered himself from the sofa to kneel directly in front of her chair. He placed his hands on the armrests, effectively caging her in, but she didn't feel trapped. Far from it. She felt . . . liberated.

"I was such a fool, Bronwyn." His voice had lowered and she wasn't sure he knew that he was speaking barely above a whisper. She had to strain to hear him. "I'm a wreck of a man and I brought you into this hell with me and ruined your life in the process."

"You didn't ruin my life," she protested, but he shook his head at her denial—not believing her.

"It sounds crazy to say that I loved you too much and that my love destroyed us, but I feel like that's what happened. I'm *toxic*. I've always known that and to even consider a fresh start with you . . ." He laughed bitterly. "I'm a selfish idiot.

"Do you love me?" she asked him quietly, and he blinked at the question.

"What?" he asked blankly.

"Well, you just said that you loved me 'too much.'" She rolled her eyes. "As if that's such a bad thing. But you used the past tense. So do you still *love* me?"

"That's a stupid question," he growled.

"It's a valid question," she dismissed.

"Of course I love you," he nearly shouted. "It's not a question of me not loving you—"

"I beg to differ," she interrupted, waving her hands at him. "It's very *much* a question of you not loving me. You never *told* me you loved me. Not once."

"Okay, when we married, quite honestly, I didn't even *know* I loved you. I told you, I'd never had anyone love me for no reason before. I didn't bloody know what love was!" His voice rose on the last three words, but she merely raised her eyebrows at him.

"Do you know what it is now?"

"Yes," he whispered. "Yes, I know."

"Well?"

"It's . . . it's . . ." He floundered for a few moments before inhaling deeply. "It's everything, isn't it? It's the quiet dinners when not much gets said. It's the sunny days at the beach. It's hearing *your* laughter in my head when I see Kayla giggling. It's seeing the love in your eyes when you watch our baby sleep. It's watching the sun rise in your smile and set in your tears. It's the contentment in seeing you eat and sleep and study and play. It's the small, everyday things, like never getting tired of watching you tuck that same stubborn strand of hair behind your ear twenty times a day, and it's the huge life-altering things like seeing *your* smile and *my* eyes on our beautiful little girl's face. It's knowing that even if you turn away from me forever, I'll always be the better for having had you in my life."

She leaned forward and stared deeply into his grave blue eyes for an endless moment before reaching out to cup his strong and stubbled jaw with her slender hands. He had trustingly laid his beautiful, wounded soul into her keeping, and she would protect it fiercely.

"There you are," she whispered wonderingly as the edges of her lips tilted up into a tiny smile. She formed her words as clearly as she could, not wanting him to misunderstand her. "I've been looking for you." His stern brows lowered in confusion, and she leaned down to press a feather-soft kiss to his sensuous lips before easing back so that he could see her face again.

"There's the man I married."

His eyes widened as her words registered. He swallowed and then swallowed again, his Adam's apple bobbing with the movement. She watched him valiantly try to keep it together, to remain strong as usual—but her steady gaze seemed to completely unravel him. His shoulders heaved as he drew in a convulsive breath, and the sound that tore loose from his chest when he exhaled again was an unmistakable sob.

"It's okay," she said, stroking one hand down the side of his face, and it was that gentle touch that undid him completely. His face crumpled, his eyes filled, and he finally, *finally*, dropped every single defense that he had built up over the years and allowed himself to weep. He tried to turn away. Even after everything that he had just revealed, his first instinct was to weather this storm of emotion alone; but Bronwyn wouldn't let him.

She put her arms around his neck and held on tight. His head dropped into her lap and she folded herself over him so that she was wrapped around him. She crooned the same soothing little sounds that she used when Kayla cried, hoping that he could feel the slight vibrations coming from her chest and throat. His weeping was raw, violent, and gut-wrenching. Her own tears had all but blinded her, but she was determined to be strong for him, and she refused to allow them to overwhelm her. This moment was for this beautiful man who was so very terrified of allowing himself to be happy.

"It's okay," she whispered into his hair. "It's okay, Bryce." The words were ridiculously inadequate of course. It was very far from okay, but she was still processing the ugly truth and trying to figure out how to deal with everything he had revealed. He was so very, *very* damaged, but his revelations only gave her deep and abiding love for him a sharply protective edge. She would be damned if she'd allow him to spend one more second thinking that he wasn't deserving of her love. She now understood that the mistakes he had made had been his twisted and misguided attempts to protect her from the monster he believed himself to be. The realization was heartrending, and her scorching tears slid silently down her face and into his soft hair.

It felt like hours later when his sobs came to a shuddering stop. For a moment he simply allowed himself to rest in her arms, before she felt the tension creep back into his big body, and he lifted himself out of her loving hold and moved to stand beside the window again. He kept his eyes averted as he self-consciously tugged at his dress shirt, which had wrinkled beyond repair. She watched as his ravaged face closed up and shook her head with a sigh before standing up and placing herself squarely in front of him, giving him no option but to meet her eyes.

She had carefully weighed all of her possible responses to his tormented disclosures and knew that there was only one way to play this without stomping all over his fragile male pride.

"You're an idiot," she said quietly, and he blinked in confusion. "I don't . . ."

"How could you even *think* that you're capable of hurting Kayla or me?" she asked, rolling her eyes to convey exasperation. "We've had some huge arguments in the past, and I've never felt remotely threatened by you."

"Bronwyn, I always walked out in the middle of our arguments, remember? It used to drive you crazy, but every time I felt myself getting too angry, I'd rein in my temper and walk out because I was so terrified that I would hurt you physically."

"Bryce, what's the angriest you've ever been with me?" she asked him gently, and he shrugged helplessly.

"When you told me you were pregnant?" His statement came out in question form, as if he wasn't entirely sure of his answer.

"No you weren't angry then," she denied. "You were afraid to allow yourself to hope and lashed out because of that fear. I know that now. I'm talking about *real* anger. The kind that makes you feel like your head's going to explode."

"I don't know." He looked confused. "I don't think that I've ever allowed myself to get too angry with you," he admitted, and she snorted, showing her disdain with a dismissive flick of her wrist.

"Please, I can recall several incidents off the top of my head. Like the time I told Rick that you enjoyed getting the occasional manicure with me. You were so furious you were practically breathing steam."

"Okay, I was pissed off," he admitted uncomfortably, looking a little uncertain. "Justifiably so, since Rick has never really let me hear the end of it. He still makes the odd snarky comment about it. But that's petty stuff. I'd hardly hurt you over something so trivial."

"Oh? Your father never beat you over trivial things then? Like a three-year-old's accidently dropping a watch into a toilet bowl?"

"It was a gold watch," he muttered.

It was a watch! she signed fiercely. "Gold, diamonds, whatever. Breaking a three-year-old child's arm because of it isn't a normal reaction. What if Kayla did the same thing? Would you hit her? Break her arm?" He paled at the question and shook his head in unconscious rejection.

"No, you wouldn't," she answered for him. "Of *course* you wouldn't."

"I don't . . ."

"What about when we were on our honeymoon and I danced with Sasha Tisdale? You nearly went purple with jealousy."

"You still remember that jerk's name?" he asked incredulously. The same jealousy flared in his eyes again, and she grinned irreverently.

"Well he was really, *really* good looking," she reminded, and he glowered, starting to look less shocked and more like the arrogant man she knew and loved beyond all reason.

"Seriously? You think that second 'really' was warranted?"

"I only left off the third one in deference to your fragile ego," she teased. "Bryce, you were beyond irrational about that dance. You were jealous and possessive but nowhere near violent. Now, I'm no expert, but from what I've read about abusive spouses, they barely need an excuse to trigger the violence. Even when you were emotionally hurtful—even *then*—you were punishing yourself more than me." She switched to sign language. *It's just not in your nature to be violent.*

How do you know that? How can you be sure? he asked, his eyes were filled with anguished uncertainty, and she cupped his jaw before going up on her toes to plant a kiss on his gorgeous mouth.

"Because even at your most irrational, when I thought you were kicking me out of the house and then after my return when you seemed to hate me so much . . . I never *once* feared you. Not once, Bryce."

"I'm so sorry," he whispered, shutting his eyes and ducking his head. "I'm so sorry. I'm sorry. I'm . . ."

She stopped his words with a soft kiss, and his eyes opened and met hers. She ended the kiss with a smile.

"I know you are," she acknowledged. "I forgive you, Bryce, and I love you *very* much."

"You do?"

She nodded.

"Of course I do. I don't think that our problems have been miraculously resolved by any means. I think that we have a long, hard road ahead of us actually. But I think that we can finally move forward."

"I've been going back to therapy," he admitted softly. "It's been . . . helpful."

"I hope that we can go together sometime," she said, and he nodded.

"I'd like that." He stared down at her with something like awe in his eyes before shaking his head in disbelief. "How the hell did I get so lucky?"

"I got lucky too, you know," she pointed out, and wrapped her arms around his waist. "Last night I said that I fell in love with a man not a superhero. But you know what? You *are* my hero, Bryce."

"How can you say that after everything that's happened and everything that you've heard tonight?"

"Bryce, if anything, tonight has taught me that you're the kind of man who would place himself squarely between his family and any threat. Of course you're a hero. Mine, Kayla's, Rick's . . . never doubt that."

Bryce stared down into the tear-ravaged face of this woman who meant the world to him and saw sincerity shining up at him. It was in her eyes and in her smile, and the relief that coursed through his body nearly buckled his knees. For the first time in longer than he could remember, he really felt like everything was going to work out. That somehow, against all odds, he had managed to redeem himself and win his wife back. The panic and fear that he'd been living with for more than two years—no, even longer than that—since they had first married, was dissipating and he felt years younger. He captured her mouth with his own and kissed her with desperation that bordered on obsessive. When he eventually felt able to let her go, they were both flushed and breathless.

"I'm going to marry you someday, Bronwyn Kirkland Palmer," he told her with a cocky grin, and she licked her lips dazedly.

"Do you have a timeline on that wedding date, Mr. Palmer?" she asked him sweetly.

"Hey, don't rush me, lady. We've only just started dating. I have big plans for this courtship, you know."

"Oh? What kind of plans?" she asked, curious, rubbing her body sensuously against his. He smiled gently before cupping her face and tilting her head back for another one of his drugging kisses.

"You're just going to have to wait and see," he muttered, his voice alive with promise.

CHAPTER SEVENTEEN

Two Months Later

"I haven't been back here since before the accident," Bryce told Bronwyn as they stepped into their beautiful holiday home in Knysna. They had arrived after dark and so had missed out on the house's spectacular panoramic views of the gorgeous lagoon and Knysna Heads. Still, the serenity of the place was reflected in the sounds of the quietly chirruping night insects and the susurration of the gentle waves lapping at the shore. Bronwyn was filled with mixed emotions as she stepped into the huge stone foyer. The last time she had been here hadn't been a happy time for her, and as she glanced around the gorgeously appointed house, all she could see was her former self disconsolately drifting from room to room like a lonely little ghost as hope faded to despair with every passing minute.

The domestic staff had been in before their arrival since the place was freshly cleaned and the refrigerator restocked for their weekend here. He hadn't told her that this was where he was bringing her, but she had easily recognized the unmistakable Garden Route and had known for hours where they were headed. The drive had become more and more tense with every kilometer that the car ate up, and the last hour had been mostly quiet without Kayla around to break the silence. They had asked Rick and Lisa to take the little girl for this weekend that Bryce had so carefully been planning for weeks.

Bronwyn wandered into the living room and he trailed after her, dropping their bags in the hallway. She made her way to the floor-to-ceiling window that overlooked the tranquil lagoon. Because of the pitch-blackness outside, she could see nothing but her own troubled reflection staring back at her, and she tracked Bryce's movements as he came up to stand behind her. He placed his hands on her slender shoulders and tugged her back until she was leaning against his chest. She went willingly into his loose embrace, her head tilting back until it rested just below his shoulder. His strong arms folded around her narrow waist, his hands rested against her abdomen, and his lightly stubbled jaw nuzzled into the nook just below her ear. She could feel his gentle, warm breath washing against the sensitive skin of her ear as he exhaled deeply.

"I know this place holds some pretty unhappy memories for you," he murmured, his lips brushing against her earlobe as he spoke. "I want to replace those memories with sweeter ones."

She dropped her hands and entwined her fingers with his.

"Will you give me the chance do that for you, Bron?" he asked thickly, and she blinked away the tears before nodding. She watched his reflection in the glass and saw the naked relief on his face at her response.

"Thank you," he said before sucking her delicate lobe into his mouth. She dragged in a harsh breath at the sensation. His hands moved to the curve of her waist, and he turned her around before she fully understood what his intention was. She had her hands braced against his broad chest and could feel the accelerated beat of his heart as he stared down into her eyes. He had looped his arms around her waist and his hands were now resting just above the curve of her behind.

"It's been years since I kissed you last," he observed urgently, his eyes dropping down to her lips and dilating when she sucked her full lower lip into her mouth to moisten it.

"It *has* been years," she agreed—even though it had been mere hours. Ever since they had started seeing each other again, they had been getting increasingly hot and heavy with the petting, and while they had gotten close to making love, they had always stopped before the point of no return. Neither of them wanted to muddy the waters with sex before they both felt that their relationship was strong enough to withstand all emotional and physical obstacles. They would not rush into bed until they were both completely ready for it. Somehow, by unspoken mutual agreement, they knew that this weekend would see them consummating their new relationship. Bryce had known it when he had planned the trip, and Bronwyn had known it when she had agreed to go with him.

He groaned and dropped his hungry mouth onto hers and just about ate her alive. Bronwyn met his desperate kiss with feverish concentration, her tongue dueling with his in a battle for supremacy. The kiss eventually gentled, and his hands lifted to cup her face as he tilted her head for easier access to her mouth. He loved holding her face when he kissed her; his thumbs were always restlessly stroking her soft skin, brushing over her cheekbones and tracing the delicate line of her jaw. After a long while, he eased up, his tongue retreated, and his mouth softened as he feathered butterfly kisses on her lips and up over her cheeks and down into her neck.

Their kiss had been mostly silent, punctuated by heavy breathing and the occasional gasp or desperate moan. Now, as he lifted his head to stare into her eyes, he smiled gently down at her.

"I love you," he whispered, and Bronwyn's face lit up as she smiled radiantly at him.

"I know you do, Bryce . . . but I never get sick of hearing those words," she told him.

"Well, since I'll never get tired of saying them, I guess we'll have to resign ourselves to making each other revoltingly happy for the rest of our lives." He stepped away from her reluctantly, and Bronwyn had to bite back her protest as his gorgeous—and visibly aroused—body moved beyond her reach. When she unconsciously raised one of her hands toward him, he *tut-tut*ted and waved a finger back and forth in front of her face

"Hands off the merchandise, lady. I have plans for this evening and I can't have you distracting me. Why don't you head up for a nap and a shower? And chat with Kayla like you've been dying to do for the last hour? Leave me to prepare our dinner."

She grinned at the thought of him bumbling about in the kitchen. He really wasn't the domestic god he seemed to think he was. He made a terrible mess and his meals were often culinary disasters, with unpalatable over- or undercooked dishes. Still, he tried—bless him—and she appreciated his efforts. He was always so disgustingly pleased with himself that she didn't have the heart to mention the occasional raw potato or the burned edges on a steak. She blew him a little kiss and headed toward the hallway, picking up her overnight bag along the way.

"Dress code?" she turned to ask him, and he shrugged.

"Casual."

She nodded and turned away again.

"Give the munchkin my love."

She flicked him a thumbs-up to acknowledge his request.

~

She made her way back downstairs an hour later, feeling refreshed after a short nap and a long shower. She had also called Kayla to say good night but the little girl had been distracted by a game she was playing with Rhys and Rick, so the call had been a little rushed. She had taken Bryce at his word and hadn't dressed up, wearing only a pair of jeans and a loose T-shirt. She hadn't bothered with shoes at all; the under-floor heating kept her feet warm enough

Whatever Bryce was cooking up in the huge kitchen smelled surprisingly good. She was a little mystified when she got to the kitchen and saw no trace of him. Curiously, she poked around a few of the scattered Tupperware containers left on the white marble top of the gorgeous stone island in the middle of the kitchen. The whole house had a spacious log cabin feel to it, with its stone floors and wooden walls and high-beamed ceilings. Unfortunately her search yielded little in the way of answers except to inform her that whatever Bryce was offering for dinner was of the stick-in-the-microwave-and-heat variety. Which could only mean that he had asked someone else—probably Celeste—to cook it. She smiled ruefully at his minor deception, but her taste buds were truly grateful.

She heard a sound coming from the living room and headed in that direction. She found him out on the large, covered balcony, which had a spectacular view of the lagoon. In fact, they were so close to the water that it actually felt like they were on a boat out on the lagoon when they stood on the balcony. In winter, they were able to enclose the space entirely by slotting in glass panes between the eaves and the balcony railing. It allowed them to still enjoy the view without being exposed to the cold wind and rain. It was a pretty mild evening, so Bryce had a couple of the panes open, allowing the night sounds and the fragrant briny air to drift in.

He was bustling around the round table that he had shifted into the center of the balcony. It was covered in a white tablecloth—the finest linen of course—and he had pulled out all the stops, bringing out the best china and silverware for the occasion. He also had a gorgeous bouquet of red roses in a crystal vase as the centerpiece of the table. He was currently struggling to keep the candles lit. Every time he managed to get one tiny flame burning, a breeze would snuff it out, and he was starting to curse under his breath. She giggled to herself when he tried again, only to be foiled by another mischievous gust of wind.

She lovingly traced the lines of his strong back with her eyes and saw that he had changed his clothes. He was wearing a pair of faded jeans that conformed beautifully to the gorgeous curve of his firm butt and a black dress shirt with a pair of running shoes. His hair was damp and a bit messy, so he must have showered sometime in the last hour.

He swore even more vituperatively than before, and she rolled her eyes before walking up to stand beside him. He was so absorbed in his task that he didn't notice her until she placed a hand on his back. He jumped before relaxing when he saw that it was Bronwyn.

"I can't get the damned things lit," he groused, gesturing to the two tall, white candles beautifully showcased in their sterling silver holders. Bronwyn twined her arm around his and sandwiched his large hand between hers. She rested her cheek against his hard deltoid and contemplated the problem, while idly playing with his fingers before straightening up and smiling at him. The living room light illuminated the balcony just enough to enable them to see each other. She held up a finger indicating that he should wait there before dashing back inside for a few minutes.

She returned with a triumphant smirk, holding up four little scented Glade candles in glass holders. They usually kept them around for candlelit baths. He grinned and grabbed a couple of the glasses from her.

"Vanilla? My favorite," he announced happily as he placed them strategically around the table. After they were lit, he frowned doubtfully at the scant light they offered. "Are there any more?" he asked, and she nodded.

I didn't want to ruin your dinner by having the whole place reek of vanilla. Everything would taste like cake, she signed.

Fair point, he acknowledged.

"I think this is perfect." She waved her arm at the table and he smiled.

"I think *you're* perfect." She snorted at that unnecessary bit of flattery, and he grinned again, sweeping her up in a hug.

"I'm starving," he growled, nipping at her neck to let her know exactly *what* he was starving for. As if the erection insistently pushing against her wasn't proof enough of that. She giggled and pushed him away.

"Down, boy," she teased. "I want to see what culinary feast you've prepared for us tonight." She didn't miss the flash of guilt in his eyes as he uncovered the chafing dishes at the other end of the beautifully decorated table.

"We have"—he cleared his throat nervously, keeping his eyes averted—"roast beef soup with crème fraîche, followed by salad with vinaigrette dressing." More throat clearing. He really was getting truly awful at deception. "Stuffed flank steak served with baby potatoes in a garlic butter sauce, and triple chocolate mousse for dessert."

Her lips twitched at his discomfort as he raised miserable eyes to hers, and when he saw her gentle smile, he heaved a huge, sad sigh.

"You know, don't you?" he asked wretchedly, and she nodded. "I'm sorry. I wanted everything to be perfect tonight, and I didn't think burned meat and hard potatoes would cut it this time." Again his gaze shifted slightly to the left of her as his cheeks lit with shame. She put a soft hand on his jaw and turned his head until he was looking at her again.

"Bryce, you're a man of many talents . . . unfortunately, cooking isn't really one of them. I love you for trying and even though those other meals weren't perfect, I enjoyed them because of the love that went into the preparation. That said, this looks truly delicious, and I'm happy you decided to forgo cooking tonight. Where did this come from? Initially I thought you may have asked Celeste to prepare something for us, but this doesn't at all resemble anything she has cooked for us before."

"Yeah, it's from a local restaurant. They delivered it earlier when the housekeeper was still here. They left very specific instructions on how to reheat everything. I hope nothing has dried out or spoiled."

"I'm sure it'll be fine." She waved aside his concern. He helped her into her chair and draped a napkin over her lap with flair. He sat down to her left and angled his chair so that he could see her face and hands clearly. The meal was divine, and they joked and fed each other as they devoured the food in front of them. They had made their way through half a bottle of delicious Cabernet Sauvignon, and as they licked the last of their chocolate mousse off their spoons, Bryce reached for the bottle to refill their long-stemmed wineglasses with the burgundy liquid. He raised his glass and eyed her expectantly. She smiled and raised hers as well.

"I know that I'm not the easiest guy to get along with, Bron," he murmured, his voice shaking. "And that when you decided to give this relationship a second chance, you also took on a whole boatload of my emotional crap." His voice wobbled, and he paused to gain control of his emotions. "I'm just so happy that you gave me another chance."

She knew that. His ebullience over the last couple of months had been hard to miss. He was still terrified of losing his temper around her and Kayla, but Bronwyn wasn't above pushing his buttons in order provoke a response from him. She trusted him not to hurt them, but she wanted him to trust himself too. Their therapist, in a one-on-one session with Bronwyn, had suggested that course of action, and they were making progress. He *had* lost his temper with her just two weeks before, after Bronwyn had ditched Paul while she was out shopping.

Recognizing how furious he was after Paul had informed him of her transgression, she had deliberately gotten belligerent in an effort to get him to lose his icy control and had then watched in unflinching awe as her ex-husband completely lost his legendary composure for the first time in her memory. He had ranted, raved, paced, growled, and even snapped a pencil, but he hadn't even gotten close to harming a hair on her head. After he had calmed down, she had smugly kissed him and murmured, "You don't scare me, big man. But I promise to be more careful in the future." He had looked a little dazed after that and slightly mollified by her words. But the look of befuddled self-discovery in his eyes had been one of the sweetest things she had ever seen. After that he had stopped carrying himself like a man tiptoeing on eggshells around Bronwyn and Kayla.

Bronwyn had learned a lot more about him over the last two months than she had dreamed possible. At first it had been a little disheartening to discover just how much he had kept hidden from her in the past, but at the same time she had recognized that he was fundamentally the same man that she had fallen in love with all those years ago.

"Sometimes," he was saying, still in that low, rough voice that shook with the force of his emotions, "I wonder how the hell I got so lucky. I don't deserve you, no matter what you say, and I am awed, humbled, and so damned grateful that you're in my life."

He cleared his throat and carefully placed his glass back on the table before, quite unexpectedly, dropping out of his chair and on to one knee in front of her. Confused by the clumsy movement from her usually graceful ex-husband, Bronwyn wasn't sure what was happening at first until he started patting at the breast pocket of his shirt. Flabbergasted, she watched as his eyes flared in panic and his hands dropped down to his jeans pockets and frantically started digging around in them. She started to get an inkling of what his intentions were and tried to hide her grin at this less-than-suave proposal.

"Damn it, I wanted it to be perfect," he was muttering to himself, but she didn't think that he was aware of the fact that he was speaking out loud. He fumbled with something small and gleaming that he pulled out of the same breast pocket he had abandoned just moments ago. When he raised his vulnerable gaze to hers once more, there was sweat beading his forehead, and his breath was coming in ragged gasps.

"I played this out in my head so many times," he confessed hoarsely. "I envisioned hot-air balloons, brass bands, and huge, extravagant spectacles. But in the end, perfection for me was having you to myself in a private place where I could beg you to end my miserable, lonely existence without you. You give my life purpose and meaning. Every beat of my heart belongs to you. I love you, Bronwyn. Please marry me." He opened the palm of his hand and Bronwyn gasped when she saw the ring lying there.

"Where did you find this?" she whispered, her eyes going misty. It was *her* ring, the one he had given her after his first proposal . . . the one she had so reluctantly sold years ago. "How did you track it down? I never even told you the name of the shop I used."

"I e-mailed pictures of the rings to just about every pawn shop proprietor on the Garden Route. It took a while but eventually one e-mailed me back with the information I needed. He had sold it to an elderly lady who said that it reminded her of her own wedding set. She's a regular customer of his and luckily had enough of a romantic heart to sell the set back to me when she heard why I needed it."

"The set? You have the wedding ring too?" she asked in disbelief, and he nodded somberly.

"Yes . . . I wasn't sure you'd want the rings back, but I took a chance that you'd recognize it as a symbol of my enduring love for you. I may not have known it but I loved you the first time I proposed and never stopped loving you. Not once. If you want something else, I could . . ."

"Don't you *dare*," she choked out the words. "Don't even think about it."

"So you'll marry me?" he asked hesitantly.

"Of course I'll *marry* you," she said with a watery smile, cupping his jaw before leaning down to plant a kiss on his beautiful mouth. "I love you too. So much!"

He started grinning like an idiot before clumsily placing the ring on her finger. They both stared down at the gleaming diamond and emerald cluster before Bryce lifted her hand to his mouth and dropped a lingering kiss on the ring.

"Don't take it off again," he whispered.

"Never," she promised fervently. "*Never.*" She kissed him again, winding her arms around his strong neck and toying with the hair at the nape of his neck. She felt him tense as he pushed his way to his feet, taking her with him. She refused to relinquish her hold on him, and he wrapped his arms around her slender waist, dragging her even closer. The kiss got hot so quickly they were gasping for breath but unable to surrender each other's mouths.

"God, I could eat you alive," he rasped, lifting his lips from hers and sweeping them down over the graceful column of her throat, over her delicate chin, until they once again landed, with searing intensity, on her open and gasping mouth. His hands moved to frame her small face, and his palms drifted down her cheeks until his thumbs brushed the underside of her jaw, where they exerted enough pressure to tilt her head back even farther in order to accommodate him more fully. His tongue swept into her mouth, and they both shuddered at the invasion. Her delicate hands molded over the strong, sculpted contours of his torso and up over his pectorals until her fingers unintentionally brushed over the small, flat male nipples, which were hard as pebbles beneath the thin material of his shirt. He hissed at the sensation, and she teasingly moved her hands away from the highly sensitive area.

"Touch me like that again." He lifted his lips only long enough to issue the rough command, and Bronwyn moved her fluttering fingers back up and over his chest, kneading and exploring hungrily along the way, until she reached her goal. She copied a move from his playbook and gently flicked the tiny nubs with her thumbs until he groaned against her lips. She was fully committed to the kiss, enjoying the musky taste of his mouth and the unbearably erotic sensation of the rasp of his tongue over hers. Her skin burned at every point of contact, but she still couldn't get close enough to him. It had just been so long since they had been together like this.

He cupped her firm behind through the denim of her jeans and hefted her up. She happily took the hint and wrapped her long legs around his waist. She kept her mouth glued to his, even while he stumbled his way into the living room and nearly dropped her in the process. He got only far enough inside to turn and brace her against a wall.

"Sweetheart, I'm so *hard* for you," he whispered. The words were completely redundant since she couldn't miss the solid ridge of his masculinity pushing up against her through the thick denim of their jeans. He shifted her until her own hot core was rubbing up against that delicious length of flesh that she could feel throbbing despite the layers of clothing between them. She wriggled and ignored his groan as she tried to lower her legs, wanting to stand. Thankfully he seemed to know exactly what she wanted, and he stepped back to allow her down. Free to do what she was aching to do, Bronwyn clumsily unbuttoned the fly of his jeans. No easy task when he was pushing up against the unyielding material and leaving her with little room to maneuver. She succeeded at her task and his rigid penis spilled into her waiting hands. She gripped him tightly and stroked him in a way designed to drive him a little crazy. He groaned, fighting to maintain his composure and kissed her gently, his velvet-soft lips firm while his tongue forged its way into her mouth. Bronwyn was helpless to do anything but open for him, and she gasped when his hot tongue immediately sought and coaxed a response from hers. Her grip tightened around him and the sound that emerged from his throat was so anguished that for a second she thought she might have hurt him. He lifted his head and stared down at her intensely.

"I love what you're doing, Bron, but I don't think I'll last much longer if you continue doing it," he warned. Bronwyn sighed and reluctantly released her prize after one last, lingering stroke that very nearly undid him if his reaction was anything to go by. It took a few moments of gasping and muttered curses before he opened his eyes again to scowl down at her feverishly.

"You drive me crazy," he said shakily before claiming her lips in a kiss that was the polar opposite of the gentle one he had given her before. It was hot, possessive, and downright raunchy.

Her hands fluttered aimlessly for a few seconds before reaching up to bury themselves in his luxurious hair. She arched up against him and he muttered something unintelligible into her mouth before releasing her face. In a move so fast it had her head spinning, he swung her up into his arms and strode toward the living room sofa.

"I'm sorry, babe," his voice was strained as he placed her on the soft sofa, kneeling on the floor beside her. "I don't think I can make it up to the bedroom. Are you sure you want this?" She rolled her eyes at his ridiculous question and pulled him back toward her. He made a half-laughing, half-groaning sound as he claimed her lips again, smothering her own happy little giggle. She had the softness of the sofa against her back and the hardness of Bryce plastered against her front. He made no attempt to hide his obvious arousal from her as he climbed onto the sofa with her and unabashedly settled between her spread-eagled thighs before grinding himself up against her hot center.

"I've missed this," he confessed, relinquishing her lips again. "I've missed us."

"Me too," she admitted, losing herself in his burning gaze.

"Gorgeous," he ground out thickly, reaching for the hem of her plain T-shirt and tugging it up and off her in seconds. Bryce stared down at her small breasts with such burning intensity that she knew she was blushing from head to foot.

"Pretty," he grunted, his voice so thick she could barely make out the word. One strong forefinger traced the delicate, scalloped edge of her shell-pink demi bra, and she sucked in a breath when the tip of his finger came within a hairsbreadth of the hard little peak of her breast. His other forefinger echoed the movement on her neglected breast, and she moaned huskily, arching herself up in the hopes that he'd touch her the way she needed to be touched. He smiled in response before placing the flat of one hand on her chest, between her breasts, and gently pushing her back down.

"No rush, babe . . . relax." He barely got the words out before dropping his lips on her mouth again for another fiery kiss. Bronwyn inhaled sharply, breathing in the delicious smell of him, before wrapping her slender arms around his back and digging her fingernails into his hard muscles.

He lifted his head and trailed his mouth down over her chin, down her delicate neck, down down down to her chest, until they reached the barely there slope of one breast. His lips traced the same lacy edge his finger had explored moments before, and Bronwyn shuddered when she felt his hot moist breath against her overstimulated nipple.

"Please," she whimpered. "Pleasepleasepleaseplease . . ."

His mouth descended onto the tight, aching nub through the satiny material, sucking so hard that the pleasure bordered on pain. Before the sensation became too uncomfortable, he eased off, regretfully dropping the softest of farewell kisses onto the delicious little morsel before moving over and gracing her neglected breast with the same treatment.

He sat up abruptly, kneeling between her widespread thighs, looking primal and fierce with his hair mussed, a flush highlighting his harsh cheekbones and his jeans unsnapped at the waist. She hungrily drank in the sight of the hard pillar of flesh relentlessly pushing up from the open fly of his jeans before shifting her gaze back up to his eyes. He was doing a bit of visual devouring of his own—dragging his ravenous gaze up and down her half-naked body with an intensity that made her quiver in response.

He dragged his shirt up over his head, not even bothering with the buttons, and tossed it aside. Bronwyn nearly moaned out loud at the sight of his well-developed upper body. Her hands helplessly reached up to trace his well-defined pecs and abs, and she watched in intoxicated fascination when his muscles bunched and leaped beneath her wandering hands. She already knew his body so well but still felt like she was seeing and discovering him for the very first time. She sat up too and hungrily sucked and licked the salty, smooth skin of his chest until he groaned painfully.

"You're so . . ." The rest of his words were muffled against the skin of her neck, which he dragged into his mouth hungrily before moving back up to her mouth like it was some irresistible lure that he could not stay away from. His hands found the clasp of the bra at her back, and she felt the garment loosen but remain sandwiched between their bodies. She moved far enough away from him to yank the offending scrap of satin and lace away, plastering her naked skin back up against his hot, smooth chest. He hissed at the feel of her against him and dragged his head up to gaze down at her pouting little breasts in unabashed hunger. They were both kneeling on the large sofa now, both topless and dressed only in their jeans. Bryce cupped her breasts and tested their slight weight in the palms of his hands before his thumbs descended onto the hot coals of her raspberry-red nipples, flicking and teasing at them while she arched her back in an effort to get them into his mouth. Not one to turn down such a very delicious invitation, Bryce complied with her unspoken demand and dragged first one sweet little nub into his mouth, and then the other. The sensation was so overwhelming that it stole the breath from her body and left the scream of ecstasy she'd been about to utter lodged in her throat.

"Sensitive," he grunted unnecessarily, his voice filled with primal satisfaction. He barely lifted his mouth from its delicious task to utter that guttural observation before dipping back down to where the creamy, berry-tipped treats awaited him. He had one strong, large hand braced firmly against the small of her narrow back. His other hand was working at the snap of her jeans, and before she knew it, he'd deftly pushed the stiff denim far enough down past her narrow hips to allow his eager fingers room to delve between her slender thighs, where they cupped the dripping-wet band of satiny material at her core.

Bronwyn ground herself up against his hand while Bryce, a consummate multitasker, still had his mouth on her overwhelmingly sensitive breasts. His fingers were burrowing beneath the line of her panties, and one *very* talented digit immediately found its way to the little knot of nerve endings at the junction of her thighs. He strummed her delicately for a few seconds, and Bronwyn convulsed violently, a strangled cry of crippling pleasure tearing from her throat. Recognizing that she was on the verge, Bryce replaced the finger with his long thumb and found the tight, wet entrance to her body, which he breeched with a gentle, yet assertive, thrust.

The combination of his thumb on her clitoris, his long finger lodged firmly inside of her, and his mouth tugging insistently at an aching nipple sent Bronwyn tumbling over the edge of insanity, and the scream ratcheted even higher as her back arched even more while her hips thrust frantically at his hand.

Her hands were digging into his broad shoulders, and Bryce stared down into her face, drinking in the sight of her prolonged orgasm like a man dying of thirst. After what seemed like an eternity, Bronwyn stopped convulsing against him and her cry faded into breathless little sobs as she melted against him. He gently allowed her limp body to slide down onto the sofa, where she lay staring up at him with wet eyes and a look of utter, shocked devastation on her face. He smiled tenderly, dropping a kiss onto her gasping lips before tugging her jeans and skimpy pink bikini briefs down her languid, unresponsive legs. He made a frustrated noise when the clothing snagged at her ankles but managed to prevail before tossing them aside triumphantly.

"Love me, sweetheart?" he asked roughly, and she smiled contentedly up into his sweaty face.

"More than you can possibly imagine," she mouthed, and he grinned happily.

"Good. I'm going to make love with you now," he proclaimed intently, and she swallowed a giggle at the solemn announcement. He looked so serious.

"Well then, stop talking about it and get on with it," she said, still fighting for her breath after her massive climax. He growled at the challenge and tugged a condom from the back pocket of his jeans before impatiently shoving them down to his knees and dropping down between her spread thighs. Bronwyn, who was starting to feel halfway normal after the emotional and physical wreckage of her overwhelming orgasm, stared up at him when his face appeared in her line of vision. The ruddy color along his stark cheekbones had intensified, his eyes looked feverish and desperate, and his hair fell down to frame his face in a wild mane. She had never seen him look more intense and focused. She raised her heavy head and looked down to where he was poised like a battering ram between her legs. She could see the head of his shaft above her feminine mound, and she felt the rest of the hard column sawing up against her cleft. An instant later and her head fell back with a moan when the intense sensations surged to life again.

The friction was driving her crazy, and she could see by the way his face tightened that it had a similar effect on the gorgeous man braced above her. Her hands moved up to his face, where she traced his lips, then his cheekbones, with wondering fingers, and he groaned helplessly. She watched as he leaned back and fumbled while putting the condom on.

"Sweetheart," he growled after he had taken care of their protection. His eyes were boring into hers intensely. "I want you to reach down between your legs and take me in your hand." She was happy to obey him, reaching down and grabbing hold of him in one of her eager hands. Her fingers could barely close around his girth.

"Put it inside," he commanded roughly, and she inhaled a shuddering breath before obediently positioning him. She moved her hips a little and hissed when the broad head slipped inside. His brow was furrowed in concentration and his eyes closed in ecstasy as he very carefully inched even farther ahead. Bronwyn groaned at the achingly familiar feel of him.

"God, this is amazing," he groaned as he sheathed himself even farther. His eyes shut involuntarily. He hissed painfully when she thrust up against him. "No, babe. Please don't move. I can barely keep it together, Bron. If you move . . ." He gulped in a breath and released it slowly before moving a little farther. Bronwyn, loving the incredible feeling of fullness, helplessly contracted around him, and he breathed a little prayer as he paused again.

"So long," he moaned, almost incoherently. "It's been so long but I want this to last." She moved her hands up to his face and angled his head until he opened his eyes to look at her.

"It's okay," she said as clearly as she could. "It doesn't have to be slow this time." He kissed her with hungry gratitude before boldly surging forward. Bronwyn raised her knees to his hips as she pushed herself up to meet his thrusts. One of his hands slid down over her naked thigh to hook beneath her knee and raise her leg a little higher. The slight change in angle had him hitting her spot with every urgent thrust and it drove her wild. She was beyond thinking about anything but this moment, this man, and his masterful ability to turn her into a ruined, incoherent mess in mere moments.

Her arms snaked around his neck as she held on for dear life while he hammered into her. His lips were nibbling at her ear, his breathing was hot, labored, and liberally interspersed with groans as he lost himself in her. Bronwyn matched his thrusts with her own, and as she found herself hurtling toward another powerful climax, she arched her back and tangled her fingers in his hair.

"Bryce . . ." Her voice broke on his name, and her breath caught as she felt herself clamping around his hardness. In that incredible moment, she completely forgot that he couldn't hear her. "I'm coming . . ." He increased his tempo when he felt her tightening, not needing to hear her in order to recognize the familiar signs of her impending orgasm. Bronwyn went as taut as a bowstring, right on the verge . . .

"That's right, my love," he encouraged breathlessly. "Come for me." He drew himself nearly all the way out, until nothing but a whisper of him remained inside of her and she sobbed in frustration, before he plunged back in, angling himself to hit her just right. That was all it took to send her screaming down into the abyss. The intense contractions of her climax were enough to send Bryce plummeting down after her with a cry of pleasure. He moved his hand from the crook of her knee and flattened it against her back to pull her as close to him as she could get, while he shuddered inside of her for what seemed like forever. Afterward, they both went completely limp, occasionally jerking as pleasurable aftershocks hit them. They remained that way for a moment, still joined together and too drained to move. Bryce was planting idle little kisses on her damp neck, and Bronwyn was stroking his sweat-soaked hair.

"You're breathtaking," he murmured into her ear before stirring himself long enough to move off her and remove the condom. She groaned in protest when he left her briefly to dispose of it in the downstairs bathroom, kicking off his jeans and underwear in the process. He was back in seconds and stood grinning down at her nude body in immense satisfaction.

"Sated, sweaty, and ever-so-slightly smug," he informed her. "That's how you look."

"That's how I feel," she confirmed lazily, lifting her arms toward him. "Why are you standing there? Come down here. I'm cold, I need you to keep me warm." He smiled tenderly and entwined his fingers with hers before tugging gently at her hands.

"Let's head up to bed," he suggested, and she pulled a sulky face.

"I don't want to move," she pouted, and he chuckled before releasing her hands to swoop down and deftly scoop her up. Bronwyn squealed and looped her arms around his neck when she felt herself slipping. He tightened his hold on her and clutched her possessively close to his chest. Bronwyn nestled her face in his neck and nuzzled his warm, delicious-smelling skin contentedly.

When he reached the bedroom, he gently deposited her on their huge king-size bed, dropping down to join her. He immediately reached for her again, seemingly unwilling to relinquish his hold on her for very long. Bronwyn loved snuggling up against his big, hard body; it always made her feel protected. They did nothing more than stroke and pet, still sated after their shattering bout of lovemaking.

"Bronwyn, I can't promise not to make mistakes, and I probably will inadvertently wind up doing stupid things that may hurt you in the future. I'm not perfect. I'm just a man and as flawed—more so—than any other man. But I *can* promise to love you with the entirety of my heart, protect you with all the strength in my body, cherish you with my mind and soul for the rest of my life and probably beyond that," he vowed. Bronwyn's cheek was pressed to his chest, and she couldn't see his face, but his voice was husky and trembling with the intensity of his emotions and the veracity of his words. "I adore our daughter and with you by my side, I'll be the best father I can be. If we should be blessed with other children, I'll adore them too."

Bronwyn raised her head from its resting place close to his heart and smiled up at him soggily. She adjusted her position sinuously until she was straddling his hips, with her hands braced against his chest. "I love you too," she reaffirmed. "Flaws and all, Bryce. The only person who ever demanded perfection from you was *you*. You're not perfect, but you're perfect for me. I'll cherish and protect your heart today, tomorrow, and forever." He reached up to cup her face with gentle hands, tugging her down for a fierce kiss.

"Forever?" he asked shakily after releasing her lips. She smiled again before tracing an *x* across his heart and then dropping her head to kiss the spot she had just marked.

"Yes. Forever."

Bryce's broad chest heaved in a shuddering sigh of contentment before he dragged her down to snuggle against his chest. Bronwyn burrowed against him and smiled drowsily when she felt him stroking her hair languidly. They were silent for a few long moments and Bronwyn was on the verge of dozing off when she heard his voice. It was quiet but filled with the awe of a man who was just now recognizing a completely unfamiliar emotion.

"I'm happy."

That was all anyone could ever ask for.

EPILOGUE

Y ou're what?" Bryce stared blankly into Bronwyn's beaming face. They were in his study, and she had seated herself in the chair opposite his desk.

"Pregnant," she enunciated *and* signed the word, but he still blinked stupidly for a few moments. Her chest heaved in a clearly exasperated sigh before she got up, rounded his desk to shout it directly into his ear. "*PREGNANT!*"

He jumped as his hearing aid squealed. He now had only 45-decibel hearing loss in his right ear after finally deciding to try that operation the year before. He still couldn't follow conversations very well unless the speaker was sitting close to him, positioned on his right side, and his hearing aid was on. The operation hadn't really changed his life much—except that his wife and daughter now sometimes felt the need to shout things directly into his ear when they felt he wasn't paying close enough attention to them. He had only done it to hear Kayla's laughter, and when he'd heard it for the first time, he had been gratified to learn that she *did* have her mother's laugh after all.

"You're pregnant?" he said on a slow exhalation of breath, and Bronwyn nodded down at him with a grin. He felt his own lips stretching into a matching grin. They had suspected that she might be even though they'd only recently decided to try for a second child.

Bronwyn had just taken on a partner at her veterinary clinic, precisely for this purpose, and Kayla had just started her second year at school. Their dramatic daughter had recently been making smart-arsed comments about not wanting to be an only child for the rest of her life. Especially since her cousin Rhys had recently acquired a baby sister and even little Lily De Lucci—whom Kayla seemed to consider both rival and friend—was a big sister twice over thanks to the twin girls her mother had given birth to a few years before. Hating to be left out of anything, Kayla had placed an order for a little brother because neither Rhys nor Lily had one.

"Oh my God." Bryce leaped to his feet and swung Bronwyn up into a hug. "That's fantastic news, sweetheart." He dropped her back onto her feet and gave her a quick, concerned once-over. "What did the doctor say? Is everything okay?" he asked worriedly.

I'm healthy as a horse. Baby's due in about seven months' time. Just before Christmas.

"You always know just what to get us for Christmas," he teased.

"I try my best." She shrugged modestly.

God, he loved her so much. They had remarried nearly five years ago, less than a month after his proposal. Their marriage, even now, was filled with surprise after surprise. He wanted to create amazing memories with spontaneous trips to Europe when she wasn't busy with work, hot-air-balloon rides, flowers, jewelry, and toys for Kayla. And even more disastrous romantic meals that he had cooked himself. In the interests of self-preservation, Bronwyn had enrolled him in a Cordon Bleu cooking course. He'd had minimal success in the class. Now, instead of merely burning steaks, he burned things like glazed duck and stuffed pheasant. He pretended not to notice his wife and daughter's exchanged grimaces when they knew that he would be cooking dinner. He was damned determined to conquer the cooking thing. He couldn't imagine not succeeding at it . . . okay, so it was taking him a little longer than he'd anticipated—years really—but he knew that he could do it.

Bryce absolutely doted on his "girls" and loved spoiling them, and Bronwyn had stopped protesting at the extravagance when she had seen how much pleasure he got out of his surprises. He couldn't imagine his life without them and was grateful every day for the miracle that had been granted to an undeserving man like him.

"You're amazing," he murmured, sitting back down behind his desk and dragging her into his lap. He was well on his way to showing her just how amazing he thought she was when the study door was flung open unceremoniously, and their daughter dashed into the room. Oliver, their excitable and yappy little red miniature pinscher, followed her into the room. Kayla was still wearing her school uniform, and her braid was an unraveling mess that created a halo of escaped hair around her gamine little face.

"Guess what?" she asked breathlessly, so used to seeing her parents snuggling that she didn't even pause on her way to his desk.

"What?" Bronwyn asked with a grin.

"Ms. Williams gave me two gold stars today!" the little girl boasted, practically bouncing up and down in excitement.

"She did?" Bronwyn smiled, signing at the same time so that Bryce could follow the conversation.

"That's fantastic, munchkin," Bryce said. He had his head on Bronwyn's shoulder and one hand protectively tucked against her flat stomach. "What for?"

I got ten out of ten for my spelling and for my math, she signed a mile a minute, her little hands practically a blur.

"Wow, I think that calls for a celebration, don't you?" he asked them indulgently, and Bronwyn nodded, knowing that he meant to celebrate more than Kayla's gold stars. Naturally they wouldn't tell Kayla about the baby for a while. She would be an unholy, impatient little terror if she found out and then had to wait months before the baby was born.

"It's definitely cause for celebration," Bronwyn agreed with a smile. "Kayla, go and have a bath and put on your prettiest dress, we're going out to dinner."

"Really?" Her beautiful blue eyes shone with pride and her parents nodded. She squealed in excitement and careened back out of the room with Oliver racing out after her.

"Thank you," Bryce whispered quietly, and Bronwyn craned her neck to meet his eyes.

"For?" she asked.

"Everything," he said expansively before elaborating. "For the small, everyday things and the huge, life-altering things." His eyes went misty, and he blinked in embarrassment. When he was able to see her face clearly again, she was smiling luminously. He watched her hands and her face as they spelled out her inevitable response, the one that never failed to bring a lump to his throat and tears to his eyes.

There's the man I married.

ACKNOWLEDGMENTS

Special thanks to my lovely beta readers; your feedback has been invaluable:

Carol

Leigh-Ann

Lorinda

Morwa

Shannon

ABOUT THE AUTHOR

Natasha Anders was born in Cape Town, South Africa. She spent the last nine years working as an Assistant English Teacher in Niigata, Japan, where she became a legendary karaoke diva. Natasha is currently living in Cape Town with her temperamental and opinionated budgie, Sir Oliver Spencer, who has kindly deigned to share his apartment with her. Please feel free to contact her (or Oliver) on Twitter at @satyne1.